'Johns is one of Australia's most popu reason—she tells great stories. She alw and then delivers them in a page-turning combination of heart, wit and wisdom ... *How to Mend a Broken Heart* is yet another cracking read from Rachael Johns ... in fact, it's her best yet.' —*Better Reading*

'Imbued with an adventurous spirit, and ultimately hope, this book transports you mentally to a vibrant and unique city a world away, yet strangely familiar. I highly recommend this book. I finished it feeling warm and cosy, if I'd just shared a wonderful adventure with two good friends.' —*She Society* on *How to Mend a Broken Heart*

'This was such a fun and rewarding read! ... If you are looking for a well-crafted romance novel by an accomplished Australian author, then Rachael Johns is your gal, and I heartily recommend this novel' —Victoria Brookman, author of *Burnt Out*

'A brilliant read from one of Australia's most popular authors, this will have you hooked from the very beginning.' —*Who* on *Flying the Nest*

'With her typical humour, empathy and wisdom, Rachael Johns has once again created characters you can't help but fall in love with and wish the best for. *Flying the Nest* might just be her best novel yet!' —Tess Woods, author of *Love at First Flight*, on *Flying the Nest*

'Writing with warmth and insight, Rachael Johns is brilliant at capturing the joy and sadness in all of our lives. I hope she has many more tales to tell!' —Anthea Hodgson, author of *The Drifter*, on *Flying the Nest*

'A really good book makes you feel like you've found a new friend—one that resonates with you, and one who you can learn from. That's exactly how I felt in Rachael Johns' new novel, *Flying the Nest* ... A disarmingly all-too-real portrayal of what happens when the traditional roles of wife and mother are turned on their head. This is a book that women will want to bond over, share laughs and tears over—a must read for every woman who has had their life take an unexpected turn.' —*Mamamia* on *Flying the Nest*

'Rachael Johns really gets women and is able to express the multilayered internal conflicts that so many of us experience, lay it all out on the page, and still make it deeply personal ... She's masterful at telling the stories of everyday heartbreaks ... *Flying the Nest* is wonderful—Rachael Johns never disappoints.' —*Better Reading* on *Flying the Nest*

'If you like your chick-lit with a dash of intelligent social commentary, *Just One Wish* is the perfect summer read. Rachael Johns's latest novel is sparklingly funny, quirky and totally of this moment.' —*Herald Sun* on *Just One Wish*

'Johns knows how to weave the experiences of different generations of women together, with nuance and sensitivity, understanding how competing contexts shape women's choices ... Exploring themes like motherhood, the roles of women, and lost love, *Just One Wish* will make you look at the women in your own life and wonder what stories they haven't told.' —*Mamamia* on *Just One Wish*

'Johns draws readers in with her richly complex characters.' —*The Daily Telegraph* on *Just One Wish*

'Rachael Johns writes with warmth and heart, her easy, fluent style revealing an emotional intelligence and firm embrace of the things in life that matter, like female friendship.' —*The Age* on *Lost Without You*

'Heart-warming and compassionate ... Any book lover interested in life's emotional complexities and in the events that define and alter us, will be engrossed in *Lost Without You.*' —*Better Reading* on *Lost Without You*

'Full of heartache and joy with a twist that keeps the pages turning ... *The Greatest Gift* will appeal to fans of Jojo Moyes and Monica McInerney.' —*Australian Books + Publishing* on *The Greatest Gift*

'Rachael Johns has done it again, writing a book that you want to devour in one sitting, and then turn back to the first page to savour it all over again. I loved the characters of Harper and Jasper; their stories made me laugh and cry, and ache and cheer and ultimately reflect on all the many facets of that extraordinary journey called motherhood.' —Natasha Lester, author of *The Paris Secret*, on *The Greatest Gift*

'The bond between Flick, Neve, and Emma blossomed as their sons grew up, but even best friends keep secrets from one another ... Fans of emotional, issue driven women's fiction will welcome Johns' US women's fiction debut.' —*Booklist* on *The Art of Keeping Secrets*

'... a compelling and poignant story of dark secrets and turbulent relationships ... I fell completely in love with the well-drawn characters of Flick, Emma and Neve. They were funny and flawed and filled with the kind of raw vulnerability that makes your heart ache for them.' —Nicola Moriarty, bestselling author of *The Fifth Letter*, on *The Art of Keeping Secrets*

'Written with compassion and real insight, *The Art of Keeping Secrets* peeks inside the lives of three ordinary women and the surprising secrets they live with. Utterly absorbing and wonderfully written, Johns explores what secrets can do to a relationship, and pulls apart the notion that some secrets are best kept. It is that gripping novel that, once started, will not allow you to do anything else until the final secret has been revealed.' —Sally Hepworth, bestselling author of *The Secrets of Midwives*, on *The Art of Keeping Secrets*

'A fascinating and deeply moving tale of friendship, family and of course—secrets. These characters will latch onto your heart and refuse to let it go.' —USA Today bestselling author Kelly Rimmer on *The Art of Keeping Secrets*

Rachael Johns is an English teacher by trade, a mum 24/7, a Diet Coke addict, a cat lover and chronic arachnophobe. She is also the bestselling, ABIA-winning author of *The Patterson Girls* and a number of other romance and women's fiction books including *The Art of Keeping Secrets, The Greatest Gift, Lost Without You, Just One Wish, Something to Talk About, Flying the Nest, How to Mend a Broken Heart* and *The Work Wives. Outback Secrets* is the fifth in her series of rural romances set in Bunyip Bay. Rachael rarely sleeps, never irons and loves nothing more than sitting in bed with her laptop and imagining her own stories. She is currently Australia's leading writer of contemporary relationship stories around women's issues, a genre she has coined 'life-lit'.

Rachael lives in the Swan Valley with her hyperactive husband, three mostly gorgeous heroes-in-training, two ravenous cats, a cantankerous bird and a very badly behaved dog.

Rachael loves to hear from readers and can be contacted via her website rachaeljohns.com. She is also on Facebook and Instagram.

Also by Rachael Johns:

The Patterson Girls
The Art of Keeping Secrets
The Greatest Gift
Lost Without You
Just One Wish
Flying the Nest
How to Mend a Broken Heart
The Work Wives

The Rose Hill novels
Talk of the Town
Something to Talk About

The Bunyip Bay novels
Outback Dreams
Outback Blaze
Outback Ghost
Outback Sisters
Outback Secrets

The Hope Junction novels
Jilted
The Road to Hope

Man Drought

The Kissing Season (e-novella)
The Next Season (e-novella)
Secret Confessions Down and Dusty: Casey (e-novella)

OUTBACK *Secrets*

RACHAEL JOHNS

FICTION HQ

First Published 2021
Second Australian Paperback Edition 2022
ISBN 9781867266426

OUTBACK SECRETS

Published by
HQ Fiction
An imprint of Harlequin Enterprises (Australia) Pty Limited (ABN 47 001 180 918), a subsidiary of HarperCollins Publishers Australia Pty Limited (ABN 36 009 913 517)
Level 13, 201 Elizabeth St
SYDNEY NSW 2000
AUSTRALIA

A catalogue record for this book is available from the National Library of Australia
www.librariesaustralia.nla.gov.au

Printed and bound in Australia by McPherson's Printing Group

FSC
www.fsc.org
MIX
Paper | Supporting responsible forestry
FSC® C001695

Outback Secrets *is dedicated to the wonderful people in the*
chael Johns Online Book Club—I love chatting books and writing
vith you all, and your passion for reading inspires me. Thank you!

SIGN OUT THE FRONT OF THE PALACE, BUNYIP BAY

Sometimes you run into people who change your life for the better.
Those people are called publicans.

Prologue

Henrietta Forward could already taste the ice-cold beer that was waiting for her back at Anna Downs station. A drink, dinner, shower and bed, in that order, was on her agenda because she was absolutely knackered. She was nearing the end of a busy few weeks aerial mustering in the East Kimberleys—one of the most remote and beautiful parts of Western Australia—and was looking forward to a few days off to catch her breath before driving across the country to the Riverina region of New South Wales.

It wasn't that she didn't adore her job; Henri only felt truly alive when she was above the earth, looking down at the varied landscapes she was lucky enough to experience, but the hours were long and by the end of a stint like this one, she was in dire need of a little R&R. Smiling down at the deep red ground below, she knew she'd never tire of the scenery or the thrill of chasing cattle. Stunning gorges and waterholes were scattered throughout the enormous Anna Downs property, not to mention boabs and eucalypts that would soon be a vibrant shade of green due to the wet. She even loved the weirdly shaped termite mounds that poked up from the earth and looked like little cities of mud-built skyscrapers. This work wasn't her bread and butter because a lot of stations up here used choppers—they made it easier to navigate the trees, although weren't nearly as kind on the cattle in her opinion—but there were still a few station owners who preferred fixed-wings and for that she was grateful.

The mobs were in decent sizes now and the ringers were starting to move them towards the yards. There was just one last bit of bush still to inspect. Henri headed over, feeling adrenaline buzz through her as she spied a couple of cattle in a clearing. If there was one thing certain about mustering, it was that where there were some animals, there'd be others close by. The hardest part was encouraging them out of the trees; once they got going it was easy enough to keep them moving, especially if she nudged them in the direction of the nearest waterhole.

Training her gaze on the destination, she angled the Cessna towards the trees—the goal to startle the cattle with the loud noise of the aircraft, which would encourage them to head in the opposite direction. She needed to get close enough to get them moving but not so fast as to cause trouble. It was better if the beasts walked rather than ran. If they moved too fast, occasionally the old girls would leave their calves behind without a backward glance, which did not make for happy station owners.

But it soon became apparent this was the least of Henri's problems. Her heart hammered at the sound of an almighty bang as she descended towards the trees.

Fuck! The engine! The prop had stopped dead.

No. This could *not* be happening, but even as she prayed to a God she hadn't thought of since Sunday School that this was all in her vivid imagination, Henri knew that was not the case. Hadn't she felt something wasn't quite right with the old Continental engine?

Earlier in the day there'd been a slight, almost imperceptible miss now and again. The engine was nearing time for a rebuild and was scheduled to be pulled and overhauled as soon as mustering season was finished, but when she'd stopped to refuel, she'd examined around the cowling, checked the oil, and everything had looked fine.

Cold fear sliced through her as she realised this was anything but fine, but she didn't have time to panic.

Her training took over and instinct set in. Using the speed she still had, Henri gained height again and set up for a forced landing, all the while scanning the area below for a suitable location. A long way from the station's airstrip, she'd need to improvise and hope like hell that fate was on her side. Her hands grew clammy on the controls, and just when she was losing hope of finding anywhere close to suitable, a small clearing presented itself.

Determined, she maintained an approach speed as she brought the Cessna lower, then switched everything off after the last flap had been applied. She couldn't breathe, her head completely consumed with the most terrifying, most important landing she'd ever made.

'Oh my God! I did it,' she shrieked as the wheels hit the ground and her heart started beating wildly.

But the danger wasn't over yet; she needed to keep her wits about her a little longer in order to brake heavily and avoid the trees that were rapidly approaching on the other side of the clearing. The small wheels, not made for such rough terrain, bounced along, the noise so horrendous Henri could barely hear herself think.

But she had to. She had to fight to keep control.

Finally, just when it looked like both she and the aircraft had survived the ordeal unscathed, she jolted in her seat, swearing again as a wheel hit something hard. She didn't have time to wonder what it was—although later she'd identify the culprit as one of the termite mounds she'd been admiring—as the leg dislodged and the aircraft slewed around madly.

It was over in a heartbeat. Her final stop anything but graceful.

It could have been a lot worse, she told herself as she sat there, dazed and trying to catch her breath. After a long day sitting in the high-decibel environment of the cockpit, the sound of silence was almost deafening. All she could hear was the ringing in her own ears.

The red dust that had been disturbed on impact settled around her and Henri stared out of the cockpit, almost unable to believe what had just happened. Although there'd been some close encounters with powerlines in her many years flying, that was the nearest she'd ever come to true calamity, possibly even death.

Suddenly her whole body started to tremble. She forced herself to unbuckle her seatbelt, remove her headset, climb out and examine just how bad the damage was. One undercarriage leg had been bent backwards and right up, lowering the fuselage closer to the ground. Bingo, she thought as she noticed oil smeared back from the engine cowl, telling her exactly why the engine had stopped.

Despite her heart still pounding, some of the shock started to abate and she actually felt slightly proud that she'd known something wasn't quite right. Disaster had threatened and she'd lived to tell the tale. Next time she'd simply have to pay more attention to her gut.

It was a good thing mustering was all but finished, because there was no way that aircraft was going up again any time soon.

Suddenly parched and knowing there was nothing more she could do here, Henri grabbed her water bottle from the baggage compartment, shut the cockpit door and started walking in the direction of the yards. It was a good distance away, but the ringers would have seen her aircraft go down and she knew it wouldn't be long before they came to her rescue.

Chapter One

Six weeks later

'Well, Cecil, we're home sweet home,' Henri said, her grip tightening on the steering wheel as she drove past the welcome sign on the outskirts of Bunyip Bay, almost four weeks earlier than planned. She'd nearly come home a few weeks ago but hadn't wanted to raise suspicion, and besides, she wasn't sure she could stand any longer than a month living with her mother.

It was years since she'd officially been a resident of this town, but her mum's family were founding members, having farmed in the district since the mid 1800s when they'd immigrated from a tiny town in Cornwall. Bunyip Bay was where Henri had spent her childhood until heading to Perth to boarding school at age thirteen. This was where her siblings and most of her friends still resided, and her answer when anyone asked where she came from. She'd adored growing up here, chasing her dad and brothers around the farm until she was old enough to muck in and help, and she'd hated her years at boarding school in the city. Not just because a lot of the girls only cared about make-up and fashion—two things Henri had no interest in whatsoever—but because she missed her dad, the aromas of the farm and the feel of the sand between her toes. Bunyip Bay was in her blood and, as she unwound her window and smelled the fresh salty scents of the nearby ocean, she felt some of the tension she'd been carrying the last few weeks start to ease.

Maybe her boss was right … maybe she did simply need a break, some time back home before she started her next contract. Some quality time in the ocean. Aside from flying, there was nothing quite as therapeutic for Henri as swimming and surfing. Of course she'd stopped at other beaches on her journey west, but she couldn't wait to take a dip in her favourite bit of the ocean.

There was just one even more important stop first.

Driving on through the main street lined with dusty four-wheel drives and even dirtier dual-cab utes, Henri smiled at the familiar sights. The IGA, the Community Resource Centre, the medical centre, primary school, the old Memorial Hall, the bowling club, her best friend Frankie's café and the iconic pub at the top of the hill where she'd spent many an errant night in her late teens, were all almost exactly the same as they'd always been. It was only The Ag Store that was new and shiny. Henri's sister Tilley and her husband owned Bunyip Bay's ag and hardware supplies, a business they'd literally built from the ground up after the old owners lost everything in an arson attack.

Even though it was only the very beginning of December, the festive spirit was already well and truly on display in the main street. There were Christmas decorations strung across the road, and koalas, kangaroos and, of course, bunyips wearing Christmas hats sat at the top of almost every lamp post. The shops had gone all out as well. Outside the front of The Ag Store stood a massive blow-up Santa Claus wearing red and green board shorts and an Akubra with corks hanging off it.

The Palace was the only building not decked out to the nines, but if Henri recalled correctly, the publican never bothered with such frippery, much to the frustration of certain people in town.

She continued on and then turned right, driving only another hundred metres or so before she came upon the local cemetery. It was barely ten o'clock but already the December sun had a bite, so Henri parked Cecil under an old gum tree, grabbed her cap off the passenger seat and started towards the entrance.

As a kid, she'd loved playing here with her siblings and friends while her parents had business in town. They'd spent many an hour making up stories about the bodies under the ground, scaring each other senseless, but back then she hadn't actually been close to anyone buried here.

Now she felt differently as she walked over the uneven ground to her father's resting place. *Now*, the cemetery felt sacred, much more so than anywhere else—even church—had ever felt.

'Hey, Dad. How's tricks?' she said, pausing in front of his grave and using the saying that had always been his.

The black marble headstone was shiny and polished, much newer than many of the others, and there were fresh grevilleas and Geraldton wax from Bungara Springs in the ceramic vase at the base, indicating that her mother had been here very recently. Henri wondered how often she came. There were also a couple of Matchbox cars that she guessed had been left—accidentally or on purpose, she wasn't sure—by one of her nieces or nephews.

She didn't have anything to leave, but she knew her dad wouldn't care. He'd always said her presence at Christmas was far more important than any presents.

Until his heart attack four years ago, coming home for Christmas had always been the highlight of her year, but although the farm ticked on with her mother and brothers at the helm, the place didn't feel the same now that he was gone. Henri and her dad had been two peas in a pod, sharing a love of aircraft, vintage cars and the ocean. They just got each other, whereas she and her mum only ever seemed to get *at* each other.

This was the first time in four years she'd be back for more than a few days, but at least it would give her a chance to properly catch up with her family and Frankie.

A lone crow perched atop a slanting headstone a few metres away squawked as if Henri was interrupting his peace. But aside from the bird and the rustling leaves of trees that were almost as slanted as the headstone—thanks to the famous local wind—the cemetery was deserted, and for that she was grateful.

Dropping down to the ground beside her father's grave, she crossed her legs and poured out her heart as if he were actually sitting here beside her. She told him everything. From her brush with death up in the Kimberleys to what had happened when she'd first climbed back in an aircraft almost two weeks later.

'I feel so stupid, so frustrated,' she confessed, picking up a nearby rock and ditching it hard. Many times over the last six weeks she'd felt like throwing or even punching something!

Henri had this weird feeling that if her dad were still alive, she wouldn't be in this predicament because she'd have called him the minute she realised there was a problem and he'd have calmed her, talked her round. She hadn't called her mother because she knew exactly what she'd have said. She'd never wanted Henri to become an agricultural pilot in the first place.

'What do you think I should do, Dad?'

Of course, there wasn't a reply, but she sat there listening to the wind and the occasional squawk from the crow until finally her sobs subsided. Then, she pushed to her feet, dusted the dirt, leaves and little gum-seeds from her shorts and started back towards Cecil.

'Oh my God!' shrieked her best friend when Henri stepped into Frankie's Café over an hour later, her ponytail still wet from what she'd intended to be only a five-minute swim, tops.

Heads looked up from all the tables and Henri recognised most of them.

Seated right beside the door was sweet old Dolce Abbott, who'd owned the newsagency when Henri was little and always gave her lollies when her dad popped in for the paper. Henri had thought she looked like one of the Golden Girls and that she was ancient back then, but she still looked exactly the same. Also at her table was the not-so-sweet Eileen Brady, her hair purple-rinsed and her expression pinched. Eileen had taught her Sunday School until Henri told her parents she'd run away from home if they made her go even one more time. It wasn't that she had anything against the content—some Bible stories were ripe with blood and gore—it was the delivery that made her want to set the church on fire. Eileen not only had a talent for making anything mind-numbingly boring but also spent at least half of every lesson telling the children they were full of sin.

'What the hell are you doing here?!' Frankie dashed around the counter and enveloped Henri in a massive hug. 'Karen thought she saw Cecil pass through town an hour ago, but I said it must be another bright orange Kombi because I thought you weren't coming home until just before Christmas.'

That was the one problem with having such a distinctive vehicle—it was hard to fade into the background. But Henri wouldn't change her faithful Kombi van for anything, even if he did have a terrible habit of breaking down in the middle of nowhere. Luckily, she usually had the skills to fix him.

'Change of plans,' she said, willing fresh tears to take a hike. Hard-nosed Henrietta Forward didn't cry—well, not in public anyway—and doing so here would be like putting a massive neon sign on her head alerting everyone to the fact that something was wrong.

Of course, she'd tell Frankie about her problem at some stage, but not now with the likes of Eileen Brady sipping her tea and eating scones and cream, just waiting for something she could turn into gossip.

'Why are you wet?' Frankie asked.

As she pulled back to take a proper look at Henri, it was hard not to miss the sparkly diamond on her ring finger. After years of being single like Henri, a journalist-slash-farmer from Mingenew had walked into her café and swept Frankie off her feet. Although he worked at the radio station in Geraldton, he now lived in Bunyip Bay and had apparently taken over the running of the *Bunyip News* from Susan O'Neil. Henri had only met Logan twice but he seemed like a good bloke and she was happy for her friend.

'I've been at the beach,' she said, surprised Frankie couldn't smell the salt on her.

'You went for a swim before you came and saw me?'

Henri shrugged. 'Priorities. But I'm seeing you before Mum, Tilley and the boys.'

Frankie nodded her approval. 'Do they know you're coming?'

'Nope. Thought I'd surprise them, although no doubt they'll hear about it before I get back to Bungara.' She glanced in the direction of Eileen Brady, who was definitely listening to their conversation. 'Anyway, what's been going on around here?'

'Oh my God, so much. You got time for a drink and we'll fill you in?'

'We?'

Frankie gestured to a table in the corner where two women were sitting. 'You remember Ruby, and you've met Stella before too, haven't you?'

Henri barely had time to reply before her friend deposited her in a seat alongside them. More greetings were exchanged, and Henri asked Frankie after her older sister Simone, who'd remarried and moved to Mingenew a year or so ago.

'Oh, she's fab—loving living on a farm, and the girls are doing well too.'

'That's great. Hopefully I'll actually get a chance to catch up with her now I'm home for a while.' Henri nodded to the paperwork on the table that included various drawings of some kind of creature. 'What's all this about?'

'We're looking at submissions from sculptors to try and decide who to commission for the Big Bunyip.'

'The Big what?' It sounded vaguely familiar. Her mum had probably mentioned it during one of their obligatory Sunday check-ins, but the truth was Henri usually switched off after the first couple of minutes.

'We're organising the creation and installation of a Big Bunyip when you come into town from the south,' Stella explained, rubbing her hand over her enormous pregnant bump. Henri probably should have asked when she was due, but the moment had passed.

'What about the Bunyip statue in the park?' She remembered when it was erected—her whole primary school had trekked down to the park for the unveiling and there'd even been a TV person from Geraldton. It had been very exciting for her eight-year-old self.

Ruby laughed. 'We're planning something much bigger than that. You know, like Wagin has the giant ram and Wyndham a big croc?'

Henri nodded; having travelled all around Australia for work, she was well aware of the many big things their country was famous for.

'We want something that will really put Bunyip Bay on the map,' Stella explained.

'Aren't we already on the map?' The caravan park had looked pretty full when Henri passed it coming into town, and the beach was already busy, even though school holidays hadn't started yet.

'The truth is,' Stella began with a sheepish smile, 'my daughter read a library book about Australia's Big Things and decided the bunyip in the park isn't big enough.'

'And,' Frankie said, 'when Heidi wants something—especially something as crazy and wonderful as a ridiculously massive bunyip—Heidi gets it.'

Stella beamed. 'These two really do spoil her. I keep telling them they need to have their own babies to overindulge.'

'Don't you worry,' Ruby said with a wink, 'Drew and I are working very hard on doing just that. In fact, I'm hoping he isn't home too late tonight so we can work some more.'

Oh God. The last thing Henri wanted to talk about was making babies. 'Sounds like this project is going to be pretty pricey. Are you guys organising a fundraiser?'

Such events were frequent around here—cake stalls, sausage sizzles, quiz and bingo nights, the annual Undies Run, locally published cookbooks … there was always something happening. If there was one thing the residents of Bunyip Bay excelled at it was raising money.

Ruby shook her head as she reached for her mug. 'No need. We received an anonymous donation just last week.'

Before anyone could say any more, the door of the café opened and a loud voice pierced the air.

'I don't believe it. Rosemary said Cecil was outside the café, but I had to come see with my own eyes.' Henri's sister, Tilley, dressed in her Ag Store uniform of black shorts and a bright red polo shirt, yanked her out of her seat and pulled her into a hug. 'What are you doing here?'

'Surprise!' Henri faux-smiled as she disentangled herself from Tilley's arms.

'Mum is going to lose her mind when she sees you. Are you home till Christmas or …' She shook her head and glared at Henri. 'This better not be a quick trip to tell us you're working for Christmas. You know how hard Mum finds the festive season without Dad, if you're not going to be here—'

Henri held up a hand. 'Relax. I'm here till the day after Boxing Day.' Hopefully by then she'd have her head straight again, because if not … *No*, that wasn't worth thinking about. 'I thought I might be able to lend Andrew and Callum a hand on the farm. They're still harvesting, aren't they?'

Tilley nodded. 'Yeah, but they're almost done. Don't worry, I'm sure Mum will find plenty of jobs for you to do, and failing that, you can always come hang out at the shop.'

By 'hang out', Henri was pretty sure her sister meant free labour.

'Speaking of Mum, I should probably head out to the farm before the bush telegraph alerts her to my arrival.' She turned back to Ruby and Stella. 'Lovely to see you both again. Good luck with the bunyip.'

'Thanks,' they said in unison.

'I'll call you,' Henri told Frankie, giving her another hug. 'I want to hear all your wedding plans.'

Frankie grinned. 'Excellent. Chat soon.'

Tilley saw Henri out to Cecil, nattering the whole way about what was going on with the business, James, and their daughter Macy. She didn't once ask if there was a reason Henri was home early, and Henri didn't know if she was happy or annoyed about that. Weren't big sisters supposed to be confidantes? Although they'd shared a bedroom growing up, the ten-year age gap meant they had never been close—not in the way Frankie and Simone were anyway.

'I wish I could come out and see Mum's face when you arrive,' Tilley said as Henri climbed into the van. 'But I'm bringing Macy out after school to ride her horse, so we'll catch up then.'

'Bye.' Henri pulled Cecil's door shut, snapped on her seatbelt and started towards home.

Ten minutes later, she slowed the van as the sign for Bungara Springs loomed on the side of the road and felt a familiar rush of love as she turned down their long gravel driveway. She jumped out and collected the mail from the mailbox her granddad had made from an old Esky, then smiled as she bumped over the cattle grid and scanned the flat, dry earth on either side. Leftover canola stalks poked forlornly out of the ground, indicating that these front paddocks had already been harvested. Although she spent most of her time in rural areas, there was nothing quite like *this* area. This farm. The place where she'd grown up. Tilley said their brothers were almost finished harvesting, but at least Henri would be able to help with the clean-up and machinery servicing.

Further on, she saw a harvester in the distance and some cattle in one of the home paddocks. She passed the sheds, where she'd spent many a freezing cold winter and sweltering summer day helping her parents, and then finally came upon the homestead, where her mum now lived alone. Callum, Andrew and their young families lived in other houses on the property, far enough away that Fiona couldn't live in their pockets but close enough that she was available for babysitting at short notice.

A couple of brown kangaroos were grazing under an old gum tree just outside the fence that surrounded the house garden, but they bounded away as Cecil noisily approached.

Henri had barely emerged from the van, when she heard her mum's voice and looked up to see her hurrying towards her.

'Good golly, is that really you, Henrietta?'

'Hey, Mum. Hope you don't mind an early visitor.'

'Are you crazy?' She threw her arms around Henri, almost knocking her off balance. 'This is the best surprise I've had all year. You're still staying for Christmas, aren't you?'

'Yes, Mum.'

'Well, then, let's get you inside and settled.'

Henri grabbed her luggage and followed her mother inside, swallowing at the sight of her dad's boots still sitting by the front door, his beloved dogs Max and Muriel resting on either side. She bent to pat the old girls, who once would have run out to greet her when they'd heard the van but were now tired and content to laze around.

'So, what's brought you home so early?' her mum asked as they sat down in the big country kitchen with a cup of tea a few minutes later. The dining table felt enormous with only the two of them. 'I thought you were working in the Riverina till mid-December?'

A lump formed in Henri's throat and she took a sip of her drink before replying. Should she tell her mother the truth?

'I … *They* … they overbooked pilots and I wasn't needed, so I thought I'd come home and see if I could be any help here.'

'Well, there's always plenty of things to do on the farm—I can definitely use you in the garden—but we'll make sure you'll get some time for some fun too. And you're not the only one who's just come home.' She grinned over the top of her teacup, clearly wanting Henri to bite.

When she didn't, she added, 'Mark Morgan has finally retired and is home to take over the family farm.'

Mark had been in Henri's year at school and unable to hold down a conversation if it wasn't about football; he had been snapped up by Essendon at eighteen.

'Apparently, he's nursing a broken heart because his WAM decided not to come with him.'

'WAM?'

Her mother nodded knowingly. 'It's what the partners of footballers are called.'

Henri snorted and covered her mouth so as not to spit tea all over the tablecloth. 'I think you mean WAGs.'

'Whatever.' She shrugged. 'The important thing is that he's single again and so are you.'

Oh my God. Henri hadn't been home five minutes and it had started already. She took a deep breath.

'Mum, I wouldn't date Mark Morgan if he was the last man on earth. He was arrogant at school and from what I hear he's only got worse.'

'Well, you shouldn't listen to everything you hear,' her mother said snootily and took another sip of her tea. 'But never mind, there are plenty more eligible bachelors in town. Wait till you meet the new pastor!'

Not wanting to start an argument with her mother this early in her stay, Henri forced a smile, downed the dregs of her tea and then headed outside to find her brothers.

Chapter Two

'Evening, boys,' Liam said as local farmer Ryan Forrester and his new husband Grant approached the bar. It was the first Saturday of December, and they were busier than they'd been in weeks.

'Hey,' Ryan said as Grant nodded a hello. 'How's things tonight?'

'Busy. Finally. It's been a bit quiet in here lately, that's for sure. Guess you guys have finished harvest too?'

'Ah huh. Thank God.' Ryan grinned and ran a hand through his unruly, dark blond hair. 'Every year it feels like it's never going to end, and I always feel kinda surprised when it does.'

'He's been a bit of a bear to live with these past few weeks,' Grant said, smiling fondly at Ryan. 'Lucky I've been busy with end of year reports and school stuff to miss him too much.'

'Sounds like you could both do with a drink then?' Liam said, already reaching for glasses.

Being the publican of The Palace for almost ten years meant he knew what most of the locals wanted without having to ask. While he poured Ryan a pint of lager and then Grant a glass of red, he asked the kinds of questions he'd never have imagined asking anyone when he was growing up in Silver Ridge,

Colorado. Questions about canola prices and broken combs on headers. Liam didn't pretend to be a farming expert by any means, but over the years he'd picked up a few things. He certainly knew enough to hold his own in conversations with his customers.

'You staying for dinner as well?' he asked as Grant pressed his credit card against the EFTPOS machine.

'Yep.' Grant glanced over to the dining room, which was filling up fast.

'We were supposed to be heading to Geraldton for dinner at the Italian restaurant,' Ryan explained, 'but then Adam called and said a bunch of them were getting together for an impromptu end of harvest celebration and …'

'Here we are,' Grant finished, lifting his glass and taking a sip. 'You know Ryan, he can never resist a good party.'

Liam laughed. 'Well, enjoy. Lara will come and take your orders soon.'

As the men headed into the dining room to join their friends, he poured another pint for Rex Carter, who was more commonly known as Sexy Rexy and pretty much a permanent fixture at the bar once the sun went down. No matter what was going on around the place, Liam could always rely on Rex and a few other townies who liked to play cards of an evening to keep him in business. The past few weeks, with most of the town stuck on headers twenty-four hours a day or driving trucks constantly up and down the main street on the way to the wheat bins, it would hardly have been worth opening if it weren't for the blokes he'd nicknamed the 'Poker Pensioners'.

'Thanks, champ,' Rex said, lifting his glass to his mouth, the froth catching on his thick, unruly moustache.

'You're welcome,' Liam replied before turning to the next patron. Normally, Rex liked to have a bit of a chat but there was no time tonight. Liam and his two backpacker bartenders—Lara and Dylan—were all run off their feet, and behind him in the kitchen he could hear Macca barking at Tegan as they worked hard to fill the many orders.

'Do you mind if I sneak off to the bathroom quickly?' Lara asked during a brief lull at the bar. 'Dylan's just taking an order to table ten, but he won't be long and I'm—'

'Go,' Liam shooed her out of the bar, then picked up a glass and began to polish it, smiling as he surveyed the crowded pub. This might not have been the life he'd envisaged for himself when he was growing up, but it was the one that had saved him.

The Palace wasn't anything like its name; when he first arrived, it had been in desperate need of a lot of TLC, but something about its rustic country decor and non-pretentious vibe had got under his skin. Not to mention the long chat he'd had with then publican, Arthur McArthur, following which he'd made an offer to the man that was too good to refuse.

Sure, the hours were crap and at least once a week he had to manhandle a lout who'd had one too many, but there were also plenty of perks. He got his beer at cost price—not that he drank that much himself anymore—and his nights were never boring. He'd made many acquaintances during his time here, people like Ryan, Grant, and even Sexy Rexy—not friends exactly, but living and working in the pub meant he got plenty of social interaction. Sometimes more than he wanted.

Over the years he'd made improvements—putting a new lick of paint on both the inside and outside of the building, handcrafting tables and chairs, overhauling the menu and introducing a jukebox, which he quickly removed when he discovered some people had dire taste in music. Spice Girls on repeat was not something he wanted to hear in his pub ever again. Now he had surround-sound stereo and only he selected the tunes—currently Kings of Leon—and he could play something softer in the dining room than the rest of the pub. Occasionally he even got in a live band, and on those nights The Palace was packed to the rafters.

He'd single-handedly transformed it from a place where only itinerant farm workers and cray-fishermen hung out for the sole purpose of getting sloshed, to somewhere locals could enjoy a nice meal with friends or family. These days many community groups chose to hold their meetings in the dining room rather than in the vast Memorial Hall; he had a quiz night once a month and themed food different days of the week. Like it had been in eras gone by, The Palace was once again the hub of this close-knit community and somewhere tourists weren't scared to go in the holiday season.

'Excuse me? What's a girl got to do to get a drink around here?'

Liam blinked, startled from his reverie at the sassy voice of a woman. If it wasn't for her exclamation and subsequent thump against the bar, he probably wouldn't have seen her—she wasn't much taller than the bar itself. But what she lacked in height she made up for in beauty—natural beauty, not the caked-on glamour variety. And she didn't look as if she cared much about fashion either. She was wearing the same shapeless blue shirt that most of the male farmers usually got around in, only on her it looked sexy as all hell.

'I'm sorry?'

'I *said* …' Her dark eyes flashed with mischief below her thick chocolate brown fringe. 'What's a girl got to do to get a drink around here? Actually … don't answer that.'

Her tone said she'd expected him to say something crass and he bit down on the impulse to defend himself. 'What can I get you?'

'A pint of Guinness, please?'

'Coming right up.' He grabbed a glass and started to pour, scrutinising her in what he hoped was a surreptitious manner. Was the pint for a boyfriend or something? She wasn't wearing a ring, but that didn't necessarily mean anything. Most of the girls around here drank wine or mixers. Although she was about the height of a pixie, she sported a 'don't mess with me' expression that indicated she wasn't in the best of moods. That only piqued his interest more.

'You're not a local,' he said as he handed over her beer. Though there was something vaguely familiar about her, as if maybe they'd met before, but he couldn't place her.

'I'm more damn local than you,' she retorted, slapping a twenty-dollar note down on the bar and taking a sip of her drink. 'Ah, that's better.' She sighed and gazed at the glass as if it had just given her the best sex of her life.

Then before he could ask her name, she tucked the change into her pocket and sashayed into the dining room, her tight, skinny jeans giving him the perfect view of her pert behind. For such a tiny package there was certainly a lot to like about her. She weaved her way through the tables, pausing occasionally to exchange a few brief words with people she passed, before settling at the large table where Ryan and Grant now sat with their friends. The sexy Guinness-drinker was the odd one out in the group—the only one who didn't appear to have a partner.

Not that *that* meant anything. Her boyfriend or girlfriend might be otherwise occupied tonight, but whether she was in a relationship didn't matter because *whoever* she was, she clearly had connections in Bunyip Bay, which meant she was off limits. When it came to romantic liaisons, Liam kept a strictly no-strings policy. In the past, he'd enjoyed a bit of fun with the backpackers who worked in the pub—people who were in town for a good time not a long time—but these days most of them were far too young for him, which meant his liaisons were few and far between.

'I wouldn't go getting any ideas about that one if I were you,' said Rex, downing the last dregs of his beer.

'Huh?' Liam tore his gaze from the dining room to the scruffy man.

'Firecracker, she is. Reckon she'd be way more trouble than she's worth.'

'Really? Who exactly is she?'

'Henrietta Forward, although call her Henrietta and I hear she'll deck you. Goes by the name of Henri. She's Fred and Fiona's youngest. Was always getting into scrapes as a young'un.'

Liam racked his mind trying to recall what he knew about her family. The Forwards owned one of the largest farms in the region. Fred Forward had died a few years ago from a heart attack. There were two brothers—both farmers—and a sister, Tilley … *now* he recalled Fiona Forward sometimes talking about a younger daughter with a mixture of pride and frustration. Hadn't she once told him her youngest was the only reason she was such a regular church-goer? That if she kept on God's good side, hopefully he'd take care of her daughter.

'She's a pilot or something, isn't she?'

Rex nodded and pushed his empty pint glass across the counter. Liam refilled it with Carlton Draught. Looking at Henrietta, you'd never have guessed she flew planes for a living—she didn't look big enough to see over the controls in the cockpit.

'So, she doesn't live in Bunyip Bay?' he asked.

'Nah. I don't think she lives anywhere. Like most in her field, she follows the work—all over Australia, probably all over the world.'

'I bet Fiona's happy to have her home for a bit.'

Rex snorted. 'From what I've heard, Fiona will only be happy when she gets her home for good.'

Chapter Three

As Henri stepped away from the bar and headed into the dining room, she took a moment to properly take in her surroundings. When she was a kid, sometimes her family had come here for dinner if her mum couldn't be bothered cooking. It had been the only place in town that served a sit-down dinner, yet it had been anything but flash. She remembered she hated the smell of greasy food, beer-soaked carpets and smoke that seemed to permeate the building even though smokers had been relegated to the front verandah by then. Most often those evenings had ended with her mum complaining all the way back to the farm about the dirty plates or the weird smell in the restrooms and her dad saying that you couldn't afford to be fussy in the country.

'Arthur McArthur's a good bloke. He does his best,' he'd always say, 'and at least we don't have to do the washing up tonight!'

The pub she was standing in now did not look anything like the pub she remembered. Although she'd been in for the occasional drink on her trips home, whenever she stepped inside The Palace she was always a bit shocked by its transformation. While the layout was still the same, the walls once stained with offensive brown patches were now a soft buttery colour, and instead of the dented old beer signs that used to hang on them, there were classy black and white prints of other country pubs from all around Australia. The floorboards were so shiny they could be dangerous and the old 1960s furniture had been replaced with beautifully designed and handcrafted tables and chairs. There were also cosy nooks with leather armchairs and sofas, and the light fittings that cast a perfect glow over everything looked sophisticated and rather expensive.

It wasn't your average outback pub—Henri could easily have just stepped off a street in Perth, Sydney or Melbourne into a funky bar—yet it had the warm, familiar vibe of a good country local, and apparently this was all down to the new publican, Liam Castle. Well, not exactly new, but in a town like Bunyip Bay you were new until you'd lived here at least three or four decades and if her maths was right, he must have only been here about one.

She glanced back to see him pouring more pints, chatting away with his customers. Henri didn't know much about him, but everyone said he was a good bloke. He had to be a patient man to put up with some of the people in this place.

'Henri, what's the hold-up?' called Tilley, from a large table in the middle of the dining room.

'Coming,' she hissed.

Everyone stood as she arrived, and she went around the table greeting them all. She'd been hoping for a night out to catch up with Frankie alone; aside from a couple of brief phone calls, her best friend had been unable to make the time for her yet. Henri understood she was busy, but she'd also really love a chance to talk to her without her fiancé or anyone else around. The only introduction needed was to Ryan's handsome husband Grant, a drama teacher who commuted from Bunyip Bay to Geraldton for work. It was good to finally meet him after hearing so much about him.

Until the two of them walked in here one night holding hands, no one had had any idea that Ryan was gay and, according to Henri's mother, there'd been much mourning and gnashing of teeth among the single ladies in town. It had been the same when Adam had married single mum Stella.

Finally sinking into a chair, she was suddenly very aware that she was the only single person at the table. There had to be something in the water in Bunyip Bay. The last couple of years everyone Henri knew was pairing off at a rate of knots. Whenever she called home, it felt like Fiona told her about yet another person she'd grown up with either getting engaged or getting pregnant, neither of which appealed to her in the slightest.

A waitress Henri didn't know came to take their orders and then conversation returned to the current hot topics in the Bay—the recent harvest, what everyone was doing for Christmas, and also the identity of the town's mysterious benefactor. Although Henri had grown up with most of these people, she couldn't help feeling a bit of an outsider as they talked. So much happened while she was away and, sometimes, she felt a little lost.

Over the years, her mum had kept her informed about Bunyip Bay's philanthropist—debts had been paid, romantic getaways gifted to couples doing it tough; there'd been an anonymous donation for a brand-new nature playground at the primary school, and the last couple of years, a generous donation towards the town Christmas tree. The latest in this long list was a contribution to the Big Bunyip Fund, which Stella, Frankie and Ruby had been discussing last week.

'So, does anyone have any idea who it is yet?' Henri asked, more to feel part of the conversation than because she had any real curiosity.

Logan shook his head. 'Nope, but my boss heard about it, and he reckons I should investigate. He thinks it'd make a good segment for our new podcast about feel-good stories from country towns.'

'I listen to that podcast when I'm on the road,' Henri said. 'I really loved the one about the drag queens saving the bowling club.'

Logan smiled. 'That was one of my favourites too. Those girls were a hoot.'

Drew picked up his beer. 'But *they* also seemed happy to talk, whereas our bloke here clearly wants to remain anonymous. Maybe your boss should respect that.'

'Who should respect what?'

Henri swivelled her head at the sound of a deep voice behind her to see Liam Castle standing there with a tray. As he leaned over and picked up her empty glass, she caught a whiff of some kind of woody cologne and inhaled deeply before she realised what she was doing. But he smelled *good*—much better than anyone surrounded by beer and pub grub should.

'The mysterious benefactor,' Tilley informed him. 'We were just discussing his latest gift for the Big Bunyip. Logan's boss wants him to try and get to the bottom of it.'

'How do you know this so-called benefactor is a man?' Liam asked as he collected the rest of the empty glasses.

All eyes around the table blinked, then Frankie exclaimed, 'Oh my God, you're right. How terribly sexist of us. Women can be rich too.'

'Do you have any idea who it could be, Liam?' asked Stella.

'Nope.' He jerked his head towards the bar. 'My clientele is more the good hardworking variety, rather than millionaires.'

Everyone laughed.

'Well, if you do hear anything,' Logan said, 'let me know.'

'Will do.'

'You really gunna pursue this?' asked Stella.

Logan shrugged. 'Look, if I don't, Garry will put someone else on the job and they might not care about the town or the people the way I do; all they'll want is to get a good story. If I do it, at least we can control the narrative.'

'You sure you're not just missing the excitement of your old job?' James said with a smirk. Until hooking up with Frankie, Logan had worked for a newspaper in Perth. 'I imagine drivetime radio and fiddling with the *Bunyip News* gets a little boring.'

'Nothing boring about radio—you should hear some of the people who call in. But wouldn't you guys like to see something in the local rag besides cricket scores, petty crimes and notices of the upcoming AGM?'

They all agreed it would be a nice change.

'Can I get anyone any refills?' Liam asked.

Henri nodded. 'Yes, another Guinness please.'

Everyone gave their orders and Liam retreated to the bar.

'You know, if this guy's—I mean *person's*—identity is revealed, they might put an end to the good deeds,' Drew said as Liam retreated to get their drinks.

'But the donations keep getting more and more outrageous,' Frankie said with a shrug. 'Maybe they want to be outed?'

'I am curious about why whoever it is does it,' Logan admitted. 'And where they got all their money from.' He looked to Drew. 'Shouldn't you be a little interested as well? I mean, what if it's dirty money?'

Drew snorted and shook his head. 'You journos have vivid imaginations. Why don't you stick to radio and writing up missing cat notices in the *Bunyip News*. I'll stick to fighting the bad guys.'

'Why do you care so much about me finding out?' Logan teased. 'You got something to hide? Didn't the benefactor give Ruby a whole load of money for new horses a couple of years back?'

'Hah,' Ruby said, 'if you're asking if Drew is the mysterious benefactor, then that would be mega news to me. And I'd be very disappointed that he hasn't forked out for the kitchen renovation I'm desperate for.'

'If you're such a good researcher,' Drew added, and Henri couldn't tell whether he was amused or pissed off, 'then you'd know that the random acts began long before I arrived in the Bay.'

She grinned as the discussion heated up and people either sided with Logan or Drew. But just when it was really starting to get interesting, Frankie put a stop to it, very obviously changing the topic of conversation.

'So, Henri,' she said loudly after Liam had delivered the next round of drinks, 'tell us what you've been up to. Any exciting stories from the sky?'

Exciting stories? Henri's stomach tightened and she reached for the comfort of her glass. 'Um … not really. I was mustering up north until November. Before that I was in Quebec spraying budworms.'

'Where are you off to next?' Logan wanted to know.

'I've got a fire contract starting up down south just after Christmas and then later in the year I'm heading over to Canada again.' At least she hoped she was.

'Wow,' Ruby said, 'you certainly get around. Don't you ever get sick of living out of a suitcase?'

'Not really. You get used to travelling light.'

'And do you get much chance for romance on the road, or rather in the air?' Grant asked, his arm wrapped around Ryan's shoulder.

Henri chose to ignore the question, taking a large gulp of her Guinness instead. There hadn't been what she'd call 'romance' in years, but people still insisted on asking and it really got her goat. She was fairly certain single men didn't get asked this question so much.

At the other end of the table, Tilley laughed. 'Romance? Much to Mum's disgust, Henri doesn't know the meaning of the word.'

'My lifestyle isn't really conducive to a relationship,' Henri explained, annoyed that she felt she had to. 'And I'm not really the settling-down type anyway.'

'Don't you want to have babies?' Stella asked, looking at Henri as if she had reindeer antlers growing out of her head.

Henri didn't want to offend the pregnant woman—not that anyone seemed to be worried about offending her! The last week at home with her mother, sometimes she'd felt like she was living in a Jane Austen novel where all anyone cared about was marrying people off. And procreating. She'd hoped for a reprieve from that tonight.

'Nieces and nephews are quite enough for me,' she said finally.

'What about sex?' This from Tilley, but everyone leaned forward a little, their eyes twinkling with interest.

She shot her sister a warning glare. 'I'm not a nun, if that's what you're asking.'

It might have been years since her last serious relationship, but she knew how and where to find someone to scratch the itch when the need arose. *And* she had a very good vibrator when the available talent didn't take her fancy.

'Yeah, from what she tells me, Henri does okay in that department,' Frankie said with a knowing wink and Henri could have hugged her.

'I bet I could find you someone,' Grant said, as if he hadn't heard a word of what she and Frankie had just said.

'Ooh yes,' Stella exclaimed as the others nodded in excited agreement. Even Frankie.

What the hell?

Before Henri could restate that she wasn't on the lookout for love, sex or marriage, Grant beamed. 'I've become Bunyip Bay's unofficial matchmaker.'

Ruby nodded. 'It's true. He's already married off Sally the vet, three teachers and a number of lonely farmers.'

He shrugged—'I can't help myself. I'm considering setting up a business on the main street'—and then winked.

'But since you're a friend of mine,' Ryan said, smiling at his husband, 'he'll be happy to give you mate's rates, won't you?'

Grant nodded. 'Of course. This'll be fun. I have a few ideas of potential beaus already. I could have you married off by Christmas.'

Once again everyone laughed and James said, 'If you succeed, you'll make my mother-in-law one very happy lady.'

Henri gritted her teeth—what part of 'I'm not really the settling-down type' did they not understand? Ninety-nine per cent of her socks were single, and you didn't see *them* crying about it! There was nothing worse than hanging out with a bunch of happy couples who didn't think anyone could be happy and content by themselves. Or thought her career so unimportant that she'd happily toss it in to return to the Bay to be somebody's Mrs, barefoot and pregnant in the kitchen. She didn't need her mum, her sister, or some guy she'd only just met sticking their noses in where it wasn't wanted.

Why on earth had she thought coming home so early was a good idea? She'd barely been back a week and already she was feeling claustrophobic and homicidal. And she hadn't had a chance to talk to Frankie about her problem. She should have gone to Bali and treated herself to a month at a spa, then flown home on Christmas Eve.

Ah, the benefit of hindsight.

'Thanks,' she said, 'but I'm not looking for marriage so I wouldn't want to waste your time. Anyone need another drink?'

Not waiting for their replies, she pushed to a stand and made a beeline for the bar.

'Another pint?' Liam asked.

Henri was about to say yes, when she changed her mind. She suspected she was going to need something stronger to get her through the rest of the evening. 'Actually, make it a whiskey. On the rocks.'

'Single or double?'

She glanced back towards the dining room where her sister and friends were no doubt plotting her wedding to some guy she hadn't even met, or worse, someone she had.

'Better make it a double.'

He raised his eyebrows. 'Not enjoying dinner?'

'Dinner's fine,' she replied, 'it's the company that's pissing me off.'

Chapter Four

As Liam poured Henri's drink, he glanced towards the dining room and couldn't hide his frown. He didn't like *everyone* in town but the people she was here with were some of the best around. Like him, most of them had experienced some kind of hardship or heartache and it had shaped them into people who gave a damn about others. He knew much more about each of them than they did about him, but that wasn't because they didn't care or weren't interested.

He slid her whiskey across the bar and watched as she downed half of it in one go. 'Want to talk about it?'

She shook her head—'It's nothing really'—and took another sip of her drink.

'I don't think we've officially met. I'm Liam,' he said, offering her his hand.

'I know.' She stared at it a few long moments before reaching out and sliding her hand into his. 'Henri.'

It was one of the most innocuous gestures there was, but it felt anything but innocuous. Just having her tiny hand in his did weird things to his insides. He held it a fraction too long, but she didn't seem in any hurry to let go either. Then again, she was quite possibly halfway to half-cut and thus her reflexes might be delayed, so he withdrew his hand and tried to collect himself before anyone noticed and started jumping to conclusions.

'Henri. Short for Henrietta?'

She made a face like she'd just tasted something nasty.

'What's wrong with Henrietta?' he asked, amused.

'What's right with it? It's too many syllables for starters and so bloody old-fashioned. Not to mention girly.'

'And you're not girly?'

She glared at him over the top of her glass. 'Are all publicans as chatty as you?'

'I don't actually know any others, and most customers would say I'm not particularly chatty.' Listening was more his gig. 'But I guess some people just inspire more conversation than others.'

'Is that so?' This earned him a smile and, as sexy as Henri was when she was scowling, her smile made him feel as if his chest was full of fireworks. 'How about we talk about you then?'

Once again, he glanced towards the dining room—talking about himself was his least favourite pastime and these days it was rare anyone even tried to get him to. Of course, there'd been a bit of interest when he first arrived in the town, but then there'd been a scandal about a group of farmers who'd had a swingers' club in the seventies and attention switched to that as everyone tried to work out who was involved. There was always something happening in a small town, and it wasn't long before Liam blended into the background. People didn't come to the pub to learn about him, they came to socialise and have fun with their mates or to drown their sorrows alone, which often led to them talking about themselves.

Honestly, the things he'd heard. Some of the locals seemed to have confused him for a priest in confession. He knew who was having an affair with who, who took medication for depression and other ailments they didn't want friends and family knowing about, who had gambling problems, who hated their job, who hated their boss, who wanted to sleep with their boss, who'd cheated on exams, who'd lied on resumes … The list of transgressions was endless. If Liam were a different kind of person, he'd be able to blackmail half the people in this town and a few beyond, but instead he tried to be a welcome ear when someone needed it and the rest of the time he kept his mouth shut.

'Shouldn't you be getting back to your friends?' he said.

'Who are you? The social police?'

Another gulp of her drink—she sure was putting them away fast, and he hoped she could handle her liquor. He took his duty to serve alcohol responsibly very seriously, but he got the feeling Henri wouldn't take too kindly to being told to slow down.

'Trust me,' she went on, 'there's plenty of time to talk weddings, bunyips and babies. Right now, I could do with a few minutes' reprieve. So tell me …' She planted her elbows on the bar and leaned towards him. 'Where are you from? That accent's American, right?'

Her question surprised him. People rarely asked about his accent; sometimes he forgot he even had one. 'Yeah. I'm from Colorado.'

'Long way from home.' She swished the ice around her glass. 'I've spent a lot of time flying in Canada and travelled a bit in the US, but I've never been to Colorado. Mountains, right? Snow? Big lakes? Cutesy small towns that look good on postcards.'

He nodded. 'That's about right.'

She glanced into her glass and then back to him. 'So, what brought you down under?'

'My mom was Aussie.'

'Really? Where was she from?'

Always reticent to talk about his family, he hesitated a moment, but something about Henri made him want to continue the conversation. 'Her parents had a farm near Dubbo in New South Wales.'

'I know that area well. How'd you end up in Bunyip Bay?'

'Well … I'd always been curious about my Aussie roots. In my mid-twenties, I decided to take some time out and this was one of the places I visited. I fell in love and never left.'

'I don't blame you. It's a gorgeous place, and as infuriating as some of the people in Bunyip Bay can be, this is one of the prettiest parts of the country. There aren't many towns that have good farming land on one side and a fab beach on the other.'

'Yeah, this place *also* looks pretty good on postcards,' he said, gesturing to a little stand on the bar, which was dusty because nobody really bothered with postcards anymore.

They shared a smile.

'Do you get to go home much?' she asked.

Home? At this one word, Liam's chest tightened. He shook his head and changed tack. 'You said you've flown in the US and Canada? Whereabouts? What exactly did you do there?'

The diversion worked. 'There's not as much flying work in Australia as there once was, so most of us travel a bit. The last couple of years I've taken a forestry contract spraying Spruce Budworm over there. After Quebec, I generally stay for a few months in the Prairie Provinces spraying fungicide on crops.'

'That's a really nice part of Canada—I went on a school trip there. You're lucky your job takes you to such cool places.'

'Yeah.' That one word was long and heavy, and Liam got the feeling she had something on her mind, but she hit him with a wry smile and said, 'It's a tough life, but someone's got to do it.'

'How long are you back here for?'

She glanced over to the table where her sister and friends were deep in conversation, then sighed. 'Almost four weeks. I don't usually get as long between contracts and I thought it'd be nice to spend a bit of time back at home, but I'm beginning to second-guess my decision.'

'Did you ever consider flying for a commercial airline?'

She scoffed. 'That would bore me to bloody tears. At that level the details disappear, but low-level flying you can see everything from an angle and height most people never get to. You see cattle feeding, the wind rustling through crops and shimmering over entire fields. On a still morning in the mountains, sometimes the fog looks like a waterfall flowing over a precipice, tumbling down into a valley in beautiful slow motion. You see amazing sunsets and sunrises, and not one day or flight is the same.'

'Flying that low in such a small plane must be pretty dangerous though.'

'Oh my God!' Her wistful smile faded and her eyes narrowed. 'Don't you start. I get enough of that from my mother, and I came here tonight to escape her.'

'I'm sorry. I just—'

'What's taking you so long?' Tilley came up to the bar and wrapped an arm around her younger sister.

Liam thought he noticed Henri flinch.

'I'm only coming back if you promise there'll be no more talk about setting me up with anyone,' she said. 'I swear if Grant mentions marrying me off one more time, I'll rip off my sock and stuff it in his mouth.'

'Henri!' Tilley scolded and Liam stifled a smile. 'No one meant any harm,' she added with a bit of a pout. 'We just care about you and want to see you happy.'

'I *am* happy.' Henri sighed and pushed her now empty glass towards Liam. 'Top-up, please?'

'How about you have a glass of soda water instead?' Tilley suggested, glaring at Liam as if warning him not to refill her sister's glass if he knew what was good for him.

Henri glared at him just as hard and although he agreed with her sister that maybe she should lay off the heavy stuff or at least slow down, he found himself unable to say no to her. Besides, she was a grown woman and he imagined being treated like a child when you were an adult would be infuriating. Without a word, he picked up a fresh glass and made her another whiskey on the rocks, slightly heavier than normal on the ice.

'Thanks, Liam.' Henri gave her sister a triumphant smile as she picked up the glass and sauntered back towards the dining room.

Tilley opened her mouth as if to give him what for, but he held up a hand. 'Don't involve me in your sister squabbles,' he said and then moved along the bar to pour Rex his final pint for the night.

With a huff, Tilley went back to join her group and Liam did his best to focus on his job, resisting the urge to glance over at Henri and see how she was getting on. At about nine o'clock, things started to slow down. Rex and the Poker Pensioners had headed home and only a few youngsters around the pool table and a couple of contract workers who were staying above the pub remained. When Tilley, Frankie and everyone stood to leave, he assumed Henri would go with them, but instead he watched with interest as she hugged them all goodbye.

He wasn't close enough to hear her and her sister's conversation, but in his years owning the pub he'd become pretty good at reading body language and theirs was tense. It looked like Tilley was trying to encourage Henri to go with her, but she was having none of it. Eventually James said something—probably about needing to get home to relieve his mother, Susan, from babysitting duties—and Tilley gave in and went with him. Henri headed to the bathroom and when she emerged again, she went over to the group shooting pool, downing shots and generally having a grand old time celebrating the end of harvest.

He guessed they were all about five to ten years younger than Henri but the high-fives she gave a couple of them indicated they knew each other, cementing the fact in Liam's mind that whether she lived here or not, Bunyip Bay was in her blood. She was part of it and it her. Damn pity, because he couldn't remember the last time a woman had walked into the pub and set his blood boiling the way she had.

Deciding it was safer to steer clear of Henri, he didn't allow himself to pay too much attention to the goings-on around the pool table, instead focusing on the few remaining patrons sitting at the bar. When things got a little rowdy, he sent Dylan over to deliver a warning and then grabbed a coffee and retreated into the office to do some paperwork, leaving the bartenders and his dog Sheila, who always slept in her basket behind the bar, to hold the fort.

As office work was his least favourite task, a massive pile of invoices awaited him. His nights were generally busy and during the day he favoured manual tasks, like hauling and replacing kegs or spending time in his workshop out the back. Being active helped keep his dark thoughts at bay, whereas when he sat down in the office, it was much harder.

He took a deep breath and sat down to tackle the paper beast.

Hours later, a knock sounded on his office door and he looked up to see Lara standing there.

'You planning on working all night, boss?' she asked with a smile.

Liam glanced at his watch and couldn't believe it was almost midnight. 'Time flies when you're having fun.'

She laughed and nodded towards the pile of papers on his desk. 'Rather you than me. Dylan's just locking up and I've checked the bathrooms are empty. Anything else you want us to do before knocking off?'

'No, thanks. You guys have a good night. See you tomorrow.'

She nodded and escaped quickly as if scared he might change his mind.

Liam filed the completed invoices and then switched off his computer. Only as he left the office did he notice the absence of his furry companion. He frowned. Sheila didn't like to be left alone, so it was odd she hadn't come to find him when Dylan and Lara had disappeared.

The pub was dark except for the lights above the bar and in the hallway, which led to the stairs up to the second floor. He whistled and called her name.

Just when he was starting to panic—could Sheila somehow have got outside?—she appeared from the direction of the pool table.

'There you are, girl,' he said as she ambled over to him. 'Come on, let's get to bed.'

But when he turned towards the stairs, she didn't follow, and he looked back to see her returning the way she'd come from.

'Sheila!' he called, slightly annoyed now. It was late and he just wanted to fall into bed. 'Come!'

Normally very obedient, she ignored him.

With a frustrated sigh, he followed her to find the reason for her reluctance lying curled up on one of the couches. He sighed. Clearly, Lara and Dylan hadn't done a very thorough scan of the pub before they shut the doors. Although the lights were off in this area, enough moonlight spilled in through the windows for him to identify the squatter as Henrietta Forward.

There were no signs of vomit and she looked far too peaceful—and gorgeous—for someone who'd drunk enough to pass out. Maybe she was just really tired.

'Hey, Henrietta,' he said, reaching out to gently shake her shoulder. 'Time to wake up.'

She made an infuriatingly cute noise and then rolled over and curled in on herself as if she were settling in for the night, but he couldn't just leave her here. The men staying upstairs would be down early in the morning for breakfast and he didn't want them to startle her. Not to mention the fact he couldn't guarantee her safety here all alone.

'Henrietta,' he tried again, his voice firmer this time.

She moaned and turned slightly towards him. 'It's Henri,' she slurred. 'What d'you want?'

She did not sound sober enough to drive.

'Sorry, Henri, but you can't sleep here. Can I call Tilley or someone to come get you?'

Her eyes snapped open, and she looked at him in horror. 'No! I'm fine. I'll sleep in my car.' But when she went to stand, she stumbled and fell right into him.

'Hel-lo,' she semi-sang as she looked up into his face. 'You have very lovely eyes.'

He stifled a smile. The same could be said for her but now was not the time or the place.

'There's one free room upstairs. Why don't you take that?' he offered. 'It'll be much more comfortable than your car.'

She palmed a hand against his chest. 'That, Liam, sounds like an offer too good to refuse. Thank you.'

Almost as if she could understand the exchange, Sheila trotted off towards the stairs and Liam put an arm around Henri, supporting her as he led her to the stairs. It took a great deal of effort—she kept stumbling and talking about how his eyes reminded her of a chocolate bar.

'Do you *have* any schocolate?' she asked, once again pausing on the stairs. 'I've got the munchies.'

'I might be able to find something, but you gotta keep walking to get it.'

'O-kay. If you shay sho, Liam.'

Eventually, they made it up to the landing and past all the closed doors as they headed to the vacant guest room next door to his apartment. Still semi-supporting Henri, he dug in his pocket for his master key and then manoeuvred the door open.

'Do you want to use the bathroom while I find you something to eat?'

She nodded, her eyes drooping again, but when he checked the shared bathrooms, they were both occupied. Dammit.

'Look, why don't you use mine quickly?'

'Thanks, Liam, you're shuch a schweetheart.'

With Sheila at their heels, he led her into his apartment and showed her into the bathroom. 'There's a fresh towel in the cupboard if you want and a new toothbrush under the sink. Anything else I can get you?'

'Can't brush my teeth till I've had my shococlate,' she said.

Suppressing a laugh, he turned to leave. 'I'll see what I can find.'

He grabbed a bottle of water, painkillers and a Mars Bar from his midnight snack stash, then waited patiently outside the door.

After about ten minutes, he tapped his foot, starting to feel a little anxious.

'Henrietta?' he called, tentatively pushing the door open and stepping into his bathroom to find it empty and the other door, leading into his bedroom, open. He found her sprawled across his bed, snoring peacefully. 'Shit.'

Guess he'd been relegated to the couch for the night.

Covering Henrietta with a light sheet, he looked at Sheila, who'd already taken her usual position at the foot of the bed. 'Keep an eye on her for me, okay?'

And then, pulling the door almost shut, leaving just enough room for the dog to get out if needed, he headed out to spend what he already knew would be a restless night in the lounge room.

Chapter Five

When Henri woke, her head seemed to have become the stage for a heavy metal rock band and her throat felt like she'd scoffed a box of Weet-bix without any milk. She groaned, opened one eye slowly—even that simple action hurt like the devil—and then the other. Nothing about this room looked familiar, and was that furry thing slumbering at her feet a dog? It didn't look dangerous and the little sleepy noises it was making were kinda sweet, but still ...

Where the hell am I?

She rolled towards the bedside table and saw her phone and bag alongside a bottle of water, a packet of Panadol and a Mars Bar. *Ugh.* She could not stomach chocolate right now.

Wincing, she sat up slowly and reached for the water. After swallowing two painkillers, she picked up her phone to find a message from Tilley.

Mum thinks you stayed with me last night. Did you sleep in Cecil or did you find alternative company? Hope you were safe and don't have too sore a head this morning. xx

Trust Tilley to add 'kisses' even when she was being all big sisterly and superior, but thank God she'd provided an alibi for their mum. Not that she should have to. At almost thirty years old, Henri was big enough to look after herself, but the moment she stepped back into Bunyip Bay everyone resorted to treating her like a child. She wouldn't be surprised if they sat her at the kids' table for Christmas lunch.

Annoyed, she deleted Tilley's message without replying and surveyed her surroundings as she tried to work out where she was and how exactly she'd come to be here. She thought back to yesterday afternoon at home … She'd been helping her mum make candles for Christmas gifts, when she'd started on at Henri again about growing up and putting down roots.

She was incorrigible—even when Henri was helping her, making an effort to spend quality time with her—she couldn't leave her alone.

Did she somehow know about the crash up north? Henri definitely hadn't told her, and she hadn't yet been able to bring herself to tell Tilley or her brothers either—but maybe her mother had a sixth sense. Or maybe Henri was just being paranoid.

Then again, this wasn't really anything new. It used to be that her mother would drop subtle hints that it would be nice to see Henri more often—saying things like she was glad she'd started her family young, well before her biological clock started ticking—but this time Henri had barely taken her first sip of tea before she'd started on at her. And since then, she'd been like a broken record and had given her lecture-slash-plea so many times that Henri could probably harangue herself.

'I know you like flying, but you've had your fun now, darling. You've seen some amazing places, had some exciting experiences, and the Lord's looked after you so far, but every time you fly it's not only *your* life you put on the line. My blood pressure hasn't been the same since you took to the skies and I went grey before my time worrying about you, young lady! Besides, your career simply isn't compatible with having a family.'

'Who ever said anything about wanting to have a family?!'

The last thing Henri needed was her mother mouthing off about her flying right now—she had enough worries of her own. But of course, her arguments always fell on deaf ears. Fiona Forward simply couldn't understand that anyone might want to take a different path than she had—marriage, four kids and even more grandchildren to cluck over. Three out of her four children had procreated—wasn't that enough?

'You know that agronomist who works with James?'

'No,' Henri said, already dreading what was coming.

'I'm sure you do. Toby Cooper—redhead, tall, lovely smile. He came to town about five years ago with his wife, but she hated country living and they've recently divorced.'

'And that's a *good* thing?' Henri glared at her.

This was why she usually made excuses about only being able to come home for a few days. It had been different when her dad was alive because he'd always stuck up for her, but now …

Having lost track of the number of eligible bachelors her mother had hinted at over the last few days, she was this close to storming out when the phone rang. She'd jumped up to answer it and almost cried with joy when Tilley asked if she wanted to come for dinner at the pub. She hadn't been able to get ready fast enough.

Yet the company at The Palace hadn't been as enjoyable as she'd hoped. She glowered as she remembered her so-called friends, sister, and even her brother-in-law prying into her life, picking holes in her choices and not listening when she'd insisted that she didn't need Ryan's husband to find *her* one!

Thankfully they'd backed off when she returned to the table, but just when she'd finally been starting to relax again, Ruby had glanced at her watch and exclaimed surprise that it was already nine o'clock. They'd all started mumbling about it getting late, as if they'd turn into pumpkins if they didn't call it a night immediately. Knowing her mother would likely still be up watching home improvement shows or the cheesy Christmas movies that had already started on Netflix, Henri ignored Tilley's insistence that she should go too and instead ended up hanging out with a bunch of people who'd been quite a few years behind her at school and were more interested in drinking games and hooking up than weddings and babies.

Oh my God! She sat up a little. Had she gone home with one of them? Most of them were barely out of adolescence and she actually used to babysit Brad McDonald. The thought of doing the horizontal mambo with him made her stomach roil and she hoped her drunken-self had had more sense than that.

How much had she actually had to drink? Right now, Henri felt like she'd been swimming in the vats at a distillery, and the fact she couldn't remember getting here wasn't a good sign.

What was *wrong* with her at the moment? Normally the prying questions of her friends and family would have been water off a duck's back, but ever since the accident she'd been tender. More on edge. Definitely defensive. Still, she couldn't let this happen again. She couldn't turn to alcohol every time someone pissed her off. A couple of drinks was one thing, but having no recall of what had happened after her sister left last night made her feel very uneasy.

In the midst of her panic attack, she heard a faint whistling coming from somewhere beyond the bedroom. Her heart jumped. Was that coffee she could smell? She inhaled deeply. And maybe toast?

Right now, plain toast and coffee felt like perhaps the only thing she could stomach, but that depended on who was making it.

She glanced around the room looking for clues. With its grey-toned walls and lack of any feminine frippery, it could belong to a bachelor, but it was much neater and more sophisticated than most of the guys she'd been with before. And it didn't smell funny either. This bed was so damn comfy, and the forest green sheets didn't feel cheap or dirty—they were as silky soft as those in a five-star hotel, not that she'd stayed in many. There were a couple of framed paintings of snow-capped mountains hanging on one wall and a family photo on the dresser. At this distance she couldn't make out the people but, hoping it would give her some clue as to whose bed she was in, she threw off the sheet to go take a look when a man appeared in the doorway.

He was tall—although pretty much everyone was taller than her—with very broad shoulders and tousled, whiskey-coloured hair, that was neither long nor short. The stubble on his jawline suggested that he sometimes shaved and sometimes didn't bother. In one hand he held a mug and in the other a plate.

The dog raised its head, and Henri could almost swear it smiled at him.

'Liam!' As recognition dawned, she remembered talking to him while he poured her drinks. Until last night, they hadn't exchanged more than a few words, but she'd enjoyed their chat much more than talking with her friends.

'Morning, Henrietta.'

Too flustered to reprimand him for using her full name, she blurted, 'What am I doing here? Did we sleep together?'

Her insides squeezed as she wondered if she'd have to go get the morning after pill from the local pharmacist who'd known her since she was a small child.

'No. We did not,' Liam said, instantly putting her at ease.

'Thank God.' She flopped back against the rather comfy pillows. 'Because when I shag someone, I like to remember.'

'And when *I* shag someone, I prefer them not to be comatose.'

Guilt swamped her and she didn't want Liam to think she was accusing him of anything untoward. The fact her Blundies were still on her feet and her skinny jeans zipped seemed evidence enough that he was telling the truth, but then … what on earth was she doing here?

'I'm sorry, I didn't mean—'

'It's fine,' he said, a little gruffly. 'Anyway, I thought you might like some coffee and toast.'

She smiled up at him. 'Thanks. I'd kill for a coffee, but do you mind if I use your bathroom first?'

He nodded towards an open door off the bedroom. 'You know where it is. I'll give you a few moments … Feel free to grab a towel from the cupboard and have a shower if you like. As I mentioned last night, there's a clean toothbrush under the sink too if you want it.'

Then the poor man slunk out of his bedroom like *he* was the one who had no right to be there. The dog hopped off the bed and followed after him.

Henri waited a couple of seconds and then fled into the bathroom and gasped at the sight of herself in the mirror. No wonder Liam had suggested a shower—with her hair standing up at all angles and her eyes puffy and bloodshot, she looked like someone ready to go Trick or Treating—but she didn't have any fresh clothes to change into.

She did however accept the offer of the toothbrush, steal some of his deodorant and splash water against her face.

As she headed back through the bedroom to collect her things, she couldn't resist pausing at the dresser and taking a squiz at the photo she'd seen earlier. A couple who looked to be in their early to mid thirties and two kids—a boy and a younger girl—smiled happily back at her. She picked it up to take a closer look.

Was the man or the boy Liam? Henri found it hard to tell, and what did it matter to her anyway?

Putting the photo back down, she grabbed her phone, shoved it into her bag, then took a deep breath and walked out.

'Hi,' she said sheepishly when she found him sitting at the kitchen counter, flicking through the *Sunday Times* as he sipped a cup of coffee.

'Feel a bit better?' he asked, looking up.

She nodded.

'Want some toast? I can make some fresh?'

'Um …' Henri felt she ought to say no—he was probably just asking to be polite—but her stomach groaned so loudly even Liam must have heard it. 'If it's not too much trouble?'

'Not at all. Take a seat.'

He stood and crossed the small kitchen to put two more pieces of bread into the toaster as Henri slipped onto a stool.

'So, if we didn't … you know … how did I end up in your bed, and where did you sleep?'

He frowned as he poured her a fresh coffee. 'You really don't remember anything about last night?'

Her face, neck and even her ears grew hot. 'Not really. I didn't do or say anything crazy or stupid, did I?'

'Not that I know of. Unless you call falling asleep in a public drinking establishment crazy?'

'Trust me, I've slept in worse places. My job has trained me to sleep anywhere.'

'Guess it's better than driving home drunk. Any sugars?'

'Two, please. And I would *not* have driven home,' she said, horrified. 'I might have had more to drink than usual, but I'm not stupid. I'd have slept in Cecil.'

'Cecil?' he asked.

'Yeah, my Kombi—he's the love of my life.'

The toast popped but Liam didn't reach for it. 'You have a Kombi van? Does it have a bed in it?'

She nodded. 'He's outside in the car park.'

Liam started laughing.

'What's so funny?'

'Last night, when I found you curled up on the couch near the pool table, I could barely wake you. I offered to call Tilley to come get you, but you told me you'd sleep in your car. I didn't know it had an actual bed in it, so I offered you a room instead.'

'Whoops.' Henri smiled apologetically. 'Didn't I mention Cecil was a van?'

He shook his head. 'All you mentioned was how lovely my eyes were and how much you wanted chocolate.'

'Oh God, I'm so sorry.'

'It's fine. Really. All part of the service. And in answer to your question, we came in here so you could use my bathroom, but you fell asleep in the bedroom instead. I slept on the couch—I promise. I'd have taken the free room myself but I wanted to be close in case … you needed anything.'

Henri guessed that was his polite way of saying he wanted to be able to hear if she started vomiting in her sleep and he needed to stop her choking to death. How utterly mortifying to have got so pissed that this stranger had to give up his bed for her.

'I promise I don't usually behave this way, but things have been a little stressful lately and my mum's been driving me crazy since I got home. I was angry at her when I arrived last night and then … never mind.' The guy might be a good Samaritan but that didn't mean he needed to hear her woes. 'I'm usually much better at holding my grog but I must have been really tired or something.'

'Seriously, don't worry about it. I've dealt with worse drunks than you. You weren't verbally abusive, you didn't tell any terrible jokes, and in the end, you didn't even throw up.'

Thank God. 'Well, I appreciate it anyway.' She finally took a sip of coffee. 'Geez, that's good.'

Liam grinned, and damn if it wasn't the kind of smile that made Henri feel a little off kilter. More likely it was just the alcohol still lingering in her veins.

'There are few things in life I take more seriously than coffee,' he said.

'We have that in common then,' she replied, returning his smile.

'What do you want on your toast?' He plucked the slices from the toaster and slapped them on a plate. 'I've got Vegemite, honey or blueberry jelly?'

'Vegemite, please.'

The moment Liam unscrewed the lid on the jar, the dog started sniffing the air.

'You've already had your breakfast,' he told her, the affection clear in his voice. 'This is for our guest.'

'Your dog's a real sweetie,' Henri said, smiling down at the odd-looking thing. Its body was speckled grey and white, but its head was mostly black with flecks of ginger.

'She's not bad.' He slathered the toast with butter and Vegemite then passed it to her.

'Thanks.' She took a bite of her toast, then frowned. 'Was it downstairs last night? Or does it stay up here while you work?'

'*It* is called Sheila. And she was asleep behind the bar.'

'She must be a very well-behaved dog. I don't remember seeing her at all.' Not that she remembered much.

'She's quiet unless a brawl kicks off and then she barks and bares her teeth. Much more effective than a bouncer.'

Liam didn't look like he needed a bouncer. Henri reckoned those broad shoulders and muscular arms would be more than capable of handling any drunk and disorderly behaviour.

'What kind of dog is she?'

'Blue Heeler Kelpie cross.'

That accounted for her multicoloured fur. 'I miss having pets. That's the one negative about not having an actual house to call home.'

'Do you live in your van?'

She nodded. 'Kinda. When I'm working on stations, the owners usually give us accommodation, and other times I stay in hotels, dormitories—it all depends on the location and the contract. But Cecil is my home. He's where I keep my few important possessions and it's handy to just be able to pull over on the side of the road and have a kip when I'm driving long distances between contracts.'

'Did you always want to be a pilot?' he asked, taking a bite of his toast.

'For sure. My dad was into aircraft—he made and collected little models—but one of my earliest memories is of an Air Tractor flying over our farm, spraying fertiliser on the canola. I remember thinking that flying so low, swooping dangerously close to the ground, must be what it felt like to be a bird. I know every kid wants to fly like Wendy and Peter Pan, but from the moment I first saw that AT, I knew the only thing I wanted to be was an ag pilot.'

'So you were a plane-mad kid, rather than a horse-mad one?'

'Horses schmorses.' She rolled her eyes. 'I honestly don't know why girls get so stupid over them.'

'Don't let Ruby hear you say that.'

'Or my niece, Macy. She's obsessed as well. What about you? Did you always want to own a pub?' she asked.

'If you mean was it what I told people I wanted to do when I grew up, then no.'

'So, what *did* you want to do?'

Liam took his time replying and it seemed to Henri that he was thinking over his answer more than necessary for such a simple question. 'Um … I wanted to be a professional surfer. Only problem was there weren't any beaches where I grew up.'

'Colorado, right?' She smiled victoriously. 'See, I wasn't that drunk last night. But yes, I imagine no beaches would be quite an obstacle to becoming a pro. Do you surf now?'

'No, you can't teach an old dog new tricks, but I swim most days,' he said. 'How often do you come back to Bunyip Bay?'

'That depends on who you ask. I think I come back often enough, but Mum would disagree. She doesn't understand that …' Henri's voice drifted off as she realised how close she'd come to unloading on Liam about her family issues again. 'Speaking of my mother, I'd better be getting back to the farm or she's liable to send out a search party.'

'We don't want that.'

He didn't know that her mum thought she'd been at Tilley's place, but she'd already overstayed her welcome. Liam had probably only been being polite when he'd offered her breakfast and was likely now wondering why she was still here rabbiting on.

She took her empty plate and mug across to the sink and turned on the tap.

'Leave that,' he said. 'I'll do it later.'

'Okay, thanks—for the coffee, the toast, and for everything. I owe you one.'

He shook his head. 'As I said, all part of the service. Come on, I'll see you out.'

The two of them headed downstairs, with Sheila trailing dutifully behind. They emerged into the main area of the pub and came face to face with a friend of her mother's. *Oh shit.*

'Henrietta!' Janet exclaimed. 'What are you doing here?'

Henri could ask the same of her, but the cleaning equipment she was carrying gave her away.

'Um …' She didn't exactly want to say she'd passed out and Liam had to put her to bed, but if she didn't come up with something, half the town would soon think that Henri Forward had spent the night with the publican. There was a lot to love about small towns, but idle gossip was not one of them.

'Henrietta stayed in room seven last night,' Liam said quickly. 'She was going to sleep in her van but since we had some free rooms, I told her to take one.'

'Oh, I see. That's very generous of you, Mr Castle.'

Henri nodded. 'Anyway, it's lovely to see you again, Janet.'

'Yes, you too, Henrietta. I'd better finish clearing up the breakfast things, but you take care, dear. I hope we'll see you at the town hall for wreath-making on Friday.'

It was an order not a question. But although Henri couldn't really think of anything worse, her mother had already asked her to go, and she wasn't a complete beast of a daughter!

'Of course, I'm looking forward to it. See you there.'

Liam opened the main door at the front and as light spilled into the building, she spotted Cecil sitting all on his lonesome in the customer car park.

'Well, thanks for everything,' she said. 'I—'

Liam held up a hand. 'Honestly, you've thanked me enough. If you say it again, it's going to start to get embarrassing.'

She laughed. 'Okay, okay, I'm going.'

Then, before even realising what she was doing, she stretched up on tiptoes and kissed him on the cheek. She quickly withdrew, but as she turned and hightailed it for her van, the scent of Liam lingered.

And man, he smelled good. A delicious cocktail of coffee, expensive soap and woody cologne.

She pushed the thought aside and climbed into the car.

Chapter Six

Mid Monday morning, Henri toed off her boots at the front door and headed into the house, the flyscreen door slapping closed behind her. After a few hours' hard labour in the machinery shed, she was in dire need of a Diet Coke.

Her mother looked up from where she sat at the table, her sewing machine in front of her and an array of brightly coloured material beside it. 'Hello, darling.'

'What are you doing?' Henri asked, as she yanked open the fridge and grabbed a can.

'Sewing the buttons on Macy's costume for the school Christmas play. You're coming, aren't you?'

Henri cringed. Usually she wasn't home in time to see the end-of-year school concert and it sounded mind-numbingly boring. She wouldn't mind if it were just her nieces and nephews—it was the thought of having to watch *other* kids dance and sing for a couple of hours that put her off. 'When is it?'

'Thursday night, day before the kids break for the holidays.'

'Yeah, I'll be there.' It wasn't like she had much else to do and it would certainly earn her brownie points. 'Anyway, I'm heading into town to pick up a new chain for the header and some sheep lick blocks. Do you need me to get anything?'

'Actually, do you mind stopping in at the IGA for some eggs? I want to make a quiche for dinner and our girls have stopped laying for some reason. I'll turn them into roast chooks if they don't get their act together soon. And maybe some more wrapping paper—I don't think I've got quite enough for the kids' presents and I want to get them done this week before they finish school.'

'Got it. Wrapping paper and eggs. I'll be back soon.'

'You're not going yet, are you?' she asked as Henri grabbed Cecil's keys off the row of hooks on the kitchen wall.

'I was planning on it, unless there's something else you need me to do first?'

'No, but …' She frowned and shook her head. 'You don't even look like you brushed your hair this morning.'

'I did so.' Well, she'd run her fingers through it and scooped it into a ponytail. But even if she'd given herself a bloody blow-dry, it would have been ruined in the heat while she'd been tinkering with Callum under the header for the last couple of hours.

'And those shorts are hardly suitable for town. They've got grease all over them. Why don't you have a shower and put a dress on or something?'

'A *dress*? Why would I wear a dress to go to The Ag Store and the IGA?' Never mind the fact that she only owned one—her Christmas Day outfit—and it was definitely not grocery or farm shopping attire. 'I'll be heading out to work again as soon as I get back.'

'Yes, but you never know who you might run into in town.'

Henri didn't need to be a genius to know she was referring to eligible bachelors. 'I'm not trying to impress anyone, Mum, and *if* I was on the lookout for a husband, I'd want a man who likes me for who I am—messy hair, stained shorts, holey old T-shirts and all.'

Her mother pursed her lips and Henri managed not to smile—she could almost see the steam shooting out her ears. 'Fine. Drive safely.'

'Will do,' Henri said smugly, tossing the keys in her hand as she left the house.

On the ten-minute drive to town, she blasted McAlister Kemp from the stereo and sang along loudly, only turning the music down as she turned into the main street. Tilley was out when Henri arrived at The Ag Store, so it didn't take long to pick up what she needed, and she decided she'd stop in at Frankie's Café for a quick bite to eat. Maybe they'd finally have a chance for more than a five-minute conversation.

She couldn't believe her luck when she found the perfect parking spot right out front, and it was only when she registered that no one was sitting outside that she remembered Frankie closed on Sundays and Mondays. She'd mentioned Saturday night that she'd be spending a couple of days with Logan at his family farm, visiting his brother and Simone. Dammit. She was beginning to wonder if she'd ever get to properly catch up with her best friend.

The IGA was pretty much deserted, but Henri nodded to the teenage boy behind the counter, grabbed a basket and set off. Having found the eggs and some very funky wrapping paper, she was humming along to 'Six White Boomers', which was playing on the stereo overhead, when she turned out of the aisle and came face to face with Eileen Brady.

Too late to turn the other way and pretend she hadn't seen her, Henri pasted on a smile. 'Morning, Mrs Brady.'

'Actually, it's after*noon* now, Henrietta,' Eileen said, tapping on her watch. 'What mischief are you up to today?'

Mischief? Henri smirked. 'Nothing exciting, just getting some eggs and wrapping paper for Mum. She goes a little crazy with the grandies' Christmas gifts and always underestimates how much she needs.'

'How lovely,' Eileen said with a sniff. 'Fiona is very lucky that she's been blessed with both children *and* grandchildren. Tuck and I couldn't have a family. It's why I dedicated so many years to teaching Sunday School—you students were like the family I never had.'

Henri decided it was safer not to comment on that; Eileen might think quite differently if she knew what the kids used to say behind her back.

Instead, she smiled blandly. 'Well, it was nice seeing you, Mrs Brady, but I better—'

'Is there something going on between you and Mr Castle?' Eileen interrupted, peering intently over the top of her ugly glasses.

'Excuse me?'

For a moment Henri didn't realise who she was referring to, but then Eileen raised her wiry eyebrows and added, 'Because Janet said she saw you yesterday morning. She said you stayed in one of the rooms above the pub, but then when Karen was taking her morning constitutional, *she* saw the two of you exchange a kiss?'

'A kiss?' Henri echoed, thinking Eileen must be referring to the peck she'd placed on Liam's cheek as a show of thanks. It was quite hilarious that this chaste gesture had been discussed around town and become evidence that the two of them had indulged in a raunchy one-night stand. Some people really needed to get a life. No wonder Henri preferred hanging around with blokes—they were far less prone to this kind of gossip.

She opened her mouth to tell the old busybody that she and Liam were just friends—although even that was a stretch—and she should mind her own business anyway, but Eileen continued before she could get a word in.

'You should be careful, dear.'

'Oh?' Henri frowned, not liking her tone. 'What's that supposed to mean?'

The wretched woman leaned a little closer and spoke in a low voice, even though they were the only two people in the aisle. 'I don't like to gossip …'

Hah! Henri deserved a medal for withholding her snort.

'But Mr Castle's a bit of an odd one, if you know what I mean.'

'No, I don't think I do.'

'Well, I'm sure you know he came to town ten years ago with nothing more than a rusty old ute and a backpack. No family has ever visited him as far as anyone can tell and he's never had a relationship. Between you and me, I wondered if he was gay for a while—I've got no problem with gays, I'm very happy for Ryan Forrester and his fancy city husband, but rumour has it, Liam gets very friendly with his female guests, if you know what I mean.' Eileen tapped the side of her nose. 'So, I guess he's straight, which makes me think he's running from something. I asked old Sergeant O'Leary to put his name through the police computer when Liam first arrived, but he refused to tell me what he'd found! Then there's that scar on his shoulder—he says it's from an accident he had as a child, but it looks suspiciously like a bullet wound to me.'

Bullet wound? Henri was struggling to keep up.

'All I'm saying is that you should be careful, Henrietta. There are plenty of men in town and a nice girl from a good family like yours could do a lot better for herself than a questionable publican.'

Questionable? Was Eileen for real? She was even worse than her mother!

Just because Liam had some scar, was single and possibly had the occasional one-night stand, he was questionable? Henri's nails curled into her fists as she remembered this was a little old lady, not some guy riling her up about not being as good as her male colleagues. Which was a pity because she'd have no qualms about slugging the latter.

'Thank you for your concern,' she said instead, her smile so fake it made her cheeks hurt, 'but as I'm sure you've already guessed, your warning is too late. I did spend Saturday night in Liam's bed, but it wasn't merely a one-night stand. I'm crazy about him.'

Eileen's eyes grew so wide Henri thought they might pop right out of her head.

What the hell? Where had that come from? She'd *meant* to tell the interfering gossip that she could look after herself and perhaps add that Liam was a far better person than Mrs Brady could ever hope to be, but instead … *Oh God!*

'Oh … well …' Eileen recovered. 'I must say I didn't think he'd be your type, but who am I to interfere with young love? Anyway, congratulations, Henrietta. I hope he won't break your heart.'

That was Henri's chance to say she'd been joking, but suddenly a plan landed fully formed in her head. And it might just be perfect. Concocting a fake boyfriend would be the ideal way to get her mother off her back. And it should stop her sister and friends from encouraging Grant the matchmaker as well. She didn't know why she hadn't thought of the idea before.

Smiling smugly, Henri bid Eileen goodbye and headed for the checkout. Now that Eileen thought she and Liam were an item, it wouldn't be long before the whole town was enlightened.

Only when she stepped outside and saw The Palace across the road did she realise the major flaw in her plan.

Liam! He would have to be in on the scheme for it to have any chance of working.

Shit. Bugger. Shit.

She stopped and stared at the pub, deliberating between going back into the supermarket and setting Eileen straight or …

Before Henri could talk sense into herself, she dumped the groceries on Cecil's passenger seat and started across the street towards the pub, ignoring the way her heart rate accelerated the closer she got.

Of course, the door was locked and there was no sign of life inside when she peered through the windows. But just as she was about to give up and head back to look for Eileen with her tail between her legs, she registered music coming from somewhere round the back. Having come this far, she followed the sound of Midnight Oil singing their classic 'Beds Are Burning' to find a large shed, its door open, the music blasting out from inside.

Curious, she stepped up to the door. It took a moment for her eyes to adjust to the dim interior and when they did, they zeroed in on the very middle of the shed where Liam was bent, shirtless, over some kind of work bench with some kind of power tool.

He didn't hear her at first, but when Sheila trotted over to her, he glanced up and switched off the machinery.

'Well, hello,' he said, turning towards her so she got the full view of his bare torso. Her mouth went dry at the sight.

Sweat glistened on his tanned chest, which had just the right smattering of dark hair, and she had the craziest urge to reach out and trail her finger down it. It was then she remembered what Eileen said and her gaze snapped to his shoulders—broad, bulky and, on the left, a scar that looked a bit like a birthmark, only it went inwards.

Could it be from a bullet wound?

He cleared his throat, and a ghost of a smile crossed his face. 'Can I help you?' he asked, putting down what looked to be a power sander.

Embarrassed to be caught with her tongue practically hanging out of her mouth, Henri suddenly forgot the reason for her visit.

'What are you making?' She gestured to the various pieces of wood spread across a large bench.

'A rocking chair,' he said, reaching to grab a black T-shirt off the edge of the bench, which he sadly proceeded to tug over his head.

Probably a good thing, because Henri was finding it hard to think straight with all that glistening bare skin.

'It's beautiful.' She stepped forward and ran her hand over one of the curved pieces. It was even smoother than it looked. And it smelled good too, reminding her of the times she used to help her dad chop wood on the farm.

'What are you going to do with it when you're finished?' She suddenly wondered if he'd made all the gorgeous furniture in the pub. 'Do you sell them? This would make the perfect Christmas present for my mother.'

'I do commissions, but this one's for Dolce,' he said. 'Don't let her know though—it's a surprise. She likes to sit out on her porch at dusk watching the world go by and she mentioned her old rocker is on its last legs.'

'That's so sweet,' said Henri, touched by the kindness he showed towards the old widow.

Liam looked slightly uncomfortable. 'Anyway, did you just come to chat about my side hustle or was there some other reason for this unexpected visit?'

All other thoughts evaporated as she remembered what she'd told Eileen. She wiped her suddenly sweaty hands on her shorts, then cursed silently as she looked down to see they were now covered in black grease.

'Um …' Heat flooded her cheeks as regret threatened to swallow her whole. What had she been thinking?

Of course, she'd have to tell her old Sunday School teacher it had been a joke. For all Henri knew Liam already had a girlfriend—the women of Bunyip Bay had to be stupid if they hadn't worked out a way to tap *that* yet! Then again, if that were the case, surely Eileen would have known, and she'd have had no qualms about telling Henri off for sleeping with someone else's man. The world might be a lot more accepting of certain things these days but as far as she knew, infidelity was definitely still regarded as a sin.

But that was beside the point—girlfriend or not, it was a ridiculous idea. Creating a fake boyfriend? It was like something you'd see in a rom-com, not something any rational person would actually try to pull off.

'Um …' she said again, then shook her head. 'Never mind. It was nothing. I'm sorry I interrupted your work.'

But as she turned to go, Liam reached out and gently took hold of her wrist, turning her back to face him.

'Why don't I believe you, Henrietta?' he said, his simmering grey eyes staring directly into hers. 'Come on, I didn't take you for a chicken. Why'd you really come?'

'Because I told Eileen Brady that you and I were in a relationship,' she blurted, trying to ignore the way her pulse raced under his touch.

'You did what?' He let go of her arm like it had burned him.

'She confronted me in the IGA—apparently everyone's talking about the fact I left the pub early yesterday morning. They think we slept together. I was about to set her straight, when she started mouthing off about you. Nothing annoys me more than people like her judging others and making assumptions. When she warned me off, saying I could do better than you and that I needed to be careful, I snapped and told her we were together.'

His eyes widened but Henri barrelled on.

'And then I realised if I told my mother the same thing, it would get her off my back. She's desperate for me to find someone in Bunyip Bay to settle down and make babies with. That's never going to happen, but if she thinks there's even a slight chance, it'll make the next couple of weeks back here so much easier. Even my friends are trying to convince me to let Grant set me up with someone and this would put a stop to *that* as well.'

Liam made absolutely no comment while she delivered her monologue, nor did his chiselled face move a muscle. Henri wasn't usually the type to get nervous, but right now her hands were sweating and she couldn't seem to stop talking. The more she tried to explain what she'd done, the more ludicrous it sounded.

★ ★ ★

'Are you insane?' Liam asked when Henri finally stopped talking to catch her breath.

She grimaced. 'Not usually, but sometimes my family and this town push me over the edge. I just snapped. Surely you can't be happy about Eileen spreading nasty rumours about you?'

'I don't give a damn what people say or think about me,' he said, struggling not to laugh. He only wished he'd been there to see the look on the meddlesome woman's face. Always quick to take pleasure in other people's misfortune, Mrs Brady was one of the few people in town he found it hard to like.

Henri hung her head. 'I'm sorry.'

'But …' He gave her a reassuring smile. 'It's kinda cute you felt the need to defend my honour.'

And that wasn't the only thing cute about her. In those tiny denim shorts covered in grease, a tank top that looked like it had been worn so much it was thin in places, and her hair pulled back in a messy ponytail as if she'd come here straight from rolling out of bed, he had to work really hard not to *obviously* appreciate her cuteness. Not to mention those incredible legs tucked into very dirty boots.

She looked up and her lips curved slightly. 'Well, sometimes I speak before I think. It's a flaw, but we all have them. Even you, I'm sure.'

He shook his head. 'Nah, pretty sure I'm perfect.'

She rolled her pretty brown eyes and her expression relaxed a little.

'Anyway.' He cleared his throat and tried to focus on the issue at hand. 'I get you want to do this to get your mom off your back, but … what exactly is in it for me?'

'Um …' Henri bit her lip, and it was clear she hadn't thought this through one bit. 'Well, is there anything you want or need?'

Geez, wrong question. There was only one thing Liam could think of off the top of his head, but he didn't think that's what she had in mind. And he didn't want to come across as a sleaze. Besides, hadn't he already established that sex with Henrietta Forward wouldn't be a sensible idea? His policy aside, he had no evidence whatsoever that the attraction was mutual anyway.

'I know.' Her whole face lit up. 'Surfing.'

'Huh?'

'Yesterday. You said you'd always wanted to surf. Well, I could teach you.'

The idea of surfing professionally had never even crossed his mind; from as young as he could remember he'd harboured ambitions to take the gourmet grocery business his parents had started and grow it into an empire. They'd had two very profitable supermarkets—one in Silver Ridge and one in nearby Monument when his parents had died—but he'd planned a chain of shops right across the state. He'd lied yesterday when he told her he wanted to surf professionally; weirdly, it was the first thing that popped into his head. Maybe because swimming was one of the many things he did now to keep himself from losing the plot. '*You* can surf?'

'Don't look so surprised. I grew up here in the Bay, you know. Flying isn't the only thing I'm good at.'

I'll bet. Liam's mind took a fast dive into the gutter.

'Dad used to be a lifesaver before he married Mum and they took over her family's farm. He taught all of us to swim and surf almost as soon as we could walk. I'm not as good as my brothers—Andrew even won some competitions and stuff—but yeah, I know my way around a wave. So, what do you say? Lessons in exchange for pretending to be madly in love with me?'

An image landed in his head of Henri standing on a surfboard. In a figure-hugging wetsuit. Or a bikini! Surfing lessons with her would definitely *not* be a good idea. This *whole* proposition was a terrible idea. For a number of reasons.

Yet, instead of turning her down, he found himself saying, 'You really think you could teach me to surf?'

'Of course. As long as you can swim and have some sense of balance, I should be able to help you with the basics before I leave.'

'Three weeks, right? That's how long we have to keep this up?'

'Just under. I'm heading south, day after Boxing Day.'

'What are you doing there?'

'Fire contract.'

'And what happens then?'

'What do you mean?'

'Well, who dumps who? It's all very well fooling everyone for a short while, but we can't keep this ruse up forever.'

She thought a moment. 'I'll dump you. We'll have a big fight because you want me to give up flying and come run the pub with you and I refuse to give up my dreams and sense of self for a mere male.'

Mere male? He raised an eyebrow at how ridiculous that sounded. 'I wouldn't force you to give up your dreams.'

She smiled at him in a way that felt a bit condescending. 'That's very sweet, Liam, but trust me, no man likes a woman he can't pin down. And anyway, it's better this way—we need to protect your business. I don't want people boycotting the pub because you dumped one of their own, and maybe if Mum sees I've tried and failed at another relationship, she'll finally give up hoping for a miracle.'

'Another relationship?' That sounded like a story he wanted to hear.

'I don't really want to talk about that, if you don't mind.'

That was a good thing—if Henrietta didn't want to talk about her past then she probably wouldn't pry into his.

'Okay.' He stretched out his hand. 'You've got yourself a deal.'

She looked at him like he was the crazy one. 'Are you *serious*? Does that mean you're actually *agreeing* to my plan?'

He shrugged, hoping he wouldn't live to regret it. His mission in life was to help people where he could, but this might be taking things a fraction too far. 'Yeah. Why the hell not?'

'Excellent.' Henri's face split into the most delightful smile as she shoved her hand into his. 'I could kiss you.'

He forced a laugh as muscles all over his body tightened. 'Maybe you should save that for when we're in public.'

'What?' Her cheeks flashed a glorious shade of crimson again, and he hoped she was embarrassed rather than mortified, that she didn't find the idea of kissing him *that* repulsive. Although perhaps it would be safer if she did.

'Well, if everyone is going to believe we're together, we're going to have to be *seen* together.'

She sighed. 'Yes, of course, you're right. The surfing lessons will be a good start, but we'll have to do other stuff too.'

'*Other* stuff?' He liked the sound of that way more than he should.

She playfully punched him on the arm. 'I meant like go on dates, hang out in public.'

'Problem is, I can't exactly leave the pub this time of year. Now that harvest is over and Christmas is upon us, we're busier than ever.'

Henri frowned a moment. 'I guess I'll just have to spend time here. But you're not open till the afternoon, right? We can have lunch at Frankie's Café. Or breakfast.' Her eyes twinkled mischievously. 'Breakfast is good because it'll look like we've spent the night together.'

Liam swallowed, then quickly banished the visual from his mind.

'You free tomorrow morning for your first surfing lesson?' she asked.

He nodded. Most mornings he took Sheila down to the beach and went for a swim anyway. 'Do I need to borrow a board from someone?'

'Nah, I'll bring you one of Dad's old ones. Thanks so much for doing this, Liam, you're a gem. I'll see you tomorrow.'

Oh Lord, he thought, his eyes once again drawn to her luscious legs and her cute little behind as she strode out of his workshop.

He glanced down at Sheila to find her looking up at him in what could only be bemusement. 'What the hell have I agreed to, girl?'

Chapter Seven

Henri drove back to the farm on autopilot, barely noticing her surrounds at all.

What the F had she just done? There was clearly something seriously wrong with her!

No way would she have come up with such a preposterous plan—never mind begged a near stranger to be her partner in crime—if she were in the right frame of mind.

She'd all but decided to deliver the stuff home and then turn around and head back into The Palace to let Liam know he was off the hook, but even before she'd parked Cecil out the front of the homestead, her mother was flying down the verandah steps towards her, and the utes parked nearby indicated they had company.

Sure enough, as she climbed out of the van her brothers appeared—Andrew carrying a mug, Callum holding his two-year-old, Joe, who was munching on a piece of coconut slice. It must be smoko time.

'There you are!' her mother exclaimed, puffing a little as she met Henri halfway.

'What took you so long, little sis?' Callum said with a knowing grin.

She hadn't been gone *that* long, had she?

'Hey, little buddy.' Ignoring her brother, she reached out and ruffled her nephew's white-blond curls. 'Is Hannah here?'

'Nope, she's volunteering at school this arvo—they're making Christmas decorations or something. So Joe's with me on the farm.'

'Never mind about Hannah.' Her mum grabbed Henri firmly by the elbow. 'Why didn't you tell me you and Liam Castle were an item?'

Ah right. That accounted for the weird welcome.

'Um … I …' Henri looked to her brothers for help, but they just grinned and shrugged, clearly finding this highly amusing. 'How'd you find out?'

'So, it's true!'

'Let me guess? Eileen Brady?' She hadn't thought the old busybody would be that fast and assumed she'd have time to tell her mother first.

Really? Have you actually thought any *of this through?*

'Yes, *Eileen*,' her mum replied, 'and didn't she gloat when she called to deliver the news? You have some explaining to do, young lady! The least you could have done was tell me yourself.'

Max and Muriel finally looked up from where they'd been dozing under the jacaranda tree, purple blossoms gently raining down on them. No doubt they thought they were in trouble because Fiona was using her loud, angry voice. The voice that had Henri running away and hiding in the dirt under the shearing shed many a time when she was little. It was tempting to turn and run in that direction now.

'Calm down, Mum,' she said instead. 'I didn't want to get your hopes up, so we were going to keep things on the down-low while we got to know each other a bit better, but—'

'She was seen,' said Andrew with a smirk.

Henri looked daggers at him.

'So, it's true? You and Liam Castle are going out?' She hit Henri with her don't-even-think-about-lying-to-me look.

Henri nodded, trying to ignore the lump that had swelled in her throat. 'Let's go inside and I'll explain.'

'Fine.' Still gripping Henri's arm, her mother all but started dragging her towards the house.

Henri halted in her tracks when Callum and Andrew followed. 'You two can go back to work, you know.'

They exchanged a look, then Andrew said, 'Are you kidding? How long's it been since you've had a boyfriend? We wouldn't miss this for the world.'

A sigh had barely escaped Henri's lips when they all turned back at the sound of Tilley's four-wheel drive tearing over the gravel.

Oh Lord, just what she needed.

'What are you doing here?' she called as Tilley climbed out. The passenger door opened at the same time and Macy emerged as well.

'Mace isn't feeling well, so I had to pick her up from school. But we're crazy busy in the shop this arvo, so I hoped you wouldn't mind if she hangs out with you, Mum?'

'Course not.' She let go of Henri's arm and went forward to take Macy's, pulling the girl into her side. 'Come on, sweetheart, let's get you into the house and settled on the sofa. But don't think this lets you off the hook, Henrietta.'

'What's going on?' Tilley asked, looking between them all.

'Haven't you heard?' Callum snorted. 'Henri's shacked up with the publican!'

She glared at him. 'I have not shacked up with anyone.' And they wondered why she usually only came home for a few days at a time.

'Oh my God,' Tilley exclaimed. 'So that's where you stayed on Saturday night?'

'She didn't stay with you?' their mum asked.

Tilley shook her head, grinning widely. 'But I should have guessed.'

'What do you mean by that?' Henri frowned.

'Well, the two of you were getting along very well at the pub Saturday night. I could have fried an egg on the heat zapping back and forth between you. In hindsight it's obvious that's why you didn't want to leave when the rest of us did.'

Henri bit down on the impulse to tell her that she'd been annoyed because of the way she'd felt almost bullied about her love-life by her and their friends, but instead she said, 'To be honest, I wasn't sure anything was going to happen then. I was just enjoying our conversation … but, well …' She felt her cheeks heat with the lie she was about to tell. 'Some things are just hard to fight.'

She expected her siblings to burst out laughing and call her bluff, and her mother to accuse her of telling porkies and threaten to wash her mouth out with soap, but miraculously they all beamed.

Fiona pressed her free hand against her heart. It looked as if she was close to tears. *Oh God.* Henri swallowed the pinprick of guilt—she'd started something now, so she may as well follow through. At least this would take her mind off the mess inside her head.

'I felt exactly the same way when I met your father,' her mum said. 'All he had to say was four little words and I was a goner. I'd have married him right there on the spot.'

'What were the four little words, Granny?' asked Macy.

'You can't swim there,' she replied, smiling tenderly at her granddaughter. 'Granddad was a lifesaver for the summer on the beach, you see, and—'

While her mother began a story they'd all heard a zillion times before, Henri took the chance to escape into the house. She went straight into the kitchen and started to make herself a sandwich—stress made her hungry. The last six weeks her appetite had gone bonkers.

'Hey, good for you, little sis,' Andrew said, pulling Henri into his side in a rare show of affection. 'I've always thought Liam was a good bloke.'

'Yeah,' Callum agreed as he deposited Joe in the highchair and gave him another piece of slice that Henri was almost certain his mother wouldn't approve of. Hannah was a nutritionist and kept a very careful eye on how much sugar her kids ate.

'Yeah, he is.' Henri took a bite of her sandwich so she didn't have to elaborate. Probably the less she said, the better.

'So,' her mother began as she arrived in the kitchen with Tilley and Macy, who didn't look too sick to Henri. 'Is this thing between you and Liam serious, then? What does he think about you being away so much for work?'

It was clear where she was going with that and although this was what Henri had intended when she'd come up with this harebrained plan, she didn't want to lead her family on any more than was strictly necessary to make it through the next couple of weeks. 'We've only just hooked up, Mum. It's not like we've had much of a chance to talk about the future yet.'

'So, Hens, I want *all* the details. What's Liam like …' Tilley wriggled her eyebrows suggestively. '*You know*?'

Henri glared at her sister. Had she totally forgotten the presence of little ears? Not to mention their brothers and their *mother*. Faking a relationship was one thing, pretending to share Liam's bed was part of that, but talking about their non-existent carnal adventures was simply not going to happen.

'I thought you were busy at the shop this afternoon,' she said pointedly. 'And Macy is looking pale. Maybe we should get her settled on the couch in front of a movie?'

Tilley sighed and glanced at her watch. 'Yes, no rest for the wicked. Will you be okay, Mace? I'll come get you later. Try to get some rest and drink lots of fluids.' Then she thrust her index finger at Henri. 'Don't think this conversation is over. It's my right as big sister to all the juicy details.'

'Good*bye*,' Henri replied as Tilley walked out the back door.

'I've always liked Liam,' her mother announced. 'Some say he's a bit of an odd body, but he's never been anything but pleasant to me. And he cleaned up the pub in a way I could never have imagined possible when Arthur owned it. You could do a lot worse, darling.'

Henri didn't trust herself to do anything but smile.

'We'll have to have him round for dinner. Or maybe we can have a barbecue one night? James and Tilley can come out, and we can have it at your place, Andrew—you have that newfangled barbecue.'

'Liam works nights.' Henri rushed to nip the idea in the bud. Being seen at the pub or around town was one thing, but actually having to pretend in front of her family for hours sounded like hell, not to mention unfair on the poor guy.

'Oh, I'm sure he can get one night off. Or we could have him round for Sunday lunch?'

'The pub's open for lunch on Sundays too,' Henri pointed out.

Her mother frowned as if trying to work out a suitable time.

'Mum, maybe you should take a chill pill,' Andrew said. 'Henri told you it's early days. It's not like they're engaged. You don't wanna scare the guy off, and they probably just want to spend some time *alone*.'

Henri gave her eldest brother a grateful smile.

Her mum sighed. 'I'm sorry, you're right. I'm just … I'm happy for you, Henrietta.' She grabbed Macy's hand again. 'Come on, you, let's go find a movie to watch.'

Then she left the room, beaming like she'd just been given the elixir of eternal life.

Chapter Eight

Henri's phone rang a couple of hours later while she was still working on the header and she wasn't surprised to see Frankie's name on the screen when she dug it out of her pocket.

'Hey there,' she said.

'Don't "hey there" me! Is it true what I'm hearing about you and Liam?'

Henri smiled—Frankie was never one to beat around the bush—but then her stomach dropped; it was one thing lying to her mother who was always pestering her, but could she lie to her best friend?

She glanced over at her brothers, who were trying to seem like they weren't eavesdropping. 'Look, I can explain everything, but not right now.'

'So, there *is* something to explain?' Frankie sounded ridiculously excited.

'Yes, but—'

'Dinner, tonight. You and me. Or will you be too busy with lover boy?'

Henri rolled her eyes. 'Lover boy will be busy working late, as you know. I'd love to have dinner with you.' She paused a moment. 'Will it be just you?' No way she was spilling her guts with Logan or anyone else there.

'Yeah,' Frankie said. 'Sorry if I haven't been very available since you came home, but it's a bit of a crazy time.'

'You don't need to explain. It's fine.' Even though she had been feeling a little neglected, she wasn't planning on admitting it. If she hadn't been feeling so tender herself, she probably wouldn't have even noticed. 'I've been keeping busy.'

'That's what I'm hearing.' Frankie laughed again. 'Anyway, I gotta go, but I'll catch you tonight at the pub. Seven o'clock, okay?'

'Yep. I'll see you then,' she said, then sent a quick text to her mum.

Won't be home for dinner tonight, meeting Frankie at the pub.

Is that code for meeting Liam? You know you don't have to make excuses to me. Macy is staying over anyway, so we won't even miss you.

Henri didn't bother replying, but sure enough when she returned to the house later, she found her mother and niece making pizzas.

'We're going to have a Christmas movie marathon tonight,' Macy told her. 'Mum thinks it's too early to start watching them, but Granny says it's never too early. What do you think, Aunty Hens?'

I think I'm glad I'm going out tonight. Most festive flicks were far too cheesy for her liking.

'Sounds like fun,' she said, squeezing Macy's shoulder before starting down the corridor to wash off the day's grime.

'Will you be staying at The Palace again tonight?' her mum called, and Henri almost tripped over her own feet.

Shit. Of course she might assume that.

'Um … yeah, is that okay?' she asked, turning back. 'I'm going to start teaching Liam to surf, so it'll be easy to be there in the morning anyway.'

Fiona gave a knowing smile as she dropped a dollop of homemade tomato paste onto one of the dough bases. 'You don't need to make excuses to stay over at your boyfriend's house, Henrietta. You're a grown woman.'

'Thanks,' she replied, silently wondering why half the time her mother still treated her like a child then.

The nerves hit the moment she walked into her bedroom. What would Liam say about this? she wondered as she threw her toothbrush and toiletries into a bag. Granted, she'd already spent one night in his apartment, but as she'd been drunk at the time, this did *not* alleviate her sudden anxiety.

This hadn't been part of the deal. And as far as she knew he only had one bed.

She gulped at the thought of them having to share it, visualising them perched right at the edges almost falling out so as not to accidentally touch each other.

Of course, she could just stay in Cecil. That way her mum would think she'd been with Liam, but she wouldn't have to inconvenience him. Again.

Feeling better, Henri finished packing and hitched the bag on her shoulder, then headed out.

As it was Monday night, the pub wasn't anywhere as busy as it had been on Saturday. Music played softly overhead; Mr Brady, Mr Porter, and another older man whose name she couldn't remember, were playing cards at a table; two blokes in hi-vis uniforms were shooting pool; Sexy Rexy was the lone patron sitting at the bar, and Liam appeared to be the only one on duty.

He looked up and what was maybe surprise flashed across his face, before he smiled and lifted a hand to wave. Tonight, he wore his uniform of faded jeans and a cream T-shirt with the Toohey's gold moose (or was it a stag?) on its crest. And he wore it well. A tiny butterfly somersaulted in her stomach as she remembered the broad chest, wide shoulders and delicious six-pack, only slightly obscured by the T-shirt. The kind of musculature you got from lifting kegs, cartons of bottles and heavy bits of wood, not from long hours pumping iron in a gym. *Real* muscles.

Henri swallowed and hitched her overnight bag over her shoulder. As she approached the bar, Liam stepped out from behind it and came up to greet her.

'Well, this is a nice surprise,' he said as he leaned forward to give her an awkward hug. 'You're looking lovely this evening.'

Pulling back, her whole body still flushed from the heat of him, she attempted her best love-sick smile—not that any of the patrons tonight would likely pay attention, but it couldn't hurt to get some practice in for when they had a proper audience. 'You don't look so bad yourself.'

A shadow of a smile crossed his lips and then his eyes drifted to her bag.

'I'm meeting Frankie for dinner. She should be here soon,' she said, then lowered her voice. 'When I told Mum I was coming here, she just assumed I'd be staying the night. Again.'

'Ah, I see. That makes sense.' But he looked like she'd just suggested he turn the pub into a shelter for feral cats.

'It's okay,' she rushed to reassure him. 'I've just brought the bag inside for appearances' sake, but I'll sneak out once everyone's gone and sleep in Cecil.'

Liam pursed his lips a few long moments, then shook his head. 'That won't work.'

'What do you mean?'

'This is Bunyip Bay. Someone's sure to notice either tonight or tomorrow morning. Janet arrives early and she might …' His voice drifted off, but Henri didn't need to hear any more.

Janet's tongue was almost as loose as Eileen Brady's.

'I could give you one of the guest rooms—there's a couple available at the moment—but she'd definitely notice that too.'

'You're right.' Henri sighed. Already there were a zillion holes appearing in this plan, but, remembering her mother's excitement this evening, she couldn't bring herself to give up on it just yet. 'I'm so sorry, but maybe I could sleep on your couch? I'm an excellent house guest. You'll barely notice I'm there.'

'Don't be ridiculous. You can have my bed. It'll only be a few nights, right?'

'Yes … but no way. I won't hear of it; you're already doing me a massive favour. A sheet and a pillow will do me just fine.'

'It's non-negotiable,' he said, folding his arms across his chest. 'You have the bed or the whole deal's off.'

Henri gave him a death stare; she didn't like being told what to do. She should have told him fine, thanks for playing, it was a stupid idea anyway. But instead she found herself saying, 'Fine. I'll take your damn bed.'

'Good.' He grinned smugly, and then reached out to take her bag.

'I can carry this,' she said, tightening her grip. She wasn't used to people doing things for her—especially not handsome men with ridiculously sexy smiles.

'I'm sure you can,' he whispered, looking intently into her eyes, 'but if you were my *real* girlfriend, I wouldn't let you lift a finger, so …'

She sighed and handed him the bag, which he carried over and dumped behind the bar, only a few feet from Sheila.

'Can I get you a drink?' Liam asked as she dropped to her knees to greet the dog.

'Um … just a lemon, lime and bitters, please. I'll have a wine when Frankie arrives, but I'm knackered after a big day on the farm, so I need to pace myself or I'm liable to fall asleep on the bar.'

'Wouldn't be the first time.'

She poked her tongue out at him, ignoring the buzz that zapped through her at his teasing and trying not to think about sleeping in his bed. She gave Sheila a final pat before taking a seat at the bar next to Sexy Rexy. Like Dolce, he hadn't changed one bit since she was a kid.

'Hey there,' she said.

He made a grunting sound, slid off the stool and hurried towards the restrooms.

'What did I say?' Henri asked as Liam pushed her drink across the bar.

He chuckled. 'Think you scared him—Rex isn't used to pretty girls paying him attention.'

'No one's in earshot right now; you don't have to call me pretty,' she said, lifting her glass to her mouth, hoping it would hide her blush.

'Just getting into character.' He winked. 'So, how'd you go telling your mom about us this arvo?'

'Didn't have to. Eileen had already done the honours by the time I got home.'

'Why am I not surprised? And how did she take it? Your mom I mean. I bet she'd prefer you were with a farmer or something.'

He was quite possibly right—everyone knew there was still a class system in the country and farmers generally thought townies a rung (or two) below them on the ladder—but if her mother harboured any such thoughts, she hadn't mentioned them. 'She was ecstatic. But then again, she'd probably be happy if I hooked up with Sexy Rexy if it meant there was a possibility of me coming home for good.'

'Let's hope he remembers to wear his false teeth to the wedding.'

Henri snorted. 'How's your day been?' After all, girlfriends were supposed to show such interest, weren't they?

'Good,' he said. 'I've been working on Dolce's rocking chair. Almost finished. Just a little sanding and varnishing to go.'

'That's awesome.'

Sexy Rexy returned to the bar and Liam was refilling his pint when Frankie arrived. She leaned in and gave Henri a hug.

'Sorry I'm late.' She didn't give an excuse. They both knew she was never on time and Henri was used to it.

'No worries. What do you want to drink? My shout.'

'I think you mean *my* shout,' Liam said.

'Way to go, girlfriend.' Frankie grinned at her. 'Didn't we always say growing up we should either marry someone rich or someone who owns a pub?'

'We did?'

Frankie nodded. 'We'll have a bottle of sav blanc, please. You can't drink Guinness over dinner, Hens.'

Henri smiled—Frankie was the only person she'd ever allow to make decisions on her behalf.

They ordered Bunyip Burgers, because it was Macca's night off and therefore the only thing on the menu, and then carried the bottle and glasses over to a table.

'I'm so excited about you and Liam,' Frankie said as they sat down. 'What happened after we left on Saturday night?'

This was where Henri meant to tell her friend that it was all an elaborate ruse to get her mother off her back, but something stopped her. Maybe it was that she couldn't help thinking about the feel of his strong arms wrapped around her, or maybe it was that suddenly admitting the game she was playing felt immature and desperate.

'We …' She shrugged and twirled the wineglass between her fingers. 'We just got chatting. We hit it off and …'

'One thing led to another?' Frankie grinned as she took a sip of wine. 'Oh, I remember that first flush of attraction. Don't get me wrong, I still can't get enough of Logan, but we've been together for almost two years … things change. I was so tired of waiting for someone, I thought I'd be alone forever, but now the thought of never experiencing that thrill of the chase again … well, it's a little depressing.'

Henri smiled. 'The way I recall it, yours and Logan's chase was rather complicated.'

'Oh boy, damn straight, but I guess that was also part of the fun. Anyway, enough about me. What was it like?'

Heat rose in Henri's cheeks. 'I don't kiss and tell.'

Frankie snorted. 'You don't need to. The expression on your face tells me everything. I guess you'll be staying at the pub again tonight?'

'Probably.'

'And your mum's okay with that? I bet she gets a bit lonely now your dad's gone?'

'Yeah.' Henri swallowed. 'The house feels so weird without him there, but she's got Macy staying over tonight. I've been crafting a bit with her, but the shows she watches in the evenings bore me to tears. She's happy for me and Liam so …'

'Crafting? You!'

'I know, I know. Don't worry, I'm not doing that much. I've helped her make a few Christmas gifts but mostly I've been working with the boys on the farm. So, what's new with you?'

'Well, I'm about to put the café up for sale.'

'What? You serious?' The café was Frankie's pride and joy, although she had recently bought another one in Geraldton because she and Logan planned to settle there.

'I'd hoped to keep both, but as you know we've been dividing our time between here and there, but we've realised it's just not realistic. With Logan's deteriorating eyesight, he can't drive at night and it's becoming a bit too much.'

'I'm sorry,' Henri said, unable to imagine how she'd feel in Logan's shoes. Just before he and Frankie started dating, he'd been diagnosed with a medical issue, which meant he was slowly going blind.

'Thanks. He's got a great attitude and doesn't let it get to him too much, but there are moments, and … we do have to make some adjustments. Besides, after the wedding we want to have a baby, so the sale and the move just makes sense.'

'A baby. Wow. So very grown up,' Henri teased just as Liam appeared to deliver two massive burgers with a side of fries to the table.

'Thank you,' they said in unison.

'You're welcome,' he replied, brushing a hand over Henri's shoulder as he departed. The skin beneath his touch tingled and she felt the effects all over her body.

She looked up to see Frankie frowning at her. 'You still planning to leave again after Christmas?'

Henri nodded. 'Of course, but don't tell Mum.'

'Won't you miss him?'

'I'll miss some things,' Henri said, playing the game. 'But, Frank, we've only just got together. Who knows what will happen?'

'Eileen said you told her you were crazy about Liam?'

Henri rolled her eyes, while silently berating her loose tongue. 'You know she has a habit of over-exaggerating.'

Frankie laughed. 'Too true. You better come back for the wedding though.'

'You know I wouldn't miss that for the world. I'll be back in Australia after my Canada contract by then.' She was thinking positively, hoping that she'd have actually made it into an aircraft at all. 'And I've already given my boss the heads-up that I'll need some time off.'

After that, they ate and talked about Frankie and Logan's wedding plans. Although such things weren't among Henri's favourite topics of conversation, it was different when it was her best friend. She couldn't help but catch some of Frankie's enthusiasm.

Somehow Henri's little flying problem never came up and she was having so much fun that she didn't want to put a dampener on the evening by talking about it. Not yet.

Eventually, Liam called last drinks and Henri couldn't believe how late it was.

She hugged Frankie goodbye and, ignoring the tightness in her stomach, crossed back to the bar. Sexy Rexy had long gone, but the hi-vis guys were still throwing back beers and balls at the pool table.

'Good night?' Liam asked as Henri approached.

She opened her mouth to reply but yawned instead, the events of the day finally catching up with her.

'You know, you don't need to hang down here and wait for me,' he said as he wiped a cloth over the bar. 'I'll still be a while. You can get settled upstairs if you'd prefer.'

'Okay, thanks.' Henri jumped at the chance. 'If you're sure.'

As easy as Liam was to talk to down here, she was already anticipating the awkwardness of the two of them alone in his apartment. Better if she was tucked up in bed by the time he joined her upstairs.

Guilt again squeezed her at the thought of taking his bed. The guy was already doing her favour enough.

'Are you sure I can't sleep on the couch?'

'Don't even think about it,' he said, pulling a key from his pocket and pressing it into the palm of her hand. 'I'll only carry you to bed if I find you there.'

She laughed nervously at the image, a weird ache passing through her at the thought.

'You know where to go, right?'

She nodded. 'Thank you.'

'No worries. Make yourself at home. There's coffee, tea and Milo in the kitchen if you want a drink before bed. There's even a packet of Tim Tams.'

The strange pain in her stomach remained as she climbed the stairs, then walked along the hallway past the guest rooms before she came to a door with a sign announcing 'Private Residence'.

It was only as she slipped the key into the lock and pushed open the door that she realised Sheila had accompanied her.

'Well, hello, girl,' she said as the two of them went inside. 'Come to keep an eye on me, have you?'

There were a couple of lamps on in the living room and Henri eyed the couch on which Liam had slept on Saturday night—it was a well-worn, chocolate-brown leather one that looked much comfier than many places she'd slept. There were a couple of matching armchairs, a bookshelf, a big screen TV and a few woodworking magazines on the coffee table. Beside the couch was a dog bed, which didn't look as if it was used much at all.

It was only the thought of Liam coming in and watching her sleep that had her venturing into the bedroom and dumping her bag there. His room was even tidier than she remembered. The bed was neatly made and the surface of the dresser now devoid of anything Liam. Most telling was the empty space where the photo of a family had been.

She frowned. Had she imagined it?

No, Henri clearly remembered standing right here and picking up the frame, gazing down at the four people, the adults smiling proudly and the little girl sticking out her tongue as the older boy held her in a pretend headlock. It was definitely a happy photo and although she hadn't had long to scrutinise it, she remembered being unsure whether Liam was the man or the little boy. He had strong similarities to both of them, although she thought the man's hair was a lot longer than Liam's was currently. If it was him ... did that mean the kids were his too?

He'd been in town about ten years, so the children in the photo would practically be adults by now. Probably unlikely, since he couldn't be that much older than her, which meant he'd have to have had them pretty young. Eileen said he never had visitors, so, whoever these people were, what had become of them? And more importantly, why was the photo no longer here?

She'd noticed a period tonight when Tegan came out of the kitchen to serve behind the bar and Liam had disappeared for a while. Had he come up and removed it then?

Henri pondered these questions as she went into the bathroom and readied herself for bed. Yes, she checked in the vanity cupboard—although not exactly sure what she was looking for, she felt it was due diligence. It wasn't that she was nosy, more that as she was staying in a strange man's house, in his bed, it was sensible to check for any evidence that he could be a serial killer or something. At least that's what she told herself.

But there was nothing bar a few bottles of shampoo, an electric razor, some antiseptic cream and a spare toothbrush.

Resisting the urge to snoop any further, she went back into his bedroom and climbed in between the covers. Sheila jumped up beside her and settled at her feet. Exhausted, Henri switched off the bedside lamp, lay back on the pillows and pulled the summer-weight doona up to her chin. Although the bedding felt clean—as if he'd changed the sheets when he came upstairs as well—eau de Liam lingered. She inhaled, long and hard, trying to work out exactly what scents she could smell, but just like him, the notes of his cologne were a mystery.

She fell asleep, wondering who Liam really was. Who were the people in the photo to him? And what had caused the scar on his shoulder?

Chapter Nine

'Rise and shine, sleeping beauty!'

Liam blinked at the sound of Henri's voice, what felt like mere millimetres from his ear, then opened his eyes properly to see her standing over him.

'What the hell?' he groaned, feeling as if he'd had less than two hours' sleep.

He couldn't believe he'd actually agreed to letting her sleep over, but he hadn't been thinking straight. He didn't seem capable of doing so around Henri. The first night she'd stayed, he'd been only thinking of her welfare, but that should have been the end of it. Instead, he'd not only agreed to pretending to be her boyfriend, but now, it seemed, to basically having her move in with him.

Shit. That had escalated fast. He never planned to have a real girlfriend live with him, never mind a fake one. His heart jackhammered. Had she woken him because she'd heard him having a nightmare? It had been months since his last one, but he never knew when they were going to creep up on him again. Stressful situations often triggered them. Perhaps the knowledge that she was sleeping only a room away and worrying about her hearing him had actually brought one on?

'What time is it?'

'Six thirty,' she replied, far too chirpily. 'The early bird catches the worm.'

He let go of the breath he'd been holding, pulled the throw blanket over his head and rolled back into the damn uncomfy couch. 'I don't like worms. And I don't get up before eight. You're on holidays, aren't you? We can go surfing later.'

But Henri was persistent. In one hard tug, she yanked the blanket right off and then gasped before dumping it back on top of him. 'Sorry!'

He was wide awake now and laughed at the shock on her face. 'You're lucky I'm wearing underwear. Normally I sleep naked.'

Although she didn't seem the type to get embarrassed about much, her cheeks turned tomato red and she opened her mouth and closed it a couple of times before she managed, 'Well, go put some pants on and I'll make us some coffee, then we can hit the beach.'

'So *that's* why you've woken me at this ungodly hour.'

She nodded. 'We made the date yesterday, remember?'

He gave her a look—he remembered agreeing to lessons, but not to an actual time.

'Stop being such a sook and get dressed. You can have a nap later if you're tired, but the waves are the perfect size for a beginner right now.'

'Are you always this bossy?' he called as she headed into the kitchen.

'Are you always this lazy?' she retorted over her shoulder.

He smiled at her sass. Waking up to a woman in the house was a novelty but flustering her had been an added bonus because he got the feeling not much ruffled Henrietta Forward's feathers.

Tossing the throw rug aside, Liam picked up the clothes he'd discarded last night and went into his bedroom to find his swim trunks. The bed was so neatly made it almost looked as if it hadn't been slept in, but he remembered all too well coming upstairs last night. He'd suspected he might find Henri zonked out on the couch, but miraculously she'd taken the bed as he'd told her to. Wanting to check on Sheila, he'd quietly snuck into his room and, thanks to the gentle moonlight spilling in through the gap in his curtains, seen the two of them sleeping peacefully. If he was honest, he'd felt a little jealous. Usually Sheila never left his side, but she'd clearly taken a shine to Henri. Either that or she was keeping an eye on the competition.

Don't worry, girl, you're the only female I need in my life.

Despite telling himself this, he'd fought the urge to climb in beside them. If Henri had been surprised to find him in nothing but his underwear, he could only imagine her horror if she'd woken up to find him lying right next to her.

Then, reminding himself that was *never* gonna happen—sleeping on the couch was too close as it was—Liam went into the bathroom to splash water on his face and brush his teeth. He ran a hand over the rough skin on his jaw and thought about shaving, but immediately rejected the idea. He wasn't trying to impress Henri; they simply needed to fool everyone else.

'Sleep well?' he asked a few minutes later when he found her in the kitchen feeding chunks of Vegemite toast to Sheila, who was supposed to be on a diet.

'Like a bloody baby. You might just have the most comfortable bed I've ever slept in. Those sheets. Where the hell did you buy them?'

'Online.'

She swooned. 'I might never leave.'

He laughed, because they both knew she was joking.

She handed him a coffee and he joined her in another piece of toast before they headed downstairs and over to her bright orange Kombi, which held two surfboards on an old-fashioned roof rack.

'Are you sure Sheila's okay to come with us? We could leave her here and I can take her for a walk later,' he said as Henri opened the door and indicated for the dog to jump up.

'Yeah, she'll be right. The bench seat's vinyl, so it's easy to clean. Over the years Cecil's seen much worse than Sheila. Trust me.'

'How long have you had the van?' he said, climbing in beside his dog as Henri went around to the driver's side.

'Since I was sixteen. Dad bought him for my birthday—he was pretty much a bomb, but we did him up together over the next couple of years.' She turned the key in the ignition and the engine spluttered a few times before finally coming to life. 'He's not the most reliable vehicle, I'll be honest. I've lost track of the number of times I've found myself stranded in the middle of nowhere with van trouble, but Dad also taught me how to fix him and most of the time I can.'

'Why's he called Cecil?'

She smiled. 'Cecil was Dad's middle name—Mum always used it when she was cross at him—but I thought it suited him more than Fred.'

It was impossible not to hear the love she had for her father and the van they'd restored together. It was impossible to ignore the pang in his chest at the thought of his own father.

'You guys sound like you had a pretty special relationship.'

'Yeah.' She nodded as she reversed out of the parking space. 'We did.'

As the pub was less than a kilometre from the ocean, there wasn't much time for small talk, and Sheila, being in an unfamiliar vehicle, was much more excitable than usual, which didn't help either. She kept trying to climb onto Henri's lap and Liam spent most of the journey trying to stop her from sticking her tongue in Henri's ear.

They were both laughing so hard by the time she stopped in the small parking area at the beach that they couldn't escape the van fast enough. Sheila's tail started swishing madly the moment she smelled the fresh salty air and although she was a good dog and stayed when told, it was clear she was struggling to be obedient as they unloaded the surfboards.

'Thanks,' Liam said as Henri handed him a long board that was thicker than hers.

They started towards the dunes, Sheila bounding happily ahead of them.

Although he came down here every day, the view still took his breath away. He and Henri had joked about Bunyip Bay being like a postcard, but a picture could never do justice to the clear turquoise water currently glistening as it rolled and crashed on the pale yellow sand. Having grown up nowhere near the ocean, he was pretty sure he'd never get sick of it. There was one lone dog walker too far away to recognise, a seagull diving in and out of the water and a couple of fishermen standing patiently with their rods waiting for a bite, but apart from that the beach was empty.

As if reading his mind, Henri said, 'It's gorgeous, isn't it? I'll be honest, sometimes I love this place more than the people. And just as I thought, the waves are perfect for beginners this morning. Come on.'

Liam struggled to catch up as she jogged a couple of hundred metres up the beach to a spot that had 'perfect curls'. He wouldn't have called himself unfit, but Henri was fitter.

'Besides surfing, do you do any other regular exercise?' he asked when they finally stopped to dump their things on the sand. Panting hard, Sheila flopped down between them.

Henri shrugged as she ripped her T-shirt over her head, revealing a demure, black one-piece swimsuit that on her perfectly toned body looked anything but demure. It felt like his shorts shrunk two sizes and he quickly averted his gaze while he removed his shirt.

'I go without surfing for long periods of time, and I don't stay in one place long enough to join a sports team or anything, but sometimes I'll do a Pilates class and I run most days.'

That'd do it.

He picked up the board, eager to get into the water before she noticed the bulge in his shorts. 'Time to hit the waves?'

'Not so fast, buddy. Beginners start on the sand.'

'Huh?'

'You don't want to become shark bait. Standing and balancing on a board isn't as easy as it looks. You need to practise on land first. Like this.'

She shimmied out of her shorts, then dropped to the ground and lay flat on the board a couple of seconds before jumping to her feet again. Her lean legs were a thing of beauty as they moved, her breasts jiggled a little with the action. If he didn't know better, he'd think she was torturing him on purpose.

'Now your turn.'

Reluctantly, Liam copied the action.

'Bravo.' Henri applauded as if he was a little kid in need of positive reinforcement.

He shot her a warning look. '*Now* can we go in the water?'

'A little more practice first.'

This time she joined him, but he still felt like an idiot jumping up and down on dry land.

'So ... I was thinking,' Henri said as they leapt about like a pair of bloody Jack-in-the-boxes, 'we should get to know each other a bit better.'

He almost lost his balance—'What do you mean?'—and hoped his voice didn't sound as choked as it felt. Not only was he beginning to second-guess this lesson, but the whole damn farce.

'Well, just in case Mrs Brady or someone tries to trip us up, we should know each other's birthdays, favourite foods, pet hates, et cetera.'

'Okay.' He relaxed a little. He could do *those* kinds of things. 'When's your birthday?'

'August third. Yours?'

'April ninth.'

Her lips twisted upwards. 'You're an Aries?'

He raised an eyebrow. 'You believe that shit?'

'What do you reckon? But Tilley's always been obsessed. She still reads her star sign in the paper every morning and always texts me mine as well, so I know the basics.'

He laughed. 'And how old are you?'

'Twenty-nine.'

'You?'

'Thirty-seven.'

They went on like this for a few minutes, exchanging more basic facts as they practised. Henri was full of surprises. In many ways she came across as a tomboy—although he didn't think you were supposed to say that anymore—but her favourite colour was purple, she loved country music and indulged in regular spa visits on her day off.

'Well, well, well, the rumours must be true!'

They both startled at the sound of a male voice and looked up to see Drew and Ruby a few metres away, hand in hand.

'Hi, guys,' Liam and Henri said as Sheila got up to go and greet them.

'Morning,' said Ruby, stooping to stroke the dog.

'Eileen was mouthing off in the post office yesterday about you two being together,' Drew said, 'but I never know whether to believe anything that old biddy says.'

Ruby shoved her elbow into his side. 'Drew!'

'What? It's true!'

Liam nodded. 'Usually I'd take anything she says with a grain of salt but yes, this time she's telling the truth.' He slipped his hand into Henri's to emphasise the fact.

'Anyway,' Ruby grinned back at them, 'we better leave you lovebirds to it. Drew's on the late shift today, so we're off to Frankie's for breakfast. Feel free to join us if you want.'

'Thanks,' Henri replied, 'but we'll be a while here yet.'

'That went well, I think,' Liam said as the couple retreated. 'I don't think they suspected a thing.'

Henri grinned as she withdrew her hand. 'I think you're right. And I also think you're finally ready for the water.'

'Hallelujah.' Strapping the safety tie around his ankle, he scooped up his board and ran towards the ocean before she could change her mind.

They ran into the sea together, yelping as the cool water hit their legs. No matter that he swam here every day, the temperature of the water always surprised him. After having practised popping up onto his board so many times, Liam didn't expect it to be too much harder on an actual wave, but the first time he attempted it, he didn't even manage to stand properly before he tumbled ungracefully into the water.

To Henri's credit, when he resurfaced, she was only slightly smirking. 'Not bad. Now get back on and try again.'

After a few more false starts—and a number of instructions from Henri about how to stand and where to position his feet—Liam finally managed to stay on for longer than a few seconds and it was one of the most amazing feelings in the world. When he sank down into the water again, he watched Henri glide along a wave until it finally crumbled into nothing. He couldn't recall ever seeing anything more beautiful.

'You must miss the water when you're away,' he said as she paddled back to meet him.

She ran a hand over her hair, droplets of water tumbling onto her already wet and glistening body. 'Yes and no. I'm usually so busy I forget how much of a thrill I get surfing. I … I get it from flying instead. It's lucky the beach is here though because if it wasn't for this, I might never come back.'

'You don't like Bunyip Bay?'

'It's not that.' She gestured around them. 'What's not to love? When I'm away I always look forward to coming home—at least I used to—but now, it always feels a little claustrophobic.'

'How so?'

She held up two fingers. 'Two words. My family.'

'You don't get along with them?'

'Oh,' she sighed loudly, 'it's not that we don't get along, not exactly. I love working on the farm with my brothers, but they're busy with their wives and kids now, and I miss Dad so much. It might sound weird, but when I'm not here, I can kind of imagine that he still is. Every time I walk back into the house, it's suddenly so obvious that he's gone, and everything feels weird.'

'I'm sorry,' he said, knowing exactly how weird the world could feel without a loved one. 'I didn't know him well, but your parents came into the pub at least once a month for dinner and he seemed like a good guy.'

'He was. The best. Mum and I clash a little sometimes, but he was always the peacekeeper between us. She's always telling me how I should live my life, right down to how I should dress, whereas Dad was proud of what I did.'

'I'm sure she's proud of you.'

Henri humphed. 'Tilley's not much better. She tells me off for swearing too much—says it's not *lady*-like—and even the boys don't really treat me as an equal. They *all* treat me like a baby yet are also constantly on at me about growing up!'

He frowned. 'I haven't heard you swear *that* much.'

'I've been on my best behaviour. Anyway, enough yakking. You're trying to distract me, aren't you?' She raised an eyebrow at him. 'I saw you catch that last wave. Not bad. But let's see if you can stay on longer than five seconds this time.'

'Hey! It was more like ten seconds.'

'Then prove it,' she said, turning and paddling towards an incoming wave.

Liam paddled after her, trying to focus on the board and the water rather than the way her arms cut through the blue with the swift precision of a professional. Somehow, he managed to focus and with each attempt, he spent even longer on the board.

'You might just be a natural,' Henri shouted to him between waves.

Her praise felt way better than it should.

After almost an hour in the water, their fingers started to shrivel up like prunes and Henri announced, 'That's probably enough for one day. Wouldn't want to tire you out.'

'Tire me out?' he scoffed. 'I'll have you know it'll take a lot more than that to tire me out. I have *awesome* stamina.'

'Is that right?' she teased as they walked up the sand towards their gear. 'I guess I'll have to take your word for that.'

Chapter Ten

On Thursday morning, Henri watched, her heart in her throat, as Liam paddled towards the biggest set he'd attempted since they'd started lessons two days ago. He was a quick learner—which was probably a good thing as she wasn't known for her patience—and she had to admit she enjoyed watching him much more than she probably should. Even if he was hopeless that would be the case—his broad shoulders, strong hips and muscular thighs were a thing of beauty, not to mention those arms—but he was actually pretty good. Not that she'd *gush* to him; it was never a good idea to blow smoke up a guy's trumpet.

He gripped the edges of the board, then pushed to a stand and she bit her lip as he quickly disappeared into the barrel. Would he come out the other side or tumble into the water and get ragdolled?

Long seconds passed and then he appeared again, still upright on the Malibu. The breath gushed from her lungs and Henri couldn't help grinning.

'Woohoo!' she shrieked, the sound lost in the waves and the wind as she paddled over to him.

'Well?' Liam asked, his board under one arm, his wet hair flopping over one eye.

'Well, what?' she joked.

'How good was that? I can't believe it; I did it.'

'Yeah, it was pretty good.'

'*Pretty good*?' His lovely grey eyes widened. 'You're a hard task-master, aren't you, Ms Forward? If I'd known surfing felt like this, maybe I'd have got someone to give me lessons years ago.'

'Okay. It was great.' She rolled her eyes, still smiling madly. His excitement was catching, almost as good as conquering a big wave herself. 'What do you want? A bloody medal? Maybe *I* should get the medal for being such a stellar teacher?'

'I don't know about a medal, but how about I buy you breakfast instead?'

'Two days in a row, Mr Castle? Tongues will start to wag, you know.'

He winked as they started towards the shore. 'Isn't that exactly what we want?'

He was right of course, but sometimes Henri found herself forgetting why they were actually spending time together. Since Monday, she'd spent two out of three nights at the pub, chatting to him down at the bar before retreating upstairs to his bed, and every morning here on the beach. They'd known each other less than a week but it somehow felt much longer. And having Liam to focus on as well as her daytime labour on the farm meant that she was finally sleeping better again.

Her heart still raced every time she thought about what had happened to her on the Riverina, but she felt much more relaxed than when she'd first arrived home.

'Good morning. How was the surf?' sang Frankie as they entered the café ten minutes later, Liam holding the door open with one hand, his other firmly clasping Henri's. All for show of course.

'Fantastic,' Henri replied, fighting a blush. As comfortable as she was around Liam, it still felt weird pretending they were together. Especially to people like Frankie.

But it wasn't only her best friend in the café. Most of the tables were taken and there was a small queue at the counter, where Frankie stood making coffees at her whiz-bang machine. Busy noise drifted from the kitchen and two waiters were rushing about, taking and delivering orders.

'What are you having?' Liam asked, retrieving his wallet from his pocket as he nodded towards the menu decoratively scrawled on a large blackboard.

'Oh, no, no, no, no, no,' Henri countered, pulling her purse from her handbag. 'This one's on me. You paid yesterday.'

'Already bickering like an old married couple,' said Sally the vet, standing in front of them in the line.

They smiled at her, both playing along.

Henri inhaled the mouth-watering aroma of fresh sourdough bread and sizzling bacon coming from the kitchen. 'I'm gunna have the big breakfast with the lot.'

Liam nodded. 'I'll have the same.'

There were a number of healthier options on Frankie's breakfast menu, but Liam and Henri had more than worked up an appetite.

Once they'd placed their order, they scored a table just vacated by the window so they could keep an eye on Sheila who was tied to a post outside, in her element, enjoying the attention of everyone who stopped to stroke her on their way past.

'Where'd you get Sheila?' Henri asked as she absentmindedly began to flick through a copy of the *Bunyip News* that someone had left on the table.

'Someone abandoned her at the pub when she was just a pup.'

'What?' Henri looked up. 'You serious?'

He nodded. 'A truckie came in for a few beers. Asked if he could bring his puppy in while he ate, and it was a quiet night, so I said it was fine. We had a good chat, seemed an okay guy.

He and the dog were staying in his truck in the parking bay just out of town. At least that's what he said. Anyway, he went to the bathroom and never came back. Didn't pay for his meal and didn't take the pup. I figured she was payment for the meal. We've been together ever since.'

'How old is she?'

Liam's brow scrunched a moment. 'Must be coming up to eight years.'

'So it wasn't that long after you arrived?'

'No.'

'I have to say, you've really turned The Palace around. I remember it being a bit of a dive when I was a kid. You said you didn't think about owning a pub when you were growing up, so what the hell drove you to buy ours?'

Liam leaned back in the chair a little. 'Will it sound crazy if I tell you that it was kind of a spur of the moment decision?'

'A little.'

'During my road trip around Australia, I was always quite taken with the old pubs in each of the towns. Locals told me stories of times when they were really happening places, yet so many of them seemed rundown, if not deserted. Then, when I drove into Bunyip Bay and saw the For Sale sign out the front, I thought … why the hell not? At first Arthur thought I was a drunk having a laugh, but when he realised my offer was deadly serious, he made me sign the contract and skipped town before I could change my mind.'

Henri smiled—that sounded right; it was always hard to sell businesses in rural areas. Especially those attached to ancient buildings that needed a lot of upkeep, which definitely described The Palace.

'I'd always been fairly handy,' Liam continued as if reading her mind, 'so I knew I could do a lot of the renovation work myself, and it felt like a fun project.'

'Weren't you planning on going back to America? What did your family think?'

'To be honest … I wasn't sure.' He took a quick breath. 'Things hadn't been easy before I left, and I was ready for a change.'

There was something in his tone that told Henri she shouldn't ask what exactly hadn't been easy, but Harriet, Frankie's niece, arrived beside them with a tray before she got the chance anyway.

'Hey, guys, here's your coffees,' she said.

Henri did a double-take. 'How are you old enough to be working here? What about school?'

Harriet rolled her eyes. 'I just finished Year Twelve. I'm heading to Perth for uni after Christmas, but Mum said I needed to do something in between. It was either help her and Angus on the farm or work here with Aunty Eff. I didn't want to break a nail, so I'm staying with her and Logan for a bit.'

Henri laughed, her eyes drifting to Harriet's perfect rainbow manicure. 'What are you studying at uni?'

'Psychology. I want to work with teens with eating disorders,' she replied, before heading back into the kitchen to collect their breakfasts.

Liam grinned as he stirred sugar into his coffee. 'Someone clearly doesn't like farming.'

'It's not everyone's cup of tea.'

'You said you always wanted to fly, but you seem to enjoy farm work as well?'

'Oh, I love it. That's why I'm an agricultural pilot. A massive part of my job relies on my knowledge of farming. I need to know about chemicals, how they work, the dangers of using them and how to apply them efficiently and safely. Crop-dusting takes up a good chunk of my time, and that and mustering are my favourite parts of my job.'

'Would you ever consider giving up flying and working on the farm?'

'You haven't been talking to my mother, have you?' she asked, her stomach clenching.

'No, I'm curious, that's all.' He picked up his mug and took a sip.

'With two older brothers, farming at Bungara would never have been a real possibility for me even if I wanted to. And I could never afford to buy my own farm.'

'Shouldn't you have just as much right to the family farm as your brothers?'

'Maybe, but I never wanted it anyway and Mum and Dad knew that, so it didn't matter.' Henri wrapped her fingers around her mug; even though she wasn't cold, she sought comfort from the warmth of holding it. If she didn't fly, she had no idea what she'd do with her life and that was a scary thought.

Harriet returned with two overflowing plates of eggs, bacon, beans, grilled tomatoes, hash browns, mushrooms and sausages. They thanked her and picked up their cutlery.

'These eggs are so good,' Liam said after taking his first mouthful.

'Bunyip Bay's certainly pretty lucky,' Henri agreed. 'With Frankie for breakfast and lunch and Macca for dinner, all meals are covered. So, tell me about your woodwork?'

'What do you want to know?'

'How did you get into it? Who taught you? I never clicked you'd made all the furniture in the pub until I saw you in your studio. Did you train as a carpenter or something?'

'No.' Liam shook his head. 'It's just a hobby—took me a while to finish all the pub stuff. I liked the subject at school, but it wasn't until I moved here that I got properly into it. A lot of what I do is self-taught. I slowly built up my tools and it's kind of addictive. The more I made, the more I wanted to.'

'If you weren't into pubs and you weren't making furniture, what did you do before you came to Australia?'

'Are you sure you're not a journo?'

'Why?' She winked. 'You hiding something?'

'No,' he scoffed. 'You just ask a lot of questions.'

'It's called conversation, Liam. Aren't I allowed to be interested in the man I'm …' She glanced from side to side and lowered her voice. 'Supposed to be sleeping with?'

His lips flickered at the edges and their eyes met in a way that made her insides warmer than the coffee. 'Fair enough. I studied business at college, and I worked in retail. Both come in handy at the pub.' He pointed his fork at her. 'What about you? Any hobbies? Besides surfing, I mean.'

Henri took a quick breath. 'Don't laugh, but, when I'm not flying, I like geocaching.'

'Geo-what?'

'It's sort of like a global treasure hunt. People leave what are called geocaches, or just caches, at specific locations and then they record the coordinates on the website, so that other members can go find them.'

'What are in these so-called caches?' he asked, frowning slightly.

'Well, usually it's a plastic container or a tin and there's a little logbook in there with a pen so people can sign that they found it. Some of the small ones don't have much else, but others contain little items people have left as a bit of fun, you know, like Happy Meal toys, novelty erasers, tourist keyrings, that kind of thing. The idea is you leave something as well.'

'I see. And what exactly is the point of this?'

She smirked at his condescending tone. 'What exactly is the point of a lot of hobbies?'

'Well, knitting provides things to keep you warm, woodwork things to sit on or use in some way, painting is relaxing and can also provide joy to others, sport keeps you fit, reading informs the mind and entertains, photography—'

'Okay, okay.' Henri held up a hand and smiled. 'The point is it's fun and you get to go visit places you might not have been or thought to go. And it makes you feel part of something.'

He nodded as if conceding they were reasons enough. 'Are there any near Bunyip Bay?'

'Yep. I've planted a couple on my last few trips home and tourists have left some too. I think there was five in the surrounding region last time I checked.'

'Maybe you'll have to show me,' Liam suggested.

'Maybe I will,' she retorted, before popping a spoonful of beans into her mouth.

By the time their plates were empty, and their coffees drunk, Henri felt they'd put on a good show for the other locals in the café and once again she'd truly enjoyed chatting with Liam.

'Will I see you tonight?' Liam asked as Harriet came and cleared away their dishes.

'Possibly not. I've promised Mum I'll go with her to the Christmas concert at the school. You got anything interesting on your agenda today?'

'Got some bookwork to do ...' He made a face. 'And I need to order stock, but hopefully I'll get some time in the studio as well. Anyway, I better go rescue Sheila, but thanks so much for the surfing lessons. I'm having fun and you're a very good teacher.'

'Thanks.' Henri felt herself blush. 'It's the least I could do, considering the way you're putting yourself out for me.'

'Ah, it's not that bad,' he said with a grin.

After a quick goodbye to Frankie, they left the café and Henri bid farewell to Liam and Sheila as they crossed the road to walk back to the pub. Then she climbed into Cecil and headed home, feeling oddly bereft.

As much as she loved working on the farm, she couldn't help wishing her breakfast with Liam could have gone on just a little bit longer.

Chapter Eleven

'How was the school play?' Liam asked Henri as they headed over the dunes towards the sand on Friday morning, boards under their arms and Sheila trotting between them. She hadn't stayed at the pub last night, which he thought he'd prefer, but he'd actually found it a little odd coming into his apartment, knowing she wasn't already asleep in his bedroom. It was crazy how quickly he'd got used to having her around.

'You know it was actually pretty cute. They put on this play called *How the Bunyip Stole Christmas* and my nephew, Silas, was the star. He made such a scary bunyip.'

'Was it a rip-off of *How the Grinch Stole Christmas* or does it just sound like it?'

Henri snorted. 'Well, there were definite similarities between the two, but I think I might actually prefer the Bunyip Bay version.'

Even Liam, who avoided all things Christmas if he could possibly help it, couldn't deny that did sound a bit cute.

'To Andrew's dismay,' she continued, 'Silas now wants to become a film star rather than a farmer.'

'Really? I thought being a YouTube sensation was all the rage among the young ones these days. Film star sounds so passé.'

'What do you know about YouTube sensations?' she asked, amused.

'I'll have you know I know about a lot of things. You should hear the conversations people have in the pub—I pick up a lot. And most of the young backpackers seem to watch more YouTube than anything else.'

'That sounds about right. Macy is addicted too. She watches horse videos on there. Apparently, there are even horse-riding YouTube stars.'

Liam raised his eyebrows as they dropped their gear down on the patch of sand that was rapidly becoming 'their spot'. 'What'll they think of next?'

'Do you have any nieces or nephews?' Henri asked, and his ribcage tightened a little. He didn't mind talking about *her* family, but his was a different story.

'Nope. You seem to dote on yours though? Do you want to have kids yourself one day?'

Henri ripped her T-shirt over her head. Despite it covering her mouth, her reply was not muffled at all. 'Hell no. Do you?'

'I don't think so.' Maybe he might have considered it once upon a time, but that was another lifetime. Things had changed. *He'd* changed.

'Well, I know so,' Henri said firmly as she removed her shorts.

He should have been getting used to the sight of her in nothing but a swimsuit, but it still made his mouth water.

'Don't get me wrong,' she added, 'I like kids. You're right, I adore my nieces and nephews, but I've never had that burning urge to procreate like so many people, especially women, seem to. Tilley was talking about her wedding and having babies before I was even born. The idea never crossed my mind until I was almost an adult and I realised that's what people just expected I'd want. I don't know, maybe there's something wrong with me?'

She sounded vulnerable, a little despondent maybe, and he felt compelled to set her straight.

'I don't think so. The world's richer because everyone is different. And hey, the earth will probably thank us for not procreating, what with overpopulation and everything.'

She nodded and her lips stretched into a smile. 'Yeah, you're right. You and me? We're saving the world, one non-baby at a time. We should be awarded for our selfless decision.' Then she grabbed her board and ran towards the water.

Grinning at the image of them receiving some kind of trophy, Liam picked up his board and hurried after her. He was probably enjoying his mornings with Henri far too much, but he couldn't help himself. Quite aside from the view—and no, he wasn't talking about the ocean—and the thrill he got whenever he managed to actually catch a wave, she was like no woman he'd ever met before. She said things how she saw them, not giving two hoots whether it was the done thing, and she often made him laugh.

He was content with his life, his daily swims, the pub and his woodwork, but spending time with Henri had been a welcome diversion from the monotony of every day. And it was always good to learn a new skill, even if surfing was one that had never crossed his mind until he'd met her. Now that he was more confident, Henri didn't spend every moment in the water alongside him. While he practised on the smaller waves, she sometimes swam out further and attempted a bigger one. Sometimes he forgot he was supposed to be practising and found himself floating on his board, watching her instead. She was so graceful and watching her relaxed him in a way nothing else did.

She often caught him and paddled back to tell him off for slacking, and if he was honest, that was fun too.

After almost an hour in the surf, they emerged from the water and trekked back up to where Sheila was patiently guarding their things.

'That was awesome,' Henri said, dropping her board on the sand and then shaking her wet ponytail. 'I can't think of a better way to start the day.'

Liam could think of *one* better way, but of course he kept that to himself. Instead he picked up his towel and tried to rub the sand from his wet hair, only to open his eyes moments later to find Henri staring at him.

He swallowed as every muscle in his body grew tight. Was she checking him out? Did she feel the heat that arced between them too or was that wishful thinking?

Before he could work out the answer or what he wanted to do about it if she did, she reached out and touched her index finger, ever so gently, to his shoulder.

His pulse raced as heat spread from that one spot throughout his entire body in a matter of seconds.

'What happened?' she asked, tracing her finger around the scar.

His heart sank. *Of course.* It *was* interest he'd seen in her eyes, but not attraction. She was simply curious, like everyone else.

'I was …' His pulse thudded as he tried to remember the story he told the town whenever he had to get his gear off for the annual Undies Run, but he couldn't for the life of him recall it.

Time seemed to drag. Henri stared at him, her finger lingering on his shoulder, her eyes swimming with curiosity.

What the hell was it?

At that moment, he caught sight of someone walking up the beach towards them and, despite being too far away to see who it was, he dropped his towel, stepped forward and took Henri's face in his hands.

Only as his mouth sank against hers, did the lie come to him.

A slingshot. He and his friends mucking around with sticks and stones when they were kids. Due to his friend's bad aim, he'd been struck hard by a rock. *That's* what he'd told everyone had happened to him.

★ ★ ★

Henri's hand dropped as Liam's moved from her face to the back of her head, his fingers curling under her wet hair. Despite the morning sun baking down on them, she shivered.

His lips had totally taken her by surprise, but it didn't take long for her body to get on board. A delicious hum buzzed through her as his tongue darted out of his mouth and teased hers open.

She let go and gave herself completely to the moment, welcoming him into her mouth as she reached up and steadied herself on his strong, broad shoulders. Her fingers tingled as they swept over his skin. He was hot and damp and there was sand rubbing between them, but he tasted of mint with the hint of coffee, and she couldn't get enough of it.

Couldn't get enough of him.

She groaned involuntarily as his hand moved slowly down her back, lingering on her hip and grazing the skin at the top of her thigh as he kissed her like both of their lives depended on it.

Every part of her caught fire and she struggled to breathe, but damn if she could bring herself to break away for oxygen. Kisses like this didn't come along every day, at least not in her world.

When was the last time she'd been *this* turned on? Hell, the last guy she'd slept with hadn't even managed to make her feel this way when he'd been buried deep inside her.

But she didn't want to think about anyone else. Not when something torturously hard was gently pressing into her belly. Her mind skipped forward a few beats as she anticipated what might come next, then, as quickly as it had begun, it was over.

Liam pulled back, picked up his towel and wrapped it around his torso. He nodded over her shoulder. 'Morning, Grant.'

'Certainly looks that way from where I'm standing,' came the voice of Bunyip Bay's self-proclaimed matchmaker.

As Grant came up beside them, Henri stood there on the sand, her heart still racing and her nipples so hard they were visible through her bathers, but unable to think straight enough to scoop up her own towel and cover herself.

Was he the reason Liam had kissed her?

Of course. She sighed and finally bent to pick up her towel, a different kind of heat flooding her. Could she *be* more of a fool?

But if that kiss was Liam pretending, she could only begin to imagine how much better it could be if his heart was in it.

She turned and summoned a smile for Grant, who was wearing tiny black running shorts and jogging on the spot. 'Hey there. How are you?'

He beamed. 'I'm great. I've been trying to set this guy up for ages, so this is a happy sight. I must admit when I heard about you two, I couldn't picture it, but now that I've seen you together … well, congratulations.'

'Thanks,' Liam said, turning a knowing smile on Henri.

Still flustered, all she could manage was a quick nod.

'You not working today?' Liam asked.

Grant shook his head. 'I've got the day off. Ryan and I are heading down to Perth to meet a possible surrogate, but I convinced him to let me take a quick run first—helps calm the nerves—while he does a couple of errands at The Ag Store.'

'Wow. Good luck,' said Liam.

'Yes.' Henry finally found her voice. 'That's very exciting. Hope it goes well.'

'We're trying not to get our hopes up,' Grant said, his expression contradicting his words, 'but I've got a good feeling about this woman. Speaking of which, I better finish my run or I'll be late. You two have a good day.'

'Thanks. You too.'

With a final wave, Grant continued on up the beach. Henri fought the urge to run after him.

'Come on, lazy,' Liam said, nudging Sheila with his toe. 'Time for breakfast. Frankie's again?'

For a second Henri thought this was directed at the dog, but then realised he was looking to her, waiting for an answer.

Food was the last thing on her mind right now. While they'd held hands and hugged many times in the last few days, that was the first time Liam's lips had touched hers and right now she wasn't sure if she'd ever be able to think straight again. Her heart rate was only just beginning to slow, but the thought of sitting opposite him and making small talk after that kiss set it racing all over again.

'Actually, I …' She racked her mind for an excuse. 'We've been here longer than I imagined, so I should probably take a raincheck and get back to the farm.'

'No problem.' Liam nodded as they gathered up their things. He seemed to accept the lie, even though they weren't any later than they'd been the last few days. 'What are your plans for today? Anything as exciting as yesterday's concert?'

She forced a laugh and tried to reply in the same easy manner. 'Thankfully no. Although I've still got the annual wreath-making to look forward to tomorrow. And the boys start shearing next week, so there'll be a bit to do to get ready for that.'

'Don't they take a break after harvest?'

'Callum and Andrew aren't very good at relaxing—I don't know many farmers who are—but post-shearing and post-Christmas, Hannah and Janai are dragging them away for a bit. Mum, Tilley and James will head down to Busselton to camp for a couple of weeks too. Getting away from the farm is the only way to get the boys into holiday mode.'

'Fair enough. Do you ever go with them?'

'No. I haven't since Dad died. It's really more for the kids. And to be honest, I don't do holidays that well either.'

They walked in silence the rest of the way to the van, then loaded the boards onto the roof.

'Do you want to come back to the pub to have a shower before you head home?' Liam asked.

She'd done so the other days to de-sand before they headed to Frankie's for breakfast. But still ... how could he act so normal after what they'd just done minutes earlier on the beach? If the skin around her lips wasn't still burning from its brush with his stubble, she'd have thought she imagined the whole damn thing.

'Nah, I'll have a shower at home,' she replied, 'but thanks anyway.'

'Okay, then I might just walk Sheila back to the pub. Will you be back tonight?'

Henri wondered if she could get away with missing a night—the thought of being in such close proximity to him again so soon had muscles she hadn't used in months twitching. But if she let one little kiss get to her, how on earth would she get through the next couple of weeks? She needed a few hours' reprieve, but then she'd be fine. Now that she'd started this, she had to follow it through.

'That's the deal, isn't it?' she said, her tone sassier than she felt.

He smiled and nodded once. 'I'll see you then. Have a good day.'

'You too.'

Once home, Henri indulged in a long, *cold* shower and then went searching for her brothers, desperate for a physically gruelling task to take her mind and body off Liam.

It was only hours later, when she was sweating like a pig and elbow-deep in sheep shit under the shearing shed, that she realised he'd never answered her question about his scar.

Chapter Twelve

Every time the multicoloured fly straps that hung above the pub door swished open that night, Liam looked up, expecting Henri.

Every time it wasn't her, disappointment fought with relief.

No matter how hard he'd tried to distract himself with woodwork and pub work, she'd been on his mind all day. Ever since that damn kiss on the beach.

Although he'd already established he felt some attraction towards her, he had *not* expected to feel the kind of intensity he had when he'd pressed his mouth against hers. He'd meant it to be a quick smooch on the lips, merely long enough to distract Henri from his scar and throw some more fuel on their facade, but somehow tongues and hands had become involved and before he knew it, his body temperature had skyrocketed.

The barely audible groans she'd made into his mouth as her hands gripped his shoulders had turned him on something chronic and it was only when he felt his erection flare that reality had landed. This was all an act. Of course she'd kissed him back; she'd clearly realised that someone was nearby, and her lies depended on putting on a good show.

His damn swimming trunks had provided little cover, but he hoped he'd managed to pull back before she'd noticed just how dedicated he was to her cause.

Then again, was anyone *that* good an actor? Could *Henri* be that good an actor? Or had she felt something just as powerful as he had?

When they were leaving the beach, he'd almost suggested she come back to the pub and they do a little private rehearsal, but she'd been eager to escape and, as there was no one in sight, he'd had no excuse to kiss her again to try and suss out the situation.

But, so what if she'd felt the same sparks? That didn't mean they should act on them.

Out of the corner of his eye now, Liam registered movement at the door again. He looked up to see a woman entering. Not Henri, but someone who looked incredibly similar to her—only a few decades older, a few pounds heavier, and with hair dyed a soft brown to masquerade her greys.

He picked up a cloth and a glass that had already been polished and started rubbing as Fiona Forward stalked towards him.

'Good evening, Liam,' she said, perching herself on the closest bar stool. He rarely saw her without a smile, but tonight her expression was pensive.

'Evening, Mrs Forward. You here for the CWA dinner?'

She nodded. 'And, please, call me Fiona. Now that we're practically family, I don't think we need to be so formal, do you?'

'Family?' He almost choked on air. No wonder Henri felt the need to make up stories.

'Well, I know it's only early days, but I haven't seen Henrietta light up talking about a man for a long while, and it's been even longer since she showed any interest in anyone in the Bay.'

'Can I get you a drink?' Liam asked, unsure how to reply to that. Lying in theory was one thing, but blatantly telling untruths to someone's face didn't sit right with him. Yet he'd promised Henri, so he couldn't throw her under the bus.

'I'll have a glass of pinot grigio, please. I came a little early because I thought it would be good for us to have a chat beforehand and get to know each other better.'

'Sounds great,' he lied, turning to grab a cold bottle from the fridge and taking his sweet time filling a glass before handing it back to her. Part of him was surprised Fiona had taken this long to drop by.

'So, tell me, Liam, what is it that you like about my Henrietta?'

'Um …' He cleared his throat. Telling her that he thought her daughter was sexy as hell was probably not the way to win over a future in-law, even if that in-law was pretend. 'What's not to like? She's funny. Smart. Strong. I like that she dances to her own beat. We're still getting to know each other and I'm loving it.'

Fiona twirled her glass around but didn't take a sip. From her expression, he couldn't tell whether his answer had satisfied her or not. The hair on the back of his neck prickled.

'Not to be too intrusive,' she said eventually, 'but as far as I recall you haven't really had a serious relationship since you arrived in town, so I'm curious as to your intentions?'

He blinked. 'I'm sorry?'

'Well, I know Henrietta's a very pretty girl—even if she does her damn best to hide it—but is that *all* she is to you? A summer fling?'

Geez, country people didn't beat around the bush.

He swallowed and glanced around for someone who needed serving, but Dylan and Lara had it covered. What would Henri want him to say?

'Well, as you said, it's only early days, but I really like her. I haven't had many serious relationships in my life because I've … well, until Henri, no one has made me want to curb my wild bachelor ways. But in the short time we've been together, she's totally got under my skin. I'm looking forward to seeing what the future holds.'

Lord, he deserved an Academy Award for that little spiel, but Fiona wasn't done with her Spanish Inquisition.

'That's wonderful to hear, but how exactly will a long-term relationship work for you? Henrietta's job takes her all over the world for long periods at a time, and your hours aren't exactly conducive to a relationship either.'

Liam tensed a little. Fiona was right—being a publican would be hard on a relationship, and hell, he didn't even want one, but it still slightly irked him that she had certain ideas about him.

'That's true,' he said after a long pause, 'but I guess where there's a will there's a way. I'm sure Henri and I will work it out.'

Apparently not happy with this answer, Fiona changed tack. 'But it's not just the lifestyle, is it?' He kept his mouth shut because it was clearly a rhetorical question. 'Being an ag pilot is one of the most dangerous professions there is. Everyone says air travel is the safest kind of transport but that's bullshit when you include agricultural flying.'

He drew back slightly at the sound of prim and proper Fiona Forward cursing, but she just barrelled on.

'Did you know that the incidence of death and injury amongst ag pilots is over one hundred times Australia's national average for all other work-related injuries? The statistics speak for themselves. I just don't understand why Henrietta insists on gambling with her life every single day when there are plenty of other, safer careers she'd be good at.'

'Maybe so,' he said, unable to resist coming to her defence. 'But if all ag pilots decided to do something safer, where would that leave farmers who need crops spraying or livestock mustered? And what about bushfires? Without people like Henri risking their lives dropping water bombs, Australia would probably lose a lot more lives to fire.'

Fiona did the sign of the cross. 'Maybe so, but if you truly care about her the way you say you do, surely you have *some* concerns about her career as well?'

Liam wanted to tell her that life had no guarantees—you could have the safest job in the world and one day some psycho could turn up wielding a gun and obliterate all you knew—but instead he nodded.

'Of course I do. From the way she talks, it can be tough being a female in what is essentially still a male-dominated industry and I truly admire her for that. But you're right, the idea of anything happening to her doesn't bear thinking about.'

The smile that blossomed on her face told him she approved very much of his answer. She reached out and patted his hand. 'This has been a good chat, Liam.'

By the time Fiona's friends arrived and she went off to join them, Liam felt in dire need of a drink himself. And that feeling was very rare these days.

'Why the long face?' he heard Lara ask, and for a second he thought she was talking to him, but then he turned to see she was addressing Jim, a retired shire worker and one of his 'Poker Pensioners'.

The man all but slumped against the bar. 'Me house is being eaten away by termites.'

Lara made a face that said exactly what she thought of that.

Stifling a laugh as he recalled Lara's reaction when she'd seen her first huntsman spider, Liam turned to the older man. 'That's no good. Haven't you had regular treatments?'

Jim looked at Liam like he was on drugs. 'Who can afford that? It's a bit like insurance—bloody rort.'

Liam raised his eyebrows. 'You don't have insurance either?'

'Don't lecture me, kiddo. I didn't come here to be made to feel worse.'

Knowing exactly what he came for, Liam went to grab a pint glass, but Lara was already on it. She filled it to the brim with Jim's favourite beer.

'That's on the house,' Liam said as she handed it to him.

'Thanks.' Jim wrapped his stubby fingers around the glass and lifted it to his mouth. 'Reckon I could go a Bunyip Burger as well.'

'No worries.' Liam called the order through to Macca in the kitchen as Lara went off to see if any of their other customers needed refills.

They were reasonably busy tonight because in addition to the usual Friday night crowd, the local CWA were also having their Christmas meeting. There was only a dozen of them, but you'd be mistaken for thinking that number was a lot greater—the women were noisier than the barely legal blokes who frequented the pub on Friday and Saturday nights to play pool.

'Is your termite problem treatable?' Liam asked as Jim turned to go join his mates.

He sighed. 'If I had the funds to fix it, it would be.'

'How much exactly do you need?'

'Just under three grand.'

'Sheesh.' Liam grimaced. Even playing twice a week as he usually did, Jim would have to win a lot of games of poker to make that kind of money when his fellow players only ever bet with five-cent coins.

'I know.' He sighed loudly. 'Where's a poor pensioner supposed to get that kind of money?'

Liam shrugged as Jim downed almost half the pint in one go. 'Maybe you could ask for some kind of payment plan?'

'When have you ever known Phil McDonald to give a damn about the little folks?' he asked.

Rex, who'd been drinking quietly next to Jim, snorted. 'You'd have more luck asking the bloody Queen for a loan.'

Liam had to admit Rex was probably right. Phil was not only the owner of pretty much the only pest control company that serviced Bunyip Bay, but he also happened to be a local farmer *and* the Shire President. All he seemed to care about was making sure the town's sporting facilities were top notch and that the road out to Glenorchy—his prized Merino sheep farm—was sealed.

'Well, good luck,' Liam said, before going into the kitchen to start collecting the steaks and parmies for the annual CWA dinner.

'You need some Christmas tunes in here,' said Karen Barker as he put a plate laden with Macca's roast veggies, cauliflower cheese and a well-done steak in front of her. 'There's only two weeks to go now, you know?'

How could he forget with everyone constantly reminding him? 'You wouldn't be able to hear them over the top of your chatter,' he retorted, his tone far lighter than he felt.

'Bah humbug, Liam. Why are you such a Grinch?' asked Susan O'Neil, her large dangly reindeer earrings rattling as she spoke. 'Wouldn't hurt you to put up a few decorations.'

His chest tightened, because they were wrong: it would hurt—so very, very much. He'd sent Lara down to the shop to buy them Christmas crackers and seeing the packet waiting on the bar to be put out on the table was bad enough. What more did they want?

'Oh my goodness! *Bah* humbug!' exclaimed Mandy Sawyer, with what sounded very much like a witch's cackle. 'Get it, *Bar* Humbug—that's what you should rename The Palace at Christmas.'

The others thought this hilarious, all except Henri's mum who told them to leave him alone.

He tossed her an appreciative smile, then left them to their laughter as he went to fetch the next lot of meals, taking a quick moment to collect himself in the kitchen. It was stupid that even after so long, just the word 'Christmas' almost had him coming out in hives, but it did. December was his least favourite month of the year and he couldn't wait for it to be over.

When Liam returned, he brought Lara with him in the hope to get in and out faster, but the women were all deep in conversation about a community garden they were hoping to start next year anyway. That was the one good thing about these ladies—they always had so much to discuss that their conversation moved on at the speed of light.

Just when he thought they'd managed to hand out the rest of the meals without drawing any further attention to himself, Eileen Brady called to his retreating back, 'What's Henrietta up to tonight?'

'She should be here soon,' Fiona Forward answered for him with a smug smile as she winked at Liam in a manner that suggested the two of them were in cahoots in some kind of secret scheme. If only she knew the truth! 'She was having dinner with Hannah, Callum and the kids first.'

He nodded as if he knew this and then retreated quickly before the women could start teasing or grilling him on his phony love-life. That was another good reason to steer clear of ever getting involved with anyone in Bunyip Bay—in a small town a romance was rarely between two people; the rest of the residents also felt it their right to have their say.

The next couple of hours passed quickly and just when Liam was beginning to think Henri wasn't going to show up after all, the fly strips parted again and there she was.

The sight of her stole the air from his lungs.

She looked different this evening and it was only when she got closer that he realised what it was. The chocolate-brown locks that were normally captured in a high ponytail were falling in soft waves around her shoulders and she was wearing lipstick. *Red* lipstick. And mascara. Her sensible boots were still on her feet, but instead of her usual jeans or scruffy shorts, she wore a knee-length denim skirt and a figure-hugging blue tank top that was almost as revealing as her swimsuit.

Praising God for the particularly warm weather tonight, Liam stepped around the bar to greet her. He'd only meant to kiss her on the cheek but couldn't resist placing his mouth on hers instead. After all, wouldn't that be what a real boyfriend would do?

'Get a room!' he heard someone shout from over near the pool table. In the dining room, the CWA ladies applauded.

Henri laughed and rolled her eyes as they pulled apart.

'You look fabulous,' he said, resting his hand on the small of her back.

'Thanks.' She grinned up at him, then whispered, 'Thought maybe I should go to a bit of effort for my fake boyfriend. Great acting by the way.'

'I'll have you know I was the lead male role in the high school production three years in a row.'

'Wow. I'm impressed.'

'You're not so bad yourself.'

'Well, although I didn't have your esteemed training, I was pretty convincing when I lied about something Tilley or one of my brothers did to me to get them into trouble.'

He forced a laugh. 'Geez, remind me not to get on your bad side! Now, can I get you a drink?'

Henri glanced towards the dining room and waved at her mum. 'I'm shattered, but I'd better have one drink. Make sure Mum gets a good glimpse of us together before I head upstairs.'

'She and I have actually already had a bit of a chat.'

'What? Really?'

'She gave me the third degree, wanted to know if my intentions were honourable.'

'Oh God,' Henri groaned. 'What did you say?'

'I told her that your flying concerns me just as much as her and that I planned to make you fall so much in love with me that you couldn't bear to spend a moment away from me because I couldn't bear the thought of losing you.'

'Hah! Do you think she believed you?'

'Hey.' He cocked his head to one side. 'Didn't you just say how good an actor I am? I reckon she's ready to add my name to the family bible.'

Her eyes crinkled at the corners. 'Did she tell you about that too or was that just a lucky guess?'

He laughed, took her hand and started back towards the bar. 'So, what's it to be tonight? Guinness or whiskey?'

'Just a glass of house white, thanks,' she said, taking the stool next to Rex and nodding hello to Lara and Dylan, who were busy serving.

Liam slipped back behind the bar to pour her wine. 'How was your day?'

'Exhausting,' she replied as he handed her the glass, experiencing what could only be described as a jolt as their fingers brushed in the exchange.

What the hell was wrong with him? He liked women as much as the next straight guy, but he couldn't remember feeling such a visceral reaction to someone since …

He froze. Since Katie.

'What did you get up to?' he asked, pushing that unwanted thought from his mind.

'I helped Andrew feed the sheep, then I dug their shit out from under the shearing sheds to fertilise Mum's roses.'

'You did all that in today's heat?' He couldn't help but be impressed.

'Don't you know we country people are tough?'

There wasn't much chance to talk after that, which was probably a good thing. Liam took dessert into the CWA ladies, cleared empties, refilled glasses, and chatted to locals as they came and went from the bar. Henri sipped her drink and quietly surveyed the scene.

'Sorry things are a bit hectic tonight,' he said.

'It's fine. I don't want to distract you.'

You might not want to, but you definitely do.

He cleared his throat. 'Can I get you another drink?'

She glanced long and hard at her near-empty glass. 'Nah, I should probably go and say hi to Mum and her friends anyway, and then I might call it a night.'

'Okay.' He slipped his hand into his pocket and offered her his key.

'Thanks.' As she took it, she leaned across the bar, grabbed a fistful of his shirt, yanked him towards her and kissed him on the lips. 'Goodnight, Liam.'

'Goodnight, Henri,' he managed as she turned and started towards the dining room.

And good luck, he thought. Those women would be like a school of piranhas begging her for information.

But then again, wasn't that what she wanted?

Chapter Thirteen

Saturday morning, following another surfing lesson with Liam, Henri left Cecil in the car park at The Palace and began the walk down the street to the Town Hall, which she could see was already surrounded by utes and four-wheel drives.

She had what could only be described as a spring in her step when she heard her mum summon her.

'Henrietta! Boy, am I glad to see you. Come here and help me with all this stuff?'

She looked up to see her mother's Prado parked out the front of Frankie's Café and jogged the next few metres to get to her. 'Hey, Mum.'

'You're looking pretty pleased with yourself this morning.'

'It's a beautiful day.' Henri gestured to the sky, which was as clear as the ocean, except for the sun, shining brightly and already casting a warm glow on the earth. 'And I'm excited about wreath-making.'

'There's more to that smile than good weather, and as for wreath-making …' She snorted. 'Don't think I'm too old to remember what young love is like. Speaking of, I had a lovely chat with your new fella last night—'

'So he told me. I'm lucky you didn't scare him off.'

'If he could be scared off so easily, he wouldn't be worth having. But I have to say, it was a good conversation.'

'Shall we get this stuff out?' Henri pointed to the plastic containers and baskets in the back of the Prado. 'We don't want to be late.'

'Late? Everyone else is blooming early. I can't believe I had to park so far away.'

'Guess they're all as excited as I am.'

As they started towards the hall, their arms laden with wreath-making supplies from her mother's prized garden, it was impossible to miss the massive For Sale sign in the window of the café.

'I wonder who'll buy it?' Fiona remarked. 'It'll be sad to see Frankie go—what with Simone now living in Mingenew and their mum in Perth, I guess it's the end of an era for their family.'

'But the Burtons are still here,' Henri said, thinking of Adam and his parents. His mum was Simone and Frankie's aunt.

'Yes, you're right,' she sighed. 'I'm sure they'll be back for plenty of visits, and I think Logan still plans to help with the *Bunyip News* until they can find someone to take over his position. Maybe that's something you could do?'

'What?' Henri was thinking about the Burtons and the tragedy that had almost torn them apart, so she must have heard wrong.

'Well, you were quite good at English at school and it's always nice to give back to the community.'

'It also helps if you *live* in the community,' she replied, thinking that her mother had finally, completely, lost her marbles.

'Well, if things get serious between you and Liam, won't you want to spend more time here? Frankie and Logan found commuting between two places too hard and they were only working half an hour apart. Liam's a good-looking man, Henrietta, you won't want to leave him alone too long.'

'Right. Of course.' Fury rose inside Henri at her mother's less-than-subtle reference to Max—the man who had broken her heart five years ago. She swallowed the urge to snap that no man—not even one who gave fake kisses as good as Liam—would ever convince her to ground herself, while inside terrified that it wouldn't be a man that did the honours at all.

Tears welled in her eyes, but she blinked them away, not wanting to cry *or* get in an argument with her mother right now.

'Oh, look, is that Faith Forrester?' she said, pointing to a tall woman retrieving a tiny baby from the back of a silver four-wheel drive, not too far from the town hall.

'Yes.' Her mum's face lit up like a Christmas tree. 'Well, Faith Montgomery now. I heard she and Monty were coming home for Christmas. That must be baby Mabel. Let's go over and help her.'

Henri wasn't sure how they were going to do that when they were already carrying more than they really could, but she followed her over to Faith anyway.

'Ooh, my goodness,' her mum exclaimed, getting right into Faith's personal space and peering down at the poor baby like it was some kind of rare species. 'If that isn't the cutest baby I've ever seen! Has she got Monty's eyes?'

'Hi, Mrs Forward,' Faith smiled. 'And thank you. Both Clancy and Mabel take after Monty. I barely got a look in. Hi, Henri, how are you?'

'Hey. Congratulations,' Henri said. 'On your wedding and your two babies.'

'Thanks. Pity you couldn't make it back for the wedding.'

'Yeah, sorry.' Since the non-event that was her own nuptials, she'd not been able to bring herself to attend anyone else's, but she was going to have to get over that for Frankie and Logan's. 'Work's pretty hectic certain times of the year. How's Monty?'

'Yeah, he's great.' Faith beamed—it seemed two kids under two hadn't put a dampener on their romance at all. 'He wasn't able to get away from the farm yet, but he'll be up in time for the Christmas Tree next weekend.'

'Did your son stay with him?'

'No. I'm not quite ready to leave my little man for more than a few hours. Clancy's with my dad today—they were off to look at the sheep when I left, but I'm hoping he'll have a nap soon and not get up to too much mischief.'

'Who? Your dad or Clancy?' Henri joked.

Faith laughed. 'Maybe both?'

'Can Henri hold Mabel?' Fiona asked.

Faith looked puzzled as she gazed at all Henri was carrying. 'If she wants to. I need to feed her soon, but maybe after that?'

Henri glared at her mother. Did she think that holding Faith's newborn would make her clucky? That would be a miracle because she didn't have a maternal bone in her body. 'How about I carry your bag instead and we get Mabel out of the sun?'

'Thanks.' Faith looked like a load had been lifted as Henri reached inside the car and retrieved a giant nappy bag, then hauled it over her shoulder without dropping even one flower on the ground.

The moment they stepped inside the hall, Faith was mobbed with hugs.

'Where's Clancy?'

'Ooh, look at her hair!'

'How was the drive up here?'

'So wonderful that Ryan and Grant are going to give your two a little cousin soon.'

The poor baby almost got squashed in the stampede. You'd think Faith had returned from a mission to the moon, but Henri wasn't complaining—it took the heat off her for a bit.

While her mother went into the kitchen to put the pavlova into the fridge, she exchanged hellos with a few people and unloaded the rest of what they'd brought onto the wooden trestle tables that were set up in rows across the hall.

'Are these the same tables that were here when we used to come to town for Brownies?' she asked Tilley, who was laying out tiny pots of glue.

Her sister nodded.

Henri recalled thinking they were on their last legs twenty years ago. 'Why hasn't the shire replaced them, or someone fundraised for new ones?'

Tilley shrugged. 'Guess there's always something else that takes precedence.'

Before Henri and Tilley could say anything else on the matter, there were more exclamations of excitement as four women, or rather one woman, two teenagers and another baby, entered the building. Henri looked up to see it was Simone McArthur—she couldn't remember her new married name—and her daughter Harriet, who was holding Simone's youngest, who had to be about two now. What on earth was she called? Lord knows her mum had probably told her a million times.

'Ooh hasn't Celeste grown,' cooed Esther Burton, going over to pluck the little girl from her big sister's arms. 'Hello, my gorgeous little great niece.'

It was still weird to see Esther out and about. As long as Henri could remember she'd been agoraphobic, imprisoned on her farm in grief after the loss of her daughter, but all that had changed two Christmases ago and she'd been making amazing progress ever since.

'So good to see you all,' said someone else. Henri couldn't see who as the women had swamped the new arrivals in much the same way they had Faith.

'Couldn't miss the annual wreath-making,' Simone said, kissing and hugging all her old friends. 'You can take the girl out of Bunyip Bay, but you can't take Bunyip Bay out of the girl. Besides, I couldn't wait till Christmas to see Faith.'

The two of them embraced then Simone snatched Mabel out of Faith's arms. 'Oh, my goodness, I could just eat her right up.'

Before long, the fuss over Bunyip Bay's returned residents died down and everyone began crafting. There had to be fifty women, ranging in age from Mabel at only a couple of months to Dolce who was well into her nineties. As Henri watched the older woman's hand shaking as she cut the stems off her flowers, she thought of the rocking chair Liam was making and smiled as she imagined her joy when she saw it.

It wasn't just wreaths they were working on; some women were making earrings, others macrame gifts and a few painting pots for plants. The annual Christmas wreath-making session was basically just another excuse to get together, chat with the girls and celebrate the year that had been. The only requirement was that you brought a dish for afternoon tea and left the hall having created *something*.

Mostly Henri just listened and tried her best not to make a total disaster of her wreath, but inevitably the conversation eventually came around to her. Or more specifically her and Liam.

Secrets were practically illegal in small towns, therefore everyone wanted to know the details. Not only how they'd got together, but also things that they'd always been curious about him.

'Has he told you much about his family?'

'I get the impression they're dead.'

'Either that or he's estranged.'

'No, I'm sure he mentioned once that his parents had died in a car accident.'

'And what about what he did before buying the pub?'

'I heard he travelled.'

'Surely he must have done something besides that?'

Most of the women clearly adored Liam, but there were a few snobs who didn't really rate him because of his profession. Whatever their stance, the questions and statements came one after the other and were directed at Henri as if she might have all the answers about the slightly mysterious publican.

But she had just as many questions of her own. Although she'd spent a lot of time with Liam over the last week, she still felt like she'd only touched the surface. Every time she asked him about himself, he told her something minor and deflected the conversation back to her. She couldn't work out whether he was being cagey on purpose, or the listening skills he'd acquired at the pub meant he'd forgotten how to talk about himself. She didn't even really know what he'd done before he came to Australia.

'Um … to be honest,' she said now, 'we haven't spent a lot of time talking. When we're alone, well …'

Thankfully, she didn't have to spell it out. Her cheeks burned as she imagined exactly what it would be like to sleep with Liam. She knew he was a good kisser, and ever since she'd seen his hands smoothing down Dolce's rocking chair, she'd had visions of exactly what they'd feel like skating over her naked skin. Despite the fans spinning madly (and loudly) overhead, the hall suddenly felt like an oven. She could feel sweat in every crevice and her bra was soaking. It was surprising the flowers weren't wilting. Perhaps a good air conditioner in the hall was even more pressing than new tables.

'I'm just going to the bathroom,' she said, pushing back against the table to stand. 'Ouch!'

She winced as she saw a large splinter of wood poking out of her thumb. Dammit, she knew these tables were dangerous, but maybe this was her punishment for lying to everyone.

'You okay?' asked Stella.

'Just a splinter. I'll be fine,' she replied, then headed into the bathroom to try and get it out.

To Henri's relief, the women didn't push her for any further information about Liam when she returned, but that didn't mean *she* stopped thinking about him.

Chapter Fourteen

Liam froze as he approached his apartment just after midnight on Saturday evening to find a large wreath hanging on the door.

What the hell!?

His fingers curled into fists and a light sweat erupted on his skin as he took in the concoction of red, gold and green ribbons, plastic berries and foliage that had been pillaged from native vegetation.

This had to be Henri's doing. Who else but a girlfriend—or rather a fake one—would feel they had the right to do such a thing?

He glanced down to grumble at Sheila, only to remember that his dog was already inside. No doubt curled up with Henri on *his* bed.

Irritation swept through him as he ripped the wreath off its hook.

She'd overstepped the mark with this. It was one thing taking his bed most nights, another to be pretending to be together—touching and kissing in public—but hanging Christmas decorations was pushing the friendship too far. No one came up here apart from his staff and out-of-towners, so this ugly, over-sized decoration wasn't aiding and abetting their farce.

The only place he wanted to see it was in his trash can, exactly where he was about to shove it.

With the offending item in one hand, he wrenched the door open with the other and stormed inside, his heart jolting at the sight of Henri on his couch, Sheila fast asleep beside her.

Why was she still awake?

And not only awake, but sitting here in tiny shorts and a skimpy tee watching stupid Christmas movies?

'Hello,' she said, as she gestured to what he was carrying. 'I see you found my Christmas wreath. Too ugly to hang on your door? Don't worry, I'm not offended.'

Dragging his gaze from the TV he turned properly to look at her, swallowing at the sight of her bare legs.

'What?' His brain catching up, he looked at the wreath, then held it up like it was a trophy. 'No, not at all. I just thought it might be better downstairs where *everyone* can see it.'

It was like someone else had climbed into his body and started operating his voice box. That was not what he'd planned to say at all, but his irritation had all but dissipated at the uncertainty that crossed her face.

He was being irrational. Henri didn't know what Christmas decorations did to him. She hadn't hung the wreath to upset him. It was probably some kind of twisted thanks for going along with her scheme.

She frowned. 'Are you sure? I know it's not the prettiest thing, but I didn't know what else to do with it. Mum's is now hanging in pride of place on our front door, so she suggested I give mine to you.'

'Thank you.' He took a quick breath. 'And yes, I'm sure. I'll hang it tomorrow morning.'

If it was outside, he wouldn't have to see it all the damn time, and it might also go towards appeasing the locals who'd latched on to Karen's suggestion they call the pub 'Bar Humbug'. In less than twenty-four hours, he'd lost count of the number of people who'd said it to him. All of them cackling as if it were the funniest thing they'd ever heard.

As if Henri could read his mind, she said, 'I notice you don't have any other Christmas decorations?'

He put the wreath carefully down on a side table and shrugged. 'I don't see the point. You go to all this effort to put them up, only to have to take them all down again. And then there's the storage—waste of good space. Christmas is really for little kids anyway and, you may have noticed, little kids aren't really my clientele.'

She raised one eyebrow. 'Sounds like a cop-out to me, Liam. The least you could do is put up a tree and throw some tinsel around.'

'You're up late,' he said, hoping to distract her from this line of conversation. 'Thought you'd be in bed already?'

She took a moment to reply, and he thought maybe she'd try to push him on the decorations, but then she simply shrugged one shoulder. 'Couldn't sleep.'

'So, you decided to watch Christmas movies instead?' He hated them almost as much as he hated decorations.

'*Die Hard* is not a Christmas movie,' she exclaimed as Bruce Willis scaled an elevator shaft on the screen.

'Ah, yes it is.'

'Why? Just cos it's set at Christmas?' She scoffed. 'Name one other so-called Christmas movie that has so much blood, gore and violence.'

Liam came up blank but wasn't about to roll over and let her win the argument. He flopped down in the armchair beside her.

'Just because there's machine guns, doesn't make it *not* a Christmas movie either. It's about McClane realising how much he misses his wife and family …' He swallowed. 'Because he wants to spend the holiday with them.'

Henri shook her head. 'He could have that epiphany at any time of the year.'

'I disagree—such epiphanies are always at Christmas. But there's also tonnes of references the whole way through, not to mention the soundtrack. And what about McClane walking on broken glass at the end? If that isn't a Christ-like sacrifice, I don't know what is.'

Henri snorted. 'Now you're really clutching at straws.'

'I'm not! Christmas is the reason for pretty much everything that happens and all of the character growth.'

'Bull. Shit. There's no sign of Santa Claus or reindeer so it can't be a Christmas movie.'

'Maybe we'll just have to agree to disagree on this one.'

Although he had to admit, as usual, he was enjoying bantering with her. Probably more than he should. It felt way too much like foreplay. He hadn't had a woman in his apartment for any other reason in the whole time he'd lived here. Well, except Janet once a week when she came to do the cleaning, but she definitely didn't set him on edge the way Henri did.

'Or we can agree that I'm right and you're wrong,' she said, smiling as she disentangled herself from Sheila and pushed to her feet. 'I'm going to make a Milo. Do you want one?'

'Sure, that'd be good.'

As she headed into the kitchen, Liam picked up the remote and flopped back into the chair. There had to be something else on the TV besides this. As he flicked through the options, he heard the fridge open and Henri whistling as she pottered about the kitchen. Over the past few nights, he'd got used to waking up to her in his space—to the sight of her toothbrush in his bathroom and her shoes by the door—but she was usually in bed by the time he came upstairs. Being here alone together at night was a whole other kettle of fish.

Just remember who she is. Who her family is! She's only here to deceive them.

When she returned, carrying two steaming mugs and a packet of Tim Tams hanging between her teeth, he noticed a bandaid on her finger.

'Thanks,' he said as he took one of the mugs. 'What did you do to yourself?'

She blinked. 'What?'

'Your finger.'

'Oh. I got a splinter from the bloody tables at the hall today. It's nothing really, but I might have got a little aggressive with the tweezers when I was trying to make sure I got it all out.'

She sat back down next to Sheila, who roused for a moment, but when she realised there was only human snacks and she was not going to be given any, immediately returned to the Land of Nod.

'You got a splinter from a table?'

'Have you seen those tables?'

He shook his head. 'I don't do many craft sessions at the hall.'

'Lucky you. Well, they're probably older than Dolce and in dire need of replacement, or at least some serious TLC, but apparently new trestles are low on the shire priority list. Lucky it was me who got it and not one of the kids.'

'Maybe if a kid hurt themselves someone would do something about it,' Liam said as he opened the packet of Tim Tams, offered her one and then took one for himself. It was good to have something to keep his hands and mouth busy.

'Oh, no, no, no, no, no,' she said as he took a bite.

'What is it?' He looked around. Was there a mammoth spider on his shoulder or something?

She thrust her finger at him. 'That is *not* how you eat Tim Tams. How long have you been in Australia? You're doing it all wrong!'

'Huh?'

Henri plucked one from the packet. '*This* is the only way to have Milo and Tim Tams. Or coffee and Tim Tams. Anything and Tim Tams really.'

He watched in slight awe, slight horror, as she bit the top off one end, then flipped it and did the same at the other end, before dipping the Tim Tam into her Milo and using it as a straw. He laughed at the undignified sound she made slurping up the liquid, then sucked in a breath as chocolate dripped onto her fingers. As she popped all that was left into her mouth all he could think about was how delicious she'd taste right this moment.

Who was he kidding? She tasted delicious regardless. Thanks to their *fake* public display of affection, he had firsthand knowledge of the fact.

'Now your turn,' she said, nodding towards the packet and smiling. Did she have *any* idea what she did to him?

Trying to stay cool, he grabbed another and proceeded to do exactly what she'd done moments earlier. He blinked as the warm Milo shot up through the Tim Tam, giving him a gooey chocolate rush. But then he took too long to act and the rest of it slipped from his fingers and plopped right into his mug.

Henri thought this hilarious.

He glared at her while secretly relishing the sound of her laughter. 'That was intense.'

'But good intense, right?'

He nodded, unable to tear his gaze from hers. Thank God there was a dog and an armchair between them.

After what felt like five hours but was probably nearer five seconds, Henri licked her lips and then cleared her throat. She felt it too, he knew it, but that didn't mean they should act on it.

'I can't believe you've lived ten years in Australia and no one has showed you how to do a Tim Tam slam before.'

'Almost eleven years,' he corrected.

'That's right ...' She settled back into the couch, placing one hand on Sheila. Once again, he found himself a little jealous as he watched her fingers absentmindedly slide through the dog's fur. 'Whereabouts in Australia did you travel before stopping in Bunyip Bay?'

'I started in Sydney, bought an old ute, explored the area where my mom grew up a bit, then headed up to Queensland and across the top, before driving down the coast and ending up in Bunyip Bay.'

For a while they exchanged stories of sights seen and people met. Henri's tales of the quirky characters she'd worked with all over the world amused him and, although he'd been exhausted when he came upstairs, her laughter as he described some of the interesting backpackers he'd met in hostels gave him a second wind.

'You can tell me to mind my own business if you want, but why haven't you had a serious relationship since you've arrived?' asked Henri.

He swallowed. 'Who said I haven't?'

She gave him a look. 'Nothing goes unnoticed in Bunyip Bay. You can't even change your underwear around here without someone finding out and making sure everyone else knows about it as well.'

Despite the tightness in his chest, he couldn't help but laugh. Were there ever any truer words said?

'Well, like your job,' he said, 'mine isn't really conducive to a relationship.'

'Don't you ever get lonely?'

'Don't you?'

She rolled her eyes. 'Do you *ever* answer a question with a straight answer?'

He cocked his head to one side. 'Do *you*?'

'Let's play a game,' she suggested.

'What kind of game?'

'Kind of like Truth or Dare ...'

It sounded like dangerous territory, but also fun. Normally he played things pretty safe, but Henri made him want to live on the edge.

'But without the dares.'

He groaned. 'Where's the fun in that? Not scared of a good old dare, are you?'

She glared at him but her eyes were smiling. 'Fine—truth *or* dare. Your turn first. What's it to be?'

'Dare. What do you want me to do? Run naked down the main street? Steal flowers from Eileen Brady's garden? Do ten Tim Tam slams in a row?'

'I *dare* you to answer this question truthfully.'

'That's cheating!'

'Do you accept the dare or do you not?'

He sighed, trying to ignore the squeeze of his ribs. 'Ask away.' She didn't have a lie detector, so he didn't have to tell the truth if he didn't want to.

'Do you get those T-shirts you wear for free?'

'What?' He blinked. He'd been expecting something much more intrusive.

'Do you get those shirts for free?' she repeated, pointing to his black polo shirt, the one with the Bundy Rum polar bear on the pocket.

'Yep. Hundreds of them. Can't remember the last time I actually had to buy a shirt. It's one of the perks of owning a pub.'

She smiled. 'And what are the other perks?'

He shook his head. 'That's two questions. I think it's my turn now. Truth or dare?' Of course she chose truth. 'Have you ever been out with anyone from Bunyip Bay?'

Her cheeks flushed. 'Um … not really. I was at boarding school since I was thirteen and then never really came back to live after that, but I had the biggest crush on Adam Burton growing up.'

He laughed. 'From what I've heard you're not the only one.'

Henri nodded. 'So, what's it to be? Another dare or truth?'

'Dare. But you can't give me the same one as last time.'

'Now I'm beginning to think *you're* the chicken, but okay. I dare you to … tell me who the people in the photo that was in your bedroom are. I wasn't sure whether the man was you or just someone that looked a lot like you. Like your dad? But if it was you … were the kids yours?'

Liam shifted in his seat. *Man*, she was good at this game. He almost said, 'what photo?' hoping he could make her think she'd imagined it, but she wasn't stupid. Perhaps it would have been smarter for him to leave it there—removing it had only drawn attention.

'I'm the little boy in the photo. And no, I've never been married. No kids either.' He didn't ask her truth or dare, just launched into the next question. 'Have you ever had any serious incidents while flying?'

Something akin to discomfort flashed across her face but she covered it quickly. 'I once got a paper cut while filling out amendments to Air Navigation Orders for CASA.'

He rolled his eyes, suddenly sensing she was hiding something. 'Did that paper cut happen while you were flying?'

She shook her head.

'Then it doesn't count. Tell me the truth, Henri.'

'Okay. Fine.' She wrung her hands together in her lap. 'But if you tell my mother I'll have to kill you.'

'Promise. My lips are sealed. What happened?'

'I've had a couple of close encounters with powerlines, but that's quite common. Sometimes they're pesky to see and it's over before you even realise. If the wire breaks, there's usually no consequences. If the wire doesn't break or jams something in the aircraft, well … it can lead to serious problems, but I've always been lucky. Then, not too long ago, when I was mustering up north …'

Liam's heart thudded when Henri's voice trailed off. 'What happened?'

'It was late in the day; we were almost knocking off and I was heading down near some trees to chase out cattle when the engine failed.'

'It just stopped?'

'Yeah.' She sucked in a breath. 'Well, there was a loud bang and then the prop stopped dead. I had to act fast and come down in terrain not ideal for landing. The trees were quite dense, but I found a small clearing. I managed to crash land, but the small wheels aren't made for the rough ground. We bounced and I skidded to try and keep control, but we hit a termite mound. It all happened really fast. One minute I was airborne, the next I'm climbing out of the wreck.'

'Geez.' Liam found his hands gripping the arms of his chair as she spoke. No wonder Fiona Forward was constantly crossing herself. It sounded like Henri was lucky to come out of that alive. 'Were you hurt?'

'Not really. I walked away with nothing but a bit of bruising.'

'How do you go back up in the air after something like that happens?'

'Well, you just gotta get back on the horse, so to speak, don't you?' Henri reached for Sheila again and suddenly looked more serious than he'd ever seen. 'A pilot I kinda knew lost his life a few years ago—but you always think it won't happen to you. You know what I mean?'

He nodded. *Oh yeah*, he knew.

Growing up, Liam had almost become numb to the bad news he saw on TV. The natural disasters, the terrorist attacks, the shootings, the wars in far-off countries … they were almost as unreal as the movies he watched. When one of them actually affected you, the shock was almost as palpable as the grief. 'You're very brave.'

She shook her head—'No. I'm not brave at all'—and swiped at her eyes as if trying to ward off tears.

He grabbed the box of tissues off the coffee table and by the time he turned back to her, she was sobbing. 'Shit, Henri,' he said, yanking out a tissue and thrusting it at her, resisting the urge to pull her into his arms. 'What's wrong?'

She sniffed a few times, wiped her eyes, sniffed some more, then, 'You asked how you go back up in the air after a crash? Well, the truth is … I haven't.'

'What do you mean?'

'I had to abandon the mustering contract because the aircraft needed fixing but they were almost finished anyway. I thought I was fine. I drove across to the Riverina where I was supposed to start a rice contract that would take me right up to Christmas.' She paused. 'But when I got there, I just froze. I couldn't even bring myself to climb into the aircraft.'

Her face crumbled and suddenly the tears came hard and fast. 'I'm so sorry. I'm such a stuff-up.'

Liam moved off the armchair, lowered himself down beside her on the couch and pulled her into his arms. 'No, you're not. Geez, what you went through … being scared to fly again sounds like a perfectly normal reaction to me. Have you spoken to anyone about it?'

'Just my boss. He was great, understanding. Told me to take some time off. See how I feel after Christmas.' Her words were muffled as she sobbed into his chest. 'I was going to tell Frankie, but I couldn't bring myself to do it. I'm just so ashamed, and I can't risk Mum finding out either.'

He didn't need to ask why.

'You're the first person I've admitted it to,' she said, pulling back. 'You won't tell anyone, will you?'

'No, course not.' He was used to people telling him things they couldn't talk about with anyone else, and he always kept their secrets. 'But what are you going to do about it?'

Henri inhaled deeply and then puffed out a breath. 'I guess if I still can't fly after Christmas, I'll have to talk to a professional or something, but … what if they can't fix me? What the hell am I supposed to do with my life if I can't fly? It's in my blood. It's not only what I want to do, it's what I *need* to do—it's almost the same as breathing to me. I don't know how to do anything else. I'm actually more scared of not flying than I am of dying, which is what makes this so infuriating.'

'If that's the case,' he said, 'then I reckon you'll get in an aircraft again. I do. What about going up with another pilot? Someone you trust. See if you can handle flying when you're not in control. You know … one step at a time.'

'I don't know. Maybe. Anyway, I didn't mean to unload on you,' she said, scrunching the soggy tissue in her hand into a ball, 'but it actually feels good to have told someone. Thank you.'

'Hey.' He shrugged. 'No problem; that's what publicans do. We listen.'

She smiled. 'Anyway, enough about me … truth or dare.'

Henri's confession had been so heartfelt and raw that he'd almost forgotten they were still playing. It was getting late, but he didn't feel he could abandon her just yet. 'Truth.'

Surprise flashed in her eyes before she said, 'How'd you get the scar on your shoulder?'

Of course it was coming—he'd distracted her once, she was bound to try again—but he had no excuse to distract her with a kiss up here. 'I fell out of a tree as a kid. A stick stabbed me.'

Shit. A tree? A stick? Where the hell had that come from? It certainly wasn't his usual story. He only hoped she hadn't been talking to anyone else about it.

'Did you have to get any stitches?'

'Eleven.' At least that bit was true.

'Why did you hide the photo?'

'Because talking about my family hurts,' he admitted, his tone cool.

Most people would take the hint at that, but not Henri. 'Was that why you left America? Did you fall out with them or something?'

Her questions felt like gunshots. Heat crept up his neck and his breath quickened. Until that moment, he'd never once felt compelled to break his silence, but weirdly he found himself considering actually telling her.

The question was … where the hell to start? He'd spent so many years not talking about his family, not ever speaking about what had happened almost exactly twelve years ago, that even when he opened his mouth, nothing came out.

'I'm sorry,' she said when the silence grew awkward. 'That was three questions. You don't have to answer any of them.'

'Yeah.' Maybe that was for the best. He pushed to a stand, unable to believe how close he'd come to spilling everything. 'It's getting late—or rather early. Maybe we should call it a night? I'm going to have a shower.'

Then, without waiting for a reply, he headed for the bathroom, hoping that by tomorrow morning, all the crazy urges he felt when she was close would have passed.

Chapter Fifteen

When Henri walked into The Palace on Sunday night, her belly wobbled as if she'd just stepped off the Gravitron ride at the Perth Royal Show. The thoughts inside her head were so loud she barely registered the sounds of Radiohead blasting from the stereo, or who else was around. She hadn't seen Liam since 3 am that morning when he'd escaped to have a shower and she'd fallen asleep on the couch.

Exactly six hours later she'd woken to an empty apartment—no sign of him, no sign of Sheila, only the faintest hint of aftershave still lingering in the bathroom. She'd dressed quickly and gone downstairs, thinking she'd find him in the office, the storeroom or out in the workshop, but she couldn't find him anywhere.

It was then that she first wondered if he'd disappeared on purpose. Had she pushed him too far asking probing questions about his family?

She'd gone home, hoping to find something outside to distract her but had been roped into helping her mum, nieces and nephews make gingerbread houses instead. Not exactly the manual labour she'd felt she needed and, although she'd been busy and distracted by the kids, she hadn't been distracted enough not to have plenty of time to stress about Liam.

All day she'd been trying to convince herself she was worrying about nothing. Perhaps he'd simply had somewhere else to be that morning and hadn't wanted to wake her to say goodbye?

Whatever the case, she'd dithered about coming in tonight, eating popcorn and watching *Elf* on TV with her mum and Macy, who was sleeping over again because Tilley and James had a Christmas function on in Geraldton. When the movie finally ended, her mother had wanted to know whether Henri was heading into town tonight, and she'd been tempted to say no and stay home, but decided it was best to face Liam and see where they stood. To apologise if she'd overstepped the mark last night.

If he wanted to end their charade, she'd understand. It had been a ridiculous idea and a lot to ask of a near stranger anyway, but the thought of not having an excuse to spend time with him anymore left her numb. Maybe she could offer to continue the surfing lessons anyway?

As the multicoloured fly strips swished behind her, Liam glanced up. Their gazes snagged and Henri's breath caught in her throat.

She'd never be able to look at the logo of an alcohol company again without her heart beating a little faster. Or eat a Tim Tam.

Ignoring the urge to turn and run away, she hitched her bag on her shoulder, held her chin high and headed towards him.

'Hey!' he said as he came around the bar and leaned in to give her a quick kiss. 'You smell like ginger.'

'That'd be because I've spent the whole day surrounded by it. I was helping Mum make gingerbread houses with the kids.'

'Yum. Did you bring me any? As your *boyfriend*, shouldn't I at least get a sample?'

She relaxed immediately. If he was joking about being her boyfriend, he couldn't be too mad. 'Sorry. Didn't think. I'll see if there's any left and bring you some tomorrow.'

'All good.' He placed his hand in the small of her back and led her over to the bar.

Henri said 'Hi' to Dylan, who was loading clean glasses from a tray onto the shelves beneath the bar, and then climbed up on a stool next to Sexy Rexy—a name as ill-fitting as ever there was, but that was country folks for you. They *loved* nicknames and they *loved* irony. She nodded an acknowledgement.

Miraculously, the town drunk didn't skedaddle away as he normally did when she attempted conversation. Maybe it was because Henri was later than usual, and he had enough Dutch courage to make talking to strange women not quite as scary.

'Can I get you a drink?' Liam asked.

'Rumour has it you make a pretty good cocktail.'

Liam lowered his head in one slow nod. 'That rumour would be correct.'

'Excellent. Then I'll have a Sex on the Beach, please.'

Where the hell had that come from? Henri didn't even know what Sex on the Beach entailed—well, not the drink variety; the literal variety she imagined would be very, very sandy and not particularly comfortable. But if the colour Liam's cheeks suddenly turned was anything to go by, then he was thinking about the latter as well.

Her Kegel muscles squeezed of their own accord.

'Coming right up,' he said, already starting to gather the ingredients.

As she watched him skilfully mix vodka with peach schnapps, orange and cranberry juice, her thoughts once again turned to last night. She couldn't remember the last time she'd stayed up that late, or rather early.

The game of Truth or Dare had made the night *feel* flirtatious, even though a lot of what she'd told him had been anything but light. It was one of the weirdest conversations she'd ever had because the serious nature of what she'd shared had felt in stark contrast to the low-level hum sparking between them.

'Here you go, one Sex on the Beach.' Liam placed a glass containing a colourful drink topped with one of those paper umbrellas in front of her. 'Enjoy.'

He kept a straight face, but Henri felt fireworks skate across her cheeks. She really couldn't work him out. Was he flirting with her or merely in character?

'Thank you,' she managed, then took a much-needed sip of the cool, sweetly delicious liquid.

'You're more than welcome.'

'I missed our surfing lesson this morning.'

'I didn't want to wake you because you looked so comfy, but I had something I had to do. Sorry, I probably should have left a note but I'm still getting used to this whole relationship thing.'

She smiled. 'You and me both. And it's fine. Glad everything was okay.'

'Of course.' He nodded slowly, his eyes trained on hers, telling her he too was referring to their conversation last night.

The knowledge that she hadn't ruined things between them relaxed her.

'Planning on watching more Christmas movies tonight?' he asked.

'Don't start that again. Unless you like being a loser, because I'm prepared to argue to the death!'

Liam's lips flickered upwards. 'Well, don't fall asleep on the couch, because I'll be a little later than usual and I don't want to wake you when I come in.'

'Oh? What are you up to?' Her ridiculous heart wondered if he was meeting someone—a *female* someone—not that it was any of her business. Unless he wasn't discreet and someone in town saw him with someone else. The situation was already complicated enough without people jumping to the conclusion that Liam had two women on the go.

He lowered his voice. 'I'm going to deliver Dolce's rocking chair.'

'I'll help you,' she offered. 'That rocking chair must be pretty heavy.'

'It's fine. I'm used to lifting heavy stuff on my own.'

'It doesn't mean you have to.' Granted, Liam was a big, muscly guy but it still wouldn't be easy to move that masterpiece around on his own. Especially not in the dark, while trying to be all stealth-like. It was the least she could do considering all he was doing for her.

'Okay. If you insist. I might close up slightly earlier than usual anyway, because it's quietened down now.'

As if fate wanted to prove him a liar, at that exact moment, there was a shout from the corner near the pool table. 'You fucking bastard!'

Even before she'd turned to see Jaxon Bird's hands wrapped around Brad McDonald's neck as he slammed him onto the table, Liam charged around the bar. Sheila, who'd been dead to the world moments earlier, was right behind him, baring her teeth. Liam launched himself at the boys, dragging Jaxon off his so-called friend and holding them both at arm's length as Sheila stood between them all. Even from the bar, you could hear her growling. Although Jaxon looked to have made the first move, Brad bounced up and down on the spot like a caged beast ready to strike, and Henri worried that Liam might become collateral damage.

'That's enough. Calm the hell down or you're both banned from the pub till next year,' he ordered.

Although Henri stilled at the authority in Liam's voice, it was like neither of the boys actually heard him.

'What the hell, man! She's my ex-girlfriend,' Jaxon shouted.

'You two were just kids when you were together,' Brad retorted. 'I'm showing her what it's like to be with a man!'

'Fuck you!' Henri flinched as Jaxon shoved Liam out of his way as he laid into Brad again. 'You hurt her, and I'll fucking kill you!'

Dylan ditched the bottle of wine he'd been holding and ran to offer assistance.

Liam grabbed both offenders by the scruff of their necks. 'I'll kill the both of you if you don't stop disturbing the peace!'

He started to drag them towards the door, shoving Brad at Dylan. The tall Welsh bartender caught him as if he were a rugby ball.

'They'll be right,' Sexy Rexy said as Liam and Dylan escorted the boys from the building.

Henri had almost forgotten he was here. Nerves pulsed from her belly up to her throat. 'I hope so.'

'Liam can handle those two babies. I've seen him deal with a lot worse.'

She prayed they'd do as they were told as she took another sip of her cocktail. 'By the way, I'm Henri Forward. Not sure we've ever been properly introduced. You work for the shire, right?'

Sexy Rexy nodded and thrust out his hand, which she shook firmly despite the fact it was warm and sticky. 'Rex Carter. I'm the chief executive officer of the Bunyip Bay Waste Recovery Park.'

'Sounds like a big job,' she said, taking a sip of her drink to hide her smile. She'd only ever heard it called the rubbish tip, and *CEO*? That was a bit of a stretch. 'Do you come here a lot?'

The man glared daggers at her. 'What are you trying to say? You think I'm a drunk? You think I have nothing better to do with my time?'

'No. Sorry. Nothing like that.' *Although if the shoe fits.* Henri tried for a placating smile. 'I was just thinking that must mean you know Liam quite well.'

His face softened. 'Yeah. You could say that. He's a good bloke. If it weren't for him, I probably wouldn't be sitting here right now, and I reckon I'm probably not the only one.'

'What do you mean?'

'After me wife up and left with me brother, I started coming here of an evening just to get out of the quiet house. Drowned my sorrows in Jack Daniels. But after a while even JD didn't make me feel any better. When I didn't show up here one night, Liam came around to my place. Broke down me door and found me passed out in me bed. He called the ambos and they got me back.' He glanced down into his glass, which was almost empty. 'Don't get me wrong, I wanted to kill him for stuffing up my plans, but he didn't give up on me. He told me how he enjoys our chats and said he'd miss me if I wasn't around. And well, it might sound stupid, but …'

'It doesn't sound stupid,' Henri said, barely managing to get the words out around the lump that had formed in her throat. She'd already suspected that Liam wasn't just a good-looking guy but also a truly good one, and this just proved it. His patrons weren't just customers to him—he cared about each and every one of them.

'These days, I only drink the light stuff,' Rex continued as he lifted the pint and downed the dregs. 'And Liam makes sure I stop before I start getting too down in the dumps. He also encouraged me to go for a promotion when it came up at the tip, and now I get to boss people instead of the other way.'

'That's great,' Henri said, glancing back towards the door, wondering what was taking Liam and Dylan so long.

Just when she was thinking that maybe she should call Drew, the fly strips parted and Liam, Sheila and Dylan stepped through.

'Oh my God.' Henri leapt from her stool at the sight of blood spilling from Liam's lip. 'Who did that to you?'

He shook his head. 'It doesn't matter. I'm just gonna go clean up.' Then he walked around the bar and into the kitchen behind.

Dylan looked at Henri. 'Can you go help him? I'm not good with blood.' When she hesitated, he added, 'Or I can go upstairs and get Lara. It's her night off but she'll be awake binge-watching *Schitt's Creek*.'

'No, course not. I'll help.' Henri slid off the stool. *Of course* as the girlfriend she should be the one patching him up, but in all the drama she'd forgotten about their charade.

She walked around the bar and into the now-empty kitchen—last orders were hours ago, and Macca and the kitchen staff had left—to find Liam leaning against a counter, an icepack pressed against his lip, Sheila standing guard right beside him; she was such a good dog. Henri wasn't sure what else she could do but offer commiserations.

'Youch, that looks painful,' she said.

He raised one eyebrow at her.

'Sorry—stating the obvious. Bad habit of mine. It probably feels even worse than it looks. Do you need any help cleaning it up?'

He lowered the icepack and angled his face towards her. 'Has it stopped bleeding?'

Henri stepped up close. 'I think so,' she murmured, resisting the urge to reach out and cup his cheek. 'Are you gunna press charges?'

'Nah, he didn't mean it. And I was young once. I know what it's like to get all worked up over a girl.'

'You're a lot more forgiving than I am,' she said. 'I didn't even know Jaxon and Brad were old enough to drink.'

'Only just. Jaxon celebrated his eighteenth here only a few weeks ago. Brad a couple of months before that. They're good kids mostly. They'll be in tomorrow to apologise, I'm sure.'

Liam washed his face and cleaned up, joking that Macca would kill him for messing up his kitchen. Then they switched off the lights and headed back out to the bar, which was now deserted.

'Bet her touch was much better than mine,' Dylan said as he finished sweeping the floor. He leaned the broom against the bar. 'I've locked up and turned off the taps. Anything else you want me to do before I go?'

Liam shook his head. 'Thanks, mate. See you tomorrow.'

When Dylan disappeared, he hit Henri with a now-crooked smile. 'You ready for our late-night delivery?'

'Are you sure you're still up for it?'

'I'm not going to let a little cut get me down, but if you'd rather not join me—'

'I'm coming,' she said firmly, then glanced down at Sheila. 'She coming too?'

'No, we'll leave her here. Don't want her to see a possum or something and start barking.'

Henri followed Liam out the back door and over to the workshop, where his red Hilux was parked. Light from a lone streetlight lit up their path and Henri felt a flicker of excitement as she realised this was the first time they'd been *alone*-alone. Most of the time they had an audience, or at least Sheila acting as chaperone.

Hopefully oblivious to the workings of her mind, Liam slid open the heavy door and flicked on a switch. She inhaled the scent of wood chips and varnish as light spilled over Dolce's rocking chair, which was waiting just inside the door.

'Wow,' Henri gasped as she took a proper look at it. All polished and shiny, it looked like something you might pay hundreds of dollars for. 'Dolce's one lucky old bird.'

'I hope she likes it.' He bent down to lift one end. 'You take the other side so you're walking forward.'

Henri did as she was told, noticing that pieces of wood were laid out across his work bench.

'What are you working on now?' she asked as they shuffled outside and carefully heaved the chair onto the tray of the ute, which Liam had already lined with a heavy blanket to avoid damage.

'Just fiddling with a few ideas.' He gestured to a thick yellow cord on her side of the tray. 'Do you mind passing me that rope?'

She picked it up and tossed it to him, then watched as he started to secure the chair, tying very impressive knots. Was there anything his hands couldn't do?

Henri swallowed—don't even go there—and focused on the job before them. 'So, what's the plan?'

'What do you mean?'

'How are we actually going to do this?'

As he finished what he was doing, he explained they'd drive the short distance to Dolce's house on the other side of Bunyip Bay but park a few houses up in front of Rex's house. 'He'll be out cold by now, so won't notice a thing. Then we'll walk to Dolce's place and quietly make the switch.'

'But why are we doing this in the dark at night? Won't Dolce know it's from you anyway?'

It wasn't like there were dozens of people in town with the skillset to create anything as beautiful as this.

Liam shrugged as he yanked at the last knot to make sure it was tight. 'I don't like making a fuss. And I thought it'd be nice for her to walk out tomorrow morning and just find it there.'

'Why not do it on Christmas Eve and make it like Santa delivered it?'

He raised an eyebrow, giving her a look that told her exactly what he thought of that idea.

'Fair enough.' Henri smiled. There was no point trying to understand the workings of a male mind and this sneaking around was kinda fun anyway. 'Then let's do this!'

Chapter Sixteen

Liam needed his head read. That's what he decided as he drove out of the car park and turned into the main street towards Dolce's end of town. The lights on all the shops made it feel as if they were driving through a silent disco and did not help the tension building in his head at all.

What had he been thinking agreeing to let Henri come with him? He didn't need her help and last night had been torturous enough. Now in the closed confines of his ute, he was struggling to think, and struggling to keep his eyes on the road when her practically bare-naked legs were only centimetres from his. A fake relationship was proving to be all-consuming and just as infuriating as a real one could be, only without the benefit of sex. His fingers twitched around the steering wheel, but he resisted the urge to reach out and place his hand on her thigh. How many days were there until Christmas? How many days until the decorations and flashing lights all around them could be taken down? Till Henri would leave again and things could go back to normal? Liam honestly wasn't sure how long he could keep it up. His thoughts about taking things further were getting stronger each moment they spent together. Right now, his cut lip wasn't the only part of him throbbing.

You simply need to remember that this is all an act!

But the problem with fake was that sometimes it felt very damn real. And sometimes when she looked at him, he wasn't so sure that she wasn't harbouring the same illicit thoughts as him. She'd ordered Sex on the Beach for crying out loud!

Maybe he should just ask her? Come right out and lay his cards on the table. See if she wanted to turn their charade into a summer fling? But if she didn't … how awkward would that make things between them? More to the point, why did he care?

Dammit, why was he losing his head over this? Until a week ago, he hadn't even known she existed.

Usually, sexual attraction was simple. He met someone he thought was hot, made sure they felt the same about him and didn't have lingering ties to anyone in town—then made his move. They enjoyed each other's company for a night (two max) and then both moved on.

The problem with Henri was she *did* have ties in town, and he already felt like he knew her better than he ever allowed himself to know any of his liaisons.

He felt like maybe they were becoming friends.

Friends. Even in his head that word felt alien. He couldn't say he'd had a proper one since leaving America. Sure, he still occasionally communicated with his childhood best friend Simon and his wife Holly, but it was mostly surface stuff. They emailed him pictures of their cute kids and liked the posts he put on the pub's Facebook page. In the early years they'd made noises about coming to visit him, but it was a long way and they didn't have the funds. He could have helped with that, but seeing them would have brought back too many memories of times when life was good. Watching Simon, Holly and their children together would only remind him of everything he'd lost.

'Wow!' Henri shrieked, jolting Liam from his thoughts as he turned into a residential street that was lit up even more than the main one, if that was possible.

He tried to ignore the tightness in his chest as he slowed the car. He should have waited a little longer until all the lights had been switched off, but as usual, with Henri around, he wasn't thinking straight.

'Everyone's really gone to town this year,' she added.

He could barely manage a nod as he surveyed either side of the road. The houses were overloaded with flashing coloured lights and front lawns littered with big blow-up decorations swaying a little in the sea breeze. The Bradys even had Santa, his sleigh and six white kangaroos on their roof. Eileen didn't like to be outdone. Still, it was only a fraction of what you'd see this time of year in the States. And without the snow and the frost, it didn't quite have the same effect. Thankfully.

As if reading his mind, Henri said, 'Whenever I see lights like this, it always reminds me of the houses you see in Christmas movies. I remember watching *Home Alone* as a kid and being so jealous of the snow and sparkling lights and wishing we went to more effort down under, and now it seems we do. Did people go all out decorating their houses where you come from?'

'Huh?' He barely heard her question, the sound of his heart thumping too loud to register anything else. *This* was why he steered clear of Christmas decorations.

'In Colorado, where you come from, are the houses all decked to the nines for Christmas?'

'Yeah,' he managed. 'They are.'

'So where is that?'

He glanced at her quickly and frowned. 'Where is what?'

'Where you come from?' she said, her tone bemused. 'What town?'

'Ah … right.' He'd never told anyone in Bunyip Bay the name of his hometown, well, almost no one. The old sergeant, O'Leary, had checked him out not long after he'd arrived because some people had apparently been asking questions. He could guess who *they* were. But aside from the cops, he didn't want people to be able to google his name and the town and put two and two together, so he'd remained vague whenever anyone asked.

'Are you all right?' Henri touched his hand gently as he slowed the ute to a stop in front of Rex's house.

As Liam had suspected, his most faithful patron's house was one of the few that was not lit up like the Rockefeller Plaza at Christmas.

He switched off the engine and the headlights. 'Silver Ridge … that's where I come from.'

'Sounds pretty.'

He could hear the smile in her voice as he turned to look at her.

'It is.' And she was too, he thought, as he met her gaze. *So pretty.* Vowing to focus on the task at hand, he cleared his throat. 'Come on, let's get this show on the road.'

They both climbed out and crept to the back of the ute. She kept watch while Liam untied all the knots.

'This is fun,' she said as they manoeuvred the rocking chair off the ute. 'I feel like a reverse burglar.'

He raised an eyebrow. 'Reverse burglar?'

'Yeah. Totally. We should have worn balaclavas.'

It was hard not to laugh as an image of Henri wearing a black mask and ski suit landed in his head. She'd make the sexiest damn burglar he'd ever seen.

Neither of them said a word as they lurked up the street, doing their best to be quiet as they carried the rocking chair between them. They were almost at their destination when the clock struck midnight and, just like that, the street went perfectly black. Well, it would have been perfect if Henri didn't choose that moment to get a serious case of the giggles.

'Shh,' he hissed, more amused than infuriated. She didn't come across as the kind of girl who *giggled*, but the more time he spent with her the more she surprised him. 'You're supposed to be helping, not getting us caught.'

'I'm sorry.' She didn't sound it, but she managed to curtail her laughter as they tiptoed up onto the porch, put his rocking chair alongside Dolce's old one and retreated quickly.

'I bet everything about Christmas is pretty different in America,' Henri said as they made their way back to the ute, passing by a house that had three white reindeer grazing on the front lawn.

Damn Christmas, couldn't she think of anything else to talk about?

'Yeah.' He forced himself to reply like a normal person. 'Summer will never feel like … like Christmas to me, neither will prawns on the barbie or cricket in the backyard.' And *that* was a good thing. 'Is that what you guys do out on the farm?'

'Not so much anymore—my brothers don't like it when I score more runs than them. When Dad was alive, he used to tell them to grow up and stop being sore losers. Mum keeps things fairly traditional foodwise. Despite the heat, she still usually goes the whole shebang with ham and turkey, roast veg, Yorkshire puddings, gravy and a steamed Christmas pudding. Once we're all stuffed silly, we flop about in the pool or head to the beach.' She looked up at him. 'What about you? What was Christmas like when you were growing up?'

His throat threatened to close over at the question, but he didn't want to keep being weird or for her to think him a grump so, somehow, he managed to tell her something.

'Well, my family wasn't huge, so Mom would invite around anyone she knew who was going to be alone for the holiday and she'd put on this enormous meal. Sometimes we'd have up to twenty strays. It was never boring.'

'Sounds fun. I guess you ate turkey?'

'Of course.' Another forced smile. 'And also the traditional casseroles—green beans, marshmallow and yams—and more pies than anyone could ever eat. Pumpkin, pecan …'

He trailed off when he realised Henri had stopped and was staring at him like he was an alien. 'What?'

'Correct me if I'm wrong, but I thought yams were sweet potatoes?' When he nodded, she screwed up her nose. 'Please tell me you don't eat them mixed together with marshmallows?'

The tightness in his chest eased a little at her horror. His smile became real. 'Don't mock it until you've tried it.'

She opened her mouth, but her words were lost as a gunshot pierced the otherwise silent night.

Fuck. His stomach dropped. How could this be happening? *Again?*

But there was no time to question fate. Instinct kicked in and Liam dived in front of Henri, pushing her onto the ground and covering her body with his. Moments later what looked like Brad's V8 Falcon hooned past, smoke pouring out of its exhaust.

At the realisation it was just the engine backfiring, breath gushed from his lungs and his heart rate tried to catch up with his head.

'Sorry. Are you okay?' he panted, gazing down at Henri, her face mere centimetres from his.

'That scar on your shoulder isn't because you fell from a tree, is it?'

'No.' He sucked in a breath. 'It's not.'

Silence stretched between them. In the distance he could hear waves lapping against the shore, and maybe an owl.

'Do you want to talk about it?' she asked eventually.

Did he want to talk about it? That was the last thing he ever wanted to do, but something about Henri had him wavering. He'd almost come clean to her last night. And after what had just happened, perhaps he did owe her *some* kind of explanation.

Rolling off her, Liam sat up, ran a hand through his hair and took a few ragged breaths.

Beside him, she slowly rose into a sitting position but didn't say a word.

'It was almost thirteen years ago,' he said after a long moment's silence. 'My family—my *parents*—owned a couple of supermarkets. Gourmet grocery stores really. We sold a lot of organic stuff, local produce, baked goods from small businesses. Dad always wanted to make it feel like you'd stepped back in time when you entered one of the stores. We were all about old-fashioned service—you got your bags packed at the checkout and then someone would carry them out to your car for you.'

In the light of the moon, Liam saw a faint smile cross Henri's face, but she still didn't speak.

'Anyway, one day … I got a call from Lacey, my little sister. I was at one of our stores and she was with my parents at the other. She was crying so hard I could barely make out what she was saying. Turns out there was a crazy person storming around the store.'

He took another deep breath and Henri gave him an encouraging nod.

'I could hear shouting and screaming. I thought she said someone was threatening to shoot Mom and Dad. Even though I couldn't believe it, I got in my car and drove over there as fast as I could. On a good day it's a fifteen-minute drive. I made it in nine and a half. Lacey stayed on the line, and I heard gunshots. She screamed. She was hysterical.' He'd never forget that piercing sound—it was almost worse than the sound of gunfire. 'She didn't have to tell me. I just knew.'

'He killed your parents?'

Liam nodded. 'I tried to go inside. The sheriff was there. But Silver Ridge … it's a small town. He ordered me to wait for back-up, but I … I had to get to Lacey. I couldn't leave her in there alone.'

That's when he lost the battle with tears. He didn't know if he could go on.

Henri reached out and squeezed his hand. Liam looked down at her hand wrapped around his and then back into her face. Her eyes were glistening too.

'It was a war zone,' he said. 'Customers. Staff. Everyone was hiding under checkouts. Hiding wherever they could. There were kids squeezed into the tiny space under the shelves where their parents had shoved them, stock scattered all over the floor. Blood. Everywhere. So much blood … I saw Mom first, then Dad. Then Lacey.'

'*No*,' Henri gasped, and he nodded.

'The bastard turned his gun on me. I honestly couldn't have cared less if he killed me. But there were two more shots before he could.'

Although the night was still warm, Liam shivered, then tugged aside the collar of his shirt to reveal his scar. The reminder of what he'd lost, which he saw every day when he looked in the mirror.

Tears were now pouring down Henri's cheeks as she gazed at it.

'He shot me at the exact time the cops shot him. He was killed instantly. His aim wasn't so great with me. It didn't matter, he'd already taken almost everything I cared about.'

Not quite everything.

But Liam didn't tell Henri about Kate. He couldn't. It was hard to believe he'd managed to tell her what he had, but there was only so much his heart could take in one night.

'Who was he?' she asked.

'Who was who?'

'The killer?'

He sighed. 'Some guy whose girlfriend had dumped him for a man who worked for us. Stupid thing was he got the wrong store. Nate worked with me at Monument. That bastard took five lives that day—two other employees as well as my family. And he got off lightly in the end. His punishment should have been so much more than death. He should be living out his years in some hellish prison, worrying someone might slice his throat while he sleeps.'

'I can't even, Liam … I don't know what to say.'

'There's nothing you can say.'

They sat in silence a few minutes before Henri said, 'What did you do … after?'

'After all the mess was cleaned up and I'd buried my whole family?'

Her eyes widened. 'You didn't have anyone else? No aunts, uncles, grandparents?'

'My dad was an only child. Mom was estranged from her family—I've never met any of them—and Dad's mother died when he was nineteen. Bowel cancer. When … when the shooting happened, his father was in residential care with dementia. He went a few months later. I'm not sure how much he understood about the shooting. Maybe grief was what finished him off.'

'Oh God,' Henri breathed.

He knew what she was thinking. That he'd lost his immediate family and then his only living relative in a matter of months.

'It was always the plan that I'd take over the running of the stores when Mom and Dad retired. I'd already started working on plans to expand across the state. But I could barely step foot in those two stores anymore, and after Pa's funeral, well, there didn't seem any point to anything.'

'So, you sold the supermarkets and came here?'

'Yeah … A local businessman bought our Monument store, and I sold the Silver Ridge one to a supermarket chain that planned to knock it down and build their own. The town wasn't very happy with me—they didn't want big business ruining their small-town charm, but I didn't care. I had to get the hell out of America. I had citizenship here because of Mom, and the best damn thing about it …'

'Our strict gun laws?' she finished when his voice trailed off.

He nodded.

She squeezed his hand again. 'I don't blame you.'

He started trembling—the shock of having spoken about this properly for the first time in a long time taking hold. 'Please don't tell anyone.'

'Why?' she asked.

'Because … because in Silver Ridge I became that tragic guy from the grocery stores who lost all his loved ones in a shooting. It changed how people behaved around me. And I don't need other people's pity as a constant reminder of everything I've lost. As if I'll ever forget. But here, here in Bunyip Bay, I'm just Liam the publican—I can live with that guy.'

Left unsaid was the fact he couldn't live with the other guy.

'It's okay.' Henri pressed her finger against his lip, just to the right of the split. It tingled beneath her touch. 'Your secret's safe with me. I promise.'

He felt the tension rush out of his lungs. Because he believed her.

'You wanna go home now?' she asked.

'Yeah.'

They stood, and as they walked in silence, Henri slipped her hand into his. She held it firmly until they got back to the ute.

'You know,' she said when they were back upstairs in his apartment and kicking off their shoes. 'Your couch is nowhere near as comfortable as it looks. But … there's really plenty of room in your bed … We could always share it?'

'Thanks,' he managed after serious hesitation, 'but I'll be fine on the couch. You take the bed. I'll see you in the morning.'

As much as he craved the feeling of lying alongside Henri, he needed to be alone a while. Besides, if there was any night his terrors were going to return, this would be it.

He only hoped Henri was a deep sleeper.

Chapter Seventeen

It was still dark when Henri woke to the smell of coffee on Wednesday morning. She rubbed her eyes and stretched to pluck her mobile off Liam's bedside table. 5.30 am. Even earlier than they usually went surfing.

After two nights at home, she'd been excited to stay over again last night, but to her dismay Liam hadn't been in a very chatty mood. Downstairs in the pub, he'd been friendly enough but even though she'd hung in the bar until closing time, hoping maybe they'd watch another movie or something, he'd made it clear when they got upstairs that he was tired and wanted an early night.

Well, as early as nights ever were for publicans. Liam kept complete opposite hours to farmers and also to her.

Henri had been tired too after two long days working with her brothers and the shearing team, but she couldn't help sensing that there was more than fatigue going on. She felt like something had shifted between her and Liam since he'd confided in her about the shooting on Sunday night. She'd come into town for surfing lessons every morning since, but even they felt different. From their very first lesson she'd started to feel like they could be good friends, but the last couple of mornings, she'd once again felt like she was teaching a stranger.

Did he regret telling her?

Or maybe she was the problem?

Remembering what he'd said about not wanting to see pity in other people's eyes, she'd tried not to change the way *she* acted around him and resisted the urge to try and get him to talk more about his family—he would if and when he wanted to—but she ached for him whenever she recalled their conversation. Even four years on she still struggled daily with the loss of her dad and the knowledge she'd never get to talk or laugh with him again. How much worse must it be if you knew you could never do that with any of your family?

As much as her mum and Tilley sometimes infuriated her, the thought of them and her brothers all being taken away from her … How did anyone ever recover from that?

A knock sounded on the door that was already partially open so that Sheila could go back and forth between them. Liam's voice followed.

'Rise and shine, sleeping beauty.' He stepped into the bedroom.

'Isn't that usually my line?' she said, trying to ignore the way her stomach turned over at the sight of him. In khaki cargo shorts and a plain black T-shirt, he looked damn delicious.

With a chuckle, he put a mug of coffee down on the bedside table and then sat on the edge of the bed. Every nerve ending in her body stood to attention and, although she was wearing perfectly demure summer PJs, she suddenly felt naked.

Wishful thinking.

Henri shook that thought from her head, sat up and reached for the coffee. 'What's going on? You're not usually a morning person. Have I turned you into a surfing junkie?'

'Not quite. And we're not going surfing today.'

'We're not?' Henri frowned. 'Then why are we up so early?'

'We're going on a road trip—and before you ask, I checked with Andrew and Callum that they could do without you in the sheds and they agree, you deserve a proper day off. I thought it was high time you showed me what geocaching is all about.'

'We don't need to go on a road trip for that,' Henri said, unsure how she felt about him going behind her back to arrange things with her brothers—she liked to make her own decisions. 'I'm happy to induct you into the geocaching family, but wouldn't it be better if we did so around here? You know … we're more likely to be *seen* that way.'

'Maybe.' He stood. 'But we're not actually looking for a geocache today. We're planting one, as you put it. And I have the perfect location in mind. Now drink that, and then get dressed. We'll have breakfast en route.'

'Where exactly are we going?'

'That's a surprise, but bring your swimsuit,' Liam said and left the room before she could ask any further questions.

Henri's gut churned—she didn't like surprises; in her experience they weren't usually good. But as Liam had gone out of his way to help her, the least she could do was go along with whatever he had planned. And she couldn't help feeling heartened that he was choosing to spend time with her. Maybe she'd imagined the awkwardness of the last few days after all.

Fifteen minutes later, they were on their way. Weirdly, the confined space of Liam's Hilux felt even smaller *without* Sheila between them, but when she asked if the dog was coming, he told her she wasn't fond of road trips.

Henri spent the first five minutes of the journey trying to get Liam to give her a clue as to where they were going. They were heading north, and he'd told her to pack her bathers, so she guessed they were staying coastal, but surely he wouldn't take her further than Kalbarri on a day trip. Then again, there were also some gorgeous waterholes a little bit further inland if you knew where to look.

Yet, no matter how hard she tried, he refused to give her any hint and after a while she gave up and they spent the next five minutes arguing over what music to listen to. Liam wanted classic rock and Henri country. Considering he wouldn't tell her where they were headed, she thought the least he could do was let her pick, but they were both as stubborn as each other. Finally, they decided to compromise and listen to Logan Knight doing the breakfast show from Geraldton instead. He was undeniably good at his job, speaking with warmth and empathy about the day's news stories and listening intently to every person who called in.

'Have you and Frankie been friends since you were kids, then?' Liam asked, when Logan mentioned his fiancée on air.

'Yeah. Our mums are friends. They love to tell stories of sitting on the breastfeeding couch at playgroup while our older siblings ran amuck outside.'

She told him how, as they grew up, they became more and more inseparable and how heartbroken she'd felt when she had to go to boarding school and Frankie had got to take the bus to high school in Geraldton instead. 'I was so jealous of her because I would much rather have stayed on the farm. Anyway, we both made new friends after that and haven't lived in the same place since, but it's always like we've never been apart whenever we catch up. What about you? Any special childhood friends you still keep in touch with?'

'Yeah, Simon. He lived next door as long as I can remember. Like yours and Frankie's, our parents were friends as well. We went to school together and rode our skateboards in the afternoons. We spent almost every waking hour together, but we were also hugely competitive. The biggest contest of all was who could get a girlfriend first. Simon won, of course. He was captain of the football team and had cheerleaders fighting over him.'

'Has Simon ever visited you here?' Henri recalled Eileen Brady saying Liam never had guests, but surely even that old busybody couldn't know everything.

He shook his head. 'He's married to Holly now and they've got a couple of cute kids, but we still Skype a few times a year.'

'Do you think you'll ever go back home?'

'Bunyip Bay's home now.' Liam shrugged and proceeded to change the subject.

Henri got the message. He might have spilled his heart the other night, but it was clear he didn't want to keep talking about it and she didn't want things to be awkward on their journey to who knows where anyway.

The next little while they stuck to safe conversation—movies, TV and book talk. Time passed quickly and before she knew it, they were slowing at a service station on the outskirts of Geraldton. They grabbed ham and cheese toasties and more coffee, and as they climbed back into the ute, Henri said, 'How much further are we going?'

'Patience, Henrietta,' Liam said.

'It's Henri.' She glared, but he didn't look remorseful in the slightest.

A few minutes later they turned off the highway and started driving inland. Henri's heart skipped a beat when she realised where they were heading.

No. He wouldn't. We can't be heading for Geraldton Airport.

'Are we going to Ellendale Pool?' she exclaimed, trying to ignore the anxiety starting to eat at her insides. 'I haven't been there in years, but it's stunning. Great place to drop a geocache.'

When Liam merely smiled, Henri wasn't sure whether she'd finally guessed correctly, or was so far off the mark he couldn't even be bothered to set her straight.

About ten minutes later, he slowed the ute again and a cold sweat erupted as he turned down the road that did indeed lead to the airport.

'What the hell, Liam? We're not flying anywhere!'

'I've booked a private flight to the Abrolhos with Geraldton Air Charter,' he said calmly. 'They'll take us up over Hutt Lagoon first and then we'll head across to the Abrolhos, where we can eat the picnic lunch I packed, have a look around and leave the old biscuit tin that I thought would make a good geocache container. I've done my research, you know.'

Henri couldn't speak as she registered what he'd just said. She jabbed her finger against the button to open the window, unsure whether it was to gasp for air or try to throw herself out of it.

'No,' she finally managed after a few quick breaths. 'Not. Happening.'

Liam just kept on driving.

'I can't. We can't do this. What if …'

'What if we crash?' he asked when her voice trailed off. 'What if we don't? What if we have a fabulous day instead? The odds of that happening far outweigh the odds of disaster.'

'You of all people should know that the odds aren't always in your favour,' she spat, too panicked to feel guilty about throwing his past in his face.

'That's true. Life is risky. And it can be short. I know how much flying means to you and so I thought maybe a step towards regaining your confidence would be to go up with another pilot—someone extremely experienced. Then, in the unlikely event that anything goes wrong, it'll be their responsibility to save us, not yours. It was just a thought.'

Did that make sense? Was it fear of flying that had stopped her in the Riverina or was it a fear of being in control? Would going up with someone else be the first step?

'I also really want to see the Abrolhos Islands, so this isn't an entirely selfless act,' Liam added. 'I've been meaning to take a day trip ever since I arrived, but you know how it is—you often forget to be a tourist in your backyard. Have you ever been?'

The answer was no—her brothers sometimes went out there on fishing trips, but she never had—but she didn't reply to his question. 'I'm not saying I'm going to do this … but who's going to fly us? I'll only even consider it if it's Wendy.'

Wendy Mann was the chief pilot and managing director of Geraldton Air Charter. Henri didn't know her well, but they'd met a couple of times; she was a doyenne of the industry and Henri had immense respect for her.

'Wendy's on holidays at the moment, but I asked Geraldton Air for their most experienced pilot after her and they assure me Glenn Baker is it.'

'I've never heard of him.'

'Well, he's been flying for over thirty years and has also won some big awards. Apparently, he started his career in WA, but then moved east for work. He and his wife have recently moved back to Geraldton to be closer to their daughter who just had her first baby.'

Henri took a few more deep breaths. He sounded experienced, and Wendy obviously trusted him, but … 'I'm really not sure I can do this, Liam.'

'Okay,' he said as he turned into the small car park adjacent to Geraldton Air Charter, a tiny terminal not far from the actual airport. 'That's fine. Do you want to get out and try or shall we just head back to Bunyip Bay?'

There was no indication of pressure or defeat in his voice, but Henri didn't want to disappoint him. And deep down she wanted to try for herself. If she couldn't even get up in an aircraft when someone else was at the controls, then she'd seriously need to seek professional help.

She sighed and blinked as tears threatened. 'I want to try.'

The smile that erupted on Liam's face was so damn beautiful and hit her right in the gut.

He parked the Hilux and then came around to the passenger side and opened her door. Not that she usually expected or waited for men to assist her, but she found herself frozen in the seat.

'It'll be okay,' he promised, offering her his hand. 'We don't have to do anything you're not comfortable with. The flight's all paid for, whether we take it or not.'

Until that moment, she hadn't even thought about money, but private chartered flights weren't cheap. She frowned as she accepted his hand and climbed out of the car. 'I'll pay you back either way.'

'Don't be ridiculous.' The door clunked shut behind them. 'I told you, I want to do this as much for me as for you.'

Henri wasn't sure she believed him but decided it was an argument they could have later.

While her head told her to get back in the ute and do anything but what they were about to do, her body somehow allowed Liam to lead her to the building, where they were met by a very chirpy young woman called Erika, and Glenn, the pilot. The latter looked to be in his mid-fifties, with a good head of salt and pepper hair, thick black glasses and smiling eyes that reminded Henri of her father.

He greeted them with a warm handshake, and she swallowed the urge to apologise for her sweaty palms. She didn't know what Liam had told Glenn, whether he knew she too was a pilot, so she decided not to mention it. Yet.

Erika went through some quick paperwork then fitted them with lifejackets. 'In the unlikely event of an emergency.'

‘Right, let’s go,’ Glenn said, gesturing to a glass door that would lead them out to the waiting aircraft, which looked to be a Gippsland Airvan, GA8. Henri mentally approved the choice—the single-engine aircraft was made in Australia and extremely reliable. ‘Would you both prefer to travel in the back or would one of you like to sit up front with me?’

Liam looked to Henri. ‘What do you want?’

‘Both in the back.’ If she was going to do this, she wanted him right beside her every step of the way, and she also wasn’t sure she could handle being so close to the controls.

Glenn nodded. ‘Righto.’

He and Liam made small talk as they climbed into the Airvan, but Henri didn’t register any of it. Her hands were shaking so bad it took three attempts to fasten her seatbelt and she could feel her heart beating in a way she never had before. Was this what it felt like when you were about to have a heart attack?

As Glenn did his final checks and then started the engine, Henri shook her head and launched for the door. ‘I can’t do this!’

The seatbelt slammed her back into place and Liam reached for her hand. ‘Can we take a moment, Glenn?’

‘Sure,’ he replied, turning his head and giving Henri what she guessed was supposed to be an encouraging smile. ‘These small girls take a little getting used to.’

Henri looked at Liam—he clearly hadn’t warned Geraldton Air Charter about her issue. Weirdly, this took a bit of the pressure off.

‘Okay,’ she said after a few moments. ‘I think I’m ready.’

No, she wasn’t ready, she thought as Glenn picked up speed and then launched the Airvan into the air. The toastie she’d eaten churned in her stomach and she squeezed her eyes shut, not daring to look out the window or into the cockpit just in front of her. Her only comfort was Liam’s fingers wrapped firmly around her own.

Once they were properly airborne and flying at what had to be about 2000 feet above sea level, Glenn began to narrate the sights below. They flew north first, towards Kalbarri, so they could look down over Hutt Lagoon, more commonly known as the Pink Lake. Henri might not have been to the Abrolhos Islands before but of course she'd flown this coast and did not feel the need, or desire, to look down.

'Wow, I've seen the lake from the ground but it's so much bigger than I thought,' Liam said.

'Yep,' Glenn replied. 'It's about fourteen kilometres long and over two wide. Big pink natural beauty that's for sure.'

'It's not as pink as I remember either.'

'The actual colour of the water changes depending on the levels of algae and also if there's a high concentration of brine prawn,' Glenn explained. 'Hutt Lagoon was named after William Hutt—a British MP who was involved in the colonisation of Western Australia—by explorer George Grey, who camped along the eastern edge in the 1830s. It was during the wet season and Grey thought he'd found a large estuary. When another explorer, George Fletcher Moore, went to investigate the following year, he couldn't find this estuary because the waters had gone down, and the mouth of the Hutt River was dry.'

After the Pink Lake, they turned and headed south-west towards the 210 islands that made up the Abrolhos archipelago. After listening to Glenn talk about the history of the three main island groups—Easter, Pelsart and Wallabi—and the 'graveyard of ships' that surrounded them, including the famous *Batavia* that ran aground here on its maiden voyage from the Netherlands, Henri finally found the courage to open her eyes.

As Glenn spoke about the mutiny that happened on the island, killing about 125 of the shipwreck survivors, Henri—still clutching Liam's hand—leaned towards her window and peered down.

'Spectacular, isn't it?' Liam said, and she had to admit it was the perfect word to describe the sight below them.

'Uh huh.' Henri had seen plenty of amazing places from the air, but that didn't mean she ever took their beauty for granted. The vivid deep blues and crisp aqua colours of the ocean, speckled with the dots of yellow and green that made up the islands and the white foam of the waves lapping at the land, finally distracted her from the fact they were actually flying. It was hard to feel fear when overwhelmed by such natural beauty.

Glenn pointed out notable islands as they flew overhead—Big Rat and Little Rat with their colourful fishing camps, boasting lots of shacks and bordered by jetties. She listened properly now as he spoke about the communities below, the small number of people who lived here all year round and the cray fishermen who spent about three months each year calling the islands home.

'There was even a school there until not so long ago,' he told them, 'but it's closed now. The lobster industry is changing, it's spread more throughout the year due to quotas that were introduced. Before the quotas, whole families would go across from March to June and the communities were thriving. It's different now, but you can still experience that kind of spirit if you visit on Anzac Day.'

'For the two-up competition? I've heard of that,' Liam said.

'Yeah.' Glenn nodded. 'It's one helluva day, that's for certain. Right. You guys ready to land?'

Liam looked at Henri but what could she say? *No, please keep flying up here where I feel moderately safe?* Eventually they'd run out of petrol and …

Banishing that thought, she nodded, then held her breath again and hoped her nails weren't digging into Liam's palm as Glenn brought the Airvan in to land on the airstrip on East Wallabi, pointing out beautiful Turtle Bay as he did.

'Magical place to swim,' he said. 'You might even see some sea lions or dolphins if you're lucky.'

'I did it!' Henri shrieked as the Airvan touched down.

Glenn pressed on the brakes, and they slowed quickly. There were no anthills here and it was a textbook landing if ever there was one. Adrenaline buzzed through her, and she couldn't help bouncing in her seat. She might not have been the pilot, but this definitely felt like a huge step in the right direction.

'You did.' Liam grinned, his expression proud. 'Well done.'

She squeezed his hand, which she hadn't let go during the whole flight. 'Thank you.'

'Don't mention it.' He extracted his hand. 'Now, let's go plant a geocache.'

Chapter Eighteen

The island was practically deserted when they disembarked. Glenn bid them farewell and flew back to the mainland for another charter, promising to return later that afternoon to collect them.

'Wow.' Henri glanced around as the plane became a distant speck in the sky. 'I feel like we're in the middle of nowhere and nowhere is paradise.'

Her hair was flapping around her face as the wind blew vigorously, but the only other sounds around them were the gentle waves nearby and the occasional cry of a bird overhead. They were standing at the edge of the red-dirt airstrip—island shrubbery and little shacks on one side, pristine ocean on the other. The sky was blue, the temperature comfortable, and Liam had to agree with her description.

'What do you want to do first?' he asked as she dug a cap out of her backpack to restrain her hair. 'We could go for a walk and find somewhere to put the geocache, or do you want to start with a swim? I brought snorkel gear for both of us and snacks. Are you hungry yet?'

He was babbling as if nervous and perhaps he was. It had seemed like a good idea—albeit a risky one—to encourage Henri to try to conquer her fear of flying, but now that they were here alone, he wondered how he was supposed to be on his best behaviour around her for the next few hours with no one but the wildlife as chaperones.

But Liam didn't need to be nervous.

It turned out they weren't completely alone on the island. Glenn and another pilot for Geraldton Air Charter returned in just over an hour with a group of tourists and, on their walk around East Wallabi, Liam and Henri ran into a couple of islanders as well.

They didn't exchange more than brief greetings with the other people over the course of the day, but when they were alone, he felt completely at ease and relaxed in her company. Yes, he was still crazy attracted to her, but the friendship developing between them felt even stronger—she knew things about him and he about her that no one else did—and he didn't want to jeopardise that.

Liam had thought he was doing fine without such a friend in his life—that he got all the social interaction he needed in the pub—but Henri made him wonder otherwise. He hoped they'd stay friends and hang out again next time she was home.

They spotted a couple of wallabies, lots of birds and a large lizard sunning itself on a rock as they searched for the perfect place to plant their geocache, before they came upon the abandoned school.

'I thought this might be a good spot,' Liam suggested. 'How about under that rusty old slide?'

'You *did* do your research.' Henri sounded impressed as he pulled an old biscuit tin out of his backpack and showed her the pencil, small notebook, Palace souvenir keyring, tiny first-aid kit and a Bunyip figurine he'd bought from the CRC. 'It's like you've done this before or something.'

'I'd never even heard about geocaching until you mentioned it, but I guess I can see the appeal.'

She smiled triumphantly. 'Told you it was fun.'

They worked out the coordinates and then Henri logged onto the app on her phone and registered their brand-new geocache. 'Considering you can only get here via air or sea, it'll be interesting to see how long it takes someone to find it,' she said.

'How'd you get into geocaching?' Liam asked as they walked back towards the beach where they planned to swim, snorkel and picnic the next few hours away.

'My dad.'

Her answer didn't surprise him.

'He heard about it from an old friend about fifteen years ago. Tilley was already married, and the boys weren't interested either, but I thought it sounded fun. We'd always go on a hunt when I was home or if he came to visit me. Dad used to collect the stupid crap from Christmas crackers to leave in the caches. Oh God, look!'

A sea lion resting on the sand not far away derailed their conversation. Liam lost track of time as they watched the beautiful creature sunning itself. Eventually it shuffled over to a rock and then flopped into the water, and he and Henri decided to do the same. For over an hour, they stayed in the cool calm water, coming up occasionally for air and to marvel over the kaleidoscope of fish and other wonders they'd seen in the colourful coral below, before finally drying off on the sand, reapplying sun cream and then getting stuck into the lunch he'd packed early that morning.

Conversation ebbed and flowed as they ate. Under the sun, soaking up its gentle warmth, they talked about everything. Annoying habits, pet hates, food quirks, the school plays he'd performed in, the many detentions she'd been given at boarding school, the instruments they'd both been forced to learn as kids. He learned that when she was growing up her friends had devoured magazines called *Dolly* and *Girlfriend* whereas she'd much preferred her parents' *Farm Weekly* and had asked for a subscription to *Australian Flying* and *Aviation* for her fifteenth birthday. He told her about breaking both his legs at summer camp and was surprised to hear Henri had never broken so much as her little toe. They even spoke about religion. They'd both gone to church while they were growing up, but Liam was now a lapsed Catholic and Henri an atheist.

'At least I'm ninety-nine per cent sure that's what I am.'

Although they covered a lot of ground, there were also stretches of time where neither of them said anything. He knew you couldn't be like this with everyone—with some people silence was so awkward you felt compelled to say absolutely anything to fill it.

When the food had been devoured, they lay on their towels, Caspian gulls soaring overhead and diving down into the sea every few minutes to fish.

Liam decided it was time to broach the subject of her flying. 'How do you feel about the fact we flew here? I know you were scared and I'm sorry if I pushed you.'

Henri turned her head to smile at him. 'No—thank you. I think it was a great first step. Sure, I was terrified at first—I wanted to kill you—but I've forgiven you. I'm glad you encouraged me and damn proud of myself for following through.'

'Me too.' He grinned. 'Do you feel less anxious about going back to work?'

She sighed. 'I don't know. I hope so. I guess I'll just have to wait and see.'

They were quiet for a while and Liam lay back, his hands resting behind his head, simply enjoying the serenity. 'Is that an eagle?' he asked when a grey and white bird that looked far too powerful to be a seagull flew high above.

No reply was forthcoming.

He turned to see that Henri had fallen asleep and he couldn't help but smile at the sight. His only concern was that the sun would burn her, so even though they were both wearing sunscreen and it wasn't very hot, he shook out his towel and lightly covered her body with it. She didn't even stir. Then he positioned himself so that his shadow fell over her face.

Liam couldn't remember the last time he'd felt this relaxed, but he couldn't nap in case they didn't wake up in time for the flight back to the mainland.

'Why'd you let me sleep so long?' she asked when he gently shook her awake a couple of hours later and told her it was time to head to the airstrip. 'We could have gone swimming again or explored some more.'

'You looked so peaceful. I couldn't bear to disturb you.'

She sighed and stretched her arms up over her head. 'Well, I have to admit, I feel very refreshed. I hope I didn't drool.'

'Only a little,' he teased.

They collected their things and walked back to meet Glenn, who was already waiting for them beside the plane.

'Well, hello, hello,' he said, raising a hand. 'Did you two have a good day?'

Liam glanced at Henri—the expression on her face could only be described as blissed out. It gave him a kick inside. Hopefully his crazy plan to re-instil her confidence in flying was working.

She nodded. 'The best day.'

'Glad to hear it, although you'd be hard pushed to have a bad one out here,' Glenn said, wiping his brow with the back of his hand. Despite the fact it wasn't really hot at all, and he'd just come from an airconditioned plane, he looked like he was burning up.

'You okay, Glenn?' Henri asked.

'Yeah.' He nodded but made a face. 'My lunch didn't agree with me, but I'll be fine. I've taken an antacid and it's only a short flight back.'

'Are you sure?' Henri said, exchanging a panicked glance with Liam.

Glenn waved away her concerns. 'Yeah, I'm fine. It's my own fault. I ate a pie for lunch, and pastry doesn't agree with me now that I'm getting older. I should know better; my wife will say it serves me right.'

Henri smiled. 'Your secret's safe with us, right, Liam?'

He nodded. 'Of course.'

They all climbed up into the plane.

'Are *you* okay?' Liam asked Henri as they fastened their seatbelts.

She took a visible breath. 'I think so, but do you mind if I hold your hand again?'

Without a word, he gave it to her.

Five minutes later, they were in the air again and Henri looked a hundred times calmer than she had when they'd taken off that morning. This time as they flew, she happily looked out the window, pointing things out as they both admired the picturesque scene below.

They had to be about halfway back when Glenn suddenly gasped and clutched his chest.

Henri's hand jolted in Liam's as she gave him a panicked look.

He let go of her hand and leaned towards the cockpit. 'Glenn?' he asked. 'Are you okay?'

'I …' He puffed out a breath. 'I'm … This indigestion is worse than usual. It's getting a bit … hard … to breathe …'

'Do you know first aid?' Henri asked before Liam could respond; she was already unbuckling her seatbelt.

'Yeah.' He did regular courses to make sure he knew the basics—in the country, you never knew how long it could take for an ambulance to arrive. Unfortunately first aid wasn't always enough. Dennis, the fourth Poker Pensioner, had experienced similar symptoms in the pub last year and hadn't walked out alive.

'Then you take care of him,' Henri ordered, already climbing into the front and positioning herself in the seat beside Glenn. 'It's okay,' she reassured him, 'I'm a pilot too. I know what I'm doing, and Liam is going to look after you. You're gunna be okay. I promise.'

Liam held his breath as he watched her scan the dual controls in front of her. *Come on, Henri, you can do this.*

* * *

Henri's hands trembled as she took over as pilot, and she felt as clammy as Glenn looked. Flashes of her last flight invaded her head and tears welled in her eyes.

Could she actually do this?

With one deep breath, she summoned every ounce of training she'd ever had. In an emergency such as this, there were three things she needed to do: *Aviate. Navigate. Communicate.* One step at a time.

Ignoring her racing heart, she scanned the instruments in front of her—the aircraft had already started a slight shallow descent. The altitude showed they'd lost 700 feet. *Breathe.* She needed to bring them up again. The moment her hand closed around the control yoke and she pulled it back to reset, her tremors abated and positive adrenaline shot through her.

This was what she was trained to do. *This* was who she was.

Power went hand in hand with altitude, so she looked to see what it had been set on the engine, reset it to 2200 RPM and put the altitude to nose on the horizon.

Yes. She could feel the force in the controls now and needed to trim it out. Her hand on the control column, she used the electric rocker switch to pull the nose up and balance out level flight.

Phew. Aviation taken care of, Henri allowed herself a quick glance over to see how Glenn was doing. He was still holding his chest and panting, but his colour seemed okay.

Either way, she couldn't worry about Glenn. Her priority was getting them back to the mainland, which meant she needed to navigate—to work out exactly where they were. Out the window she could already see the coastline, and a look at the distance-messaging equipment showed they were 180 nautical miles from Perth on a northerly bearing. They could be on the ground in fifteen minutes.

She reached for the radio to communicate their whereabouts to Perth Centre, inform them she had a medical emergency on board and needed immediate radar vectors, air traffic control clearance and priority landing at Geraldton Airport.

'What's the aircraft's call sign?' she asked Glenn, hoping he was capable of replying. 'I'll have them organise an ambulance to meet us on landing.'

He took his hand off his chest. 'Don't think that's necessary, sweetheart. No need to fuss.'

'*Fuss*?' A suspected heart attack wasn't a fuss.

'Think it was a false alarm anyway,' he said with an awkward chuckle. 'Breathing's fine again. Damn indigestion. Never having another pie for lunch in my life.'

Henri stared at the man who, five minutes ago, she was worried might not make it to the ground alive.

'Are you sure you're okay?' She thought about her dad's heart attack—she hadn't been anywhere near him when it happened, so she wasn't in the position to save him, but she'd never forgive herself if she ignored the warning signs and Glenn deteriorated. 'Better to be safe than sorry.'

'I'm fine,' he assured her. 'I'll go see my doctor as soon as we get back, but maybe you should take us to the ground, just in case?'

That didn't sit right with Henri, and she looked to Liam for backup, but he was gazing casually out the window as if nothing had happened.

And that's when it clicked.

'Hang on … Did you really have a pie for lunch, Glenn?'

He gave her a sheepish grin. 'Nope, they really do give me terrible indigestion and I've learnt my lesson. I stick to salad sandwiches on rye bread now.'

'What the hell!' She glanced back at Liam, who was now grinning from ear to ear, then back at Glenn, who looked as healthy as anything. 'Did you two set me up?'

The older pilot snorted and then started laughing.

'How about you just focus on landing the plane and we'll talk about this when we're back on the ground,' Liam said calmly.

Part of Henri wanted to tell him to take a hike, but now that she was back at the controls, another part of her desperately wanted to see if she could finish what she'd started.

'I'll deal with you later,' she told him before turning back to Glenn. 'You're sure you're okay with me doing this?'

'Course, love, and remember, I'll be right beside you every step of the way,' Glenn said.

And he was. As she flew them back to the airport it felt so good. Better than good. She soon started the descent, then not long after slammed on the brakes as they touched down on the runway. It just happened to be one of the smoothest landings Henri had ever done and she couldn't wipe the smile from her face. Glenn congratulated her.

Only when the engine was switched off did she turn back to glare at Liam.

'I can't believe you did that to me,' she spat, her heart still racing from the excitement. 'You're lucky I don't murder you with my bare hands right this very second!'

'I'm proud of you, Henri,' he said with a smile. 'I knew you could do it.'

Warmth bloomed inside her as she grinned back at him. Murder was actually the furthest thing from her mind.

What she really wanted was to kiss him.

Chapter Nineteen

'You're going to make gingerbread by *yourself*?'

'Keep your voice down!' Henri hissed at Tilley, glancing around The Ag Store, not wanting to draw the attention of the customers. Thankfully there weren't many; this wasn't really the place to buy Christmas presents. 'And yes, I am. I want to do something nice for Liam.'

After what he'd done for her yesterday, the man deserved biscuits!

Tilley raised her eyebrows. 'That's sweet in theory, but also very brave. You know the way to a man's heart is through his stomach, but it's also a way to quickly turn him off. No guy likes a woman who can't cook.'

Henri wanted to tell Tilley that she *could* cook but maybe she'd be better at it if she hadn't grown up with her and their mum undermining every attempt. Instead, she bit out a terse, 'What century are you living in?'

Tilley turned and called through to the office where her husband was sitting at the desk. 'James! Would you have married me if I couldn't cook?'

'That depends,' he fired back. 'Would you still have been good in bed?'

Tilley's cheeks flared to almost the same colour as her red Ag Store polo shirt and Henri couldn't help but snort. Sometimes she loved her in-laws more than her actual blood relatives.

'Do you even have a recipe?' Tilley asked.

'Of course I have a recipe. Haven't you heard of Google? I'm using Nigella's—you always say you can't go wrong with her. I just bought all the ingredients from IGA.'

'Okay, that's a good one, but don't overwork the dough—it should be firm but not tough. And be careful not to put too much flour in or—'

Henri held up a hand. 'Correct me if I'm wrong, but was it you or me that made seven gingerbread houses with Mum recently?'

'The way Mum tells it, you spent most of the time pinching the dough.'

'Forget I asked,' Henri spat, more than a little annoyed now. 'I'll improvise and use glasses to cut the dough.'

She'd meant to sneak the necessary equipment from home but hadn't been able to find it and didn't want to ask her mother for fear she'd get a similar lecture to the one Tilley was giving her now. Or worse, that she'd insist on helping her. Henri wanted this to be a gift from her; the whole idea of doing it in Liam's kitchen was so she didn't have someone breathing down her neck the whole time.

'I'm sorry,' Tilley said, reaching out to grab Henri's arm as she turned to storm out. 'I'm just—'

'Overbearing and egotistical?'

'I was going to say, just not used to this new side of you, but I suppose that fits as well. It's what you get from being the eldest of four kids.' She smiled sheepishly. 'This loved-up you is new to me. I'm not used to you having anyone you want to bake for.

But of course you can borrow my cutters. And anything else you need.'

Henri's shoulders loosened. 'Maybe a few trays? I didn't see any when I searched Liam's kitchen earlier and I don't want to borrow from Macca because I want this to be a surprise. Liam's working in his studio today, so hopefully by the time he finishes, I'll be done too.'

Tilley nodded. 'That's a lovely idea. I'll just go get my house keys.' She headed into the office, returning with a bunch of keys attached to a unicorn keyring. 'So, things are clearly going well between you and the spunky publican?'

Henri's stomach did some sort of gymnastics as she took the unicorn. She didn't know if it was guilt at lying or nerves because the lies—at least on her part—were starting to turn into truth. 'Yes, better than I thought possible. I really like him.'

Yesterday had been truly amazing. Undoubtedly one of the best days of her life. Quite aside from conquering her fear of getting in another aircraft, they'd walked, they'd talked, they'd snorkelled and sunbaked, and she'd almost forgotten that the rest of the world existed. She'd felt closer to Liam than she did to anyone else.

There'd definitely been moments during the day when she'd thought something real might be about to happen between them, but if he'd felt it too, he'd been on his best behaviour—both while on the islands and later when they were back at the pub.

She kept telling herself she was glad about this. As attracted as she felt towards him, did she really want to ruin what could be a burgeoning friendship? Coming back to Bunyip Bay would be even better if she knew that when she did, she could hang out with Liam and Sheila, pick up their surfing lessons and their friendship exactly where they'd left off.

'Hello? Anyone home?'

Henri blinked to find Tilley waving her hand in front of her face. 'What did you say?'

'I *said*, you still owe me all the juicy details. Should I come to the pub, and we can have a drink tonight? Mum said you've been spending *every* night there.'

'Not *every* night, but yeah, okay. Do you want to have dinner together?'

'At home or at the pub?' Tilley asked.

'Pub, and don't tell Mum. If she thinks I'm meeting you, she'll want to join us.' Both Tilley and her mother were better—much more bearable—one on one.

'Does seven work? That'll give me a chance to make sure James is feeding Macy something vaguely nutritious.'

'Seven's good. I'll see you then.'

After driving out to Tilley's place on the edge of town to collect what she needed, Henri returned and then parked Cecil a little up the road from the pub so as not to be seen. Hopefully by the time Liam came in from the studio to shower and get ready to open the pub later that afternoon, her gingerbread would be cool enough to eat.

And, let's face it, also that it would actually be edible.

She crept in the back door, snuck up to his apartment and let herself in with the key she'd stolen on her way out, only feeling mildly guilty about being there alone and uninvited. Resisting the urge to snoop or pluck his pillow off the couch, bury her head in it and inhale his woody scent, she went into the kitchen and set to work, putting baking paper on the trays, carefully measuring the exact quantities of ingredients into a bowl and then lovingly mixing it all together. It smelled and tasted so good Henri thought she deserved a medal for only eating a tiny chunk before wrapping it all in clingwrap and putting it in the fridge, and she felt immensely proud of what she'd achieved.

See, Mum? See, Tilley? I can cook.

She'd make sure to save a couple of biscuits for each of them to prove it.

After cleaning up the kitchen, there was still an hour and forty-five minutes to go before she could roll out the dough and start cutting. What on earth was she supposed to do with herself in that time?

You could go downstairs and see Liam.

Yet, as much as the idea of watching him work appealed—especially if he was shirtless again—making her presence known would defeat the point.

She wandered into the living area, thinking she'd see what was on TV, when her gaze caught on the bookshelf. Aside from a couple of old favourites, which she returned to time and time again for comfort and kept on a tiny shelf inside Cecil, all Henri's books were on her e-reader, so it was a novelty having so many at her fingertips. Her device was more practical for travelling, but she did miss the smell and feel of actual print novels.

She trailed her fingers along the spines and shrieked when she came across the recent release of a favourite author that she hadn't had the chance to read yet. As she plucked it from the shelf, she saw another couple of books that surprised her. Liam had to be the last person she'd have expected to have copies of *The Baby-Sitters Club*. She remembered Tilley and Frankie devouring these books, but they'd never interested her. Had they belonged to his little sister? Curious, she opened the first and frowned down at the inscription scribbled in juvenile handwriting on the front page.

Dear Liam—Happy Birthday. Luv Katie.

The second had an almost identical inscription. His sister's name was Lacey, so who the hell was Katie? She must have meant something special for him to have kept these books. Ignoring the ridiculous dart of jealousy that shot through her, Henri went over to the couch and collapsed onto it.

She started to read, but her mind kept drifting from the story. It kept returning to Liam. To their magical day yesterday. To the way her insides turned to mush every time she saw him, like she was some teenage girl with a silly crush.

After a while she gave up, grabbed her phone and checked how long was left on the timer. The recipe said to let the dough rest in the fridge for at least two hours—there was still an hour and ten minutes of that to go—but was it *really* necessary to wait that long?

'Guess there's only one way to find out,' she said to herself, dumping the book on the coffee table and heading back into the kitchen.

Chapter Twenty

Did I leave the TV on? Liam wondered as he approached his apartment later that afternoon to hear the sounds of Christmas carols coming from within.

But the moment he stepped inside—Sheila pushing past him, already sniffing the air—he discovered something even more disturbing. There were actual Christmas carols wafting from the kitchen where Henri appeared to be doing some kind of baking, if the flour scattered over every available surface was anything to go by. It almost looked like it had snowed.

What on earth was she doing here in the middle of the afternoon?

Cursing under her breath, Henri's mood seemed in complete contrast to the cheerful tunes currently torturing his eardrums. Her head was bent and her hands manically kneading some kind of pale brown concoction.

He took a moment just to observe. Just to let the fact she was cooking in his kitchen settle in. He watched Macca cooking all the time, but it never felt like this. This felt so … *domestic.* A sight he never expected to see. A sight he never wanted to see.

His chest grew tight, and he found himself struggling to breathe. First, she'd hung that bloody wreath on his door, then she'd somehow managed to get him to spill most of his secrets, and now this.

This was too much.

Marching right into the kitchen, he jabbed his finger against Henri's phone to silence the music. Who in their right mind actually liked Mariah Carey singing about what she wanted for Christmas anyway?

'What the hell are you doing?' he demanded.

Henri spun around and Liam got his first proper look at her. He raised his eyebrows, but it was impossible to be angry when someone was standing in front of you looking like *that.* Her hair was streaked with flour and had all but fallen out of its ponytail, there were stains all over her shorts and T-shirt, a sheen on her brow and even more flour on her face.

She was a total mess and also totally adorable. Something dangerous shifted inside him as Henri's flour-covered hand flew to her chest.

'Oh my God! You almost gave me a heart attack. You shouldn't sneak up on people like that.'

'Maybe if you weren't blasting Christmas carols so loudly, you'd have heard me.'

She shrugged. 'Maybe, but you can't make gingerbread without Christmas carols. According to my mother, it's the law.'

He stared past her to the weird-looking shapes scattered throughout the sea of flour. '*They're* gingerbread cookies?'

'They're supposed to be,' she said despondently as she gazed at the mess on the kitchen bench.

He wasn't sure whether she was angry, frustrated, upset, or a combination of all three.

'What are they for?'

'You,' she said simply.

This one word squeezed at his heart. 'You're making *me* gingerbread cookies?' Katie was the last person to cook him anything Christmas-related—eggnog cookies—the day before the shooting.

Henri nodded and wiped her brow with the back of her hand, smearing even more flour across her forehead. 'Remember? I owe you some, and I always keep my promises. But I also wanted to do something to say thank you … for yesterday, for taking a risk and pushing me to get in that Airvan. As much as I could have killed you at the time, if it wasn't for you forcing me out of my comfort zone, I'd still be wondering if I'd ever be able to fly again.'

'That's really sweet of you.'

'You might not think so when you taste them. That's if I can manage to actually get any shapes onto the tray without the dough crumbling. I'm not sure if my mistake was adding too much flour, kneading it too much, or not leaving the dough to rest long enough.'

He smiled. Now she definitely sounded frustrated.

'It's not funny!'

Liam glanced around the kitchen again. 'Oh, that's where you're wrong. I think it's very funny.'

Henri picked up a cookie cutter and hurled it at him. 'Jerk!'

Luckily, he was a good catch.

She scowled as his fingers closed around her weapon. 'I'd like to see you do better.'

He took a step towards her. 'Actually, I'm not a bad baker. When I was a kid, my parents were always busy in the shop right up to Christmas, so my little sister and I used to bake all the cookies and treats for Christmas Day.'

Which meant he *could* offer to help … but right now, baking was the very last thing on his mind. All the good intentions he'd had regarding Henri flew out the window.

Ignoring the warning voices inside his head that this wasn't a smart idea, Liam closed the rest of the distance between them, palmed his hands against her floury cheeks and yanked her mouth to his. A low, sweet noise sounded in her throat, before her hands landed in his hair and her tongue pushed into his mouth.

Hello, Henrietta.

He shoved her up against the kitchen counter and they kissed like a couple of savages. It was only when they heard the sound of Sheila's paws scraping on the benchtop that they finally pulled apart, turning to see the dog getting stuck into the big pile of dough, clearly thinking all her Christmases had come at once.

'Down, Sheila! Out. On your mat,' Liam yelled. 'Now!'

The dog skedaddled out of the kitchen, her head hung low in shame. He felt bad for all of two seconds before he turned back to Henri and all thoughts but having her vanished.

'I'm not. Sure. If you. Noticed.' Her words came in short, sharp bursts as her chest heaved up and down rapidly. 'But we. Don't actually. Have an audience right now?'

'Oh, I noticed,' he growled, his desire kicking up another notch as he gazed at her mouth. Now her lips looked red and deliciously swollen and knowing he'd made them that way had him feeling all primal and powerful. 'Do you have any objections?'

She shook her head. 'Absolutely none whatsoever.'

Liam wasn't really a religious man, but he praised the Lord as he dipped his head, desperate to taste her again. Although this wasn't in the plan, the last week and a half had felt like the longest game of foreplay in his life. He'd been a fool thinking he'd ever be content being just friends with Henrietta Forward and he was more than ready for this to progress to the next step, but Henri stopped him with a palm against his chest.

'What about your lip?' She reached up and swept her finger tenderly across it. His skin buzzed beneath her touch and every last muscle in his body tightened. 'Does it still hurt?'

Right now, he didn't give a damn about his lip. 'No. It's fine.'

'In that case …' She walked her fingers back up his chest and this time it was she who kissed him.

Things got back to hot and heavy pretty damn fast. Their bodies pressed so tightly against each other, it was a miracle their hands managed to get a look in, but Liam's fingers trailed down her neck and slid between them, skating over the edge of Henri's breasts before taking each one in the palm of his hands.

The gasp that shot from her mouth into his was like a dart of desire right to his core. He tried to ignore the erection that flared—half of him already desperate to be inside her, the other half wanting to explore every last nook and crevice of her body first. That's if he could manage to take his hands off her breasts. They felt deliciously full and heavy in his grasp and when he swirled his thumbs around her nipples and then squeezed, her moan almost sent him over the edge.

'Man, Henrietta, you're gorgeous,' he uttered, pulling back slightly as he dragged his gaze down her body, imagining the gift that awaited him once he'd peeled off her clothes. He couldn't wait to touch and taste her *every*where. When he'd come upstairs less than half an hour ago, he'd been planning on taking a shower and a quick nap before opening the pub, but now he felt anything but tired.

Shower! At that thought he remembered how hot and humid it had been out in his studio. He couldn't expect her to get naked with him smelling like this.

'I'm all sweaty and gross,' he groaned, reluctantly pulling back.

'You and me both,' she said, smiling as she gestured to her clothing.

Once again, his gaze skimmed down her beautiful body. 'Yeah, you're right. You're a very dirty girl. Maybe next time you should wear an apron.'

She smirked—'I'm pretty sure there won't be a next time'—and he wasn't sure whether she was talking about the baking or what they were about to do, but in that moment he didn't care.

'Just let me take a super quick shower,' he said, already reaching for the bottom of his shirt.

'I could join you?' Henri suggested. 'As you said, I'm dirty too, and in the interests of saving water and all …' Her voice drifted off as she walked her fingers up his now-naked torso.

That was all the encouragement Liam needed. The thought of having Henri hot, wet and naked had him grabbing her hand and dragging them both towards the bathroom. They were almost there when a heavy knock sounded on his apartment door.

They both froze. Henri's eyes widened, a question on her face.

He shrugged. It wasn't Janet's day to clean his apartment and aside from her, no one else came up here. Just his luck that someone chose *now* to stop by.

The urgent knock came again, and this time Lara's voice joined the cacophony.

'Liam! Are you in there? Liam?' she yelled in her strong Welsh accent. 'This is an emergency!'

Despite the desperate pitch of her voice, he still wanted to ignore her. Frustration coursing through his body, he dropped Henri's hand, pressed his lips quickly against her forehead and then stalked over to the door.

He hoped Lara had a damn good reason for interrupting. The pub better be on fire or something, because Liam couldn't remember the last time he'd been *this* turned on.

'What is it?' he shouted as he pulled open the door to see her standing there soaking wet.

'There's a burst water main just outside the pub. Water's coming in through the back door. It's already flooding the kitchen. Macca's in a rage.'

Liam swore. Now his cook wasn't the only one!

Chapter Twenty-one

As the door slammed shut, Henri sighed and leaned back against the wall, taking a few moments to catch her breath.

Liam had kissed her. Properly this time, not just because someone was watching. And she couldn't be more pleased. Up until then, she'd thought he'd been giving his all when they'd smooched on the beach or kissed goodnight downstairs for the benefit of the patrons, but now … now she knew that all those kisses had only been a prelude for what his mouth was actually capable of.

And his hands. *Oh God.* She'd had fantasies about what else he might be able to do with those hands, but her imagination had nothing on the reality. Even through her bra and a whole layer of clothing, the way his fingers played her nipples almost made her come right there in the kitchen.

Damn water main! She actually stamped her foot, causing Sheila to startle.

'Sorry, girl.' Her heart rate finally starting to slow again, she went over to the dog and dropped down to stroke her. She still looked forlorn from being yelled at. *Poor love.* 'How long do you reckon water mains take to fix?'

Sheila cocked her head to one side as if to say, *Do I look like a plumber?*

Henri sighed as she reached out to stroke the dog. She was right; they'd have to call Sam or the Water Corp and who knew how long they'd take to arrive. Maybe she should go downstairs and offer to help? Then again, she probably only knew fractionally more about plumbing than Sheila did.

As tight as her whole body felt—as desperately as she wanted Liam to be here right now with her—perhaps this was a blessing in disguise. It would give her a chance to do a little prep. If they were going to cross the line, and it looked as if they were, she wanted to be in tiptop condition. It had been a few days since she'd bothered to shave her legs, and even longer since she'd pruned downstairs. A delicious shiver snaked down her spine at the prospect of what lay ahead.

Normally she wouldn't worry too much about impressing a guy, but she found she wanted everything to be perfect for him. For *them*.

A spring in her step, she headed into the bathroom, found a pack of disposable razors under the sink, stripped off her clothes and turned on the shower. Or at least she tried to, but nothing came out.

Dammit. Of course, the water would be switched off.

She deliberated only a moment before yanking her clothes back on. If she was quick, she could go home, wash her hair, shave every inch of her body and come back before he even knew she was gone. She rushed back into the kitchen, grabbed the bin from under the sink and swept all her biscuit attempts right into the garbage, not feeling even one ounce of disappointment as she did. Not everyone could bake, but Henri had plenty of other talents, and tonight she planned to use them!

Without water, it was hard to leave the kitchen spotless, but she did her best to return it as close to its pre-gingerbread state as possible, then she tossed Sheila a treat—one specifically for dogs this time—and hurried downstairs out to her van. She ignored all the commotion coming from the back of the pub, telling herself that she'd help with the clean-up when she returned.

The road to the farm was practically deserted, which was a good thing because traffic would have distracted her from her fantasies. All she could think about as she drove was the feel of Liam's hands and mouth on her body and her fantasies of having them on her again.

Lost in her own bubble of bliss when she pulled up at the homestead, Henri didn't notice her mother on the far side of the front garden watering the roses, or the hose stretched across the path, as she climbed out of Cecil and ran towards the house.

Like an out-of-body experience, she heard herself squeal before she actually felt the pain stinging her ankle, but then it was unlike anything she'd ever felt before. Her eyes filled with tears as she lay on the brick pavers trying to work out what on earth had happened.

'Henrietta!' Her mother's footsteps were loud as she hurried over and knelt beside Henri. 'Are you okay?'

She was too stunned to speak as her mum helped her into a sitting position.

'Why were you in such a hurry? Didn't you see the hose? Oh goodness, look at your hands and knees.'

Henri glanced down and saw grazes all over her legs, but it was the absolute throbbing at her ankle that really concerned her.

'What are you doing?' Fiona shrieked as Henri tried to get up and test her weight. 'You don't want to get dirt in those cuts on your hands. Here, let me help. We'll get you inside and cleaned up.'

Reluctantly, she allowed her mother to put her hands under her arms and try to help her stand, but it felt like someone was stabbing a knife into her ankle.

'I can't,' she yelped, her tears flowing as she flopped back onto the ground. 'My ankle. It feels like it's broken.'

'Stay there. I'll get an ice-pack and the first-aid kit, and I'll call your brothers to come help.' She glanced at her watch. 'The medical centre will be shut by now and they'll probably want an X-ray from Geraldton anyway, so I'll drive you straight there.'

Henri barely registered anything her mother was saying—all she could think about was what this could mean for her next contract. All the worst swear words exploded from her mouth. Finally, when she was excited about getting in the air again, this had happened! How was she supposed to get from one job to the next with a broken foot? Never mind fly. She'd have to stay here with her mum, longer!

Oh Lord. That thought was almost as painful as her ankle.

Whereas half an hour ago Henri had been dreaming of doing all sorts of wonderfully wicked things to Liam, now she could actually kill him. And her libido. If she hadn't been so distracted by the prospect of bonking his brains out, she'd never have been so clumsy as to trip on a damn hose.

'Andrew's in Perth doing some Christmas shopping with Janai and the kids,' her mum said on her return, dropping down next to Henri. 'But Callum's on his way.'

'Thanks,' Henri managed, cringing as her mother laid an ice-pack across her ankle. No doubt her brother would find her clumsiness hilarious, but she couldn't even bring herself to care.

'Geez, you've done a very good job, haven't you, sweetheart? This one's *twice* as big as the other and there's already bruising.'

Henri glared at her—did she think that was helping?—and reached for the first-aid kit now on the ground between them.

Fiona snatched it back. 'I'll clean you up. Just try and relax.'

Relax? Henri snorted. Her ankle still throbbing, she barely noticed the sting as her mum wiped the dirt from her grazes.

Callum's ute appeared in a cloud of dust just as they were finishing the first aid.

'Home for a couple of weeks,' he shouted as he ran over, 'and already you're causing drama.'

She didn't even have the energy to glare at him, but she was grateful for his strength as he lifted her into his arms, carried her over to the four-wheel drive and deposited her in the passenger seat.

Callum looked to their mother. 'Will you be all right on your own with her? I was helping Hannah fix the chook pen, but I can call and tell her we'll have to finish later.'

'No,' Henri told him. 'We'll be fine. I'm sure Mum can go in and borrow a wheelchair or something when we arrive.'

'Okay then. Take care, little sis,' he said as he closed the car door.

Although Fiona was a very cautious driver, the gravel track out to the road made the beginning of the journey bumpy and with every jerk of the vehicle, Henri's ankle pulsed in pain. The journey to Geraldton seemed to take twice as long as usual.

When they arrived, Fiona parked right out front and hurried inside. She returned five minutes later with a wheelchair.

'You're not a very good patient, are you, love,' she tsked as she assisted her out of the car and into the chair, Henri muttering and cursing the whole time.

'How would you like it if *you* broke *your* ankle?' she snapped back.

Fiona looked suitably chastised. 'Maybe it's not as bad as you think?'

Oh Lord, how Henri prayed she was right. She hated feeling so helpless and the prospect of not working for however long it took to get back on her feet made her want to scream.

Once inside, she was triaged and then sent to sit in the waiting room with a whole bunch of other people. Glancing around, it looked as if she wasn't the only one with possible breaks, but everyone else with a parent hanging around appeared to be a decade or two younger than her.

'It's a miracle you got to thirty without breaking anything,' said Fiona, as if noticing the same thing. 'Anyway, it looks like we might be here a while. Should I go get us some coffees? Maybe some chocolate?'

'Good idea,' said Henri, more because she felt stifled with her mum sitting beside her than that she actually felt like eating or drinking anything.

As Fiona went off to hunt for vending machines, Henri glanced up at the TV in the corner of the room. It was playing *The Holiday*. Even though rom-coms were not at all her thing, this happened to be one of her favourite Christmas movies, second only to *Die Hard*. After their debate the other night, Henri had to concede that Liam was right, not that she'd ever admit it to him.

She sighed at the recollection, not only of that particular conversation, but of the last few days—the many conversations they'd shared either on the beach during their surfing lessons, late at night when they were all alone and only yesterday during their magical trip to the Abrolhos. They hadn't all been fun and flirtatious—their conversation the night they delivered Dolce's rocking chair had been one of the most emotionally draining she'd ever had with anyone—but there'd not been a moment in his company that she hadn't enjoyed.

And now she'd gone and stuffed it all up.

If she couldn't even put pressure on her ankle, how the hell was she going to drive into town to see him? Never mind climb those stairs to his apartment or continue their surfing lessons. And if her ankle ached every time they'd gone over a pothole, how was she supposed to finish what they'd started in the kitchen? She'd need some bloody strong painkillers to forget the agony long enough to dance the horizontal mambo.

Argh! Maybe this was punishment for lying!

One thing was for sure, Eileen Brady would certainly think it her just deserts.

Chapter Twenty-two

As the fly strips swished open for the umpteenth time Thursday night, Liam looked up and his heart stilled. It was like Groundhog Day, but different. He felt on edge as he waited to see whether Henri would return. Anxious. Nervous. Excited. Hopeful.

Or at least he *had* been hopeful, but with every minute that passed, every person who came through the door who wasn't her, that hope faded. He glanced at his watch. Just after ten o'clock. It was starting to look like Henri wasn't coming at all. If she'd changed her mind about getting naked with him, she only had to say. She didn't need to run away, which, judging by the evidence, was exactly what had happened.

While he'd been dealing with the water mains drama, he'd been too busy to think about the fact that Henri hadn't come downstairs to help. But when he'd traipsed upstairs three hours later in even more of a state than he'd been when he'd found her in the kitchen, her absence suddenly hit him.

And he'd done something he never usually did with women—he started second-guessing his behaviour. Had he misread the signs? Had Henri not felt the same way he did? Or had she simply had second thoughts?

Liam went over and over the events of the afternoon. He'd thought about that kiss nonstop ever since and he kept coming back to the same conclusion—she'd definitely kissed him back. Those moans ... you couldn't fake them. And hadn't it been *her* suggestion to share the shower? If that wasn't an invitation to seduce her, he didn't know what it was.

He shook his head. It had been a manic day on so many levels. They'd been on the back foot all evening with the kitchen opening late because of all the gunky water. Liam hadn't even been sure they were going to manage to serve meals at all, but Macca and the rest of his staff had worked like mad to bring it back up to scratch. The last thing he needed on top of all *that* was a confusing woman who gave off totally mixed signals.

Maybe it'd be a good thing if Henri was a no-show. After all, she might not *live* in Bunyip Bay but that didn't change the fact that this town was her home. That meant anything between them would always be more complicated than a one-night stand or a fling. Bamboozled by the insane chemistry that arced between them, he'd almost lost sight of that for a while.

Glancing at the row of taps in front of him, Liam seriously considered pouring himself a beer. He didn't usually drink on duty—hell, he didn't usually drink 364 days of the year—but the urge felt strong tonight and as things were starting to calm down, one drink wouldn't hurt. After today, he deserved it.

He was reaching for a glass when Drew and Mike walked into the pub, dressed in their uniform blue and looking as if they'd too had a long day.

Liam tipped his head as they strode towards the bar. 'Evening, boys. Is there a problem?'

Drew gestured to his partner with his thumb. 'The only problem is that Mike here isn't man enough to relieve his bladder on the side of the road and—'

'It's not that,' Mike interrupted, turning red like a beetroot. 'Aren't you the one always saying we need to show a good example?' He turned to Liam. 'Do you mind if I use your bathroom? We were driving through town and thought it'd be quicker than unlocking the cop shop.'

'Go ahead,' Liam said, managing to control his amusement until Mike had disappeared. 'That guy is a character.'

'That's one word for it.' Drew leaned against the bar. 'Anyway, how's Henri?'

'What do you mean?' Something in his voice made Liam's chest cramp.

'Her ankle.'

Liam swallowed. *Thank God*—an ankle wasn't too bad.

'I was in The Ag Store just before closing and Tilley was on the phone to Fiona. Couldn't help hearing that Henri tripped and broke it,' Drew said, giving Liam a funny look, no doubt wondering why her boyfriend seemed to be in the dark.

'Oh *that*. Yeah. Poor thing.'

'Have you seen her since it happened?'

'No.' He shook his head, desperate to ask *what* exactly had happened but not wanting to give away the game. 'Had a bit of an emergency here this arvo and thought it'd be best to let her rest anyway.'

Drew nodded as if this made perfect sense and Liam exhaled slowly. 'How's things out there tonight?'

That was why Henri hadn't come in tonight, although it didn't account for why she'd disappeared this afternoon. Had she hurt herself here? In the pub? Perhaps in a rush to escape what they'd almost done upstairs? He'd been so preoccupied dealing with the water damage that a bomb could have gone off and he wouldn't have noticed. But *no*. That couldn't be possible. If she'd broken her ankle, she'd have had to call out for someone to help. Surely her rescuer would have alerted him?

Needing to know, he yanked his mobile out of his pocket only to realise he didn't have her number. They'd spent every morning and almost every night together for the best part of two weeks—she'd slept in his bed, baked in his damn kitchen; he'd shared things with her he hadn't shared with anyone in years, and yet not once had he thought to ask for her number. *Idiot.*

When Mike returned to the bar, the two policemen left and Liam realised he hadn't heard one word of Drew's reply.

Was it too late to ring Henri's mum's place? He checked the time. It was now almost ten thirty—definitely too late. Most farmers were subscribers to the 'early to bed early to rise' philosophy, and after the day Henri must have had, it was highly likely she was already asleep as well. He'd simply have to wait until the morning to talk to her.

The next half hour dragged, but finally Liam called last drinks and not long after that, locked the doors.

'Henri not coming in tonight?' Dylan asked as he, Liam and Lara headed for the stairs.

'Oh my God!' Lara said, her hand rushing to her mouth. 'I'm so sorry, but Henri called during the dinner rush. We were so busy I asked if you could call her back.'

'What?' Liam's heart squeezed. 'Did she leave her number?'

Lara and Dylan both frowned.

'Don't *you* have it?' Lara asked.

Shit. 'Of course I do. Sorry. It's been a long day and I'm just tired.'

'Yeah, you can say that again,' Dylan said, taking Lara's hand. 'See you tomorrow, Liam.'

'Goodnight, guys.'

Chapter Twenty-three

Liam didn't sleep well that night, but for different reasons than usual. Henri's absence made his apartment feel eerily quiet and much bigger. Sheila had whined all night, making him think she too must be missing their house guest, or maybe she was still in a mood with him for yelling at her earlier that day. He'd given her a couple of treats after dinner and lots of cuddles to try and make up for it, then they'd both slept in his bed, between sheets that were now infused with the scent of Henri. At first, he'd imagined her lying there beside him. Thoughts of her naked body and exactly what they would have got up to that afternoon if they hadn't been rudely interrupted filled his head.

But after a while he started visualising her lying in another bed fifteen kilometres away. Was she awake? Was she in pain?

And then it really hit him: Henri had broken her ankle!

He sat up in bed, startling Sheila awake and she barked.

Would this mean Henri couldn't go back to work yet? Would *that* mean she'd stay longer in town?

Eventually, at about six in the morning, Liam threw off the covers and gave up. Luckily after too many years of sleepless nights, he was used to functioning on less than full energy levels.

Thank God for coffee, he thought, as he switched on his machine. After caffeine and a few pieces of toast, he and Sheila headed down to the beach for their morning swim. This was more to pass the time until it was a reasonable hour to go visiting than because he needed the exercise, but being in the water wasn't the same without Henri.

On his way back to the pub, Liam made a detour to collect some flowers from Dolce's garden, then he spent a couple of hours working in his studio before showering and finally allowing himself to head out to the Forwards'. He'd never been there before; in fact over the ten years he'd been in the Bay, he'd only visited a handful of actual homes. Mostly he kept to himself, using the pub as an excuse to avoid social invitations. Still, he had a general idea of the direction most people lived—including the Forwards—and when a large wooden sign with 'Bungara Springs' printed in bright red and currently bordered in gold tinsel loomed into view on the side of the road, he knew he'd come to the right place. He turned down the gravel drive and bumped along, passing sheep grazing in the dry paddocks on either side, until he came to a fork in the track. Thankfully, another wooden sign pointed him in the direction of 'Fred and Fiona's Place'.

He smiled sadly as he thought of how Henri must feel whenever she saw her father's name there.

Not much further and he came upon a large, red-brick farmhouse with a paradise of a garden out the front. On either side of a cobblestone path were two jacaranda trees in full bloom, and there were numerous garden beds overflowing with native bushes and others a contrast with bright-coloured roses. Liam pulled up just outside the white picket fence that bordered the homestead. He plucked the flowers and a box of chocolates he'd picked up at the IGA off the passenger seat and then headed for the gate. Two old border collies wandered over to him from where they'd been resting under a jacaranda when he started up the path towards the house.

'Hey there, buddies,' he said, pausing a moment to let them sniff him. Their tails wagged furiously but he wasn't sure if their excitement was for him or they could smell Sheila on his clothes.

When they'd calmed a little, he continued on and climbed the three steps onto the verandah. His heart pinched at the sight of the tinsel wound along the posts from one end to the other. Like many of the houses in town, it was covered in tiny lights and he could imagine all too well how festive it would look at night, but thankfully it didn't have the same effect during the day. A large wreath similar to the one Henri had made for him hung on the front door and he tried not to focus on it as he raised his hand to use the knocker.

Instead, he focused on the other things that made this farmhouse exactly how he imagined one should be. The pairs of boots lined up beside the door, the two old cane armchairs, a box of firewood and—

The door peeled open to reveal Fiona Forward.

'Hello.' She looked from his face to the flowers and back to his face, smiling brightly. 'I've been expecting you. Come on in.'

Liam blinked. 'You were?'

'Well, of course,' she replied, ushering him into the house. 'I imagine you were busy yesterday evening, but I knew you couldn't stay away from my girl today. She's in her bedroom feeling sorry for herself, but I'm sure your arrival will cheer her up.'

Fiona started down a long wide hallway with high ceilings and dozens of framed family photos hanging on the walls, but Liam didn't have time to look at them.

'I didn't take my shoes off,' he called as he hurried after her.

'Oh, don't worry about that. A little dirt never hurt anyone.' She paused in front of a door that had multicoloured wooden letters stuck to it, spelling out 'Matilda' and 'Henrietta'.

'Visitor for you, darling,' Fiona said as she pushed it open.

Henri looked up from where she was lying on one of two single beds on either side of the room. Her eyes flashed with surprise. 'Liam?'

'I'll leave you lovebirds alone.' Fiona all but pushed him into the room and pulled the door shut behind them.

'Hey.' He smiled at Henri—she did indeed look sorry for herself—and then glanced to her feet. The left one was bare, but the right was bandaged and propped up on three pillows. There were wooden crutches leaning against the bed. 'Heard you were in the wars. What exactly happened?'

'I tripped over a hose,' she admitted, then pointed to the flowers still in his hand. 'Did you steal those from Eileen's garden?'

'What, these?' He glanced down at the colourful bouquet. 'No. No stealing necessary. They're from Dolce's garden and she was more than happy to oblige.'

'Are they for me?'

'Nah.' He couldn't resist teasing her. 'They're for your mum, but she didn't give me a chance to give them to her yet.'

Henri crossed her arms over her chest. 'Good, because I don't like flowers anyway.'

Smirking, he put said flowers down on the dresser and held up the chocolates. 'What about these?'

She thrust out her hand. 'Give 'em here.'

Chuckling, he tossed them to her and as she tore off the plastic wrapper, he sat down on the edge of her bed. 'You know … you're kinda cute when you're cranky.'

'You'd be cranky too in my position,' she said through a mouthful of chocolate. 'My mother is driving me insane with her fussing and I can't even run away.'

'Sometimes I get cranky for a lot less. Does it hurt?' He gestured to her bandaged foot, which looked twice the size of the other.

She sighed loudly. 'What do you think? Luckily, the doc gave me some really strong painkillers.'

'Is it really broken?'

'No, thank God. Hurts like hell, but it's not torn or broken—I just did a really good job of spraining it. I should be back on my feet in a couple of days, a week max. For a moment there, I thought I was gunna have to pull out of my next contract.'

'You're still going?'

'I hope so. The doc says if I spend the next week resting, I should be okay.' At least that's what Liam thought Henri said but her mouth was once again full of chocolate.

He wasn't sure how he felt about that. On the one hand he was happy for her, on the other he found himself a little disappointed. He'd sort of got used to having her around.

Unsettled, he took a moment to check out the room and realised it was divided in two distinct halves. One side decidedly feminine—pink frilly bedspread piled with cushions, purple walls and a rainbow mural—the other, the total opposite. Henri's bed, which boasted a doona with old-fashioned planes all over it, occupied this side and the walls here were lime green and covered with old country-music posters and photos of aeroplanes.

'I'm guessing you used to share this room with Tilley?'

'Yes,' she groaned. 'It was painful. I was so excited when she got engaged to James and moved into town with him, but Mum refused to let me redecorate and take over. I think she was hoping all that pink stuff would rub off on me.'

He reached out to pick up a photo frame on her bedside table and smiled down at the image of a slightly younger Henri standing in front of a small plane, mostly blue with a yellow stripe down the middle, propeller at the front and a miniscule cockpit. There was a large hangar in the distance and a smile on Henri's face that reminded him of her expression yesterday afternoon when he'd just kissed the living hell out of her.

'What kind of plane is this?' he asked, not sure how to broach the subject he really wanted to talk about.

Henri gazed fondly at the photo. 'That photo was taken on one of my very first proper jobs—it's a radial powered Dromader. You have to coax them into life until an idle is established. Most of them bleed a bit of oil down the side of the aircraft, bad ones can haemorrhage. I actually flew one again in the Esperance bushfires in 2015 and the oil bleed was so bad that after a couple of hours, the windscreen was partially obscured by a trail of oil right up the side of the fuselage. Every time I refuelled, I also had to put fifteen litres of oil into the engine.'

'So you don't fly these aircraft now?'

She shook her head. 'Very rarely. Mostly I fly AT502s or Thrush 510s. Both are 500 US gallon machines. The AT802s are mainly used when I do fire contracts, as they can hold 500 US gallons, but even they're being used for some ag flying now. Last time I was topdressing in Victoria, the company I was with used Beavers—they're Canadian aircraft and I quite like them too.'

He had no idea what she was talking about, but he nodded as if he did.

'Sorry ...' she said. 'I get a little excited when I talk shop.'

'Hey, don't apologise.' It was good to hear her talking so passionately about flying again. He reached out and cupped her cheek in his hand. 'You're not boring me at all. Promise.'

She met his smile with one of her own. 'That's sweet of you to say.'

Liam wasn't sure whether it was the chocolate or the plane talk that had improved her mood, but he was glad she seemed a little happier than when he arrived.

'You know ...' She gestured to the box of chocolates in her lap. 'As much as I appreciate these, you didn't have to come all this way.'

'You make it sound like I trekked across the Simpson Desert to get to you. It's barely a ten-minute drive and I wanted to check you were okay. I would have come last night but by the time Drew mentioned you were hurt, it was too late to come out.'

'I'm sorry for worrying you. I did call as soon as we got back from the hospital. I left a message with Lara.'

'I know. Unfortunately, she didn't remember to tell me until *after* we'd closed.'

'Whoops.' A gorgeous blush tinted her cheeks. 'I had no idea when I asked you to help me the extent you'd have to go to.'

He slid his hand over her jaw and down her neck to her collarbone. 'It hasn't been *that* much of a hardship.' Her skin felt like velvet, and she shivered beneath his touch.

'I'm glad to hear it.'

'But,' he began, 'I thought I made it clear yesterday that I think it's time to make things a little bit more real?'

'Are you suggesting what I think you're suggesting, Liam?'

Her tone told him she didn't mind if he was.

'Uh huh. Kissing you. Surfing with you. Flying with you. Spending all this time with you ... it's driving me crazy, but I don't want to lead you on. This wouldn't be ... You need to know ...'

He swallowed—why was it so hard to lay his cards on the table? He'd done it time and time again with other women.

'I'm not interested in a relationship,' he managed eventually. 'All I can offer is a …'

Henri raised an eyebrow as he tried to find the right expression. 'A fling, Liam? Is that the word you're looking for? One-night stand? No-strings-attached bonking? Fuck buddies?'

'I …' He didn't know what to say to that. Didn't know whether she was amused or pissed off.

'Because that's more than fine with me. Your touch would have to be pretty damn magic to have me start fantasising about white weddings and happily ever afters if that's what you're asking. I'm too selfish for a relationship anyway. My career will always come first.'

'Me too. That's good.' He nodded. 'By the way, I lied. The flowers *are* for you.'

She grinned. 'Excellent, because I lied when I said I didn't like them. But now we've got all that sorted, are we just going to keep talking? Or are you gunna shut up and kiss me?'

'Well, since you asked so nicely.' He pushed her back onto the mattress and lowered his head to hers.

A knock sounded on the door.

Chapter Twenty-four

Henri cursed as her mother's voice followed quickly after the knock on her bedroom door.

'I don't want to interrupt anything but … I was just wondering if you're going to stay for lunch, Liam? It would be lovely to have you join us.'

Henri fully expected him to say no, so she almost fell off the bed when he called back, 'Sure, that would be lovely, thanks.'

'Excellent. I'm just putting it on the table now. Come on out when you're ready.'

'Are you crazy?' she hissed as they listened to her mother's footsteps patter back down the hallway. Were they not in the middle of something here?

'What?' Liam shrugged one shoulder as he hit her with the most infuriating grin. 'I'm hungry and it felt rude to turn her down. Shouldn't I be trying to stay on your mother's good side?'

Ah, that's right. The stupid farce.

Henri felt like crying. Would she and Liam ever be able to follow through on what they'd started? Then again, did she really want to have sex with him for the first time on her tiny childhood bed with her mother just down the hall?

Still, as her heart rate returned to normal, she couldn't help being disappointed. She didn't want to sit through lunch making small talk with her mum; she wanted Liam to whisk her back to the pub so they could both have their wicked way.

'Come on,' he said, climbing off the bed and reaching for her crutches. 'Let me help you.'

Not usually one to accept assistance so easily, Henri didn't object as he slipped his arm around her back and lifted her into a stand.

'You smell so good,' she whispered, leaning into him, resisting the urge to lick his neck. Her mother was a good cook, but nothing she could possibly serve would taste as delicious as him. 'What cologne do you use?'

'Nothing. Just soap and a can of whatever deodorant is on special at IGA.' He handed her the crutches, and she missed his touch as she allowed them to take her weight.

She sighed. 'Come on, let's get this ordeal over and done with.'

Liam gave her a look. 'It's only a bit of lunch.'

But where Henri's mother was concerned, nothing was ever *only* a bit of lunch.

'Let's hope so,' she said as Liam crossed the room and opened the door.

He walked right beside her as she hobbled down the hallway and into the dining room, which was adjacent to the massive country-style kitchen.

'Such a shame about Henri's ankle, but it's great that you can join us for lunch,' said Fiona.

'Why is *that* on the table?' Henri cried as she spotted one of their family photo albums resting between a jug of water and her mother's beloved dog and cat salt and pepper shakers.

'I thought Liam might like to see some photos of when you were a kid.'

'Of course he doesn't,' Henri snapped.

'Actually, I do,' Liam said, an annoying twinkle in his eyes. 'Very, *very* much so.'

If she were more mobile, she'd grab the album and hurl it out the window, but she still hadn't completely conquered the crutches so that would be near on impossible.

'You two sit down,' Fiona ordered as she headed into the kitchen.

'Is there anything I can do to help?' Liam called.

'Of course not. You're our guest.' She sounded offended to have been even asked such a question. 'Sit down and relax.'

Liam helped Henri into a seat, then he took the one beside her. He'd barely been sitting five seconds when she felt his hand land on her thigh, just below the bottom of her short denim skirt. She inhaled sharply as her damn Kegel muscles jumped to attention.

Her mother returned carrying a steamy hot quiche in her oven-mitted hands. 'It's lovely to have you here, Liam.' She set it down in the middle of the table. 'I've always wanted to ask how you came to buy a country pub?'

'Um … it was kind of a spur of the moment decision. I'd been travelling for a few years and thinking about stopping and opening some kind of business but wasn't really sure what. When I stopped in Bunyip Bay, I saw the For Sale sign outside The Palace and it just felt right.'

'How so?'

'Mum, stop asking so many questions.'

'It's fine.' Liam gave Henri a quick smile. 'Well, I guess I just liked the feel of the town, and I saw the potential in the old building. While I was driving around Australia, the old pubs, some really rundown and derelict, others beautifully restored, really intrigued me. I guess I was excited by the challenge of bringing The Palace back to life.'

'Well, you've certainly done that,' Fiona said as she began to dish up the quiche. 'Don't you agree, Henrietta? Remember how dirty and dingy it used to be?'

Henri nodded, even though she now had a feeling this wasn't the full story. People didn't just buy pubs on the spur of the moment. Then again, if her whole family were obliterated in one go, who knew what kind of crazy thing she might do.

'Some salad?' her mother asked Liam.

As he nodded, she added, 'Must be pretty tough work though. Long hours, late nights, seven days a week. Hard to get away for a break.'

'I wouldn't say it's any more gruelling than farming,' he replied.

'But all those long nights!' she exclaimed. 'And when was the last time you took a holiday?'

'True, I work nights, but most of my days are my own and as for vacations, have you seen the beach recently? People come *here* for holidays.'

At this, Fiona had to concede a smile.

'Henri and I went to the Abrolhos on Wednesday—that was amazing.'

'Ooh, yes, I saw the photos she put on Facebook. I haven't been in years. I guess you must meet some interesting characters in your job too?'

Liam nodded. 'Interesting is an understatement. I promise I'm never bored. You should hear some of the stories I've heard from people passing through.'

'I can imagine,' she said as she handed him a plate. 'I hope you like quiche.'

'What's not to like?' Liam removed his hand from Henri's knee to pick up his cutlery and she felt her skin go cold.

Knives and forks clinked against crockery as they all began to dig in. Everyone except Henri—she merely pushed the food around her plate with her fork. Usually, she'd have seconds of her mum's homemade quiche, but today the only thing she was hungry for was sitting right beside her.

'This is delicious,' Liam said after a couple of mouthfuls.

Fiona beamed. 'Thank you. It's a secret family recipe. Speaking of family … I can imagine yours weren't very happy when you decided to stay in Australia.'

Henri tensed, wishing her mother would just mind her own business; then again, Liam was the one who'd accepted her invitation. Perhaps an interrogation served him right.

'My parents are both dead,' he said, reaching for his glass of water.

Her mother blinked, then gave him a sympathetic smile. 'Oh, I'm so sorry.'

He nodded. 'Thank you.'

Awkward silence lingered a few long moments and Henri racked her mind for something innocuous to say when her mother tapped on the album. 'Would you like to see some photos from when Henrietta was growing up, Liam?'

'Are there any embarrassing ones?' he asked.

She beamed. 'This is Henrietta we're talking about … pretty much all of them are embarrassing. She was constantly getting into sticky situations, not caring about what anyone thought.'

'In that case …' Liam grinned as if someone had just told him he'd won a million dollars. 'I definitely want to see.'

Clearly delighted, Fiona abandoned her lunch and opened the thick hand-crafted scrapbook—during the height of the scrapbooking craze, she'd made one for each of her children. The baby photos came first, and Henri couldn't help the warm flush when Liam gushed about how cute she was.

'She was my chubbiest baby,' her mother told him, 'until she started to crawl, and then she didn't stop moving. She was always running, climbing over furniture and up trees. See how she's wearing red in almost every photo?'

As she pointed to the jumper two-year-old Henri was wearing, Liam nodded.

'Well, that was so we could always see her in the distance. She was constantly escaping the house, wanting to be off with Fred or her older siblings, and we discovered she was easier to keep track of when she was wearing bright colours.'

Liam laughed as Fiona flicked the page and Henri's tiny, pale bum flashed up at him from where she was bent over a paddling pool.

'Two seconds after that photo was taken, she fell right in. And, if I remember correctly, it was the middle of winter, but Henri didn't feel the cold. She was always running around naked no matter what the season. When she was seven, she went to visit Fred and the boys in the shearing shed—in the nuddy. I told her to put some clothes on, but she never has listened to me. Learnt your lesson that day, didn't you, darling?'

'What happened?' Liam asked, turning his amused grin on her.

Fiona answered for her. 'We'd started shearing a day early and there was a shed full of contractors. They thought it was hilarious.'

Oh my God. Kill me now.

But at that moment Liam's hand found its way back to her leg and this time he squeezed it gently. Pheromones overcame her.

Over the next few moments, his boldness increased. Henri swallowed. Could her mother see what he was doing? As her legs fell apart of their own accord, she was ashamed to realise she didn't even care! It was impossible to resist the sensations that were flooding her body at his touch.

The embarrassing stories continued with each turn of the album's pages—tales of her using hair removal cream thinking it was moisturiser, of trying to pee standing up like her brothers and being annoyed when she couldn't—but she barely heard her mother's voice. She'd thought only women were supposed to be able to multitask but right now, Liam seemed to be doing a much better job at it than she was.

'*Ah* …' Henri moaned involuntarily as his fingers inched up her leg.

'Are you okay, Henrietta?'

Liam pulled back his hand, a slight smirk on his face. 'Yeah, you okay, Henri?'

She'd want to kill him if she didn't want to kiss him so bad.

'Um … um …' For once in her life she struggled for words. 'Sorry, just … it's my ankle. I think the painkillers must be wearing off.'

'Oh, sweetheart.' Her mother sighed sympathetically. 'Do you want me to get you some more?'

'I don't know.'

What she really wanted was for her to miraculously vanish. Either that or for her and Liam to magically teleport back to the pub like the characters in *Harry Potter*. If they didn't get the chance to finish what they'd started soon, she was going to combust!

'I was supposed to be having dinner and Christmas drinks with Esther and Dave Burton tonight, but maybe I should cancel,' Fiona said with a frown. 'I'm sure they'll understand that I need to stay home and take care of you.'

'No!' Henri and Liam exclaimed at the same time. She couldn't stand the thought of any more of her henpecking, but it would be good for her mother to get out too. Now that her dad was gone, she needed her friends more than ever.

'I'll look after Henrietta,' Liam added, reaching to take hold of her hand—this time in full view. 'I can take her back to the pub with me now. I'll take good care of her and this way, you can enjoy your night out without worrying.'

Pleasure rolled through her like bushfire eating up a crop and she hoped 'taking care of her' was code for something else.

After packing Henri another overnight bag, they couldn't get out of the house fast enough. Her bag on Liam's shoulder, she hobbled out to the car, Liam and her mother shadowing her all the way to his ute.

'You know, in my day,' Fiona said as he opened the door for her and took her crutches, 'we only stayed over at a gentleman's house if there was a ring on our finger.'

'Mum!' Honestly, she really was the worst—she'd been encouraging Henri to stay with him most nights. 'We've only just got together. It's not time to book the church just yet.'

Liam smiled. 'There might not be a ring on Henrietta's finger yet, Fiona, but that doesn't mean I'm not looking through jewellery catalogues.'

Then, *OMG*, he actually winked.

Her mother gleamed and Henri coughed, almost choking as Liam slammed the passenger door shut.

'Was that too much?' he asked as he climbed into the driver's seat beside her.

'Nah, it was perfect. It serves her right for meddling so much in my life, but it also means when I dump you, it'll definitely be me she's angry at, not you. She'll probably cook you some casseroles to help ease your broken heart.'

'Well, if her casseroles are as good as her quiche, then that's something to look forward to. But won't that defeat the purpose?'

'What do you mean?' she asked as they bumped along the gravel drive.

'I know you wanted her off your back while you're home for Christmas, but won't this just make her more frustrated and angry at you?'

'Hopefully, she'll finally realise I'm a lost cause and be over the disappointment by the next time I visit.'

Liam nodded. 'And when will that be?'

'Probably not till October for Frankie and Logan's wedding. I've got a month between contracts and I'm heading back to Canada for their summer, but I'm hoping to pick up something else to keep me busy in between.'

Henri glanced at him, but his face was trained on the road, so she couldn't see whether his expression was one of disappointment or relief. What *would* happen when she next visited Bunyip Bay? Would he want to pick things up where they left them? Or would one saucy weekend be more than enough?

Speaking of …

'Can't you drive any faster?'

He reached out and squeezed her knee. 'Hey, easy, tiger. I want to get us both back to the pub in one piece. Didn't I just tell your mother I was going to take care of you?'

'Yes, but we both know that was a ruse,' she said, licking her lips as she gazed down at his hand and recalled the liberties it had been taking at the table.

Although Liam didn't say anything, she saw the speed dial shifting upwards.

Teasing them both, she slowly spread her legs and smiled as she saw his gaze drift from the road down to her thighs. His hand inched ever so slightly upwards, skating the skin mere inches from her knickers.

Yes, please. She closed her eyes and leaned her head back against the passenger seat, but instead of doing what she was hoping, he lifted his hand off altogether.

What the? Her eyes blinked open as Liam changed gears.

Damn manual cars. And damn country towns. If they weren't in dire risk of someone seeing them, she'd order him to pull over the car and finish what they'd started right now.

Instead, Henri forced deep breaths through her lungs and tried to ignore the burning desire building inside of her as Liam got them back to The Palace as quickly and safely as possible. When they finally turned into the car park, she'd never been more relieved to see the old cream-brick building.

'Stay there,' Liam ordered, then rushed around to help her.

'Thanks,' she muttered as he handed her the crutches from the tray of the ute.

She slipped them under her arms and began to hobble, silently cursing because it was impossible to go at any great speed with these damn things. She'd had them less than twenty-four hours and they already felt like a thorn in her side.

As if sensing her frustration, he said, 'You know what. Forget those; I'll come back for them later.' Then, before she realised what he was doing, the crutches were back on the ute and Liam had scooped her up into his arms.

Her hands closed around his neck, her face mere inches from his as she once again inhaled the intoxicating scent of him.

'Hello,' she whispered.

'Hi,' he whispered back as he strode towards the front door. Although she was smaller than most people and it probably wasn't that much of a hardship for someone as large, fit and strong as Liam to carry her, it still made her feel more feminine—more desirable—than she ever had in her life. And she liked it.

Maybe her sprained ankle was a blessing in disguise.

'You okay there?' he asked as he skilfully unlocked the door and manoeuvred them inside, kicking it shut behind them.

Henri nodded, glad the pub hadn't opened yet, so they didn't run into anyone as he carried her through, upstairs and all the way to his apartment.

'Hey, gorgeous girl,' he cooed at Sheila when she greeted them at the door and followed them into the bedroom where Liam lay Henri gently down on the bed.

'Comfy?' he asked as he straightened again. He wasn't even panting!

She grinned up at him. 'Couldn't be comfier. I'm exactly where I want to be.'

'Excellent. Can I get you a drink or anything? Something to eat?'

'We just had lunch.' Not that she'd eaten much, but that wasn't because she wasn't hungry. Now, she was ravenous.

'Right.' He nodded. 'I'll go grab the crutches and your bag then.'

Was he *serious*?

'They can wait,' she barked, patting the spot beside her. 'Why don't you grab yourself and lay down right here instead?'

A pained expression crossed Liam's face and for a second doubt seized Henri's heart. Had she misread the situation? Maybe her strong painkillers had caused her to hallucinate and everything she'd thought had happened back at her place had been a fantasy.

'Is something wrong?' She hated the neediness in her voice.

'I saw how much you were struggling on your feet. I don't want to hurt you.'

Oh God. Relief and something else akin to affection washed through her. 'So you do want me?'

'*Want* you?' Liam ran a hand through his hair and stared intently at her. 'Henrietta, I've wanted you since the moment you walked into the pub. Why else do you think I said yes to your crazy scheme? When I'm around you, I don't think straight. But you had a serious accident yesterday … I don't want to do anything that might make it worse.'

She held up a finger. 'One, don't you dare call me Henrietta ever again, and two—if you're not gunna let your sore lip stop us, then I'll be damned if I let my stupid ankle.'

The doctor had told her to avoid hot showers and anything else that might increase swelling for the first twenty-four hours—she guessed that might include heartrate-accelerating sex—but she wasn't going to let those instructions hinder her pleasure either.

Liam took a step towards her. 'Are you sure?'

'I've never been surer of anything in my life.'

Chapter Twenty-five

Liam grinned. 'Give me one moment.'

He whistled for Sheila to follow him out of the room. Henri heard the telltale sounds of him rifling through a packet of dog treats that lived on the kitchen bench and then moments later, he returned, shutting the door behind him.

'Didn't think we needed an audience,' he explained as he toed off his shoes, then crossed the room and came to sit down beside her.

'Good thinking.' Desperate to feel his naked body, she reached for the waistband of his shorts, but he caught her wrist before she got there.

'Not so fast, *Henrietta* Forward,' he said, his voice low and his eyes full of heat as he grabbed her other wrist, lifted both her arms over her head and then pinned them down against the bed. 'I intend to take this slow and make the most of it.'

Then, his fingers traced down from her face, over her neck, skating the curves of her breasts. The coil deep within her tightened and her hips lifted involuntarily off the bed.

'You're so freaking gorgeous,' he said, dipping his head to kiss her before she could tell him that he was pretty freaking gorgeous as well.

She felt his scrumptiously hard body pressing against her and, as his tongue nudged open her lips, Henri welcomed him inside, loving the feel of his mouth consuming hers. While they kissed, Liam continued his exploration of the rest of her body. Lifting himself slightly so he could slip a hand beneath her T-shirt, she gasped into his mouth as his hand connected with her bare skin, inching slowly up to cup first one breast and then the other.

Henri barely moved. She didn't know what was happening—it wasn't like she was a virgin—but every place he touched felt as if it had never been touched before and she felt utterly helpless as his fingers twirled her nipples into hard and needy buds.

'Perfection,' Liam said, lifting his mouth from hers. 'But I want to see them.'

'Then you'd better take off my T-shirt,' she managed.

And he did just that, taking not only her shirt but ridding her of her bra as well, hurling both over his shoulder before dropping a kiss on her belly button and then licking his way right back up to her breasts. His tongue twirled around her right nipple before sucking it into his mouth.

It was nice—*better than* nice—but Henri wanted in on the action as well. She wanted to feel the hard planes of his chest, she wanted to take him into her mouth and make him squirm in the same delicious way he was making her.

Again, she reached for the waistband of his shorts but once again he shifted out of her grasp.

'Patience, Henrietta,' he said. 'I'm not even nearly done yet.'

'I told you not to call me that,' she snapped, her voice huskier than she meant it to be.

He smiled. 'It's a very pretty name. I don't know why you don't like it.'

Before she could utter any further objections, he grabbed hold of *her* waistband and slowly peeled her skirt and knickers down her legs, taking extra care around her sore ankle.

When she was lying there on his bed, completely naked—except for her bandage—he smoothed his hands back up her legs, every inch of her skin tingling in his wake. 'Are you enjoying yourself, Henrietta?' he asked with a smug smile.

'Uh huh.' She nodded, barely able to get the words out. 'Enjoy' didn't even come close. Perhaps there was something to be said for slow, after all.

'Good,' he said, before spreading her legs wide and putting his mouth exactly where she felt the most need.

Within seconds she was putty in his hands. Or rather his mouth.

'Oh God!' she cried out, her hips bucking and her fingernails digging into his shoulders.

His tongue delved deeper. Her breaths came faster. Pleasure rippled through her, building to a wonderful crescendo. She couldn't remember the last time someone had done this to her but, she thought as Liam took his sweet time, maybe she'd been settling for less than she should.

'Holy shit,' she said, minutes later as she lay there, thoroughly played, trying to catch her breath. 'Just. Holy. Shit.'

Liam crawled back up and lay alongside her, his hand coming to rest on her belly. 'I like the sound of holy shit, *Henrietta*.'

She laughed. The truth was when he said 'Henrietta' she didn't actually mind it. And after *that*, she reckoned he'd earned the right to call her whatever he damn well pleased.

'Your turn now,' Henri purred, sliding her hand into his shorts.

Her fingers closed around his hard, silky length, and she tried to sit up so she could remove his clothes, but pain shot through her stupid ankle. She winced.

Concern filled Liam's face. 'You okay? Is it your ankle?'

She nodded.

'Do you want to stop?'

She glared at him. 'Don't ask stupid questions, just take off your own bloody shorts.'

Not needing to be asked twice, he yanked them off and his boxers as well and … *Wow!* Of course, she'd seen him shirtless before, but being this close, and knowing that right now his beautiful body was hers to do with as she pleased made her even hotter than she already was.

She wanted to taste him like he'd tasted her, but didn't trust her ankle not to ruin things, so instead she wrapped her fingers back around his erection and started to play.

Liam leaned against the pillows and closed his eyes and, as she moved her hand, she watched the expression on his face go from anticipation to ecstasy. It had to be one of the most beautiful things she'd ever seen.

'Henrietta!' he gasped as she felt him start to twitch. He grabbed her wrist. 'Enough. I want to finish this inside you.'

He turned and retrieved a condom from his bedside table, then positioned himself above her and sank right on down, giving them both exactly what they wanted.

And yes, it was a little awkward with her ankle, but he was careful and tender, making her feel like the most precious thing on earth.

'How's your ankle?' he asked when they finally caught their breath.

'Never been better. How's your lip?'

'Absolute agony, but it was absolutely worth it.'

Hours later, Henri woke to the sound of her phone beeping with a text message. She glanced around Liam's bedroom. There was no sign of him, Sheila, or the sun that had been blazing in through the windows when they'd returned from the farm. The window was open, and the warm, salty breeze wasn't the only thing drifting into the room. She could also hear Liam's signature rock music and the noise of his patrons chatting and laughing downstairs, not to mention smell something delicious wafting up from the kitchen.

Her stomach rumbled as she stretched across to grab her phone from the bedside table. Just like the first morning she'd woken up in his bed, it was right next to her, along with a bottle of water and a packet of painkillers, although this time the painkillers were for a different reason. Leaning against the wall right next to the bedside table were her crutches and overnight bag. He was so bloody thoughtful.

Smiling, she glanced at the screen and shrieked at the message that flashed up at her.

How's things upstairs, sleeping beauty?

Henri snorted and texted a reply.

How'd you get my number?

Face recognition worked while you were sleeping, and I sent a message to myself.

Before she could decide whether she should be annoyed by that, another message was incoming.

Anyway, answer the question. Do you like cheese?

Who doesn't like cheese?

Good answer. What about bacon?

Same as cheese.

And beetroot?

I'm ambivalent about beetroot but you're making me hungry.

Henri waited for a reply, but when almost two minutes passed and none came, she struggled out of bed and hobbled into the bathroom. As much as she loathed the crutches, she wasn't about to do anything silly that might set back her recovery, so for the next week, she and these two wooden aids would have to make a truce.

She decided she might as well take a quick shower. Balancing on one leg, she carefully removed the bandage, turned on the taps—not too hot, following doctor's orders—and then frowned. She couldn't exactly *hop* into the shower. With the wet tiles that would be asking for trouble. But could she use her crutches in water?

Ah, to hell with it. Wood dried, didn't it?

Henri grabbed the crutches and tentatively stepped under the water. It wasn't the most relaxing shower she'd ever had, but it did the trick, and when she shuffled back to Liam's bedroom—barely managing both crutches and a towel—she found him sitting on the bed, waiting for her.

'Are your crutches wet?' he asked, clearly amused as he rushed to help her.

'Yep. I wouldn't recommend showering with these things, but I was desperate.'

'I could have helped you,' he said. Once she was settled on the bed, he rested the crutches back against the wall.

'Are you kidding? No thanks.' It had been bad enough last night with her mum—she'd felt like she was three years old again—no way she wanted Liam playing nursemaid.

'Yesterday you seemed quite excited about the idea of us sharing a shower.'

'Yesterday a shower would have been sexy, today …' She shook her head and pointed to the tray sitting in the middle of the bed. 'Never mind, is that a Bunyip Burger?'

He nodded.

'Please tell me that's for me, because if not, I'll fight you for it.'

He grinned as he lifted the tray and placed it on her lap. 'It's for you. Although if the fight led to make-up sex, maybe it'd be worth it.'

'Trust me,' Henri said, lifting it to her mouth, 'bringing me one of the best burgers this side of the equator pretty much guarantees you sex anyway.'

She should probably get dressed before eating, but … priorities.

'Oh my God, this is so good,' she moaned after the first mouthful.

'Macca certainly knows how to make a burger.'

'What does he put in the patties that gives it that extra …' She couldn't think of the right word. 'That extra something?'

'That,' he said, 'is a state secret.'

'You tell me, you'll have to kill me?'

'I can't tell you, because even *I* don't know.'

'What? You serious?'

'Yeah. I know a lot of secrets about lots of things in this town, but that's not one of them. Macca guards his "extra something" with his life. And that's why I treat him like a king. The Palace menu wouldn't be the same without him.'

'So … these *other* secrets?' Henri asked, her interest piqued. 'Care to share any with me?'

He winked. 'They wouldn't be secrets if I did that, now would they?'

'Tease.'

As she got stuck into her dinner, Liam sat down on the edge of the bed and turned his attention to her ankle. She was kinda getting used to the sight of it, but it was the first time he'd seen it in all its bruised and swollen glory.

'Geez. You don't do anything by halves, do you? Is it still really sore?'

'A bit,' she admitted through another scrumptious mouthful.

'Shouldn't you still be wearing a bandage?'

'Yeah, but I took it off to shower. I'll put it back on later.'

'Let me. It'll be easier if someone else does it.'

'Okay, thanks,' Henri said. 'I left it in the bathroom.'

Liam stood and returned a few moments later, re-rolling the bandage. He sat back down on the bed and ever so tenderly took her foot in his hands. Despite the pain, her skin tingled, and desire began to build inside her as he slowly wrapped it up.

By the time he'd finished, the burger was gone, leaving only chips on the plate.

Liam gestured to them. 'I forgot to ask whether you preferred sweet potato fries or normal ones, so I brought some of each.'

'I like both.'

'Good,' he said, smiling as he picked one up and fed it to her.

Honestly, this was her best trip home in years, she thought, as her lips closed around the deep-fried goodness. She must have been a very good girl this year for Santa to deliver her this present—a man who not only made her toes curl but also fed her hot chips in bed.

I could definitely get used to this.

Her heart stilled at this thought. *No, Henri—you cannot get used to this. He isn't a gift that you get to keep forever. He's more like a library book you can enjoy but then you have to give back. So … just enjoy him while you have him.*

Pushing the almost empty tray aside, she hit him with her most seductive smile and said, 'When do you have to go back downstairs?'

Liam glanced at his watch. 'Probably now.' But instead of making a move to leave, he reached out and tugged at her towel. 'Then again, perhaps I can spare another five minutes?'

'We better make this fast then,' Henri said, dragging his face back down to hers.

Chapter Twenty-six

'You took your time,' Lara said as Liam slipped back behind the bar half an hour after he'd told her and Dylan he'd be gone five minutes, ten max.

'I had to help Henri re-bandage her ankle.'

Dylan wiggled his thick dark eyebrows. 'Is that what the kids are calling it these days?'

Lara laughed. 'Young love.'

Liam shook his head, hoping his cheeks weren't as red as they felt. He almost said 'it's not love', but bit back the words just in time.

'Things under control down here?' he asked instead.

Dylan nodded. 'Pretty much. The guys at the pool table were getting a little rowdy but Macca went out and threatened to never cook for them again and they shut the hell up.'

Liam glanced that way to see a bunch of about eight young men crowded around the table. Jaxon and Brad were at opposite ends, clearly keeping their distance from each other. When they'd turned up with their other mates this evening, he'd been in such a good mood that he'd reneged on the ban.

Was that really only last Sunday? In some ways it felt like a month. Since Henri arrived, time seemed to have warped somehow. He couldn't believe they'd barely known each other two weeks—probably because they'd been spending so much time together, it felt like so much longer.

'You look like the cat that got the rat,' Rex said after downing the dregs of his last pint.

On autopilot, Liam grabbed his glass and refilled it. 'That's it for you now,' he told him.

As Rex lifted the beer to his lips, Liam removed the empty plate in front of him and took it into the kitchen where Macca was putting the finishing touches on desserts for a table of tourists in the dining room.

'I'll take those,' he offered, eager to keep busy, while at the same time hoping his guests wouldn't linger too long that night.

Usually, he loved his job and didn't mind if people chatted in the dining room long after they'd finished eating, but already he felt the pull to head back upstairs.

'Who's having the sticky date pudding?' Liam asked the family sitting at table four.

The youngest—a girl who looked to be about eight—shot her hand into the air. 'Me, me, me.'

'We're sharing it,' added her mother.

He put it down in front of the kid, who immediately picked up her spoon and dug in. 'Good luck with that,' he said to the mom as he distributed the other desserts.

On his way back to the bar, he took an order for two more sticky date puddings and three servings of his signature dish: apple pie. Macca and his kitchen hands made absolutely everything they served up from scratch, except for Liam's apple pie. It was the one thing he baked himself and the locals had told him it beat the one Frankie served in her café.

What nobody knew was that it was his dad's recipe and baking it every week was the one time he allowed himself to ponder happy family memories.

Perhaps he should take Henri up a slice? Then again, that could be dangerous. Watching her devour Macca's burger had been excruciating enough. He didn't think he could control himself watching her eat his pie.

Control? scoffed a voice in his head. *Is that what you call what happened upstairs when you took her dinner?*

Shut up, he replied as he went to collect empties.

He was returning to the bar when his phone beeped in his pocket, and he grinned when he saw the message from 'Henrietta'. She'd probably kill him if she knew he'd put her full name in his contacts, but that was a risk he was willing to take. He rather liked the glare she gave him whenever he used it.

Things busy down there?

He glanced from the dining room to the pool table and the casual lounge area in between. There were very few vacant spots, and everyone looked settled in for the evening.

Yep. What you up to?

Just watching YouTube videos on my phone.

Her phone? That didn't sound like much fun—he should have moved the TV into the bedroom for her. It annoyed him he hadn't thought about it because hadn't he told her mom he was going to take care of her? If he was honest with himself, it was more than that. Henri made him *want* to take care of her.

His grip tightened on the phone, but he pushed his anxiety aside, telling himself he'd do the same for anyone. Well, not *exactly* the same, but he liked looking after people—it was the main reason he'd bought the pub. And Henri would be gone soon anyway.

Need anything else? A drink? Dessert?

They the only options on the menu?

God, are you always this wicked?

Maybe you should come upstairs and punish me.

He snorted. For such a tiny package, Henri was definitely a handful, but as much as he wanted to abandon his duties and race upstairs, it *was* a busy night, and he didn't trust himself to come back down if he did.

LOL. Hold that thought. I'll try to close up early.

Try hard.

Shoving his phone back in his pocket, he did his best to focus on work but he poured drinks on autopilot and every conversation he had for the rest of the night was half-assed. Knowing Henri was still upstairs in his bed made concentrating on anything else almost impossible.

Finally, the last customers left and, under the ruse of going to make sure Henri didn't need any more painkillers, Liam accepted Dylan and Lara's offer to finish cleaning up. Sheila could barely keep up with him as he bounded up the stairs and she was puffing by the time he opened the door. Liam slid off his shoes, flicked off the lights and headed into the bedroom to find Henri asleep, her phone still in her hand playing some stand-up comedy video and the light from his bedside lamp spilling across her face.

Man, she was cute. With her hair spread messily all over the pillow, she looked like a pixie in his giant king-size bed.

He gently eased the phone from her grasp, half-hoping she'd wake up, but as he swiped off the video and put the phone aside, she merely rolled over and curled in on herself, her hands clasped together just under her chin. She didn't even wake as Sheila climbed up on the bed and snuggled in beside her; then again, she'd had a very hectic twenty-four hours.

So had Liam, but he wasn't feeling tired at all. It appeared hormones pumping through your body had a similar effect to caffeine.

Resisting the urge to wake her, he tucked the light sheet over her shoulders. His fingers brushed against her smooth skin and every muscle in his body tightened. It took every ounce of self-control he possessed not to touch her again.

Instead, he went into the bathroom, shucked off his clothes and stepped into the shower. A cold shower. But once the cool water had dealt with one problem, another struck.

Where the hell was he going to sleep?

His grip tightened on the sponge as the water pummelled him. He hadn't shared a bed with anyone since Katie. When he slept with a woman, he usually managed to convince her to take him back to her room. Then, after the obligatory post-sex cuddles and a bit of light conversation, he made his excuses and went back to his own apartment. To his own bed.

The bed where Henri was currently fast asleep.

The knot in his stomach pulled tighter. It wasn't that he had anything against spending the whole night with someone, not exactly. It was more that he didn't want to subject anyone to his night terrors or have to explain *why* he had them. Over the last thirteen years, although their intensity had never waned, their occurrence had been sporadic. Sometimes he'd gone whole months without waking up sweating, screaming, kicking and thrashing about, his thoughts smack bang in the middle of the worst day of his life, but he never knew when they were going to rear their ugly head again.

Tonight could very easily be the night.

He didn't want to scare Henri but was also worried about accidentally hurting her if the terrors did strike. He'd seen a counsellor once when he'd first started having them and his doctor had diagnosed him with PTSD, and she'd told him there was a possibility that he could accidentally injure himself or even someone else in the midst of one of his episodes.

He turned off the shower, grabbed a fresh towel and started to dry himself a little more vigorously than necessary as he tried to work out what to do.

After everything they'd done that afternoon, what would Henri think if she woke up and found him sleeping on the couch? Maybe he could say he hadn't wanted to disturb her or accidentally knock her ankle and make it worse? Or that with her and Sheila spread out there'd been no room for him?

Yeah right. Only a fool would buy that story—the king-size could fit the three of them and then some—and Henri was no fool.

Snoring. Yes!

He'd tell her he snored terribly and didn't want to subject her to that. Surely she wouldn't be able to argue with that?

Relaxing a little, Liam finished drying himself, brushed his teeth and headed for the couch. But even though he was knackered, even though it was dark and deadly silent in his apartment, sleep refused to come.

After half an hour of tossing and turning, he sat up and punched his pillow. He *wanted* to sleep beside Henri, and although that set off alarm bells in his head, he couldn't help himself. He wanted to lie his naked body alongside hers, to feel the warmth emanate off her and to find out whether she made cute little noises while sleeping. Did she snore? Did she lie completely still, or did she move about a lot? Would she hog the sheets?

There were so many Henrietta questions he wanted answers to, but could he risk it?

If only he had some kind of barometer that could predict when a nightmare might strike. The thought of exposing that side of himself to someone left him cold. But then again, Henri already knew about the shooting. If he did have a nightmare, at least he wouldn't have to explain that all over again.

Maybe it *was* worth the risk. Sheila would be there as well, and he'd seen the way the dog doted on Henri—if the worst happened and he did get violent, she wouldn't let him do any harm. Not that Henri would either. She might be small, but what she lacked in size, she more than made up for in strength and determination.

Less than a minute later, Liam crept back into his bedroom, placed his pillow quietly down next to Henri's and then gently lifted the sheet and eased himself beneath it. Sheila raised her head in a brief acknowledgement from the bottom of the bed, but Henri didn't move.

He lay there frozen for a few moments. Was this a terrible mistake?

Yet just when he was contemplating heading back to the couch, he felt a hand slip into his and squeeze it ever so softly.

A rush of warmth spread from that spot right through his body and, for the first time in so many years, he rolled over and curled his body around someone else's. Henri sighed and snuggled back into him, her cute little ass pressing against his groin.

Liam smiled and pulled her even closer. Even if he didn't get a wink of sleep tonight, it'd be worth it. Because right now, he couldn't think of any place he'd rather be.

Chapter Twenty-seven

Mid Sunday afternoon, Henri was lying in Liam's bed trying to read, but she kept having to re-read whole pages. It wasn't the book's fault; she wouldn't have been able to concentrate on anything. She couldn't wipe the crazed smile off her face. It had been there ever since she'd woken up for the second morning in a row to find Liam sleeping naked beside her, the sun sneaking in through the gap in the curtains and casting light across his beautiful face. His lovely square jaw. His sexy stubble. Not to mention his glorious body, barely covered by the sheet. His torso had been completely exposed. His powerful shoulders, broad chest and lean stomach were an utter work of art and her fingers itched to reach out and trail all over him.

She knew she couldn't stay here forever and would have to go back to the farm eventually, but right now she simply wanted to enjoy this bubble of bliss.

He'd woken to find her staring and she hadn't been even the slightest bit embarrassed to have been caught perving. They had less than another week left together, and she didn't want to waste one second of that time.

They'd stayed in bed until he'd had to head downstairs to open the pub for Sunday lunch.

Since then, she'd napped, flicked the channels on the TV, which Liam had moved into the bedroom for her yesterday, and sent him naughty text messages. He'd brought her sustenance—a massive plate of Macca's renowned roast beef with all the trimmings—and chatted to her while she ate, before reluctantly heading back downstairs.

Not even an unannounced visit from her mother just after lunch had been able to dim her high, although she had to admit that interruption had been slightly awkward.

'Hey, lover! Missing me already?' she'd called when she heard the apartment door open about five minutes after he'd reluctantly trekked downstairs.

Seconds later he appeared in the doorway, but he wasn't alone.

Heat rushed to Henri's cheeks. Standing next to him was her mother, clearly having come from church as she was wearing her Sunday best and the pearls she kept for special occasions.

After Liam had made his excuses, her mum sat down on the edge of the bed where an hour earlier he'd been giving it to Henri good. If her wearing one of his T-shirts and the ruffled sheets weren't a dead giveaway of what they'd been up to, the bird's nest that was her hair would have sealed the deal.

But if her mum did suspect anything, she didn't say a word. She was on her best behaviour in fact, talking excitedly about the annual Christmas Tree event due to take place on the beach later that afternoon, and also the menu for Christmas Day.

'Does Liam have any allergies?'

That was probably something you should know about the person you were intimately involved with, but she had no effing clue. Henri thought back over the past week and the things they'd eaten together—Milo (so he couldn't be allergic to dairy), Tim

Tams (so not sugar—could you be allergic to sugar?), burgers, chips, a roast, scrambled eggs—and there were lots of food groups covered. The only things they hadn't eaten were nuts and seafood. Both of which could be hugely dangerous.

'Pretty sure Liam eats everything,' she'd told her mother, while making a mental note to check with him later.

Henri was thinking about this conversation when she heard the apartment door open again. This time she didn't call out for fear Liam might be bringing her another visitor—possibly Tilley. As she'd been in too much pain to go downstairs on Friday night, their dinner had to be postponed, so her sister was probably still chomping at the bit for gossip about her whirlwind romance.

'Well, hello there,' she said as Liam appeared alone. Actually, she purred—*seriously*, what was this man doing to her? 'To what do I owe the pleasure of this visit?'

Like a man on a mission, he crossed over to the bed and whipped off the sheet. She felt her grin explode on her face in anticipation.

'It's time to get dressed. We're going out.'

'Out?' Disappointment warred with confusion, but then something else got in on the action. 'You mean like a date?' Although Henri's tone was light and almost mocking, her heart did a tiny jig at the thought that perhaps he was whisking her off to Geraldton for a romantic dinner at one of the restaurants there.

Liam cocked his head and raised an eyebrow. 'I'm not sure going down to the beach with the whole town is my idea of a great date, but …' He shrugged. 'Each to their own.'

She tried to ignore the stupid disappointment that flooded her—since when did she want romantic dinners anyway? Eating burgers naked in bed was more than enough for her. 'We're going to the Christmas Tree? But what about the pub?'

'It'll be dead until later tonight anyway because everyone will be on the beach. Macca, Lara and Dylan said they'll take care of things so that I can take you. They practically ordered me to. Fiona mentioned it when she was leaving, and the others thought you might want to see all your nieces and nephews getting gifts?'

Henri nodded. Although she'd told her mum she wasn't going because the thought of having to hobble about on her crutches didn't appeal, the annual Christmas Tree was always fun and a good opportunity to catch up with old friends.

'Besides,' Liam added, 'being seen together at an event will perfectly consolidate our mission.'

That was true. Even though the Christmas Tree was for the kids, it wasn't only young families who migrated to the beach for the late afternoon excitement; it was a whole community celebration. But Henri felt a weird discomfort inside her at the mention of their relationship being fake.

She swallowed. 'Maybe, but I'm not sure I'm really up for it. I'm still struggling to walk, and I don't think sand and crutches mix well.'

'That's where I come in,' he said, taking her hand and not only assisting her to stand, but also taking her weight as he helped her get dressed.

Then, before she could object, he'd scooped her into his arms and carried her down the stairs. Like Liam said, the pub was deserted, except for Dylan and Lara who were talking to Sexy Rexy at the bar and a couple of old guys playing cards at one of the tables.

'Have a fun time,' Lara called as Liam strode past them towards the door. 'Don't do anything I wouldn't do.'

Henri waved at them then hissed into his ear, 'This is ridiculous. I could have used my crutches down here at least. You can't carry me around all night.'

'Just watch me. And try to enjoy yourself in the process.'

And honestly, it was hard not to while her arms were looped around his neck and his face so damn close that all she could think about was kissing him.

Somehow she resisted, as he bundled her into the Hilux. Less than two minutes later, they turned into the car park down by the beach.

'Geez,' he breathed, his eyes scanning for a parking spot. 'I've never seen it so packed down here. People weren't kidding when they said this was the Bay's biggest event of the year. I didn't even know this many people lived in here.'

Henri laughed. 'There'll be some tourists as well, but haven't you ever been to the Christmas Tree before?'

He shook his head. 'Haven't had any reason to until now.'

They found a spot not too far from the main event and Henri waited for Liam to come around to her side to help her out. He paused to grab a backpack from the tray and slip it over his shoulders, then he lifted Henri out, so they could join the hordes of people flocking over the dunes towards the sound of Christmas carols already being played by the only band in town.

'How's the ankle?' asked Frankie as she and Logan came up beside them.

'Getting a lot better,' Henri replied.

Frankie winked. 'At least you've got your knight in shining armour to take care of you.'

'Yeah, I'm pretty lucky,' Henri agreed as she met Liam's gaze.

'I reckon I'm the lucky one,' he said, and she didn't know whether he was just saying that for the benefit of their audience or whether he meant it. It was getting harder and harder to tell what was real and what was fake.

'Are you taking photos for the paper?' she asked Logan, nodding towards the camera hanging around his neck.

'Yep.'

'That's great.' Henri was surprised he was able to with his deteriorating eyesight. Then again, Frankie said he wanted to do as much as he could while it was still possible.

He lowered his voice slightly. 'It got me out of playing Santa Claus at least.'

'Who's SC this year?' When she was little, the role had always been played by Bob Emerald, a local farmer, but when he died about four years ago, others had started taking turns.

'Ryan,' Logan replied.

Henri raised an eyebrow—not only was he about five decades too young for the role, he didn't have an ounce of padding anywhere on his body.

Frankie smirked. 'I think the last few years Santa has sent his hot grandsons to Bunyip Bay rather than come himself, but I'm not complaining.'

'Who would?' Henri said as they crested the dunes and looked down on the already crowded beach.

'Where do you wanna sit?' Liam asked as Frankie and Logan headed over to the small marquee to find Ruby, who was in charge of organising the evening's proceedings.

Henri scanned the sea of people, picnic blankets, fold-up chairs and hundreds of blue eskies for a familiar face.

Before she could reply, her mother's voice pierced the air. 'Yoo-hoo, over here!'

'Sorry, but Mum will kill us if we don't sit with them,' Henri said, nodding towards where she stood about ten metres away, waving her hands in the air like a lunatic. The rest of her family were either sitting on the sand surrounding their matriarch or playing not too far away.

Liam started towards them. 'It's fine. I like your family.'

'They're okay in small doses.'

He chuckled as he lowered her into a fold-up chair that Tilley vacated as they arrived. Greetings were exchanged—all Henri's nieces and nephews came up to say hello before scattering again to join their friends—and then Liam tugged the bag off his back. She watched as he pulled out a picnic rug, spread it across the sand, and then proceeded to conjure even more, as if he'd borrowed Mary Poppins's magic bag for the occasion. In addition to the rug there was an array of delicious-looking snacks.

'Wow,' Henri exclaimed as he held up a bottle of beer and popped the top. 'You've really thought of everything.'

'Actually, Macca did,' he confessed as he passed it to her. 'I asked him to put together a few things and, as usual, he excelled himself.'

'I think I'm falling in love with Macca,' Henri said with a sigh.

'I might be jealous if I wasn't already in love with him myself.'

Everyone laughed and then settled into conversation. Well, half the adults were able to chat; the others had to have one eye on the water at all times, making sure the kids didn't get wet before the arrival of the guy in red. As Henri relaxed and sipped her beer, she realised that the Christmas Tree was probably much more enjoyable for those without kids than those with them. She lost track of how many times one of her nieces and nephews wanted to know, 'How long till Santa gets here now?'

She almost snapped that he wouldn't arrive at all if they asked again, but to their credit, her sister, brothers and in-laws had much more patience. At the sound of a baby screaming, Henri looked over to where poor Faith and Monty were sitting with Mabel—how her tiny lungs could make that much noise was a mystery!—and a little boy struggling in his dad's arms as he pointed towards the water.

'Soon, Clance,' she heard Monty say as he glanced towards the dunes, clearly as eager as the kids for the gift-giving to kick off. Clancy was likely too young to know or care about Santa, but the unwritten rules were no swimming until after the official proceedings.

Stella's daughter Heidi, with her thick-rimmed glasses, blonde pigtails and a smile that looked far too big for her face, tried to help Monty placate his son, but Clancy was having none of it.

'Thanks for trying, Heidi,' Faith said, reaching across to squeeze the little girl's hand. 'He'll be okay.'

Defeated, Heidi climbed into Adam's lap. He was sitting next to Stella, who was waving a paper fan against her face and gulping a bottle of water as if it was vodka.

Henri felt a weird pang in her chest—was she jealous of them? Of Faith and Stella? *No*, she didn't want what they had. She didn't want kids and a husband, but she had to admit that sometimes she did get lonely, especially late at night or on weekends when she was far from home and working with practical strangers. The companionship and always having someone to talk to, to come home to, must be nice. Cecil was a fabulous listener, but sometimes it'd be sweet to have someone who actually talked back.

At the sound of laughter, Henri's attention returned to her own family.

'That's hilarious,' James said, thumping Liam on the back. 'Tell us another one.'

Henri looked from her fake boyfriend to her brother-in-law—what on earth had she missed?

'Well,' Liam began, 'an Aussie walked into an American bar, ordered two beers—one for himself and one for his four-legged friend …'

He went on to explain that the bartender poured the drinks, said it was the ugliest dog he'd ever seen and then asked the breed. The Aussie replied, 'It's a long-nosed, short-eared, long-bodied, short-legged water hound. Best bloody fighter I've ever had.'

'The barman laughed his ass off, then challenged the Aussie's hound to fight his prized bulldog that had apparently never lost a fight. A thousand dollars my dog can beat yours. Of course, the funny-looking hound tore the bulldog apart, and as the bartender parted with his cash, he shook his head. What breed did you say it was again?'

When Liam delivered the punchline—'a long-nosed, short-eared, long-bodied, short-legged water hound, but in Darwin we just called them crocodiles'—Henri snorted and joined in as the rest of her family laughed once again.

'Where do you find all these?' Tilley asked.

Liam shrugged. 'Ever since I bought the pub, I've been collecting them.'

'I don't remember the last time I laughed so hard,' her mum said, grinning broadly at him before offering one of her home-made yo-yos.

'Thanks, Mrs Forward.'

'I told you, it's Fiona,' she reprimanded, still smiling and slightly blushing as she shook her head.

'Sorry.' He grinned as he lifted the biscuit to his mouth. 'Thanks, Fiona.'

Oh God. Mum *really* liked him. For her, feeding people was a sign of affection. And Henri couldn't blame her mother, or the rest of her family—Liam was very likeable indeed.

Guilt crept into her heart, but before it could really take hold, an emergency siren sounded and chaos erupted. Shrieking kids dashed towards the sound and parents scrambled up off the sand after them. Henri couldn't see from where she was sitting but knew from past experience that the local fire engine had just entered the car park.

Sure enough, minutes later there was a deep 'ho-ho-ho' as Ryan Forrester, aka Santa Claus, appeared, a large red sack over his shoulder and a couple of volunteer firies escorting him. Someone wolf-whistled and Henri laughed as she spotted Grant snapping photos on his phone. Predictably, Eileen Brady scowled at him.

'Do you want me to carry you over?' Liam asked as Ryan made his way towards the tinsel-covered marquee, waving and 'ho-ho-hoing' to the kids who parted like the Red Sea as he passed by.

'Maybe you can just support me while I walk?'

But Liam was having none of it. As he lifted her into his arms again, her mother grabbed the fold-up chair she'd been sitting on and followed after them to join the crowd that was now gathered on the sand in front of the marquee where Ryan sat on a tinsel-covered lifeguard's chair, two enormous towers of presents piled on either side of him.

Ruby used a microphone to address the animated crowd. 'Welcome, everyone, to our annual Christmas Tree.' The noise hushed. 'I know you're all very excited to see Santa Claus, but I need you to sit as quietly and patiently as possible while you wait for Mrs O'Neil to call out your name.'

She gave a few more housekeeping instructions, then turned to her assistant. 'You ready?'

Susan O'Neil nodded but as she opened her mouth to read out the first name, Ruby held up a hand. 'Hang on. Where's Logan? He's supposed to be taking photos.'

She glanced towards Drew and Mike, who were standing at opposite sides of the marquee looking very official in their uniforms. When they both shrugged, she tried Frankie, who was right at the back next to Henri and Liam.

'Um?' Frankie glanced around frantically.

'He's here,' yelled someone across the other side of the crowd.

'Sorry! Coming!' Logan shouted and wound his way through the kids to the front.

Ruby glared at him and then gave the nod to Susan to begin.

'I'll kill him later,' Frankie muttered under her breath.

'What's going on?' Henri asked.

Frankie dropped down beside her and spoke quietly so that only Henri and possibly Liam could hear. 'He's on the scent of the mysterious benefactor. He was hoping with so many locals in one place, he could talk to a few more people. Did you hear he or *she* has struck again?'

'No?' Henri had been focused on very little but the sex machine kneeling beside her.

Frankie nodded. 'You know Jim Nash? His house was infested with termites and he couldn't afford the treatment to get rid of them. Well, on Friday, one of Phil McDonald's guys just turned up. Told Jim someone had dropped an envelope into Phil's mailbox with cash for the exact amount and a typed note saying what it was for.'

'Wow. Hard to track cash, I guess.'

'Yes, but the benefactor doesn't always give cash. For the really big amounts, it's always an anonymous cheque from a bank in Geraldton. Logan's tried to get the staff to tell him who comes in for the cheques, but of course they won't.'

'So, is that what he's trying to find out now? Who banks in Geraldton? That has to be half the town.' Although why anyone went into an actual bank when you could do everything online these days, Henri had no clue.

Frankie nodded.

'Who did Jim tell about his problem?' Henri whispered, finding this conversation marginally more interesting than the repetitive giving and receiving of presents.

Frankie rolled her eyes and sniggered. 'Literally everyone. He was in the supermarket and the doctor's surgery the day he got the quote, complaining about how expensive it was.'

'And the pub,' Liam said, confirming he'd been listening. 'He was mouthing off about it the other night. I gave him a free beer and burger to shut him up.'

'So, Logan's really going to try and out this person?' Henri asked.

'No, although he agrees with his boss it would make a good story and I think it's really annoying him not knowing—journalists can't stand unanswered questions—but he's decided that if he can pitch a story about all the things the benefactor has done, focusing on the people and groups who've received donations, maybe his boss will be happy with that.'

'You reckon that'll work?' Liam asked.

Frankie shrugged. 'Who knows? But I'm hoping so. I get Logan needs to keep his boss happy, but I don't really want to upset the apple cart here just before we leave.'

Laughter rippled through the crowd and Henri looked back to the front to see Faith and Monty trying to get Clancy to stay on Ryan's lap long enough for a photo. The poor toddler looked terrified, and she guessed this would be a story told in their family for years to come.

She slipped her hand into Liam's and leaned closer to him. 'Thanks for coming with me, or rather bringing me here.'

He squeezed her hand and met her gaze. 'You're welcome. I hope you're having fun.'

'I am.'

There was another half-hour of present-giving and at least a dozen kids bursting into tears as soon as they got close to Santa Claus, and then the official part of the event was over and everyone dispersed to various parts of the beach.

Henri was surprised when Stella's daughter ran up to them and threw her arms around Liam, almost whacking Henri with the bright pink fishing net Santa had given her in the process.

'Hey there, Heidi girl,' he said, gently yanking one of her pigtails. 'How you doing?'

She pulled back and held up the net as if it were a trophy. 'Liam, come help me use my new toy.'

'That doesn't look like a toy. That looks like a serious crab-catcher.'

Heidi giggled as Liam pushed to his feet and looked to Henri. 'Will you be okay? I won't be long. Do you want me to take you back to the picnic rug first?'

'I'm fine here. You two enjoy yourselves.' Henri waved them off, bemused.

She was alone all of five seconds before Grant dropped onto the sand beside her. 'Hey there. Mind some company?'

'Of course not. Ryan did a fab job playing Santa by the way.'

'I reckon. Sexiest damn Santa Claus I've ever seen,' he said with a wink.

Henri couldn't argue with that, and although on one level Grant's cheerful, bouncy personality irritated the hell out of her, she found herself warming to him. 'Do you miss the city?'

'Not so much. There's actually more happening here than I imagined, but I'd have moved to Timbuktu to be with Ryan.'

'How'd you guys meet?'

'Mutual friends,' he said, and then told her the story of how it had been hate at first sight. 'He thought I was a show pony and I thought he was a country bumpkin, but we couldn't fight the chemistry.' Grant nodded towards the water. 'You know how it is?'

Henri followed his gaze to where Liam was holding Heidi's hand as she scrambled over the rocks.

She nodded. *Oh yeah, she knew how it was.*

She'd been trying to fight that chemistry since the day she'd proposed their charade. Normally she didn't like losing anything, but this was one duel she was glad she'd conceded.

'There must be more than chemistry for you to have moved all this way for Ryan?'

Grant nodded. 'Of course. Once we started talking, getting to know each other, we found heaps in common. He truly is my best friend in every sense.'

'Really?' On the surface Henri couldn't see what the flamboyant drama teacher and the rugged but handsome farm boy had in common at all.

'We both have similar values, our sense of humour is almost identical, we like the same movies and music, we both care about health and fitness—although whereas I favour running, Ryan prefers footy training. I guess most importantly we're on the same page about what we want for the future. We value family above all else and want lots of kids.'

Henri nodded—it was impossible not to feel warm and gooey inside listening to Grant talk about Ryan.

'What about you and Liam?'

'Huh?'

'He's really good with kids …' Grant gestured towards Liam and Heidi. 'Do you guys think you'll have any?'

At that moment, Ryan—no longer wearing his Santa outfit—dropped down onto the sand beside them.

'Steady on,' he said, wrapping an arm around Grant. 'Liam and Henri are still in that blissful, can't-keep-their-hands-off-each-other stage—children are probably the last thing on their minds right now.'

'Sorry.' Grant gave a sheepish smile. 'I forget not everyone's as clucky as we are.'

Henri smiled back. She reckoned these guys were proof that you could still be in that touchy-feely, can't-get-enough-of-each-other stage *and* want to procreate. The two weren't mutually exclusive, but neither did they always go hand in hand.

'It's fine,' she said. 'I don't mind, but I meant it when I said I don't want kids, and Liam doesn't either.'

Grant looked as if he couldn't even comprehend such a thing, but Ryan grinned and said, 'Perfect match, then.'

'How did you guys go in Perth meeting the surrogate?' she asked.

Grins to rival Heidi's spread on both their faces.

'Really good,' Ryan said, taking hold of Grant's hand.

'Lizzie is the most sublime being, and she's agreed to have a baby for us,' Grant finished.

'Wow. That's fantastic. Congratulations.'

'Thanks,' they said in unison as Stella Burton came up beside them.

Henri looked up to see her hands resting on her back in an aim to support her massive belly.

'Do you want to sit down?' She looked like she needed the chair even more than Henri did.

Stella shook her head. 'Thanks, but if I get down again, I'm not sure I'll be getting up. I almost broke Adam's back when he tried to help me stand five minutes ago.'

Henri grimaced. 'When are you due?'

'Five days ago.'

No wonder the poor woman looked fed up. What if she went into labour on the beach?

'We've tried everything to get this baby out—hot curries, whole fresh pineapples, raspberry leaf tea, and …' She lowered her voice. 'Lots of sex. *Nothing* has worked. I'm pretty sure I'm going to be pregnant forever and I couldn't miss seeing Heidi get her present from Santa.'

At the mention of her daughter, both women looked towards the water where the little girl was still playing with Liam.

'She's such a great kid,' Henri said. 'You should be super proud.'

'Oh, I am.' Stella smiled as she rubbed her belly.

'Does she know Liam well?'

'Quite well. The first time we had dinner at the pub and he came to take our order, Heidi was instantly taken with him. She wanted to go sit at the bar so they could chat, but of course, she couldn't, so between busy periods he came across and sat with us and coloured in. He's such a gem.'

Henri smiled at the thought of Liam's big hands with a thin colour pencil in them.

'We'll catch you both soon,' Ryan said as he and Grant stood. 'Gotta go spend some time with my cute niece and nephew.'

'Heidi likes everyone,' Stella continued once the boys were gone, 'but she's always had an affinity with people who've suffered terrible sadness in their lives. She was the same with Adam's mum.'

Henri slowly turned her head to look properly at Stella. She couldn't know the particular sadness that Liam had gone through, could she?

As if reading her mind, Stella added, 'I don't know much about Liam's past, but it's hard not to see the heartache in his eyes sometimes. Maybe I notice more than most because I've had my own share of disappointments, but …' She blinked and rubbed her belly again. 'Anyway, what I'm trying to say is, I'm glad he's found you. He's such a valued member of the community and he deserves happiness. And I'm looking forward to getting to know you better now that you'll probably be spending more time in town as well.'

That was when the guilt really twisted in Henri's stomach. She and Liam weren't only deceiving her mum and Eileen Brady, but their friends and the whole damn town. Lovely people like Stella who didn't deserve such dishonesty.

'Mum! Mum! Look!'

Heidi bounced up to them, flicking water as she thrust her little cupped hands at her mother. 'We caught a crab.'

'I can see, honey,' Stella said as Liam arrived carrying the net.

'Can I keep it?'

While mother and daughter wandered off to find Adam and get his opinion, Liam dropped a hand on Henri's shoulder. 'People are starting to leave, and I've heard a few say they're dropping kids at grandparents and then heading to the pub for drinks. I should get back to help. Do you mind if we make a move?'

'Of course not,' she replied, still unsettled.

Liam went over to gather their things and brought back most of Henri's family to say goodbye—half of them announced they'd be at the pub soon too—then he picked her up and traipsed up the sand towards the car park.

'Is your ankle hurting?' he asked, as he turned the key in the ignition.

'What? No, it's fine.'

'You just seem a little … I don't know … agitated?'

She rubbed her lips together before confessing, 'I'm feeling guilty.'

Liam frowned. 'What about?'

'Us. Our lies. Everyone's so happy to see us together and I just … I can't believe I ever thought it was okay to lie about it. Maybe it's time to tell them all the truth?'

He switched off the ute and shifted in his seat to face her. 'Henri, it's up to you what you want to do. If you want to come clean to your mum and everyone, that's fine. But I think you're forgetting something.'

'What's that?'

'We're not lying anymore. At least not about being … intimate.'

The way he said this last word gave Henri goosebumps. She swallowed—what they did between the sheets certainly felt real enough. 'I guess you're right.'

'Always,' Liam said cockily as he reached out to briefly cup her cheek, before sliding his hand behind her neck and drawing her head to his.

Their lips met and, as she opened her mouth and gave herself wholeheartedly to the kiss, every molecule in her body melted and all thoughts of guilt and uncertainty evaporated. In the far crevices of her mind, a little voice declared that Liam had probably ruined her for all future flings, but she pushed that voice aside.

Right now, nothing else mattered except this moment.

Chapter Twenty-eight

The pub was heaving with people—everyone drinking, laughing, singing along to Liam's playlist, some even dancing. It was his favourite sight in the world, yet he'd lost track of how many times he'd glanced at his watch since coming back from the beach four hours ago. He wished time would just hurry the hell up so everyone would disappear and he could once again be alone with Henri.

Every muscle in his body clenched in anticipation.

He'd thought after their recent shenanigans that his need for her might be waning but that didn't seem to be the case at all. That kiss in his ute this afternoon had to be one of the hottest of his life. If half the town hadn't been lingering nearby at the time, he might have had her right there in the middle of the car park.

But it wasn't just the sex. Everything about her attracted him—her strong, feisty nature, her terrible cooking skills, the way she ate Tim Tams as if it were an Olympic event, not to mention her expertise in the air. Watching her take control of the plane had been one of the sexiest things he'd ever seen. Her competence and courage awed him. He'd had more fun with Henri in their short time together than he'd had in the last thirteen years, but without even realising it, she'd also challenged him. The fact he'd taken her to the Christmas event on the beach this afternoon was testament to this. No way he'd have done that for anyone else. He wasn't about to start playing carols in the pub or wearing reindeer ears on his head anytime soon, but it hadn't been as painful as he'd imagined. Not with Henri there beside him.

He *should* be worried about feeling so much for someone, but she was leaving in a week so he simply wanted to make the most of the time they had left.

His eyes kept drifting over to where she was sitting at a table with Stella Burton, who couldn't be on her feet for long either. When she and Adam had first walked in this evening, Liam had made the mistake of asking if she should really be out in her condition. That question had earned him an icy glare from Stella and a 'you're game' from Adam.

'This is probably my last night of freedom for who knows how long. I intend to make the most of it,' she said, before promptly ordering a glass of water.

Sitting with Stella and Henri now were a number of other locals, including Mark Morgan, recently returned AFL hero. You'd think he'd returned from a war-torn country the way some of the women in town were going on. And not just the women.

Henri laughed at something he said and Liam felt a pang in his chest. Normally, he was quite happy to be a spectator to the goings-on in the pub, but tonight he resented that work was keeping him away from her. Tonight he wanted to be at that table beside her, chatting with the group and being the one to make Henri laugh.

'*Hello*. Earth to Liam. Can I get some drinks?'

Liam blinked to see Monty standing at the bar, waiting. Lara was already serving and Dylan was off collecting empties. 'Sorry. Of course. What would you like?'

'Another bottle of sav blanc and three more pints of Carlton, please.'

'Coming right up. How's things down in Mount Barker?' Liam asked as he grabbed the wine from the fridge.

'Living the dream,' Monty replied, a broad grin on his face as he glanced over to where Faith and Ruby had joined Henri and the others. He gave Liam a quick rundown of what they'd been up to in the two and a half years since they'd moved.

'Good to hear things are going so well,' Liam said as he filled the pints. He'd always liked Monty and had been as stoked as everyone else in town when he and Faith had finally realised that—as well as being the best of friends—they were meant to be together.

'But it's great to be back in the Bay for Christmas,' Monty added. 'And as much as I adore the rugrats, it's so good to have a night out with Faith and a proper chance to catch up with everyone. Hope Clancy and Mabel aren't giving Frank too much grief though.'

Liam smiled; it was hard to imagine Monty's father-in-law—a tough Aussie farmer if ever there was one—taking care of a baby and a toddler, but of course he didn't say that. 'I'm sure he'll be fine. You should just enjoy your night.'

'Thanks, mate. That's the plan. By the way, I heard about you and Henri. Wasn't sure I actually believed it until I saw you guys on the beach this arvo, but I'm happy for you both. She's a great chick.'

'What didn't you believe?'

'Well, no offence, but I've never seen you, you know, serious about anyone. And since Max, far as I know, Henri's the same. Long before I got together with Faith, Henri's mum tried to get us together, but it was clear she wasn't interested in settling down anymore.'

Anymore? Henri had always given Liam the impression that she'd always been happily footloose and fancy-free, but Monty's words made it sound otherwise. He almost said, 'Who's Max?' but caught himself just in time. Max was clearly someone he—as Henri's boyfriend—should know about.

'Here, let me help you with those,' he said instead, grabbing two of the pints before Monty could argue.

Henri glanced up and smiled at him as he delivered the drinks to their table. He couldn't resist the urge to lean down and steal a quick kiss.

'Having a good night?' he asked, resting his hand on her shoulder.

'Yes. What about you? It's so busy.'

'I like busy. Your ankle not giving you too much grief, is it?'

'Only the occasional twinge, actually.' She lifted her near-empty pint glass. 'Guinness is good medicine.'

He grinned and took it. 'I'll go get you another.'

'My hero,' she said as he turned to go.

Had Max been her hero too? Liam desperately wanted to ask who Max was, but now was hardly the time or the place. If this Max bloke was important enough for Monty to mention, talking about him might upset Henri. Still, as he went back behind the bar and poured another pint for Rex, he found the mysterious man was all he could think about.

Max. Max. Max. Who the hell was Max?

He racked his mind trying to think of all the Maxes in Bunyip Bay and could only come up with two: one of the Poker Pensioners was Max, and Sara and Jake McDonald had recently had a baby they'd called Maxwell, but neither of them were likely contenders.

'Thanks, Liam,' Ruby said as he handed her a glass of prosecco.

He contemplated asking if she knew Henri's Max, but then again, she'd only been in town a couple of years herself and the way Monty had spoken, Max and Henri were a while before that.

'No worries. Drew working tonight?' he asked.

She nodded glumly. 'Highway patrol. Again. He says it's starting to get crazy out there with people travelling for Christmas.'

Liam offered her a sympathetic smile. 'And how's your mum doing?' Lyn had been diagnosed with Motor Neurone disease a couple of years back and was currently touring Australia with Ruby's dad, Rob.

Ruby sighed and looked morosely into her glass. 'Rapidly deteriorating unfortunately. She and Dad will be home early in the new year. He's going to need me and Drew to help look after her from now on, I think.'

'I'm sorry to hear that.' It was a miracle Lyn had managed to go on as long as she had. 'Let me know if there's anything I can do to help. Anything.'

He wholeheartedly meant it but didn't actually register Ruby's reply as the sight of Henri shuffling towards them on her crutches distracted him.

'What are you doing?' he asked, rushing around the bar to help her. Although she'd insisted he bring her crutches downstairs so she wouldn't be a nuisance that didn't mean he expected her to use them. He knew how important her recovery was for starting her next contract and he didn't want her to do anything to hinder that.

'Coming to get my *medicine*,' she replied.

'Ah sorry, I completely forgot.'

'It's fine. As much as I enjoy your Florence Nightingale routine when we're alone …' Her suggestive smile made him gulp. 'I can fly a plane, so I think I can manage crutches.'

He leaned in close. 'Ah yes, but maybe I like carrying you.'

She winked. 'Only one place I want you to carry me right now. How long till you can get rid of all these people?'

'Too long,' he sighed, glancing again at his watch. 'Start praying for a fire or an earthquake or something?'

'I'll pray for a fire and an earthquake *and* something else.'

Although Liam let Henri make her own way to the bar, he waited until she'd rested her crutches against it and safely manoeuvred herself onto a stool before he returned behind and poured her pint.

'You did a fabulous job with the Christmas Tree this arvo,' Henri said as Ruby turned to go.

'Thanks. I'm just glad it's over. I'm knackered. In fact, I think I'm going to drink this and call it a night. Do you want me to carry your drink back to the table first, Henri?'

She shook her head. 'Nah, thanks, but I think I'll sit here for a while and keep Liam company.'

'Well, see you guys later then.'

'Bye,' they said in unison as Ruby departed.

When Henri lifted her glass, Liam checked to see whether anyone was listening before leaning in a little closer, just in case. 'Who's Max?'

Her mouth fell open and her hand froze midair. 'Who told you about … about Max?'

'Monty mentioned him. He sounds like someone who had a big impact on your life.'

She shook her head. 'Not really. He's no one important.'

But the way her nostrils flared slightly and her gaze didn't quite meet his told him otherwise. 'If he's not important, you won't mind telling me about him?'

'Why are you so desperate to know? You're not *jealous*, are you?'

'Jealous?' Liam scoffed as something squeezed inside him. The cold hard truth was that even if he didn't want anything serious with Henri himself, the thought of any other man touching her made him want to punch someone. 'I just don't want to be caught out again.'

'Fine.' She took a long gulp of Guinness. 'Max was … Max and I were … His family own a station up—'

A loud exclamation of 'Oh my God!' stopped him from hearing anything else about Max.

The pub fell silent, and Liam looked over to see Stella, her hand pressed against her mouth, a man he didn't recognise standing in front of her.

'Who's that?' Henri said as they watched Stella haul herself out of her seat and throw her arms around the man. She started sobbing and Adam looked on warily as if he weren't sure what to do.

'I have no idea.'

Time seemed to stand still as every single person in the pub stared at them. Who on earth was this man holding Stella so tightly? Could he be Heidi's father?

No, Liam shook his head; it was common knowledge that there was no love lost there.

'Oh my God!' she shrieked again and pulled back from the man's embrace. 'I think my waters just broke!'

'What?' Adam looked down and even from behind the bar, Liam could see that, sure enough, poor Stella looked like she'd wet herself and there was a small pool of water at her feet.

Good grief. He'd had a feeling she shouldn't be here tonight.

'Have you had any contractions yet?' Adam asked, placing a hand on Stella's back as Liam made his way towards them.

She shook her head and then immediately groaned and clutched her stomach. 'But … I … think … this … is one.'

Adam, looking like he was about to faint, glanced around at the concerned faces as if waiting for someone to tell him what to do.

Frankie stepped in. 'We need to get her to hospital.'

'It's half an hour to Geraldton,' Logan said. 'Don't second babies come a lot faster than first ones?'

Ruby, who'd not quite made it out the door before the drama started, spoke at the same time. 'We should call an ambulance.'

'I'm on it,' called Henri and Liam looked back to see her with her phone to her ear.

That's my girl, he thought, before blinking that thought away and focusing on the problem at hand.

With half the town in the pub, there were already three local volunteers on site. Unfortunately, they'd all been drinking so couldn't fetch the van, but they did what they could to make Stella comfortable while they waited for some other St John's volunteers to arrive.

While Lara went to fetch clean towels and a pillow, 'just in case', Liam and Dylan cleared the pub of everyone except Stella's close friends and Adam.

'I'm her brother,' said the man who'd arrived just before Stella's waters broke as Liam tried to get him to leave. 'I'm not going anywhere.'

Her brother. Wonders never ceased—as far as Liam knew, Stella had given up ever hearing from him.

Henri approached Liam as he was talking to the man. 'Is it okay if I wait in your office with Sheila? She seems a little distressed by all this.'

He nodded. He wished he could go with her but as this was his turf, he wasn't going to leave until he made sure everyone was okay.

Chapter Twenty-nine

'Talk about drama,' Henri said to Sheila as she hobbled into Liam's office, the dog following closely at her heels. Was the breaking of Stella's waters God's answer to their prayers? It was amazing how fast a woman going into labour had scattered the men. She laughed inwardly at the recollection of Sexy Rexy almost tripping over his own feet in his efforts to escape. The blokes Liam called his 'Poker Pensioners' hadn't been far behind. Of course there'd been a few lingering busybodies, but he'd sent them packing.

He hadn't asked Henri to leave, but she'd decided to make herself scarce anyway. Babies were cute enough, but she definitely didn't need to see one born and she didn't think Stella needed an audience either. She had Adam, Frankie and Ruby to support her. For Stella and the baby's sake, she prayed the ambulance would arrive before things progressed too much further, but also so that she could finally be alone with Liam again. As much as she'd been enjoying hanging out with her old friends, there was really only one person she wanted to spend the evening with.

Leaning her crutches against the desk, she lowered herself carefully into the swivel chair behind it. It was the first time she'd actually been in the office and, like Liam's apartment, it was clean and neatly ordered. He'd obviously made the desk, which looked as if it should be in some kind of art gallery rather than the back office of a country pub.

As she smoothed her fingers along the beautifully carved and polished wood in admiration, Sheila flopped at her feet. Henri pulled off her shoe and rubbed her good foot against the dog's soft, warm fur. Not being able to have pretty things like this desk or a pet were definitely downsides to her itinerant lifestyle.

She saw how much Liam loved Sheila and the dog was never far from his side, whereas Henri couldn't even get a bloody goldfish. Even if she could fit a small tank in Cecil, who'd look after it when she went to Canada?

'I'll just have to make the most of you for the next few days, won't I?'

Sheila looked up briefly, made a sort of rumbly noise as if agreeing, and then dropped her head back down onto her paws.

'Fuck off, Adam!'

The exclamation startled both of them and Sheila jumped to attention, her head cocked to her side as she stared at the open door. Henri grabbed her collar as Stella continued to scream.

'It's your fault I'm in this predicament. Where the hell is that ambulance? I don't want to have this baby in a bloody pub!'

Sheila barked towards the door.

'It's all right,' Henri said, trying to calm her, all the while wincing at the sound of Stella swearing and shouting. Not that she had anything against curse words—truth was she rather liked them—but sweet, serene Stella who she'd been chatting with on the beach only hours earlier, didn't look like she had such language in her.

Which only made Henri wonder why any woman would do this to themselves. The sounds she could hear right now were enough to make her want to go and have a hysterectomy. Or, at the very least, a drink.

If only she hadn't left that Guinness out on the bar—she could really do with it right about now.

She glanced around looking for something to distract her, but Liam's office was annoyingly sparse. There wasn't even a magazine lying around. In all the commotion, she'd left her bag and her phone at the bar, which meant she couldn't even amuse herself playing Solitaire or scrolling Facebook. She could sneak out and get them, but her crutches made sneaking almost impossible.

Henri barely heard her own sigh over the sound of another ear-piercing scream, followed by more swearing and a deep, guttural moan. In desperation, she yanked open one of the desk drawers, looking for a book or something else that could distract her. She lifted a pile of catalogues, hoping to find a hip flask of whiskey or something, but her efforts were fruitless.

Argh. Did the man even drink? Now that she thought about it, she'd never seen him so much as take a sip of beer. What kind of pub owner was he?

In lieu of actual alcohol, Henri opened one of the catalogues and tried to lose herself in its pages instead. It wasn't ideal, but it was better than nothing.

Just as she was coming to the end of the first catalogue, she heard someone shout, 'The ambulance is here.'

Well, hallelujah. She snapped the catalogue shut and opened the drawer to shove them all back in. She noticed two scraps of paper had fallen onto the floor: a yellow Post-it note, and what looked like a prescription. She plucked them up, respecting Liam's privacy and not reading what the prescription was for, but briefly registering the words 'JMC Office Supplies' and '$3211' scrawled across the Post-it as she put them both back into the desk drawer.

Fifteen minutes later, Liam appeared in the doorway of the office and Henri's heart somersaulted in her chest. She couldn't have been more delighted if it was one of the Hemsworth brothers.

'Is Stella gone? Is the baby gunna be okay?' she asked as Sheila got up to greet him.

'Hopefully they'll both be. Mandy and Karen have taken her to Geraldton; fingers crossed they don't end up delivering in the ambulance.'

Henri made a face. 'Better than in the pub, I guess.'

'Hell yeah, I was worried there for a moment. Never a dull moment in the Bay, that's for sure. You hightailed it out of there pretty fast.'

'I'm not good with blood. Or babies.' She shuddered. 'Especially ones that are covered in blood and gunky birth stuff.'

'Lucky you're good at many other things then,' he said with a smirk. 'Are you ready to call it a night?'

'You're closing the pub?'

'Yep. Everyone's gone. Our prayers were answered.'

Henri grinned. 'That's the best news I've heard all night. Maybe we should send Stella a thank you note.'

'Good idea,' Liam agreed as he took one predatory step towards her. 'But, right now, I have other priorities.'

'Oh?' Henri's stomach flip-flopped at the heat in his gaze. 'Like what?'

'Like this,' he said as he bent and plucked her out of the chair.

Her arms closed around his neck. 'And this,' she whispered, before pressing her mouth against his.

Their lips locked, Liam started towards the door but instead of walking through it, he slammed it shut with his foot. The sound reverberated through her body, making everything between her legs tingle in anticipation.

Seconds later, they were back at his desk.

It wasn't quite like the movies where some dashing hero sweeps everything off in one fell swoop. Not that Liam wasn't dashing, but he sat her carefully down on the edge of the desk and pushed his computer aside equally as carefully before he stepped back between her legs. Henri had no complaints. She appreciated his respect for his property. It showed a maturity that had been missing in most of the men she'd slept with.

To show said appreciation, she reached for the hem of his shirt and ripped it right over his head. He returned the favour, taking her tee and then her bra in much the same manner.

She said something indecipherable even to her own ears as she touched his hot, bare skin, her fingers skating down the ripples of his muscles. Liam pushed her back against the desk and smiled down at her, before dipping his head and sucking one nipple into his mouth, just the way she liked it. Henri briefly wondered if maybe his desk was so damn neat because he was in the habit of doing this with other women, but then another—more pressing—thought struck.

'Have you got condoms down here?'

'Shit.' He lifted his head. 'They're upstairs.'

As infuriating as this news was—she wanted him right here, right now—it was also strangely comforting. If Liam made a habit of taking women on his desk, surely he'd be better prepared.

'Then, let's make getting up there a priority,' she told him.

He plucked her T-shirt off the floor and yanked it over her head. She'd barely finished threading her arms through the holes before he'd scooped her up again.

They started towards the door and Henri reached out to turn the knob. 'Did I hear that guy say he was Stella's *brother*?'

'Ah huh.' Liam started for the stairs, Sheila padding behind them. Poor dog—neither of them had even spared at thought for her when they'd been getting hot and heavy in the office.

'I wonder what the story is there? I didn't even know she had a brother.'

'They're estranged,' he explained, a tiny bead of sweat appearing on his forehead as he began the climb up to his apartment.

'At least, she's estranged with her parents—they disowned her when she decided to go ahead and have Heidi—and as he was quite young when that happened, they made it impossible for Stella to keep in touch with him as well.'

'Wow. I can't believe Mum never told me any of this.'

They reached the landing and Liam marched towards his door at the other end of the corridor.

'I don't think it's common knowledge,' he said.

'How do *you* know?'

'I'm a publican. People talk. They tell me things. I listen. It's my job. Wanna get the key out of my pocket?'

'Is that just an excuse to get me into your pants?' she teased, her hand already sliding in.

'Would it be a problem if it was?'

She pushed the key into the lock. 'Truth is, you don't actually need an excuse.'

'Glad to hear it,' he said, as he shoved open the door and carried her inside.

Sheila stalked past them towards the bed she only slept on when she was sulking or in trouble.

'I think she's pissed off with us.'

'We'll make it up to her later,' Liam said as he headed for the bedroom.

He wasn't quite as gentle as he had been downstairs as he virtually threw her on the bed, then rid himself of his clothes—shoes and all—in record time. Henri's mouth went dry as he lay down beside her and she trailed a hand slowly down over his hard chest, then closed her fingers around his erection and gave a teasing squeeze. 'Had Stella been looking for her brother?'

Liam groaned. 'You really want to talk about Stella now?'

'I'm just curious,' she said, and began to move her hand up and down.

'She's been trying to get in contact with him for a while, but she wasn't having any luck. Her parents moved not long after she had Heidi and she couldn't find him on social media.'

'So, you're not the only one not on Facebook then,' Henri said. 'I seriously thought you were an anomaly.'

'You looked for me on Facebook?'

'Maybe.'

But Henri had the feeling he wasn't really listening anymore as she swirled her thumb over the tip of his penis. Smiling, she took him into her mouth.

A little while later, he dragged her back up so they were face to face. 'That was …' He didn't finish his sentence, crushing his mouth against hers and showing her his appreciation instead. As his tongue ravaged hers, he moved his hand back down between them, cupping first her breast, before sliding further. Another indecipherable word escaped her lips as his fingers snuck beneath the waistband of her shorts.

'What did you say?' Liam asked, amused, his finger gliding back and forth over the cotton of her knickers.

'Tell me some secrets.'

He hesitated a moment. 'You promise you won't tell a soul?'

'My lips are sealed. I'm like a vault.'

'Tuck Brady likes to wear women's clothes.'

She jerked her head to meet his gaze. 'No *way*.'

'Uh huh … and Eileen's clothes are too big for him, so she steals them from the charity shop when it's her day on roster.'

'I'm scandalised! What else?'

He hooked one thick finger under the edge of her knickers, and she gasped.

'Susan O'Neil and Frank Forrester are secretly seeing each other.'

'Oh my God? Seriously?' Surely Tilley would know if her mother-in-law was bonking the grouchy widow.

Liam nodded as he dipped his finger inside her. He barely even moved it, but pleasure ricocheted right through her body.

'Frank confessed to me one night when he was wondering if it was too soon to take her on a dirty weekend away.'

'Oh God. To Broome?'

'That's right.'

Henri remembered Tilley saying she had to water her mother-in-law's garden because she was meeting some old school friends up there for a 'girls' weekend. Was that a lie?

As hard as it was to concentrate while Liam's hand took delicious liberties between her legs, this gossip was too thrilling to ignore. 'Tell me something else.'

'Well … you know how Logan pretends to be a respectable journalist, an upstanding member of the community?'

She nodded, terrified but also desperate to hear otherwise.

'It's all a front. He's actually involved in an organised crime gang that traffics drugs.'

'What?! Does Frankie know? How can you—'

Liam snorted and the penny dropped.

'Oh my God.' She thumped her hand against his chest. 'Was anything you told me true?'

He pressed his lips against her cheek as he began to move his finger again. 'As much as I like you, Henrietta, I too am a vault.'

'Beast!' She tried to ignore the warmth that flooded her at his confession that he liked her as she remembered the conversation on the beach this afternoon. 'Just tell me one thing—do you know who the mysterious benefactor is?'

'To be honest …' Liam began. 'I'm not really comfortable talking about other people while my fingers are deep inside you. Seems a little …' He upped the pressure. 'I don't know … kinky?'

'Sorry,' Henri quipped, struggling to think straight herself now anyway. 'I forget how bad men are at multitasking.'

'Oh, I can multitask, Henrietta.' He touched her in a spot that was almost impossible to ignore. 'I just don't want to.'

Then, in one swift move—for once forgetting to be gentle with her ankle—Liam yanked her shorts and knickers down her legs, positioned himself above her and thrust into her. Henri gasped and, in a matter of seconds, she could no longer remember what on earth they were talking about.

It was only once they were lying side by side, both staring at the ceiling, their chests heaving as they waited for their breath to return to normal, that they realised they'd forgotten the condom.

'It's okay,' she assured him, 'I'll get the morning after pill.'

Chapter Thirty

Liam and Henri were lying in bed, feeling pretty damn fine about life, when his phone beeped with a text message.

'Who'd be messaging you at this time of the morning?' she murmured, her voice mellow with sleepiness and satisfaction.

He pulled her even closer and held her tightly. 'No idea.'

And right now, he didn't really care if it was Elvis Presley risen from the dead because he didn't want to move a muscle.

'Stella!' They both realised a few seconds later.

'Maybe it's Adam or one of the ambos,' Henri wondered.

Both of them now curious, Liam got out of bed and bent to pick up the jeans he'd discarded off the floor. When he pulled the phone from his pocket, he saw a message from Karen.

Thought you might like to know …

'She's had the baby,' he said, speaking as he read. 'A little girl. Mandy delivered it in the ambulance only five minutes after they left.'

Henri sat up. 'Oh my God. Are they okay?'

'Apparently.' Goosebumps spread across his skin as he finished reading the message. 'She says Stella was amazing and the little girl plump and rosy. They're settled in Geraldton now and Karen and Mandy are on their way back.'

He glanced up and saw that Henri was wearing a grin as big as his felt.

'I can't believe a baby was almost born in your pub!'

'I told you things were never dull around here.' If the ambos hadn't arrived when they did, Stella and Adam's new daughter would have been born downstairs tonight. There'd been a lot of exciting times over the last ten years, but *this*? This took the cake.

'Bet you never thought that would happen.'

'She wouldn't have been the first baby born here.'

'Oh?' Henri's eyes widened and Liam gestured to Sheila who'd snuck up onto the bed. 'She's had two litters downstairs. Both very smooth deliveries thankfully, and gorgeous healthy pups.'

Henri laughed. 'First human baby then. Anyway, I feel like this deserves a celebratory drink or something? I know it's late—or rather early—but I'm not sure I can sleep just yet.'

'I know what you mean.' He could actually feel the adrenaline pumping.

'We should toast the baby,' she suggested.

'I've got a better idea. You wait there.'

Liam tugged on his jeans and headed downstairs, tapping out a message to Karen as he went.

Well done, superstars. Drinks and dinner on me next time you and Mandy want a night out.

He switched on the light as he went into the pub kitchen, crossed over to the industrial-sized fridge and took out a dish with half an apple pie.

One plate or two? he wondered as he grabbed a knife to cut the pie. These were the types of decisions you deliberated over at midnight when something out of the ordinary had happened and you'd broken all your own rules. Not only did he rarely have sex in his own apartment, he certainly never suggested food and conversation afterwards.

In the end, he went with one plate, two spoons and a hell of a lot of ice-cream.

A few minutes later when he re-entered the bedroom, he saw that Sheila had quickly taken his spot on the bed.

'Shove over, girl.' The dog moved down a fraction.

'Is that what I think it is?' Henri asked, eying the plate in much the same way she'd been looking at *him* not long ago.

Liam had thought he was spent but her expression had his desire springing to life again. So much for scratching the itch; if anything, it felt like it was getting worse.

Summoning self-control, he climbed back into bed beside her, presented the plate and let the pie speak for itself.

She picked up one of the spoons. 'I don't have much of a sweet tooth, but I make exceptions for apple pie.'

He watched and waited, his breath bated, but the noise she made a few seconds after she slipped the spoon between her lips exceeded his expectations. It sounded like a damn orgasm.

'Oh. My. God,' she moaned as she came down from the first mouthful and stabbed her spoon aggressively into the pie for another.

Liam grinned. Every muscle in his body clenched. Watching her eat pie had to be one of the most erotic things he'd ever seen. It made him want to go downstairs right now and bake a dozen more pies and then feed them to her, one by one.

He reached for the other spoon, in dire need of something to occupy his hands and mouth, but Henri tapped him away like he was a pesky mosquito.

'I hope you don't plan on sharing this.' She held the plate up against her bare chest, drawing his eyes to her breasts.

'Well, I *am* pretty hungry,' he said, dipping his head and taking one tight nipple into his mouth.

'Oh God, Liam.' She tried to push his head away. 'I don't think I can stand apple pie and you at the same time. I'll explode.'

'Then you'd better put on some clothes.'

She laughed. 'Pass me my shirt then.'

He looked around for her T-shirt but, unable to find it, offered his instead.

'Thanks,' she said, barely putting down the pie as she pulled on the top.

Although surprised he'd lost out to his pie, he couldn't be disappointed at the sight of her in his shirt, which was equally as arousing as the sight of her scoffing his pie.

After another mouthful and another tormenting moan, she scooped up another spoonful, but this time offered it to him.

'Why thank you.' He leaned towards her and closed his mouth around the offering, enjoying the act of being fed by Henri even more than the taste of the dessert.

'You're right. Macca is a king. This pie deserves to win prizes. This pastry …' She sighed. 'I finally know what the expression "melt in your mouth" means.'

'Actually, I made this.'

She snapped her gaze from the bowl to his face. '*You* made this?'

He nodded, feeling his chest swell ridiculously.

'Wow. I knew you were pretty good with your hands already, but this … *you* are a king. Where did you learn to cook like this?'

'In my dad's kitchen,' he said.

'Your father baked as well as ran two successful supermarkets?'

'Yeah. Baking was his stress relief.' Liam swallowed. He was so used to *not* talking about his parents. 'When we were little, he and Mom used to take turns being home with us while the other one was working. Whenever we were with him and we were fighting or just doing whatever annoying things kids do, he'd sit us both up on the kitchen counter and make us cook until we forgot the problem. I always knew when Dad had a bad day because he'd bake late at night when we were all in bed. I remember when I was a teenager and constantly hungry, I actually used to hope he'd have a shit day so that the next afternoon there'd be something delicious to eat when we came home from school. As I got older, baking became my outlet as well. My friends used to tease me about it, but they never complained when they were eating.'

Henri smiled as she put the now empty bowl down on his bedside table. 'I'm impressed. My dad barely knew how to make scrambled eggs. Did yours do all the cooking in your house?'

'No. He mostly did sweet stuff—pies, cheesecakes, he even made his own donuts—and Mom did what she called the boring but necessary cooking. She made the best spaghetti I've ever tasted. Even better than Macca's.'

'Wow. Must have been good. What was she like?'

'My mom?'

Henri nodded.

A lump swelled in his throat. 'Well, Macca would say she was mad as a cut snake. She had two settings—asleep or on speed. Don't think I ever saw her sitting down when she was awake. She wasn't houseproud at all because she always said there were better things to do with her time than tidying, except in the bathroom. Mom reckoned the bathroom was the one place she got to properly relax—she didn't really spend money on much, but her one indulgence was expensive bath sheets. Heaven forbid if any of us used one of her soft, fluffy ones. We'd always know when she was having her me-time, because she'd sing so loudly in the bath.'

Henri laughed. 'Nothing wrong with singing in the bath, or the shower.'

'True, but Mom used to sing all the damn time. Songs from really cheesy musicals, like *Oklahoma* and *Singin' in the Rain*. There was usually a different one each week and it drove Lacey and me crazy because she'd sing wherever we were. Like on the sidelines at one of our hockey games.'

'Was she any good?' Henri asked.

'Yes, actually, but it was still mortifying. Not that Mom worried about that. Nothing embarrassed her; in fact I think she thrived on it. You should have heard some of the conversations she had with me.'

'Well, go on.' Henri poked him. 'You can't say something like that and not tell me. What *kind* of conversations?'

'Probably the most memorable one is the day she told me all about female pleasure.'

'What?'

He grinned. 'I was like, fourteen or something. Lacey had heard someone talking about masturbation at school and asked Mom what it was. Thinking I knew everything about everything, I decided to take it upon myself to explain. I told her it was something only guys do, and Mom stepped in and told me I couldn't be more wrong. Then she proceeded to explain, drawing diagrams and all, how females got pleasure during sex and that they could self-pleasure just as well, if not better than men. She said women don't *need* men, despite what society wants them to believe, but a good man was worth his weight in gold, and if I wanted to be a good man, I should remember one thing: Ladies always come first.'

By the time he finished Henri was laughing so much she was actually crying.

'Oh my God! My brothers would have died if Mum ever tried to talk to any of them about stuff like that.'

'Well, my mom had no embarrassment filter.'

'I reckon I'd have liked her,' Henri said, wiping her eyes with the bottom of his shirt.

Mom would have liked Henri too. They were similar in a lot of ways—both independent and passionate, and they shared a similar dry sense of humour. Sometimes when Henri said something, it took Liam a moment to realise she wasn't being serious.

'What about Lacey?' Henri said. 'What was she like?'

And although Liam had already shared more than he ever had with anyone since leaving America, somehow, he found himself talking openly about his family. And actually enjoying it. He shared memories with Henri he rarely even allowed himself to think about because they hurt too damn much.

He told her about how his parents were one of the most in love couples he'd ever met, and yet couldn't go five minutes without bickering about something. He told her about the family board-game nights they'd had every Wednesday and how even though he and his sister moaned and groaned about it, they'd secretly loved them just as much as their parents. He told her about pets they'd had, vacations they'd been on, the over-the-top birthday parties his mom had thrown.

The words came naturally, and Henri listened, smiling and laughing in all the right places, only occasionally making comments herself.

'Your parents sound like very special people,' she said, squeezing his hand.

'They were.'

'I reckon they'd be super proud of what you've done here in the Bay.'

'Not much to running a country pub,' he scoffed.

'But this place is so much more than just a country pub to the people of Bunyip Bay—The Palace is the hub of the community. And I can see how much you care about everyone too. You didn't call the cops on Jaxon and Brad. Sexy Rexy told me how if it wasn't for you, he probably wouldn't even be alive right now. And I bet he's not the only one. As you say, you listen to people when they need an ear. You make time for everyone, from Heidi right through to Dolce. This town is so damn lucky to have you.'

'Don't think I've forgotten about Max,' he said, embarrassed enough to want to change the subject. 'You were about to tell me about him when Stella went into labour.'

Henri shrugged. 'He's honestly no one.'

'Then why are you so reluctant to talk about him?'

She sighed. 'How about we make a deal? I'll tell you about Max, if you tell me about Katie.'

Ice skated down Liam's spine, and he sat up straighter. He'd never told anyone in Australia about Katie.

'How do you know about her?' he asked, failing dismally to sound nonchalant. Was Henri some kind of mind-reader?

'When I was looking through your bookshelves trying to find something to read, I spotted your *Baby-Sitters Club* books, took a look inside and saw the inscription.'

'Okay,' he conceded, only because he found himself desperate to know about Max. 'I'll tell you, but only if you tell the Max story first.'

'Fine.' She exhaled loudly, blowing her fringe out of her face. 'I met Max when I was flying in the NT. His family own a massive station not far from Katherine. We had a whirlwind romance. I was smitten and he proposed after four weeks of us being together, so I thought he was too. Two years we did the long-distance thing. I always did the mustering season with his family, but the rest of the year I followed the work. Although I visited whenever I could, it was never for long, and sometimes months went by when we didn't see each other except on Skype. We were going to get married on the station—all my family and friends were travelling up—and then two weeks before our wedding, the night before I was due up there, his sister called me in tears.'

Liam's heart skipped a beat as he imagined where this was heading. Lots of accidents happened on farms, and stations in the outback were a long way from medical assistance. 'Did he die?'

'No.' Her nostrils flared. 'Although after I found out what he'd done, he was lucky I didn't dismember him. Apparently, he'd been sleeping with their casual workers, sometimes even tourists who came to stay on the station. Keri, his sister, didn't know how many women there'd been for sure, but it was definitely not just a one-off.'

'Bastard! Did you confront him?'

'Damn straight I did.' Henri reached out and ran a hand over Sheila's fur. 'He didn't deny it and I wouldn't say he apologised either. He thought I was overreacting cancelling the wedding. He said I was lucky to have him because not many blokes would put up with a Mrs who worked away from home most of the year, that no red-blooded male could go such long stretches without sex. I should have accepted that he had needs that had to be fulfilled when I wasn't around.'

Liam realised his fists were clenched, his nails digging into his palms. 'Hadn't he heard of his right hand?'

She snorted. 'Apparently not. Although that would probably have required too much work on his part.'

'If he was so desperate to get laid, how often did he visit you?' Max should have been travelling to the ends of the earth to see her, not the other way around.

'Once or twice. In hindsight, it's easy to see I was the one making most of the effort.'

'It sounds like you're better off without him.'

'Oh I am. Hundred per cent. I'm just thankful I found out before we tied the knot.'

'How long ago was this?'

She took a moment as if calculating in her head. 'Just over six years.'

'And have there been any other serious relationships since?'

'Nope. Turns out Max was right. Most men do want a partner who's around on a daily basis.'

Henri sounded resigned to this, but it didn't seem fair that she had to choose between love and a career. What man had to make such a sacrifice? Liam bet most of her male colleagues had girlfriends or wives faithfully waiting for them at home. And surely there was a guy somewhere who'd see that Henri was a woman worth waiting for too.

Not him, of course. But someone.

'Anyway,' she angled herself a little on the pillows so that she was looking directly at him, 'enough of my sorry story. Tell me about Katie. Why did she give you *Baby-Sitters Club* books? Forgive me if I'm being judgemental, but I can't imagine they were the types of books you *chose* to read?'

Suddenly he wished he'd brought whiskey upstairs when he got the apple pie. 'You ever do anything when you were a kid to get a guy to notice you?'

'When I was a *kid*?' She raised her eyebrows. 'Less than two weeks ago I made up a crazy scheme about needing a fake boyfriend to get a guy to notice me.'

He laughed—if he didn't know Eileen Brady, he'd suddenly be worried.

'Well, when I was about eleven, I got it in my head that if I pretended to like *The Baby-Sitters Club*, it would give me something to talk about with my neighbour who was super into them, and who I'd had a crush on since I knew there was a difference between boys and girls.'

'Did it work?'

'You saw the books, didn't you? Katie and I became good friends—totally ruined my street cred with the boys but these are the sacrifices you have to make for love.'

It was Henri's turn to laugh. '*And*?'

'And what?'

'I'm not buying that's all there is to that story. You kept the books, which tells me Katie was more than a childhood crush. Did you guys ever get together?'

This was where he could lie, but that didn't feel fair after she'd just ripped open her wound for him.

'Yeah, we did. We were friends for years first—I read the whole damn series of books, even though they made me want to poke my eyes out. And then in high school, I got her an after-school job at the store. I can't exactly pinpoint when we became a couple, we just kind of did.'

'So you went to the prom together? Did your school yearbook say "couple most likely to get married" or something? All that American shit?'

'Hey! It's not shit. I'll have you know we not only went to the prom, we were crowned prom king and queen.' He still had the sash in the bottom of his wardrobe to prove it.

'Do you have photos? I'd kill to see them.'

'No,' he lied.

'So, how long were you guys together?'

'Eight years. We did long-distance too, while we were at college, but we both came back to work in my family business.'

'Oh my God.' Henri's smile faltered and she slapped a hand against her chest. 'Katie didn't die in the shooting too, did she?'

'No. Nothing like that. She was at the Monument store when it happened as well.'

'Thank goodness,' she breathed, then reached out and squeezed his hand. 'You know, you don't have to tell me any more if you don't want.'

'It's fine. There's not much else to tell.' He withdrew his hand and yanked it through his hair. 'Long story short, Katie found someone else. She married him and I sold up the businesses and moved to the other side of the world. Happy ending for both of us.'

'She found someone else after the *shooting*? She left you after you'd lost all your family?'

The incredulity in her voice had Sheila lifting her head to see what the fuss was about. He could tell Henri thought Katie was no better than Max.

'It wasn't her fault,' he said, feeling defensive on the part of the woman who'd been the love of his life for almost a decade.

'If you think that, you're far more charitable than I am,' Henri said, and then tried to stifle a yawn.

Liam reached for his phone to check the time. He couldn't believe it was almost 3 am. What on earth had possessed him to spend half the night sitting in bed with a woman, eating apple pie and talking about his damn feelings?

That simply wasn't something he did, yet here they were.

And he was the one who'd fetched the pie and opened the conversation about previous relationships. His chest cramped at the realisation.

'Guess it's time we call it a night. I need my beauty sleep.' He tried for lighthearted as he slid down the bed to rest his head on the pillows.

What he really felt like doing was tearing back the sheet and going to sleep on the couch, but what kind of a dick would that make him?

Henri reached over to switch off the bedside lamp and then snuggled into him. 'Goodnight,' she whispered before placing a quick kiss on his bare chest.

The room went black, and the only noise was the distant waves coming in through the open window and his own heavy breathing as Liam lay there, unable to get to sleep.

'You awake?' Her question startled him about five minutes after they'd said goodnight.

He swallowed. 'Yeah, why?'

Maybe she wanted to jump his bones one more time before dawn. And maybe he'd let her. It might help the tension currently pulsing through his veins.

'I just remembered something I need to ask. Do you have any food allergies?'

'Huh?' That was the last thing he'd been expecting. 'Why?'

'Mum wants to make sure there's nothing on the menu Christmas Day that could give anyone an anaphylactic shock. Ever since she accidentally—'

He pulled sharply away from her. 'I'm not spending Christmas Day with your family.'

'What? But that's part of pretending to be in a relationship with me.'

'I *never* agreed to that.'

'My boyfriend would come to Christmas lunch—Mum would expect it. Isn't the pub closed anyway? Do you have somewhere else to be?'

'I draw the line at Christmas,' he said, ignoring her question. 'I've gone along with this farce in every other way, but I don't do Christmas with anyone. And that's not negotiable.'

'*Farce*?' Hurt flashed in Henri's eyes. 'I … What do you usually do Christmas Day?'

'I drink.' He'd told her almost every other damn thing about himself—she might as well know the ugly truth. 'I drink until I get very, very drunk and then I drink some more until I pass out.'

'But I've barely seen you drink at all.'

'It's better that way.' Then before she could ask him why or try to convince him to change his mind just this once, he threw back the covers, stormed from the room and headed downstairs.

He made himself a whiskey and Coke—lighter on the latter—leaned against the bar and took a long, large gulp.

What had Henrietta Forward done to him?

Chapter Thirty-one

Henri blinked back tears as the door slammed behind Liam and Sheila, who'd scuttled off the bed after him as he'd fled the room.

What the *hell* just happened? One minute she'd been content in his arms after one of the best nights she'd had in forever, the next he'd been shoving her off as if she had some kind of contagious disease. All because she'd mentioned Christmas.

The tears broke forth and she swiped at them madly. Henri Forward did *not* cry over men. Not anymore, and especially not ones who were acting like wankers!

And Liam definitely had. Talk about overreacting. If he didn't want to be her plus-one for lunch, so be it. He didn't have to storm out like a toddler!

Sure, she'd been surprised at first, but that didn't mean she wouldn't have come round if he'd given her a few moments to digest the news. She wasn't unreasonable, she was simply tired, not to mention shocked by his aggressive reaction.

As she lay there wondering when he might come back, she tried to make sense of the way he'd behaved. Was he having second thoughts about their fling? Maybe he'd simply had enough of her and no longer wanted her in his space? Or maybe there was something deeper going on. Everything had been fine until she'd mentioned Christmas.

Oh my God. Of course.

She sat up quickly as everything clicked into place. Liam never put up Christmas decorations in the pub or played festive music. It was a local joke that he was a bit of a Grinch. She'd even heard people calling The Palace 'Bar Humbug'.

The town didn't know why he was like this, but maybe she did. Her heart felt heavy. What an insensitive fool she'd been.

Of course he wouldn't want to spend Christmas Day with *her* family when he'd never see any of his own ever again. As much as the idea of anyone being alone at Christmas didn't sit right with Henri, she *did* understand and the tears scrolling down her cheeks morphed from angry to melancholic.

She needed to talk to him. She needed to tell him she understood and that it was okay. If he didn't want to do Christmas with her family, that was fine. If he wanted to be alone she'd respect that, but maybe she could suggest the two of them spend the day together instead? They could go for a drive and do some more geocaching. There were still four days until Christmas; surely her ankle would be better by then.

Her mother wouldn't be pleased, but right now she was more concerned about Liam than anything else.

Already feeling a little better, she switched on the bedside lamp, threw back the sheet and swung into a sitting position, only to realise her problem.

Her crutches were still downstairs in the office.

She glanced around for something to use in lieu of them but found nothing. Using the bed for support, she pushed herself to a stand and then, slowly lifting her good foot off the ground, tested her weight on the bad one.

Pain shot from her ankle right up to her hip. Swear words spewing from her mouth, she flopped back onto the bed. She couldn't help thinking that if her ankle was still this bad, maybe it wouldn't be better by the time she had to leave the day after Boxing Day.

But she'd worry about that later. Right now, her only concern was checking on Liam. Making things right between them again.

Absentmindedly rubbing at her ankle, she eyed her mobile sitting on the bedside table. This wasn't the kind of conversation she wanted to have over the phone, but what choice did she have? She could hardly hop all the way downstairs, and what if he wasn't there? For all she knew, he could have gone into the studio or further afield.

She sighed and reached for the phone, her finger only hovering a few moments over his name before she pressed call.

Moments later, a ringing sounded from the floor on the other side of the bed.

'Dammit!' She threw her mobile down.

Of course he hadn't taken his; people in a state like he'd been in didn't think about stuff like that, but hopefully that meant he hadn't gone far.

And, he'd have to come back eventually.

Predicting she wouldn't be able to sleep until he did, Henri picked up her book and once again attempted to immerse herself in the pages.

* * *

Whiskey burning his mouth, Liam slammed his glass down onto the bar and stared into it as if it might have the answers to the mysteries of the universe. It didn't. He knew *that* from experience, yet still he lifted it back up and took another sip.

Just in case.

Seconds later, repulsion washed through him as the liquid slithered down his throat. What a total asshole he'd been to Henri. She didn't deserve the way he'd stormed out like a spoilt brat, simply because she'd made an assumption he'd join her family on Christmas Day. And it wasn't a crazy assumption either. They were, after all, trying to fool her mother into thinking they had a future together. They'd come *this* far; would it have killed him to help her out one more day?

It was just a day after all. It might be the only day of the year he blocked out the rest of the world and let himself properly mourn his family, but did it have to be *that* day? He could always close the pub for two days in a row instead of the usual one and make Boxing Day the day in which he drank himself into a stupor.

He could also use it to mourn Henri's departure, to mourn what had turned out to be an unexpected couple of weeks and undoubtedly the best sex of his life.

But no, aside from the fact he wouldn't be able to avoid decorations and carols and other Christmas traditions that always brought the worst possible memories, spending such a monumental day with a woman's family was all kinds of serious. And after their deep-and-meaningful conversation upstairs less than an hour ago, things already felt far too serious for his liking. They were supposed to be having meaningless sex, but the problem was it felt anything but meaningless. In their short time together, she'd rocked his world in a way that a fuck buddy was not supposed to do.

He lost his head around her. Take tonight for instance—the last time he'd had sex without protection was his very first time. He'd been a fumbling teenager, believing that risking pregnancy was better than the mortification of having to buy condoms.

But it wasn't just the sex. He thought of the last couple of nights when he'd slept all the while holding Henri close. Not only had he not been visited by horrible flashbacks from his past, but he'd also had the best sleep he'd had since the shooting. Maybe he was just exhausted; it had only been a few nights. Didn't necessarily mean anything.

Perhaps he was all over the place simply because this time of year messed with his head. Everything always felt worse in December. He'd been insane to embark on an affair this close to the anniversary of his family's death.

Liam picked up the glass again, and only when he tried to lift it to his lips did he realise his hands were trembling. No, trembling didn't even come close—they were honest-to-God convulsing. As if he were a junkie coming down from a high. And in a way that's how he felt. He wanted Henri like an addict wanted their next hit.

This was not good.

It was too much. He had too much feeling pumping through his veins. He should go upstairs and apologise, but he didn't want her to see him like this.

Still, sitting down here in the dark, trying to numb his emotions with booze wasn't a good idea either. He'd spent years working hard not to become that person and he didn't want to throw it all away.

Slamming the glass down, he whistled to Sheila, who'd curled into a ball in her usual spot behind the bar, and then he headed outside. Usually the warm, salty evening air in Bunyip Bay was like a balm to his soul, but tonight even being in the open air felt claustrophobic.

He picked up his pace as he headed towards the beach so that by the time he got there, he was running. He didn't stop as his feet hit the cool sand; he wanted to run until his calves and lungs burned so hard that he couldn't think about anything but the physical pain.

Although mostly dark on the beach, there was already the hint of dawn lighting his way just enough to see where he was going. Sheila ran alongside him, tiny crabs scuttling away into the ocean as they approached. He must have gone a couple of kilometres before she collapsed in exhaustion. Liam didn't notice straight away, and by the time he sensed he was alone and turned to look, the dog was a good hundred metres behind him lying in the sand.

'Fuck.'

He sprinted back towards her, almost tripping over his own feet in his desperation to get to her. He'd never forgive himself if the old girl had a heart attack or something because he'd pushed her too hard.

The hundred metres felt like a hundred kilometres, but finally he dropped to his knees and put his hand against Sheila's thankfully heaving side. She lifted her head slightly to look up at him, before flopping it back down onto the sand.

'Thank God,' he breathed, burying his head in her speckled fur as tears spilled down his cheeks.

What a night. Yet, although his calves were burning and his heart still racing, his mind had not switched off. His head was still full of Henri and how right it felt having her around, having her in his bed of course, but also in his heart. As much as he didn't want to admit it, he suddenly knew with absolute certainty that he hadn't felt this intensely about someone since Katie.

But he and Katie had been kids—practically babies. Two friends learning about sex and intimacy and what it meant to be a couple. Two innocents who perhaps didn't even know the meaning of the word love.

Love?

Blood rushed to his head, and he saw spots in front of his eyes. Is *that* what he felt for Henri?

No, he couldn't. They'd known each other such a short time and he didn't allow himself to get to know the women he slept with.

But that there was the problem. Henri had snuck under his defences when they were merely pretending to be together. The difference between her and other women he'd slept with was that they'd become friends. Almost without him realising. One soul-baring conversation at a time, she'd succeeded in knocking down almost every one of his walls.

And this realisation scared the living hell out of him. Because love hurt. Love meant opening your heart to the possibility of loss. Losing his family and then Katie had almost destroyed him, and—thanks to her career—Henri would have to be one of the worst people in the world to fall in love with. Even though he'd tried to help her overcome her trauma, he hadn't forgotten the statistics her mom had parroted at him.

The incidence of death and injury among ag pilots is over one hundred times Australia's national average for all other work-related injuries.

Henri was one hundred times more likely to die than everyone else he knew. That may not be a rational thought, but it still felt like a punch to the guts.

Because he loved her. Whether or not he wanted to admit it, he was abso-fucking-lutely head over heels and there was nothing he could do to stop it.

But was the happiness he felt when he was with Henri—the lightness that had been absent from his life since the shooting—worth the risk? The thought of not being with her was almost as terrifying as the thought of being with her.

He would never be the guy that asked Henri to stop flying, so he'd always be on edge every time she was out of his sight. Every time she was up in the air, his heart would be up in his throat, wondering if he'd ever see her again. Ever hold her. Ever talk to her again.

He sighed and shoved his fingers through Sheila's fur, looking for solace and maybe some kind of answers in her warmth.

But it wasn't the dog that brought clarity; it was the realisation as he stared out at the vast, choppy ocean that he was almost in exactly the same spot, almost ten years to the day, that he'd decided to take his own life.

That couldn't be a coincidence. It had to be a sign. A reminder.

When he'd stopped in Bunyip Bay after coming down the north coast of Western Australia, he'd been almost certain this idyllic spot would be his last. He'd been contemplating suicide for almost three years; travelling to Australia had been his last-ditch attempt to find meaning in his life. But as much as he'd enjoyed seeing all the amazing sights—the Great Barrier Reef, Uluru, the beautiful gorges of the Kimberleys—none of it gave him what he was looking for.

He was exhausted. He was tired of running. He couldn't handle the pain any longer and the thought of facing yet another Christmas alone had finally pushed him over the edge.

His first couple of years in Australia, he'd stayed in youth hostels—not that he needed to, but it felt extravagant splashing out on fancy hotels or resorts just for him, and the shiny marble bathrooms and fluffy white towels always reminded him of his mom. It didn't feel right to be enjoying such luxuries when she couldn't, when none of his family could. Generally, he liked the people he met at hostels more than those he shared the elevators with in five-star hotels anyway.

But Christmas in hostels was unbearable.

Yes, there were lots of other single people without family to spend the day with, but for most of them that was simply because they were having an adventure far from home and they partied hard while making the most of it.

Liam never felt like partying anymore, least of all in December when every single decoration, Christmas carol and Santa hat reminded him of the worst day of his life.

So that year, he hadn't booked anywhere to stay. He'd decided he wasn't going to need it anyway. Unless he took his life in a hotel room, but that didn't seem fair on whoever found him. He'd contemplated the best way to do it, always stumbling at the thought of the stranger who would discover him. What if a kid found him? He already felt enough guilt on earth; he didn't want to take even more into the afterlife with him. Not that he believed in an afterlife, but that was beside the point.

He'd been thinking about exactly this as he swam in the bay and had come to the conclusion that swimming out as far as he could go, until he could swim no more, and letting the ocean take him would be the best option. It was unlikely anyone would ever notice him missing. Perhaps a shark would get him and if not, hopefully his body would drift somewhere far, far away where nobody would ever find him.

And what better place to say goodbye than in Bunyip Bay, which had to be one of the most beautiful beaches he'd seen across all of Australia?

Feeling calmer than he had in years, he'd gone to The Palace for his final meal and a few beers, planning to come back down to the beach that night and swim out to the horizon. If he hadn't met Arthur McArthur, he felt certain he'd have followed through, but the old publican had seen something in his eyes.

When he'd brought him his dinner and a pint, he'd sat across the table from him and asked him questions that his therapist had asked him in the early days, but without the tone or the watching of the clock that had always made him feel like shit.

Arthur had listened. Really listened.

Liam couldn't even explain it, but there'd been something about Arthur that had made all the difference to him. He suddenly saw an alternative option—a path where he could try and make a difference to others in the same way.

He hadn't killed himself, obviously. Instead, he'd bought the pub and thrown his heart and soul into running it, but neither had he forgotten that dark, dark time. He'd made a life for himself here, but he worked hard every day to keep his demons at bay—he swam, he made things, he helped others, and he also took anti-depressants.

His demons. Demons that had pushed Katie away.

Demons that could hurt Henri in the same way. The last week had been fun, but it couldn't stay that way forever. If they got together properly, there would be days, weeks, when he struggled to get out of bed, and that was the kind of burden Henri didn't need in her life. Possibly he was jumping the gun; he wasn't even sure she felt the same way about him as he did about her, but he couldn't take the risk.

Liam sat with Sheila, watching the sun come up, and then, his heart heavy, he did what he needed to do. This wasn't just about self-preservation.

Most importantly, it was what was best for Henri.

Chapter Thirty-two

Sometime just before dawn, Henri managed to fall asleep and didn't wake till just after nine to the feeling of someone hovering nearby. Suddenly remembering how last night had ended, she opened her eyes, expecting to see Liam, and shrieked at the sight of her sister standing there instead.

'What the hell are *you* doing here?'

'And it's lovely to see you too.' Tilley smiled as she held up her crutches. 'Liam called—he said you needed a lift home. He sent these up with me, because although he might be happy carrying you around like a baby, I'm not breaking my back on your account.'

Her words were clearly meant to be funny, but Henri didn't laugh. 'Liam *called* you to come and get me?'

'That's what I said.'

'And he's downstairs?' She wondered if he'd come back into the apartment at all. But surely she'd have woken up if he did? 'You *saw* him?'

'With my own eyes.' Tilley's smile dimmed a little as uncertainty crept in.

Henri's heart deflated. He was obviously okay—he hadn't drunk himself to oblivion or driven into a ditch; he just didn't want to see her. His actions made that glaringly clear. It was surprising he hadn't packed her bag himself. Of course that would mean he'd actually have had to come up here and face her. Instead he'd sent Tilley to come and evict her. What a coward!

She could refuse to leave, stage some kind of protest, but she had more dignity than that.

'What's going on? Have you guys had a fight or something?'

Henri couldn't help snorting bitterly. 'Can you technically have a fight if you're not actually in a relationship?'

Whoops. She hadn't meant to say that out loud, but the cat was out of the bag now. What did it matter anyway?

'Hang on.' Tilley rested the crutches against the bed. 'I thought … I don't … you're *not* together?'

'No. That was all a ruse.'

'Huh?' She shook her head. 'Then why are you wearing his shirt and sleeping in his bed?'

Henri sighed. 'It's a long story.'

'I'm listening. Macy's at Caitlin's house and I don't have to be at the shop until lunchtime.' As if Tilley's big-sister voice wasn't insistent enough, she also rose her eyebrows and crossed her arms.

Henri knew there was no point trying to lie and she didn't have the energy anyway. 'Can I tell you in the car? I just want to get out of here.'

'Okay, fine.'

Henri instructed Tilley to collect her things and stuff them all into her overnight bag and in less than two minutes, they were on their way.

Tilley closed the apartment door behind them and they began the walk of shame. Would Liam be downstairs? Would they run into him on their way out? Henri didn't know if she wanted that or not. While part of her yearned to yell and scream and give him what for—for treating her like she was the kind of pest Phil McDonald dealt with—a much bigger part of her was this close to bursting into tears.

Which was ridiculous and only irritated her further. It had to be the shock and rage combined with pure mortification, because a non-relationship shouldn't hurt this damn much and she refused to consider that she might be falling in love with him. She didn't do love any more than she did crying.

Getting down the stairs with her crutches required monumental effort. Twice, she almost tripped. More than once Henri wanted to whack her sister with her crutches, but in the interests of getting out of the pub as fast as possible, she resisted.

Downstairs, there was no sign of Liam. There was no sign of anyone, except for Janet, who was cleaning up in the dining room. Henri prayed her mum's friend wouldn't see them, but of course she had no such luck.

'Henrietta! Matilda! Is that you girls?' she asked, which had to be the most stupid question because Janet had working eyes last time Henri checked and she was only a few metres away from them.

'Hi, Janet,' Tilley slightly raised the hand that was carrying Henri's overnight bag.

'What are you two up to?'

Tilley looked to Henri, then back to Janet as if she wasn't sure what to say.

'Henri can't drive because of her ankle,' Tilley said eventually, 'and she needs—'

'I've got somewhere to be.' She was becoming quite the champion of fabricating the truth, although she *did* need to get the morning after pill. But there was no way she could ask for that at the local pharmacy—for sure someone would overhear and, although it was no secret that she didn't want kids, she didn't want her dirty laundry being discussed on the main street.

Imagine if she *was* pregnant. If Liam had reacted this badly to her request for him to spend a few hours at the farm on Christmas Day, she didn't dare think about how he'd react if she were actually up the duff.

Not that she'd be at all happy about that either. Though if there were a man she'd consider it for, it would be him. If it meant waking up every day in Liam's bed, she might even give up flying.

Oh my God. Give up *flying*? A cold clamminess cramped her chest. *Shit!* Usually an expert at keeping sex separate from emotion, she'd failed dismally this time.

She'd gone and fallen in love instead.

For the first time since Max, Henri couldn't help wishing she had a career that didn't make a relationship impossible to maintain. But it was all a moot point anyway, because she'd gone and fallen in love with a man who was as emotionally unavailable as the wood he crafted into beautiful art.

At first, she'd put his reticence down to the loss of his family—some kind of self-protection against that kind of hurt again, maybe even some kind of survivor guilt. But last night when he spoke about Kate, it became clear there was so much more to it. He was still hung up on her. Probably still in love with her. Henri didn't buy for a moment his line about her marrying someone else and him moving to Australia being a happy ever after for everyone!

She wished with every last molecule that made her that she could be the woman to heal him and help him move on from the hurts in his past, but he'd made it blatantly clear that he didn't feel the same way about her, and she wasn't going to make a fool of herself chasing after something that wasn't meant to be.

She felt Tilley's hand against her arm. 'You okay? You look like you're about to faint.'

'I'm fine, it's just my ankle. Hard being on it too long.'

Tilley nodded. 'Of course. I'm sorry, Janet, but I've got to get Hens to the car.'

Henri was already hobbling towards the door, and despite the crutches, her sister had to walk fast to keep up with her as she headed for the four-wheel drive.

'What exactly is going on?' Tilley asked, once the crutches were safely deposited across the back seat and she'd climbed into the driver's side. 'You're acting very weird.'

'You said you don't need to be at the shop till lunchtime? Can you take me to Geraldton, please?'

'*Geraldton*? Why? Do you need to do some last-minute Christmas shopping or something? We've actually got some pretty cool gifts at The Ag Store—I'm trying to expand the business.'

'No. I don't need presents. I … I need to get the morning after pill.'

'Hang on …' Tilley had just turned the key in the ignition, but instead of reversing like Henri willed her to, she turned and scrutinised her. 'I thought you said you and Liam weren't actually together, so how could you possibly need—'

'*Please*, just take me and I'll explain everything on the way.'

'Fine. But you're buying me a coffee when we get there, because playing taxi was not what I had in mind for my kid-free morning.'

Henri breathed a sigh of relief; coffee she could do.

'Time to start explaining, little sister,' Tilley said when they were two minutes outside of Bunyip Bay and Henri still hadn't said a word.

'You know that first night I stayed over at the pub?'

Tilley nodded. 'Sure, the night we all had dinner and I was trying to get you to come back to my house because I was worried that you'd drive home drunk.'

'I would never drive home drunk! Just because I'm the youngest, you all treat me like a baby, but I'm not stupid.'

'*Sor*-ry,' Tilley said, sounding more like a teenage girl rather than the almost forty-year-old woman she was.

'Anyway,' Henri continued, 'I did spend the night in Liam's bed but not for the reason I said later. I was so tired that the drinks went to my head and I passed out on a couch in the pub. I guess Liam found me there when he closed up and he took me upstairs and put me in his bed.'

'He didn't take advantage of you when you were drunk?!'

'No, *of course* not. Liam would never do anything like that. He slept on his couch and then made me breakfast the next morning. That would probably have been it, if I didn't run into Eileen Brady at the IGA afterwards.'

Henri explained everything—how the town busybody had started casting aspersions about Liam, which got her goat and caused her to make up something outrageous.

'That's crazy,' Tilley said as she sped up to overtake a massive road train. 'Why didn't you just tell her she was being a narrow-minded, judgemental bigot? It's not like you to hold back your opinions.'

'Because the moment I said it, it suddenly seemed like a good idea.' When Tilley hit her with a sideways glance, Henri continued, 'Since I got home, Mum had been blathering on again about me finding a suitable match, you know how she does—listing off potential husbands without any care as to whether the guy is actually someone I'd choose for myself—'

'I'll admit she can be a little intense sometimes, but she—'

'*You're* not really any better. That night I had dinner with you and Frankie and everyone in the pub, you were all ganging up on me about my non-existent love-life. The moment I lied to Mrs Brady about me and Liam, I realised it was the perfect way to get you all to leave me alone.'

'I'm sorry.' Tilley sounded genuine this time. 'None of us meant anything by it. We just love you and we worry about you being alone and away from home all the time.'

'I'm *fine*. I like my job but when I come home for the holidays, it'd be nice if I didn't have to put up with everyone trying to fix things in my life that aren't broken.'

'I'm sorry,' Tilley said again.

'Would you stop apologising? It doesn't matter now anyway.'

'Okay. And Liam agreed to this?'

'Obviously,' Henri replied, realising how crazy it was that he actually did. Perhaps he'd always intended to seduce her into a fling? 'Don't you believe me?'

'Oh, I believe you,' Tilley said, sounding amused. 'It makes so much more sense than what you originally led us to believe.'

'What do you mean?'

'Well, if you'd said from the beginning that you'd had a one-night stand with Liam, I'd have totally bought it, but the way you made it sound like a relationship heading for commitment after being back in town five minutes? That didn't ring true for two people who, up until then, all evidence pointed to being commitment-phobes.'

'I'm not a commitment-phobe, I'm a realist.'

Tilley didn't comment on this. 'It might have been more credible if you hadn't started staying over there almost every night, but that felt like you were trying too hard to look legit.'

'Why didn't you say anything?'

Tilley shrugged. 'Maybe I'm not actually as interfering as you seem to believe. I wasn't sure what you were up to, but it also wasn't my business, and every time I saw you together I thought maybe I was wrong.'

'Do you think Mum suspected anything?'

'Noooo. She's so desperate for someone who lives in the Bay to sink their claws into you and keep you here that she only saw what she wanted to.' Tilley glanced across at her. 'What are you planning to do when you leave? Are you going to keep pretending to be together indefinitely?'

'No. I was going to tell Mum on Boxing Day that we'd decided to end things. I was going to say we broke up because Liam, like her, didn't want me to keep flying.'

'Oh, she'll hate you and love him for that.'

'That was the idea. Hopefully she'll have forgiven me by the time I come home again.'

'If not, you can always stay with Liam.' Tilley cackled as if that was the funniest thing ever. 'So, you've just been staying over at his place because of the charade?'

Henri looked out the window, so Tilley couldn't see her face. 'Something like that.'

'Well,' Tilley said, indicating to go around yet another road train. 'This story has made my day. I wish you came home more often, Hens; you certainly make life more exciting.'

Henri didn't bother replying, and instead switched on the radio. The latest song by Lady Gaga filled the car. Neither of them said anything else until they were just passing the 'Welcome to Geraldton' sign, then Tilley reached out and shut off the music.

'Hang on,' she said, looking away from the road long enough to frown at Henri. 'If all this was just a ruse, then why do you need the morning after pill?'

Busted. Heat flooded Henri's cheeks, but it wasn't embarrassment so much as anguish. She couldn't bring herself to tell her sister the whole truth—it would be too painful to say aloud.

'Well, pretending to be together meant a lot of fake kisses and a lot of fake touching. We got a little carried away last night.' If Tilley chose to believe it was *only* last night, that was her prerogative.

'Carried away as in you had *sex*?'

Henri didn't need to look at her sister to know she was grinning like a lunatic.

'Yes! What else would I mean? But it was just that. Just sex. It doesn't mean anything, so don't go reading anything into things,' she snapped and pointed up ahead. 'I think there's a chemist just off the corner on the next road.'

'Don't bite my head off,' Tilley said after another minute's silence, 'but you seem pretty wound up over a one-night stand that didn't mean anything.'

'I'm just annoyed we forgot to use a bloody condom and I have to go and sort it out. I'm also annoyed that I can't do it myself because of this damn ankle.'

Henri was fairly certain her sister didn't buy the story but for once Tilley didn't push the issue, and for that she was grateful.

Chapter Thirty-three

By the time Liam opened the pub that evening, the whole town knew that he and Henri Forward had called it quits. He'd known the moment he saw Lara's face when she came down to start work and the first words off her tongue confirmed it.

'Are you okay?' Her head cocked to one side, she reached out to squeeze his arm.

It was all he could do not to shake her off.

'Why wouldn't I be?' he said, focusing on putting the float into the register so she couldn't see his face.

'I heard about you and Henri. I'm so sorry.'

He slammed the register shut a little harder than he meant to and the clang of coins inside echoed in the otherwise quiet bar. Sheila looked up from her usual spot and glared at him.

'Who told you?'

Turned out that Lara had heard the news from Melinda at the post office, who'd heard it from Mike the cop, who'd heard it from none other than Eileen Bloody Brady. How that woman found out he had no clue, but he guessed Henri must have told someone, and it took off from there. Good news travels fast in the country!

He wondered what exactly she'd said—whether she'd confessed the whole thing had been a farce or if she'd gone with her original plan, just a few days earlier. He briefly contemplated calling Henri so they could get their stories straight, but immediately saw this for what it was. Merely an excuse to hear her voice.

His phone had felt heavy in his pocket all day. Almost every second he'd been berating himself for handling things the way he did, wondering if she'd ring or at least reply to the message he'd sent saying he was sorry, but he didn't think it was a good idea to keep seeing each other. He wasn't proud of that message, and a real man wouldn't have sent her sister to do his dirty work, but he honestly hadn't trusted himself to follow through.

Of course, she hadn't replied. She was either fuming or simply didn't care, and he desperately hoped it was the latter.

The only action his phone had seen all day was a text from Sally reminding him Sheila was due for her heartworm injection and a sales rep wanting to talk to him about a new brand of non-alcoholic gin.

'Do you want to take the night off?' Lara asked, coming back behind the bar as the fly strips parted to reveal a couple of tourists. 'I'm sure Dylan wouldn't mind working. And Mondays are usually quiet, so we'll be fine to hold the fort.'

She was right—Mondays and Tuesdays were his slow nights, which is why he made do with a skeleton staff. But he didn't *do* nights off, and the last thing he needed was to spend the evening upstairs alone with nothing but Netflix, Sheila, and a tub of cookies and cream ice-cream like some kind of pathetic character in a rom-com.

'Thanks, but I'll be fine.' He forced a smile for the couple as they stepped up to the bar. 'Good evening, welcome to The Palace. What can I get for you?'

Only two hours later he was wishing he'd taken Lara and Dylan up on the offer.

Mondays might usually be dead—even this close to Christmas—but tonight there was a steady flow of locals dropping in to see him. Most of them didn't even order a drink!

Clearly Henri hadn't confessed to the charade, and he didn't know how many more 'sorry to hear things didn't work out with you and Henri Forward's he could take. Not to mention the casseroles that arrived along with the sympathy—sweet, but totally unnecessary considering he had a cook on the payroll. By 6 pm the fridge was overflowing with containers. Even Eileen Brady had delivered him a large tuna mornay. Although he guessed it was more because she wanted to grill him on what had happened than because she actually cared, he managed to thank her politely and not berate her for this whole damn mess being partly her fault!

Not that the casseroles wouldn't be delicious—these women knew how to cook almost as good as Macca—but Liam's appetite had vanished along with Henri and his enthusiasm for doing anything. He'd tried his best today to continue as normal, to do the things he usually did to fill his day and keep his mind healthy—swimming, woodwork, cleaning out the storeroom until the cement floor actually sparkled—but still the hours had been long and painful. Just the thought of not seeing Henri tonight, of not seeing her any night, made everything seem pointless.

He knew he'd made the right decision—she deserved so much more than he could give—but how could doing the right thing feel so bloody wrong? He told himself it was still early days. That it might *feel* like twenty years since he'd seen her, but it wasn't even twenty-four hours.

For the first time in his life, he found himself counting down to Christmas. He'd be okay after he'd taken his annual day to reset and, after Henri was gone, perhaps his heart would stop hitching every time someone stepped into the pub.

He retreated to the kitchen as much as possible—thankfully it was Macca's day off, so Liam needed to be in there flipping burgers anyway—but there were only a few orders for dinner and every time he came out there was someone wanting to pry into his business under the guise of concern. From what he could gather, Henri had explained very little. He was tempted to tell everyone that it had all been a joke, but he didn't want them getting angry at her for fooling them all.

'It was a mutual decision,' became his mantra. 'Although we get along well and had a lot of fun together, we realised our lifestyles weren't compatible long term. I'm fine, honestly.'

At about eight o'clock, Lara cleared her throat as she looked through the hatch into the kitchen. 'Really sorry, Liam, but I need to pop to the loo. Are you okay to man the bar?'

'Of course,' he replied. He couldn't hide away forever. 'I'll be out in a sec.'

Thankfully the pub was empty, except for Rex and the tourist couple who'd come in earlier—they were making a night of it. That was the joy of being on vacation, every night was a Friday. They could stay as long as they wanted; Liam didn't think he'd be getting any sleep tonight anyway.

He nodded to his most faithful patron's near-empty glass. Was it his second or third pint of the evening? Had Lara served him while he'd been in the kitchen? 'Want another one?' he asked, taking a risk.

Rex's bushy eyebrows rose, making Liam think the nightly quota had already been met, but he was too braindead to worry. 'Don't mind if I do. Thanks, mate.'

As Liam went to grab a fresh glass, he noticed something out of the corner of his eye. Or rather a lack of something. Or rather someone. Slamming the glass on the bar, his heart shot to his throat. 'Where's Sheila?'

Rex shifted on his stool and gestured to the door. 'Over there. Guess the old girl wanted a change of scenery.'

Liam let out a long breath at the sight of his dog sitting just inside the pub like one of those heavy stone doorstop statues. His heart squeezed—he wasn't the only one who'd fallen for Henri, but at least he knew the reason for her absence. If only he could explain it to Sheila. Would she understand? He suspected life wasn't so complicated in canine country.

Almost wishing he were a dog himself, he picked up the glass again and put it under the tap as Rex downed the dregs of his previous pint. It was the first thing that amused Liam all day and he stifled a smile. Rex had to be one of the stingiest people he'd ever met and always drank every last drop to make sure he got his money's worth.

'You'll never guess what I found at the tip today,' Rex said as Liam placed the full glass in front of him.

'What's that?' The last time Rex had been excited about a tip find, it had been a blow-up, plastic sex doll with a hole in it, and not the kind of hole most people wanted in such a doll! Another time it was a bunch of old spoons—the cheap kind that tourists buy on vacation. Sure, one man's junk was another man's treasure, but Liam didn't think there were many people who'd get worked up about the things Rex did.

His mind drifted, wondering what Henri was doing right now. Watching some stupid Christmas movie? Making a voodoo doll that looked the spitting image of him? A tiny part of him wondered if she might show up as usual. If maybe because he hadn't answered her calls she'd decide to have it out with him face to face.

Rex banged his fist against the bar, startling Liam from his rumination. 'Are you even listening to a word I'm saying?'

'Maybe if you ever said something interesting I would!'

The moment the words were out, Liam regretted them. The hurt that flashed across Rex's face only made him feel more like pond scum than he already did. He was pretty much the guy's only friend and friends listened, even to the boring stuff.

'I'm sorry,' he said. 'What was it you found?'

'Ah, never mind.' Rex took another sip of his beer, the froth lingering on his unruly moustache. 'What's going on here tonight anyway? Why all the casseroles? And why the long face? Has someone bloody died?'

'Not that I know of.'

'Well, *something's* got your goat. Has it got to do with that Forward girl?' Rex glanced at the large tarnished watch on his wrist—another tip find. 'She's usually here by now, isn't she?'

Liam nodded. 'I don't think she's coming tonight.'

'Don't tell me there's trouble in paradise?' Rex asked. 'Didn't I tell you that one was bad news?'

'She's not *bad* news. It just didn't work out.' He wouldn't hear anyone say a bad word about her and told Rex the same as he'd told everyone else, while praying some other drama would happen in the Bay soon and he'd stop having to talk about his.

'Man, I'm sorry to hear that,' Rex said when Liam was finished. 'I was only joking about her being trouble. We've had a few chats over the last coupla nights, and I was starting to worry I was falling in love with her myself.'

Liam smiled sadly. What could you do? Henri Forward was all too easy to fall for.

'Is there anything I can do to help? I know women usually like talking about shit like this and I probably don't know the right words to say, but we could shoot some pool if you want? Try to take your mind off her.'

'Thanks,' Liam said, touched by the offer—he didn't even know if Rex could play pool. 'It's okay, I'll be fine, but maybe you could take some of the casseroles off my hands?'

'Really?' Rex smiled more broadly than Liam had ever seen, revealing a dimple in each cheek that looked quite out of place on such a weathered, often sullen face.

He nodded. 'You'd be doing me a huge favour.'

So, after Rex had finished his pint, he left The Palace with a swagger in his step and enough nutritious home-cooked dinners to feed him for a month.

Liam felt some consolation that at least someone was happy and his heartbreak was not completely in vain.

* * *

'Mum, can you teach me to knit?'

'What did you say?' Henri's mother looked up from where she was ironing pillowcases in front of the TV. When her dad was alive they'd both kept typical farming hours—early to bed, early to rise—but now that she was alone, her mother seemed to have taken to staying up late binge-watching the home renovation shows that had been his favourites. Henri guessed it was one way she still felt close to him. Tonight's episode appeared to be a Christmas edition set in the North Pole, which boggled her mind.

Crutches still under her arms, she ventured further into the room. 'Can you teach me to knit, please?'

Her mum switched off the iron, picked up the remote and muted the television. 'Do I have wax in my ears, or did you just say you wanted to learn to knit?'

Henri nodded.

'Wow.' She took a moment, steadying herself on the ironing board, clearly letting this staggering news sink in. 'I thought you'd gone to bed?'

That's what Henri had told her at dinner—that she needed an early night—but although she *was* exhausted, it was more to get away from her mother's fussing than anything. She'd taken one look at Henri when Tilley delivered her home and known something was wrong. What was it with mother's intuition? Henri had explained that she and Liam had broken up—not giving any reason why because she couldn't bear to explain everything—and requested to be left alone.

Of course, giving someone space wasn't something Fiona Forward was capable of. Half an hour later she was in Henri's room with a large bowl of chicken soup—as if such a dish had heart-healing properties. She didn't have the *flu*. And who made soup in the height of summer anyway? Soup wasn't the only offering either; there'd been cups of tea and slices of cake at regular intervals throughout the afternoon.

But after dinner, when her wish for peace had finally been granted, Henri found that lying on the single bed where Liam had kissed her so deliciously was not good for the soul. She'd kept picking up her phone and torturing herself by re-reading the last text he'd sent her.

Not that she needed to re-read it; it arrived when she was standing in the queue at the pharmacy waiting for the morning after pill and she now knew it off by heart. It was much shorter than the memory verses Eileen Brady had made her learn at Sunday School.

I'm sorry, Henri, but I can't help you with your charade anymore.

That was it. After all they'd done together all she deserved was a brief text?

Maybe if she could think about it logically, she'd realise that a simple text message was all that was required—they weren't even dating—but it still made her blood boil whenever she thought of it. Whenever she thought of him. Which was constantly.

That's why she'd hobbled out to the living room—she couldn't stand being alone with her thoughts any longer. She wanted someone, something, *anything* to distract her from herself.

'Couldn't sleep,' Henri said, flopping down onto the ghastly floral couch that had been bought the year she turned five.

'Missing Liam?' Mum asked gently.

'Missing the functionality of my left ankle more like it!'

All day she'd longed to be able to throw herself into work around the farm, but because of her stupid ankle she was housebound, and because of stupid Liam she was heartbroken—a state she'd vowed she'd never allow herself to be in again, which made her angry and self-loathing as well as sad. It certainly wasn't the Christmas she'd had in mind when she'd come back to Bunyip Bay, and she'd think twice before doing it again.

Next year she'd make sure she was as far away as possible. Timbuktu was looking good.

Her mum raised an eyebrow as if she didn't buy the whole ankle thing but didn't push the point. 'Okay,' she said, 'so you want to learn to knit?'

'That's what I said.' Henri had never sat still long enough to learn before, or had any desire to, but … desperate times and all.

'Crochet is easier. Do you want to start with that?'

Henri shook her head. She didn't want easy, she wanted something that required all her brain power so there wasn't any room left to think about Liam.

Without another word, her mother left the room, returning a few minutes later with the big wicker basket where she stored all her needles, patterns and spare yarn. She sat down on the couch next to Henri, plonking the basket between them.

'Pick a colour,' she said, gesturing to the balls of wool.

Henri plucked one at random—it didn't matter what colour it was.

'Now, what do you want to make? Scarves are easy to start with. Or you could try a dishtowel.'

Henri hadn't thought about making anything in particular. 'A *dishtowel*? What the hell is a dishtowel?'

'It's a tea towel, only made with wool.' When Henri screwed up her nose, she added, 'They work just as well and add a more personal touch to the kitchen.'

'What's a hard project?'

'Well, I have a book with some fabulous jumper patterns, but they're all fairly intricate and require a bit of skill.'

'I want to do one of them. The harder the better.'

'Why don't I just start by teaching you the basics and then, if you like it, you can choose a design and attempt something bigger. We'd have to buy wool especially anyway.'

'Okay,' Henri relented and picked up two thick wooden needles. These would make good weapons, she thought, rolling them between her fingers.

As if reading her mind, her mother took them off her and dumped them back in the basket. She picked up a metal pair that were much thinner instead. 'It'll be easier to learn on these.'

Then she took the wool Henri had chosen, looped it over the end of one of the needles and tied some sort of knot, before proceeding to create lots more little loops.

'Hang on … what are you doing?' Henri didn't want to sit here watching her mother knit!

'Relax, I'm just casting on for you. Trust me, you're not the first person I've taught to knit, and this is the hardest thing for a beginner to learn. Once you've mastered garter and purl, then I'll teach you how to cast on.'

Henri tapped her good foot as her mother cast on twenty-five stitches—*how hard could it actually be?*—and then proceeded to show her how to do garter stitch.

'Holding the needles like this, thumbs at the front and the rest of your fingers behind, you slip the right needle under the first loop and then behind. Then you bring the wool up and loop it over the back needle, like so. Holding the wool firmly, you pull the back needle down, slip it under the loop and then slip the loop right off the left needle. Voila!'

Voila?! Who even said that?

'Then you do it again until you get to the end of the row.'

Henri all but snatched the needles off her mother. 'Okay, my turn.' Then she stared at them frozen in her hands. 'What was the first step again?'

She repeated the steps slowly while Henri tried to follow them, but when she finally got the wool to go the right way, she pulled on the needle too vigorously and about five stitches unravelled right before her eyes. Her mother recast and then, gritting her teeth, Henri tried again, but she just couldn't seem to follow the supposedly simple instructions.

'Maybe there's a YouTube video or something I can watch?'

'Probably, it seems everything is online these days, but give yourself a break. It takes practice to get the hang of it. And patience.' Unsaid was the fact that Henri possessed very little of the latter, but she suddenly realised that for the last ten minutes she'd not thought once of Liam or the text message.

'Okay,' she said, taking a deep breath and trying again.

But it was hopeless. *She* was hopeless. Legitimately the worst. No sooner did it seem she was maybe getting the hang of it than she'd drop a whole stitch or somehow manage to do two at once. Spitting a word that usually made her mother flinch, Henri hurled her attempt across the room as tears rushed to her eyes. Why had she ever thought she could do this?

'This is stupid. What's wrong with me? Why can't I do anything well?'

'Oh, Henrietta.' Her mother picked up her hand and squeezed it. 'There's nothing wrong with you. And you're good at lots of things. I don't know anyone as good as you at flying.'

Was that actual pride she detected in her mum's voice? *No*, she had to be imagining it. And was flying really the only thing her mother could think of? If only she knew what had happened up north, she probably wouldn't even say that.

Henri snatched her hand back. 'And we all know what you think of me flying! I'm not good at the things *you* think matter—I'm not good at people, I'm not good at relationships, or love.'

'Oh, darling … Maybe it isn't over between you and Liam. Maybe this is just a hiccup, and you can work it out.'

'I don't think so.' Henri shook her head, losing the battle with tears. If she could have stood up and fled the room she would have, but her crutches were just out of reach.

Her mother stood instead and crossed over to the old piano that nobody used anymore. Its only function now was as a display unit for photo frames, trinkets and a fabric covered tissue box. She picked up the box and brought it back to Henri.

'Thanks,' Henri managed as she took one and buried her face in it.

As she tried to pull herself together, she felt her mum's hand rubbing gentle circles on her back, something she hadn't done since Henri was ten and crying because a boy had beaten her in the cross country.

'What happened between the two of you?' she asked after a while. 'I thought things were going so well. Why did you break up?'

'The truth is, Mum, it was never actually a thing in the first place.'

Her brow creased. 'What do you mean?'

'It's a long story.'

'Shall I get us a cup of tea?'

A bit like soup, her mother thought tea fixed everything. 'Do you have anything stronger?'

She patted Henri's knee. 'I'll see what I can find.' And then she headed out into the hall.

'Hopefully this will do the trick,' she said when she returned a few minutes later, carrying two glass tumblers that looked suspiciously like they contained whiskey on the rocks. 'There's still some of your father's Jack Daniels, but we didn't have any soda water.'

The whiskey had to be over four years old. Did alcohol go out of date? Henri couldn't remember but her heart ached at the thought of her dad. She wished it was him here now comforting her. Then again, if he were still alive, she'd probably never have got with Liam in the first place because he'd have put a stop to Fiona nagging about her finding the perfect bloke before everything go so out of hand.

'It's perfect,' she said, snatching one of the glasses and taking a much-needed gulp.

Her mum sat down beside her, and Henri felt a flicker of a smile as she lifted her glass and took a sip. She rarely drank but when she did, she was much more of a wine or G&T person. Henri had been questioning whether it was a good idea to come clean, but guilt swamped her at the sight of her mother drinking whiskey. For her.

Besides, she needed to get this off her chest—she was finished with lying, it was exhausting—and so she told her mother everything. All that she'd told Tilley and then some, confessing not only to the charade and the sex, but also that their fling had somehow morphed into something else. At least on her side.

'I guess I was doing such a good job of acting that I even fooled myself. I thought that what we felt was just physical and that I could do it without getting hurt, but … I guess I was wrong.'

When she was finished, Henri braced herself for a lecture about how lying never ended well, but it didn't come. Instead, when she looked at her mother, she saw tears in her eyes.

'I'm so sorry,' she said. 'I'm sorry that because of me, you felt you needed to pretend. And I'm sorry that because of me you ended up getting hurt. I didn't realise how pressured I was making you feel. I know it's no excuse, but I always had the best intentions. I just want you to be happy, but I forget sometimes that happiness isn't the same for everyone. It's hard for me to understand that you don't want love, marriage and babies.'

Henri shook her head. 'Of course I want that, Mum—well, not the babies, sorry, and not necessarily marriage either. But companionship, love, I want those things—however, life isn't a Danielle Steel novel. It just doesn't work that way for everyone, and I don't want to sacrifice who I am to get it. If I ever do settle down, it'll be with someone who's happy for me to continue to do what I love and wants to work with me to make that possible. That guy is not Liam.'

Before her mother could say anything to that, she added, 'And it's not anyone who you might think is right for me. I need you to stop trying to direct my life and just accept me for who I am. I want coming home to visit to be a joy, something I look forward to, not something I dread because I'm not living up to *your* dreams for me. You never even ask me about my work, all you do is try and get me to stop. And every time you suggest a local guy that would be perfect for me to settle down with … well, it makes me feel like shit.'

'Oh, honey,' her mum gushed, 'you are everything I want you to be and so much more. I'm so sorry I ever let you believe otherwise. I just love you so much and, I'll be frank, doing what you do frightens the living daylights out of me, but I know it's who you are, and I know that my fear is foolish. That the boys or Tilley are just as likely to have something terrible happen to them in a freak accident, but I can't help it.'

'It's not foolish,' Henri said, thinking it was definitely best not to mention her near-miss in the Kimberleys. You didn't need to be a mother to understand that it must be terrifying to have incubated something, birthed it, raised it and then had to send it out into the world to fend for itself.

But despite her assurance, her mother started sobbing anyway. For a moment Henri sat there like a stunned mullet gaping at the sight—her mother was so strong, she could only ever remember her crying when her dad died—but then something snapped. She shoved the wicker basket onto the floor and pulled her into a fierce hug. 'You're not supposed to be the one crying, I am.'

Although she'd bawled so much today that maybe she was all out of tears.

If only she was all out of heartbreak as well.

'I love you so much, Henri, and I'm so proud of you. Don't ever doubt that.'

No, apparently she wasn't out of tears, because at her mother's shortening of her name, great, unexpected waves of emotion overcame her, and they burst forth like a dam that had only just been managing to contain itself. She clung to her mum like she hadn't done in years. After a while it became hard to tell who was comforting who, but Henri knew two things for sure. She'd never felt so vulnerable in her life—not after Max's sister had called and told her about his indiscretions, not even when she'd had to crash land—and she'd also never felt closer to her mother.

'Do you want to give up and call it a night?' her mum asked when their sobs finally subsided and they'd almost used up the whole box of tissues.

With a sniff, Henri took one more sip of her now watery whiskey and then picked up the knitting needles again. 'No, I'm determined to conquer this, but you can go to bed if you want.'

'I think I'll sit with you a little longer, if you don't mind.'

'Not at all.'

Half an hour later, after much cursing and many more false starts, Henri finally got the hang of it, and as she methodically knitted row after row, her mother talked animatedly about various town committees and the disagreements members were having.

As usual, Henri didn't know all the people she was talking about, but it was exactly what she needed.

Chapter Thirty-four

Two days to go. Forty-eight hours until Liam could shut the pub and retreat into himself. It couldn't go fast enough. For the first time ever, he was thinking that maybe he'd take an extra couple of days on top of Christmas, get away from Bunyip Bay and go camp someplace with Sheila where he could really clear his head. The fresh air and peace and quiet would be good for the dog as well. Janet could take care of the paying guests and Macca, Lara and Dylan could handle the pub. Or he could just close and give everyone a proper vacation. He hadn't quite decided yet. Decisions were just another thing that felt too hard right now.

The only person who'd really be put out by him closing was Rex, but it wouldn't be the worst thing for him to go dry for a few days.

These were the thoughts going through Liam's head when Logan Knight came into the pub, alone, just after six o'clock on Wednesday night.

'Evening, Castle.' Logan tipped an invisible hat as he approached the bar. He didn't acknowledge Rex as he claimed a space two stools away from him. People rarely did; he seemed to blend into the background.

'Knight,' Liam said. 'On your own today?'

'Yeah, Frankie's watching Christmas rom-coms while she does the books. I thought I'd take a walk, get some fresh air.'

Liam didn't blame Logan. He couldn't think of anything worse than paperwork and rom-coms. Especially Christmas ones. 'Can I get you a drink?'

'Yeah …' Logan squinted as he looked behind the bar to the row of bottles. It was clear he was struggling to make out the labels and Liam fought the impulse to help him as he knew he wanted to hold onto as much independence as he could. 'Actually, I'll just have a pint of lager, thanks.'

'Coming right up.' He grabbed a glass and began to pour.

'Good day?' Logan asked, drumming his fingers on the bar. He looked at Liam with a weird, slightly smug expression—as if he knew something that Liam didn't.

'Not really.' It had been almost impossible to drag himself out of bed this morning. If not for Sheila needing to be exercised and fed, he probably wouldn't have bothered. Not that she seemed to be interested in either, which is why he'd forced himself up and taken her to the vet, for her annual shots but also to see if there was anything else wrong with her. Sally had listened as he relayed the dog's symptoms—'she's lethargic, off her food, doesn't want to go for a walk'—and then he'd paid a fortune on all manner of tests. She'd called him just before he'd opened the pub to say that although she was still waiting on one test, the rest had come back clear, but she suspected she knew what the problem was.

'Apparently Sheila might have depression and have to see a pet psychologist.'

He'd expected Logan to laugh at this—it was certainly the only thing that Liam had found funny over the past four days. No, not funny. There was nothing funny about depression, but he'd never known animals could suffer it too.

Instead, Logan whistled, 'Ooh, that sounds pricey. One of Frankie's cats had to have a tooth out last month and it almost broke us.'

Liam shrugged—money was the least of his problems.

'You told anyone else?'

'No.' Why would he? The last few days his staff had been steering clear of him as much as they could—he'd overheard Dylan telling Lara that he was acting like a grumpy bear and her saying Dylan should cut him some slack because he was still cut up over Henri. Had there ever been a more apt description than 'cut up'? It was exactly how he felt—as if someone had come along and chopped his body into little pieces, yet still expected it to function normally.

'Well, people that come in here love Sheila—she's like the Red Dog of Bunyip Bay.'

Liam couldn't help but raise an eyebrow—Red Dog belonged to the Pilbara and roamed freely, whereas Sheila was very much *his* dog and never went for a walk without him.

'You could put a tin right here on the bar …' Logan slapped it with his hand. 'Ask everyone to throw in their change for Sheila's psych fees. All adds up, you know.'

'I don't need handouts.'

'No.' Logan grinned and lifted his glass to his mouth. 'I don't think you do, *do* you?'

Heat crept up Liam's neck. He had an awful feeling the journalist's visit wasn't purely social. He glanced along the bar, looking for someone to serve but there was only a couple at the other end and Dylan had them covered.

'Can I get you another drink?' he asked, even though Logan had barely touched the first one. 'Or something to eat? Parmies are Deal of the Day. Or a burger? Everyone likes Macca's burgers. But there's plenty of other options. Vegetarian even?'

Logan's smirk grew at Liam's babbling. He lowered his glass to the bar. 'Maybe later. There's something I'd like to run by you first?'

'Oh?' It came out high-pitched, like a little girl had said it.

'Yeah. So, you know how I've been researching for a podcast episode about all the mystery gifts and donations that have been happening for years in town?'

Liam couldn't bring himself to nod but it was clearly a rhetorical question anyway.

'Well,' Logan continued, decent enough to keep his voice down, 'I've listed all the incidents that have occurred, right back to what I believe to be the very first nine years ago—a Bali holiday for Jane and Steve Morgan after she had a stillbirth—and I've finally worked out what the common link between them all is.'

Logan paused and Liam wasn't sure whether it was dramatically for effect or because he was waiting for a confession. He certainly wasn't going to give the game away until he was completely certain the journalist was barking up the right tree.

'Well, are you going to enlighten me?' Liam asked, shrugging one shoulder as if he were only mildly interested.

'I think *you* already know that the common factor is that every single person or organisation who has been blessed by our mysterious benefactor has, in the days or weeks leading up to the event, had a drink or a meal or come in for a meeting, right here. In The Palace. *Your* pub.'

Liam's insides turned to ice. He had to steady himself on the bar as Logan's smile grew so wide you could see the tiny gaps between his teeth.

'I guess the game's up.'

Both Liam and Logan turned to look at Rex who had just uttered those five words.

Logan blinked and shook his head slightly as if seeing the other man for the first time. 'Where'd you come from?'

'So, what are you going to do now?' Rex asked, ignoring Logan's question. 'Interview me on the radio? Write an article about me? Do you need a head shot?' He palmed his hands against his face and turned it slowly from side to side. 'Which is my best angle, do you reckon?'

'Why would I need a photo of *you*?' Logan said.

'Because I'm the mysterious benefactor,' Rex replied, jabbing his thumb into his chest and speaking in a tone that suggested Logan wasn't altogether right in the head. 'Isn't that what we're talking about?'

'You!?' Liam and Logan exclaimed in unison.

'*You're* the mysterious benefactor?' Logan added as Liam struggled to contain the laughter bubbling inside him.

Rex sighed. 'That's what I said, isn't it? For a journalist, you're pretty slow to catch on. Who the hell did you think it was?'

'I …' Logan looked at Liam, then back at Rex; he appeared to be stumped for words.

Lara came up beside Liam. 'What's all the excitement over here?'

'You know the mysterious benefactor?' he said.

'*No.* I thought that was the whole thing about a mystery—no one does know.'

'Well, it's a mystery no more.'

Lara's eyes widened. 'Who is it?'

Still grinning, Liam pointed to Rex, who beamed at the bartender.

'No way! Where'd you get all your cash?' Lara asked the question that Logan still seemed too shocked to ask.

Rex shrugged, nursed his beer in his grubby hands and told them exactly where.

By the time he'd finished his story, a crowd had gathered around the bar and Logan had recovered enough to interrupt with specific questions and take copious notes. For a man who usually disappeared into the furniture, being the centre of attention made Rex sit taller and hold his head higher.

Later, when Logan had finally gone off to type up his article and the crowd had dispersed, Rex pulled out a scruffy wallet that was barely holding itself together with a few loose threads to pay his tab.

Liam held up his hand and shook his head. 'Your drinks are on me,' he said with a wink. 'Tonight, and always.'

Chapter Thirty-five

'Now that's a sight I never expected to see,' Tilley said as she entered the farmhouse kitchen just after midday on Christmas Eve, delivering a big box of fresh vegetables for tomorrow's lunch.

Henri looked up from where she was sitting at the table knitting, keeping her mother company while she made the pavlova base, jelly for the trifle and her own version of mince pies. She poked her tongue out at her big sister.

'Henrietta has quite a talent for knitting, actually,' their mum said, smiling across at her. 'She picked it up very fast.'

That wasn't completely true, but she appreciated the praise nevertheless and she *had* been knitting pretty much nonstop since she'd started. While it didn't completely quieten her thoughts or ease her pain, it was surprisingly therapeutic. After making two dishtowels and a scarf, she'd stumbled across an organisation online that collected knitted pouches for orphaned wild animals and mittens for koalas hurt in bushfires. It felt good to be knitting for a purpose besides her own distraction.

Tilley came across and squeezed Henri's shoulder. 'I'm impressed, little sis. And how are you feeling?'

'Fine,' Henri lied as she finished another row. 'I'm not using my crutches as much anymore.'

They all knew Tilley hadn't been asking about her ankle.

'Matilda, do you have time for a cup of tea?' their mum asked, wiping her hands on her navy CWA apron.

Tilley glanced at her smart watch. 'Probably not—we're inundated with deliveries today and I promised James I'd help the courier get through them this arvo—but a quick one won't hurt. Have you got any cake to go with it? I haven't had a chance to eat all day.'

Of course there was cake—their mother practically had a different cake for every day of the year.

Tilley all but collapsed into a seat next to Henri and sighed when her mum poured the tea and placed a china cup in front of her. 'Ah, there's just something about tea that soothes the soul,' she said as she lifted the cup to take a sip.

Henri reached for her can of Diet Coke. 'Where's Macy?'

'Liarna's mum has taken them to the pool. There's a big inflatable, Christmas carols and games there today. I tell you, that girl has a better social life than me.'

Henri and her mother chuckled in agreement.

'So, Mum, do you still want me to cook the potato bake at home tomorrow morning before we come over?' Tilley asked.

She nodded. 'Yes, please. There won't be any room in our oven with the two turkeys and all the roast veggies.'

'Why do we need potato bake?' Henri said, reaching across the table to take a slice of carrot and chocolate cake. 'Aren't we having roast potatoes?'

'Yes,' sighed Tilley, 'but Macy doesn't like roast potatoes, so we decided on another option.'

'Okay then.' Whatever. Henri was pretty certain that when they were kids, you ate what you were given or went hungry, whether you liked the texture or not, but she didn't want to sound like she was a hundred years old by stating that. It was no skin off her nose anyway.

As her mother and sister went through the Christmas menu for what had to be the billionth time—you'd be forgiven for thinking Prince Harry and Megs were coming—Henri refocused her attention on her knitting.

'It's Sexy Rexy,' Tilley said about ten minutes later.

'What's Sexy Rexy?'

Tilley sighed in frustration. 'The mysterious *benefactor*, Mum! Keep up.'

Henri hadn't really been listening to the conversation, but now her head snapped up. '*Sexy Rexy* is the mysterious benefactor?'

'Am I speaking another language?' Tilley laughed. 'That's what I keep saying. I was in the café this morning and everyone was talking about it. Somehow, through all Logan's research, he worked out that all roads led to Sexy Rexy. And apparently the old drunk came right out and admitted it in the pub last night.'

'Where on earth did Rex Carter get the money for all that stuff? Did he have a rich relative die or something? It doesn't make sense. The man buys all his clothes from the op shop, and have you *seen* his house?' Their mother screwed up her nose. 'I wouldn't let one of the dogs live there.'

Tilley shrugged. 'Well, apparently he won the lottery a while back—ten million or something. And I guess he just isn't too fussed about material things or luxury himself.'

'Why would you buy lottery tickets and then not treat yourself if you came into big cash?' her mum asked. 'As much as I love Bunyip Bay, if I came into millions, I'd buy myself one of those mansions overlooking the beach in Cottesloe. The least I'd do is totally renovate this place.'

'I guess he gets a thrill from helping others,' Tilley surmised. 'And maybe his house is a palace on the inside. I don't think anyone ever visits him.'

She nodded. 'True, but those *clothes*? They're not from a rich man's wardrobe.'

'Not everyone takes such pride in their appearance like you do, Mother, and he clearly didn't want anyone to know. If he'd suddenly been seen in Gucci and Armani hauling rubbish at the tip, people would have been suspicious.'

'That's another thing! Why is he even working there? Can't be for the love of it.'

'Who knows? Maybe he likes it, or maybe it's part of his cover, although apparently he didn't seem very upset about being found out.'

'Imagine if you won the lottery.' A wistful look came over their mum's face.

'Have you ever bought a lotto ticket in your life?' Henri asked.

'No, but now that I know it's actually possible for regular people to win, maybe I will.'

'Yeah, maybe I will too. Hey! We should all go in as a family,' suggested Tilley. 'Do the same numbers every week? Use the kids' birthdays or something?'

'Good idea. Will you be in our syndicate, Henrietta?'

'Yeah, sure, Mum.' Henri popped another piece of cake into her mouth, but while her mother and sister started dreaming about what they'd do if they became millionaires overnight, she was still stuck on the whole Sexy Rexy revelation.

Her mother had been right when she said it didn't make sense. Whoever the mysterious benefactor was, they had to be someone who had their finger on the pulse of whatever was happening in town. As far as she knew, Sexy Rexy pretty much kept to himself. He wasn't involved in any clubs or committees and the only places he frequented were the tip and The Palace. It would be more believable if Eileen Brady was the culprit.

The Palace! Perhaps it did make sense. Sexy Rexy had been there every day Henri was, always perched on that same stool at the bar. Liam joked about him being part of the furniture, so he'd be in prime position to overhear when people were lamenting their woes to their friends.

Who'd ever have thought? It just showed you truly couldn't judge a book by its cover.

Had Liam known all along? He must have. How often had he told her he knew all the secrets of Bunyip Bay? And this had to be one of the longest-kept secrets of all!

She thought back to the times she'd heard anyone mention the mysterious benefactor around him. There'd always been something slightly off in his responses. That first night in the pub—Liam had come by when they'd been discussing the mystery and when someone mentioned 'him', Liam asked how they knew it was a man? Then someone had asked if Liam had any idea who he/she was, and Liam had replied with something like 'my patrons are more the hardworking type than millionaires'.

Clearly, he'd been trying to throw everyone off Sexy Rexy's scent.

And then there was the whispered conversation with Frankie during the Christmas Tree. She'd noticed something a little off in Liam's tone, like he was trying too hard to sound like he didn't know anything. It was why later that night when they were alone, she'd asked him directly if he knew who the person was, but he'd brushed her off.

No, he hadn't brushed her off. He hadn't answered at all and then he'd distracted her with sex. Not that she'd complained at the time.

Thoughts of Sexy Rexy vanished as a wave of sadness swept through her at the reminder that Liam would never distract her in such a manner ever again. She'd probably never even *have* sex again because the thought of letting anyone else touch her just wasn't worth thinking about.

'Will I see you tonight then, Hens?'

'What?' She startled at the sound of Tilley's voice and her chair scraping on the kitchen floor as she stood.

'At church?'

'Oh, right.' Henri hadn't been planning on going to the Christmas Eve service, but she looked across the table to see her mum smiling expectantly. After how good she'd been to her since their chat the other night, she couldn't bring herself to disappoint her. It wouldn't hurt her to sit through a few carols and a lecture—sorry, *sermon*—about the gifts Jesus gave to the world and the love and peace we should bring to each other not only this time of year, but always, blah, blah, blah. And she was fairly certain Liam wouldn't be there—even if he didn't have the pub, it was the *Christmas* Eve service, and he didn't *do* Christmas. He'd made that blatantly clear!

'Yep, I'll be there. With bells on,' she said with a fake smile.

Henri didn't wear bells or any kind of festive fashion, but she was in the minority. As she hobbled on her crutches alongside her mum to join the hordes of people heading towards the church—most of whom only graced the old building with their presence twice a year—she noticed almost everyone was wearing either a Christmas T-shirt, headband or earrings. And there were at least fifty Santa hats heading inside, not all of them on children!

Since when were you allowed to wear Santa hats in church? Standards had dropped a lot since she used to come here as a kid.

The dress code wasn't the only thing that had changed, Henri thought, as she and her mother joined her brothers, their wives and kids, who were waiting for them just outside the church. It sounded like there was a rock band playing inside.

'Is that the choir? Are they singing "Christmas Where The Gum Trees Grow"?' She hadn't heard that song since she was a kid and that was in school, *never* at church. Whatever happened to 'Silent Night' and 'We Three Kings'?

'It's the new pastor,' her mother explained at Henri's obvious shock. 'He's trying to make religion more fun, more accessible. And it's working; attendance is going up every week.'

'I think it might have more to do with him though,' said Janai.

'Why's that?' Henri asked.

Janai grinned. 'I take it you haven't seen Campbell yet?'

'I don't think so.'

'Oh, you'd know if you saw him,' added Hannah with a smirk. 'Let's just say I didn't know they made priests like that!'

She and Janai giggled like a couple of schoolgirls.

'He's not a priest, he's a pastor,' Andrew grumbled, which made Henri very, very curious to meet this new guy.

'Where's Matilda and James?'

'I'm sure they'll be here soon, Mum,' Callum said as he bounced a squirming Joe in his arms, 'but maybe we should go inside and sit down? We can save them some seats.'

All agreed that was a good idea. It was still warm, and although Henri guessed inside might not be any cooler with all these people, she already needed to rest her ankle.

They had to stop every few seconds to say 'Merry Christmas' to someone so it took them a while to get seated—the church was jam-packed like a tin of sardines—but they managed to get four pews together, saving space for Tilley, James and Macy. They parked Henri's crutches along the floor in front of their pew so they didn't get in the way. She'd stopped using them around the house the last few days but didn't want to take any risks at the eleventh hour.

She used the paper order of service she'd been given when they entered to fan her face as she watched the choir—they were now singing Paul Kelly's 'How To Make Gravy', of all songs—and waited for the service to start.

Tilley, James and Macy rushed down the aisle just as the music faded.

If looks could kill, the one their mum gave them as they slipped into the pew beside her would have been the end of them. 'Where on earth have you been?' she hissed, her cheeks flaming red.

'Sorry,' Tilley panted. 'There was a late delivery. Rex's doing, I guess. Trestle tables for the hall. We'd just closed up the shop, so thought it was easier to get the truck driver to drop them—'

She held up a hand. 'Shh. You're here now, that's all that matters.'

A tall blond man, who looked as though he spent more time in the gym than he did praying, stepped up to the pulpit. Henri had to concede her sisters-in-law were right—he was rather hot, in a polished, Scandinavian kind of way.

'Welcome, everyone, to our Christmas Eve service,' said Campbell, his voice booming throughout the church.

Good-looking or not, she could just tell from the way he spoke that he liked the sound of his own voice and suspected this was going to be a long night.

She sighed and flapped her program near her face again, then stopped and stared down at her hand. Although the bandaid was long gone, there was still a bit of a red lump on her index finger from the splinter she'd got at the wreath-making session.

The splinter she'd got from the trestle tables.

The splinter that Liam had seen.

The splinter she'd told him had been caused by the old tables at the Memorial Hall.

Had he mentioned them to Sexy Rexy?

Argh. No matter what topic, her mind always came back to Liam.

While Campbell droned on at the front, Henri lost the fight to try *not* to think about him. She should have brought her knitting, she thought, as she closed her eyes and lost herself in memories of the time they'd spent together. It felt like so much longer than it had actually been. In such a short time, they'd done so much. They'd surfed, they'd laughed, they'd talked, and they'd almost had sex on his desk right there in the pub. She'd never felt such an urgency to have someone that she would have done it anywhere!

She probably shouldn't be thinking about such things while sitting in church, but then again, everything else seemed to have changed, maybe that wasn't frowned upon anymore either.

Oh my God! The thought died in her head as another crashed into it.

She jolted, knocking against her crutches on the floor and causing a bit of a clatter that earned a glare from her mother.

That night in Liam's office. The Post-it note she'd picked up off Sheila.

JMC Office Supplies. Three-thousand and something dollars.

Henri leaned forward and tapped her sister on the shoulder. 'Do you know how much those tables cost?'

'What? How would I know how much they cost? We just delivered them.'

'Wasn't there an invoice or something with them?'

'Girls, be quiet,' their mother hissed as she turned around to glare at Henri yet again.

Ignoring her, Henri tapped Tilley again. 'Do you know who the tables were from?'

Tilley rolled her eyes. 'Sexy Rexy, I guess.'

'No, the *actual* tables. What company supplied them?'

'I don't know.' She shrugged. 'Some office supply place in Perth?'

'*Girls! Please!*' Fiona looked like she was about to burst an artery.

Henri flopped back against the pew as the current Sunday School kids marched to the front to perform the nativity.

Maybe she was jumping to conclusions. Liam's note could have referred to anything. He ran a business—it was probably the name of the company he ordered all his paper and printer ink from or something.

Yet, no matter how much Henri tried to put the idea out of her head, she couldn't get rid of the feeling in her gut that perhaps Logan had got the wrong person.

Like Sexy Rexy, Liam was always at the pub, and the timing was right. The random gifts had begun a couple of years after he'd arrived. Or at least, that's when someone had made the connection and the mysterious benefactor had become a local legend. Everyone thought he'd come to town with nothing but a ute and a backpack, but he had to have had *some* money to have renovated The Palace the way he had. There'd been no expense spared and yes, he'd made the furniture and done a lot of the improvements himself, but it still wouldn't have come cheap. Then there were his bedsheets, which made her feel like she was lying on silk.

His parents had owned two successful businesses. Who knew what other investments they'd had as well? With Lacey dead too, Liam would have been their only beneficiary.

Beneficiary? Benefactor?

She *knew* she was onto something. Liam made so much more sense than Sexy Rexy did.

Before Henri could think through her decision, she yanked her crutches up off the floor and pushed to a stand. Maybe she wanted to know if her hunch was right, maybe she just wanted to see him one last time. She wasn't sure, but either way, she couldn't sit here thinking about this a moment longer.

'Where are you going?' her mother hissed, grabbing hold of Henri's wrist as she started out of the pew.

'There's someone I need to see.'

She raised an eyebrow. 'Will you be back for supper?'

'Probably.' Henri wasn't stupid enough to think this was going to change anything—it might even make things worse. 'But if I'm not back by the time you need to go home, I'll stay at Tilley's tonight.'

And then she hightailed it out of there as quickly as anyone on crutches possibly could. She almost tossed them aside as she negotiated the church steps, but The Palace was at the opposite end of the main street, and she wasn't a complete and utter lunatic. It was only when she was halfway there, puffing and panting up the hill, that she realised she could have borrowed her mum's car. Having not driven since twisting her ankle, the thought hadn't even crossed her mind. Too late to turn back now, she continued on; every step felt like an effort, and she almost stacked it again a number of times.

But finally, she was there.

The multicoloured fly strips flapped about the entrance in the wind. Taking a deep breath, she swung her crutches towards them and then pushed herself inside.

And there he was. Standing behind the bar as always. Delicious as ever. Chatting to Sexy Rexy as he polished a glass.

Oh God! She shouldn't have come. One look at Liam and all the hurt she'd been working hard to push deep down shot back up to the surface. She stood in the doorway frozen, feeling like she was lingering between two worlds and she didn't want to be in either of them.

But before she could make a decision to turn and flee, an excited bark sounded as Sheila bounded towards her.

Chapter Thirty-six

'Sheila!' As his dog darted out of the bar with more spring in her step than she'd had for days, Liam looked to the entrance to see what had excited her.

Henri.

His heart jolted and he reached out to steady himself on the bar. He wasn't sure whether he was horrified or thrilled to see her. Sheila, clearly the latter, jumped up at Henri, landing her paws right into the middle of her stomach.

'Shit!' Liam watched in alarm as Henri stumbled backwards and fell onto the floor, her crutches clattering down beside her.

Snapping out of his shock, he rushed over to help her. He couldn't tell if she was laughing or crying by the time he got to her, but Sheila was in her element, bestowing sloppy, wet kisses all over her long-lost love's face.

'She really missed you,' Liam said as he restrained the dog with one hand and held out his other to help Henri.

She merely stared at it and then her eyes narrowed. '*You're* the mysterious benefactor, aren't you?'

'What?' Her question took him totally by surprise. Since Sexy Rexy's confession last night, he'd been more relaxed about his secret than he had since Logan had started sniffing around a few months ago. He honestly could have kissed the man. 'Haven't you heard—it's Rex Carter?'

'Yeah, whatever. I may not have known you long, but I can tell when you're bullshitting.'

'What makes you think—'

'Oh, it's obvious in hindsight,' she cut in. 'I can't believe no one ever twigged before. But the enlightening moment for me came just now when Tilley mentioned that a whole load of new trestle tables had been delivered to The Ag Store for the hall. An anonymous donation attributed to Sexy Rexy, Bunyip Bay's new hero.' She held up her finger and pointed at the red mark. 'You ordered them when I told you about my splinter, didn't you?'

'I …' His shoulders slumped and he let out a resigned sigh. 'They weren't supposed to get here until *after* Christmas.'

When Henri Forward would have been far away, unable to make the connection.

She just stared at him as if now that she knew the truth, she wasn't quite sure what to do with it.

'Have you told anyone?' he asked.

'No. Not yet,' she said, and he breathed a sigh of relief. 'But why do you do it? How do you choose who to give money to? How have you managed to keep it a secret so long? And why don't you want anyone to know it's you?'

He glanced around—the pub was deserted except for Rex, the usual young blokes by the pool table and a couple of families of tourists finishing up dinner in the dining room, but he still didn't want to risk anyone overhearing.

'I'll tell you,' he promised, 'but not here.'

'Okay. Where?'

'In my office.'

'Now?'

Liam nodded and offered his hand again to help Henri stand. In the days since they'd last been together, the sparks hadn't faded at all. He tried not to react as he touched her and suspected from the way she refused to meet his gaze that she was doing the same. The moment her crutches were safely tucked under her arms again, she scooted off to his office, Sheila dashing after her.

He followed and then closed the door behind him. It wasn't a small office, but with all the tension and chemistry in the air, it felt claustrophobic. As Henri lowered herself into his chair, all he could think about was the last time they were in here, yanking desperately at each other's clothes.

'Can I get you a drink?' He could do with one himself.

She shook her head, then changed her mind. 'Actually yes, I'll have a glass of cold water. That hill is deadly.'

He frowned. 'Where'd you come from?'

'Church,' she supplied, which made sense because it sounded like Campbell had conned almost everyone into attending the Christmas Eve service. Liam had suspected that was the reason the pub was practically empty tonight.

'And you walked *all* that way? With crutches?'

'I'm not sure walked is the word, but I'm here, aren't I?'

Yes, here she most definitely was, and she sounded almost as surprised as he was. He nodded and went to get her drink, relishing a few moments away from her to get his head together.

Lara and Dylan jumped apart as he returned to the bar. He raised an eyebrow at their obvious canoodling on his time, but it wasn't like they had much else to do and he didn't really care anyway.

'Will you guys be okay out here for a few minutes?' he said as he grabbed a glass for Henri.

'Sure,' they said in unison.

'Is Henri okay?' added Lara.

'She's fine,' he replied, with no idea whether that was true or not.

'You look like shit,' Henri told him as he put the glass down on his desk in front of her a few moments later.

'Thanks.' He pulled up an empty milk crate and sat opposite her. 'It's been a tough couple of days.'

'Because you were so close to being discovered? Why did you choose Sexy Rexy to cover for you? Surely you could come up with someone slightly more believable.'

'I didn't choose him. The moment Logan confronted me, he just put his hand up. I couldn't believe it. I didn't actually think anyone would buy it, but Rex is a pretty convincing storyteller. If I didn't know the truth myself, I think even *I* might have believed him.'

'So, what? He knew it was you all along?'

Liam nodded. 'Yeah, I spoke to him briefly after Logan left and he told me he's suspected for years. I guess he's more observant and with it than anyone gives him credit for. He worked out long before Logan did that all the people and groups who received money or some other form of assistance, had been in the pub prior. I told you people talk to me. Well, he overheard some of them too. They tell me things they're too scared or ashamed to admit to anyone else. Especially when they've had a few.'

'But …' Henri pressed the cold glass against her forehead. 'If they tell you, then wouldn't some of your beneficiaries have guessed?'

'I make sure I'm very subtle. If possible, I wait a little after someone talks to me before I help them. And I'm careful about delivery.'

'Yeah. How do you do that? Frankie said sometimes there are cheques—how has no one from the bank seen you?' she asked before taking a gulp of the water.

'I never collect the cheques myself. I've got a solicitor in Geraldton who helps me. I take cash out when the amount isn't too big. It sounds complicated, but I've got a system and it worked until Logan's boss decided he wanted to get to the bottom of it.'

'Okay …' She nodded and then gave him a small smile. 'So, are you loaded or something?'

He blinked, but Henri's lack of propriety was one of the things he loved about her. 'Let's just say I bought the pub with spare change. The supermarkets my parents owned were sold for a couple of million each and Mum and Dad both had good life insurance. That, on top of the money from our house and my parents' share portfolio, mean I'll never have to worry about money again.'

'How do you choose who to give to? Do you have criteria or something?' She sounded more like a journalist than Logan himself.

'No, no criteria. I just help where I can.'

Henri glanced around. 'This is a nice place, and your apartment is comfortable, but you don't live like a man with millions. Apart from your bedsheets. What are they? 1000-thread count or something?'

'Yeah, I don't scrimp on bedding—I'm a terrible sleeper, so I figure I should do everything I can to try and help in that department.'

'I think I fell in love with your sheets before I fell in love with you.'

Her eyes widened as if she hadn't meant to say that. His skin tingled. The weirdest sensation filled his chest. It was both the best news and the worst news he'd ever heard.

'You *love* me?'

'Never mind about me.' She downed the rest of the water like it was vodka, but her cheeks were even redder than they'd been when she arrived. 'We're not done talking about you yet. Why?'

'Why what?' He was still hung up on the love thing. His own heartache had been bad enough to deal with these last few days, but he'd consoled himself that Henri didn't feel the same way about him.

'Why do you do it?' she asked.

'To make a difference. To help people.'

She shook her head. 'I'm not buying it.' She leaned forward and looked him right in the eye. '*Why*?'

'Because ...' He let out a long, deep breath as heat rose on the back of his neck. 'Because it helps me deal with the guilt. I was supposed to be working at the Silver Ridge store that day, but ...' He shook his head—the reasons didn't matter. 'I should have been there. I should have stopped the guy. I should have saved them.'

'Oh, Liam.' Henri's eyes filled with tears. 'The shooting wasn't your fault. You can't stop some people doing crazy things.'

He shrugged. 'Maybe. But why did *I* get to live? My little sister hadn't even graduated high school. She hadn't had a boyfriend. Mum and Dad loved what they did but they had big plans to travel the world together when they retired. None of them got to do any of those things. I guess spending their money on helping other people goes a small way to making me feel like their deaths weren't in vain. Stupid, I know.'

'It's not stupid. It's not stupid at all.' She sniffed and wiped her eye with the back of her hand. 'Can I ask you one more thing?'

He nodded.

'Is it because of the guilt that you won't allow yourself to get close to anyone—because if your parents and sister can't have a loving relationship, why should you? Or is it because Kate hurt you by falling in love with someone else when you needed her the most?'

She had it all wrong. Familiar guilt filled him, and he struggled to find the right words. 'It's not either of those things,' he admitted. 'It's not because Kate hurt me. It's because I hurt her.'

'What?'

'I was the one who broke us, and I can't risk putting anyone else through what I did to her.'

Henri frowned. 'What do you mean? You didn't cheat on her? Abuse her?'

He could tell from the tone of her voice that she didn't believe him capable of such things and he was glad of that, but he didn't want there to be any doubt. 'No, of course not.'

'Then why? I won't tell a soul that you're responsible for the anonymous gifts and donations, but *please*, tell me exactly what you mean?'

'After I lost my family, I went through a very dark patch. I threw myself into work to try and numb the pain, but it didn't really work. I made big mistakes, stupid decisions, and then I kinda just checked out. Most days I couldn't even get out of bed. Kate took over the management of both stores and ran herself ragged, while I stayed at home, refusing to see anyone, do anything. I barely ate, I stopped shaving, I didn't even shower.'

'You were depressed,' Henri said quietly.

He nodded. 'Yeah. Kate got me to see a therapist, but things had changed between us by then. My mental health was too big a burden. It was like there were three people in our relationship—me, her and the black dog. It got her down too. She felt helpless, and eventually she found the companionship and intimacy I was no longer capable of giving her, with someone else. I'm happy for her. Truly. She deserves someone who doesn't drag her down.'

'Do you see anyone about it now? Do you take something?'

'I'm on medication, yes. Maybe I always will be.'

'How did you cope after Kate left? Surely that would have been a crippling blow?'

'Yes and no. I didn't blame her, but I felt like her leaving gave me the freedom to sell up the businesses and get away from Silver Ridge. I hoped that fleeing far from the scene of the shooting and doing some travelling would help me heal.'

'Why do I get the feeling it didn't?'

Damn, she was perceptive. 'You're right; it got worse. Much worse. I travelled almost on autopilot, each place making me feel more guilty for being able to do what my family never could.' He paused. 'It was Christmas Eve ten years ago when I drove into Bunyip Bay …'

* * *

Henri held her breath as Liam spoke—everything he'd said so far made sense and it only intensified her feelings for him. The knowledge he lived through what he did every day and still managed to be a beacon of light for those who came into the pub, only made her love him more.

'I don't think I told you, but the shooting … it happened … my family were killed on Christmas Eve.'

Oh God. It made something that was already impossible to comprehend even worse.

'The shop was covered in lights and decorations, carols were blasting from the speakers as the shots were echoing through the store. Every time I see a Christmas tree or hear so much as a "ho ho ho", it takes me right back to that day. I didn't think I could take it any longer, so that Christmas I decided to end it all.'

No. Bitter cold flooded her lungs—the thought of the world without Liam wasn't something she wanted to contemplate. Somehow, she managed to withhold her gasp, not wanting to interrupt him.

'I'd seen a lot of Australia and although almost every place I went to was amazing, I still couldn't help feeling it should have been me who died. I was exhausted, tired of the demons in my head, and I couldn't see any reason to keep living. I came here, to The Palace, for one last meal and I met Arthur McArthur. We talked like I hadn't talked to anyone since the shooting and when I thanked him, still planning to finish it all that night, he said simply, "No need to thank me, it's my job." I realised that's what I wanted. A vocation that gave me meaning and the power to help others. Being a publican might not be the obvious choice, but just an hour with Arthur showed me it had given him the kind of purpose I was looking for. If I could help one person the way he helped me, my life would be worth it.'

'And you have,' Henri said, thinking of the conversation she'd had with Rex Carter. 'And then some.'

The smallest blush crept into his cheeks.

'I'm so glad you met Arthur that night.' Henri wished he was closer so she could take his hand.

'So am I.'

'So today is ten years since you made the decision to live?' she said.

'Yeah. But it's a decision I've had to make every single day since. I'm not cured, Henri. I can't guarantee I'll never follow through.'

Every part of her ached at his words. For the first time in her life, she found herself wanting to stay in Bunyip Bay—she wanted to be here every single day so that she could make sure Liam never got so down again that he *did* follow through.

'I'm sorry, Henri,' he said, his tone heartfelt and his expression solemn. 'I'm sorry for abandoning you without an explanation the other day. I overreacted. I should have just told you that I couldn't do Christmas lunch. Instead, I was a complete and utter ass.'

She nodded. 'Yes. You were.'

But now she knew why. And now she berated herself for not making him talk to her sooner. You weren't supposed to give up on love—you were supposed to fight to the bitter end. Instead, Henri had let her hurt and stupid pride stand in the way.

Yet still something told her he wouldn't have run away, he wouldn't have given her nothing but a vague text message if he didn't care. If there wasn't something about her that scared him. And that gave her hope.

'Hypothetically,' she said, curling her ponytail around her fingers, 'if it weren't for your mental health and if I didn't work away most of the year, do you think you might ever have developed … feelings … for me?'

'Feelings?' Liam looked pained, then something seemed to snap. '*Feelings*?' he repeated, his tone incredulous. 'Henrietta Forward, I have *all* the damn feelings for you! That's why I lost the plot. You make me crazy. You could work six months a year on the moon for all I cared. It wouldn't matter to me. I'm not some fickle fool like Max who'd cheat on you because you weren't always around. I'm not scared of long-distance. If I wasn't terrified of hurting you, I'd call you every day, send constant text messages … but this is for the best, I promise you.'

He ran a hand through his hair and shook his head. 'You're not the only one who fell in love, Henri, but love isn't always enough.'

He loved her too?

Her heart felt as if it might shatter, but this time because it was suddenly too full.

Not caring about her ankle, she shot up and hobbled around the desk, then dropped herself into his lap and wrapped her arms around his neck.

'Yes, it is,' she said forcefully. 'Love *is* enough! And you need to remember—I'm not Kate. I'm older than she was, and I know the score. You're a different person than you were then too. You've managed your grief and your depression for *ten* years, but you don't have to do it alone. Not anymore. *Please.* Let me be part of your life. Let me be your friend, lover, sounding board and support. Don't push me away because of some misguided, self-sacrificing sense that it's the right thing to do!'

And then she kissed him because she was terrified of what he might say and at least wanted to taste him one last time before he smashed her heart into a zillion pieces all over again. For long, painful moments, it was like she was sitting on a wooden soldier, desperately trying to give it mouth-to-mouth.

And then—just when all her hope was slipping away—Liam slid his hands up into her hair and kissed her back. Tears poured down her face. She was crying over a guy.

And it was absolutely worth it.

'I'm not man enough to say no,' he said, holding her tight against him when he finally broke their kiss. 'I hope you don't regret this, Henri.'

'I won't,' she replied with absolute certainty. And then she started to laugh.

'What? What's so funny?'

'You know how I told you your touch would have to be pretty damn magic for me to start fantasising about a happily ever after with you?' She shrugged. 'Well, turns out it is.'

His lips curled into a smile and then he too burst out laughing as he crushed her against him again. It was the most beautiful sound Henri had ever heard.

'Can I stay the night?' she asked when their amusement had contained itself. 'You don't have to come to the farm for Christmas, but—'

'I'm coming,' he said before she could finish her sentence. 'That's if the invitation's still open.'

'Of course it is, but … are you sure?' She didn't want to do anything to hurt him.

He cupped her face in his hands and stared at her in a way that made her feel more wanted, more cherished, more *loved* than she ever had in her life.

'Yep. I'm sure. Apart from Arthur, I've never told anyone what I told you tonight and you're the first person I've wanted to talk to about my family. You give me hope. It's time to try and live a normal life again.'

Then Liam went out to close up the pub early and while he argued with Jaxon and Brad—who told him it was far *too* early for last drinks—Henri checked her phone and saw a text from Tilley.

Where are you, sister dear? Mum's getting frantic.

Tell her I'm staying at the pub tonight.

O.M.G!!! Does that mean things are back on between you and the Bay's sexiest publican?

Smiling down at her phone, she tapped out a reply.

They sure are. And you can tell Mum we'll have an extra for lunch tomorrow after all. See you then.

Chapter Thirty-seven

'Liam! *Liam!* It's okay.'

A cop's hands landed on Liam's arms, trying to restrain him, but he shoved him off. There were blood and bodies everywhere. He needed to get to her. He needed to get to her before … *No!*

Pain ricocheted through his body as if he were the one who'd been shot. Sweat poured from every pore in his skin as he tried to get to her, but he was frozen.

'No!' he screamed and started tearing at his own hair. How could he have let this happen again?

'Liam. Wake *up*!' The cop shook him hard, but the voice didn't sound like it belonged to a man. And then a dog barked.

Jolting awake, he blinked open his eyes to see Henri leaning over him and Sheila standing at the end of the bed, alert. He sat up and turned to scrutinise Henri, her face only partially visible due to the moonlight outside.

'It's all right,' she said, brushing her fingers against his forehead to wipe the sweat. 'You just had a bad dream.'

Again. They weren't over. But this one had been different from the others. If anything, this one had been worse. 'Are you okay? I didn't hurt you, did I?'

'I'm fine. It's you I'm worried about.' She took his clammy hand and held it against her chest. 'I'm sorry—I don't think you're supposed to wake someone who's having a nightmare, but you seemed so distraught. I thought—'

'It's okay. I'm glad you woke me.' Liam inhaled and exhaled slowly, trying to temper his pulse. 'But I'm sorry you had to see that.'

'There's no need to apologise. Having a bad dream isn't something to be ashamed of. Let me get you a glass of water,' she said, throwing back the sheet and heading out of the room.

He took a few more deep breaths as Sheila flopped back down, resting her head on his thigh. By the time Henri returned he was almost breathing normally again.

'Oh my God,' he said, suddenly remembering her injury. 'Your ankle. I should have got it myself.'

'It's a lot better now.' She handed him the glass and climbed back into bed beside him.

'Thank you.'

Henri adjusted the pillows behind her. 'Is this what you meant when you said you weren't a good sleeper?'

'Yeah.' He nodded and put the now-empty glass on his bedside table. 'Often it takes me hours to get to sleep because it's late at night, when I have nothing else to do, that my brain starts churning through all the thoughts that I haven't allowed it to dwell on through the day, but that's almost better than the nightmares. Right after the shooting they were unrelenting, but they've become very sporadic over the last few years. Until just now, I hadn't had one in over six months. I was kind of hoping I was done.'

'Oh, Liam.' She snuggled up close and rested her head on his shoulder, almost squishing Sheila between them. 'What happens in these nightmares?'

'I see everything again exactly as it happened that day.'

She squeezed his hand.

'But this one wasn't quite the same as usual.'

'What was different?'

'This time it was you.'

Henri lifted her head and turned to look into his eyes. 'What do you mean?'

'This time you were in the store, and he had the gun aimed at you. I could tell he was about to kill you, but ...'

'But you couldn't get to me?'

'No.' He swallowed, his body temperature soaring again at the memory. 'And then, this plane swooped into the store and ... it picked you up with its actual wings, and the roof of the building parted like the bloody Red Sea and the plane flew off with you in it.'

Her expression grew even more serious. 'Are you worried about me flying, Liam?'

A minute ago, he'd been burning up, but now his heart turned to ice.

Could he lie to her? He *knew* what the nightmare meant. It was his subconscious reminding him that he could lose her too. And he'd heard her stories, heard about her brush with death up north, knew it was possible.

'Yeah,' he admitted after a few long moments. 'I'm terrified. Almost as terrified as I am about me hurting you.'

'I'll get a job in Bunyip Bay,' she said, complete conviction in her voice. 'I could help you here, at the pub?'

He only hesitated a moment. 'No fucking way. That would only happen over my dead body! You're not stopping flying.

This only works—*we* only work—if you keep doing what you love. I won't let you change who you are in your soul because of me. It's me who needs to change. I need to grow some balls and start living properly again. And I will.'

'I would give up flying for you,' she said, 'but I love that you won't let me. I promise I will fly the safest I ever have. I'll triple check everything and I won't ever take any stupid risks. Okay?'

He nodded and rolled over so they were face to face. 'I know you won't, because now you won't just have your mother, but also me to deal with if you do.'

She laughed and kissed him on the lips. 'But you have to promise me one thing in return too.'

'Anything.'

'If you ever feel even the slightest bit low, you'll call me. If I'm not available because I'm in the air, you'll leave a message and I'll call you back the minute I touch the ground.'

'Deal.'

'Promise me you won't try and handle your demons alone anymore.'

'I promise.'

'Also … you said you saw a therapist?'

'Yeah, a couple of times, in Colorado. Didn't really help.'

'I think you should try someone again,' she said. 'Maybe the first therapist wasn't right or maybe you weren't ready, but you've still got things to work through. I'm here for you—always—but I'm not an expert and I … *Please*, just give it another shot. There's no shame in asking for help.'

'Didn't I just say I'd do anything for you?'

'Yes, but I want you to do this for yourself as well.'

He nodded. 'I'll call someone tomorrow.'

'Well, I'm not sure you'll be able to find anyone open *tomorrow*, but next business day works for me.'

'Tuesday then.' He pulled her close, unable to recall ever having such a raw and honest conversation. But with Henri it felt okay, more than okay. It felt right. 'You know absolutely everything about me now,' he said.

'Good. Because I don't want there ever to be any secrets between us.'

'Me either.' He kissed her forehead and then reached across to switch off the lamp. 'But now I think we should try and get some more sleep.'

'That, Liam Castle, is the best idea you've ever had.'

Chapter Thirty-eight

Henri woke on Christmas morning to the sun blazing in through the bedroom window and Sheila snoring softly at her feet. She smiled and cocked an ear to listen for sounds of Liam pottering in the kitchen or in the bathroom.

There were none. Not a squeak. And no tantalising aroma of coffee or toast either.

The apartment felt eerily still.

A sinking feeling descended on her as she recalled everything Liam had told her yesterday and then his nightmare. He'd scared the bejesus out of her last night when he'd been thrashing around beside her, sweating and shouting words she couldn't comprehend, but she'd thought he was okay after their conversation.

What if he hadn't been? Her blood went cold.

Was this what being hit by a tonne of bricks felt like?

She shot out of bed, not giving one thought to her ankle, and dashed through the apartment—checking first the bathroom, then the kitchen and the living room. She even checked the spare room, which she'd never been in before but found jam-packed full of boxes. He wasn't there either.

'Where the hell is he?' she screamed at Sheila who was shadowing her every step.

As the dog stared up at Henri like she was a crazy person, she froze.

Liam never went anywhere without his faithful companion and this realisation only compounded her fears. What if he'd …?

No. She couldn't allow herself to think like that or she wouldn't be able to think straight enough to find him.

Call him. Maybe he's just gone for a swim or something?

Telling herself this would be it and trying to stay calm—or at least not get any more *un*-calm—she dived on her handbag and yanked out her phone.

The blasted thing had died.

'Shit!' She glanced around but of course Liam didn't have a landline up here. Who did anymore? And even if he had, she didn't know his number off by heart. So much for technological advances making life better.

Lara and Dylan. She didn't know what time it was, but it felt bloody early; still she couldn't worry about disturbing them. Not when Liam's life might be at stake.

She quickly threw on shorts and a T-shirt, not even bothering with underwear. But when she emerged from the apartment into the corridor, she realised she had no idea which door belonged to the English backpackers.

Shit.

Then another thought struck. Maybe Janet was downstairs giving the guests their breakfast. Or maybe … maybe that's where Liam was! Surely he wouldn't expect Janet to work on Christmas Day?

She hobbled down the stairs as fast as her still dodgy ankle would allow but the pub was like a ghost town. No Janet. No Liam. No anyone. Clearly guests had to fend for themselves today. Henri was heading for the phone in the bar to call Tilley and Frankie and beg them to come collect her so they could search far and wide, when she heard something. She stopped and listened hard, recognising the faintest sound of rock music coming from outside.

The studio!

Henri didn't even remember getting from the pub to the door of the workshop, but the relief that swept over her as she stepped inside and saw Liam bent over a rocking chair was like nothing she'd ever felt before.

'Oh my God!'

He turned at her shriek and rushed over. 'What is it? Are you okay?'

She started pummelling his chest with her fists. Up until that moment she'd been too panicked to cry but the tears burst free now.

'Whoa!' He caught her wrists. 'What's the matter?'

'I thought you … When you weren't there … and Sheila was … I thought …'

He pulled her hard against him and cradled her head against his chest. 'Didn't you see my note?'

'What note?' She sniffed and pulled back to look at him.

'It said I was down here working. I left it next to you on the bedside table.'

She shook her head. 'I didn't see any note.' She'd been too distressed to register anything but his absence. 'And what kind of person works on Christmas morning anyway? How long have you been down here?'

'I'm sorry,' he said, wiping a tear as it slid down her cheek. 'I didn't mean to scare you. I woke up early because there was something I needed to finish.'

'Huh?' What on earth could be so important that he'd chosen it over waking up with her?

He turned and pointed to the rocking chair, which was, if anything, even more beautiful than the one he'd made for Dolce. 'It's for your mom.'

She gasped. 'You serious?'

'Yeah. I started it the day after we delivered Dolce's.'

'Wow.' She took a moment to just gaze at it. 'Were you still going to give it to Mum after we … broke up?'

He nodded. 'I was going to deliver it to her in the new year, but I thought you might like to give it to her for Christmas instead?'

'Hell yeah. This is much better than the ugly vase I bought her. I'm shooting right to the top of her favourite child ranking. And you, you are going to be very much in her good books as well.'

'I like the sound of that. Your mom can be scary sometimes. A bit like you.'

She laughed and wrapped her arms around him. 'Is it ready now?'

'Yep. All done. Was just giving it one last polish.'

'Good. Because I think we've still got a few hours until we have to be at the farm, and I have an idea of what we can do to fill in the time.'

He slid his hands up under the back of her T-shirt—which was actually *his* T-shirt—and palmed them against her bare skin. 'And what would that be?'

⋆ ⋆ ⋆

They were almost late to lunch, and although Henri didn't seem to care, Liam didn't want to make a bad impression. He was anxious enough as it was about actually celebrating Christmas for the first time in thirteen years.

'Are you okay?' Henri asked, as the sign for Bungara Springs appeared ahead.

'I think so,' he nodded, despite the tightness in his chest.

He hoped so, but now that they were this close, the enormity of doing Christmas—of celebrating Christmas, of spending it with someone else's family—felt more than a little overwhelming.

She reached out and squeezed his knee. 'We don't have to do this if you don't want to. I want to spend today with you, but that doesn't have to be with my crazy relations if that's too much, too soon. They'll understand.'

Liam wasn't sure they would but that was beside the point; he wanted to do this, for Henri, but also for himself. He wanted to be a part of a family again, he wanted to feel like he belonged.

'No, we're doing this,' he said firmly, squeezing the hand that was still resting on his knee. 'You're not using me as an excuse to get out of Forward family festivities. I'm hoping to hear lots more embarrassing stories from your mother.'

Henri laughed. 'Why do I have a bad feeling about this?'

'Remind me how many nieces and nephews you have,' he said as they bumped along on the gravel track towards her mom's place.

'Seven.'

'Sheesh! How am I ever going to remember all their names?'

'Don't worry about that. I'm sure they'll be too busy fighting over their presents to even notice you.' She pointed to a gum tree as the homestead came into view. 'Park over there, under the tree.'

He did as she instructed. 'Shall we take the rocking chair in now or—'

'We exchange gifts after lunch. We'll leave it till then. Hopefully no one wonders what's under the tarpaulin.'

They climbed out of the ute and almost got ambushed by Nerf guns as they headed through the garden gate.

Henri gasped and pulled him back out of the way as a line of kids ran past them. 'Oh my God, I'm so sorry,' she said, her face pale, as she surveyed the tiny foam bullets scattered all over Fiona's usually immaculate garden. 'I'll get them to stop. They can play with something else.'

'No! Don't. I'm fine,' Liam assured her. If he was honest, the sight was a little triggering, but he didn't want his issues to affect some innocent little kids enjoying themselves. 'Really. They're just toys. Don't ruin their fun.'

And the sight was pretty amusing. He couldn't help chuckling as the very smallest child—who was maybe too little to join in—toddled along behind the others, collecting them all up. At least he was trying, but his hands were so tiny he could only hold a few before he dropped them again.

Henri finally smiled. 'That's Joe. Callum and Hannah's youngest. Don't tell anyone, but he's my favourite.'

'I don't blame you. That's one pretty cute kid.'

As predicted, none of the children appeared particularly interested in their arrival and so, hand in hand, they continued on towards the house.

'Wow,' Liam said as they stepped up onto the verandah and his gaze fell upon a ridiculously long table, with a smaller one off to the side. The chairs around it didn't all match but aside from that, it looked like something out of a movie or a magazine. White tablecloth, gold runner down the middle, red and green cloth napkins, cutlery wrapped in ribbon, festive-patterned plates, Christmas crackers, glittery glassware and vases filled with native flowers from the garden. And this was only the beginning.

'Did I forget to tell you Mum goes all out?' There was a twinkle in Henri's voice as she squeezed his hand. 'If you think this looks good, wait until you taste the food.'

At that moment, the screen door opened and Callum and Andrew emerged from inside. They both wore shirts that looked as if Hawaii and the North Pole had had a love child. Maybe next year, Liam would get one too.

'What took you guys so long?' asked Andrew.

'Mum's stressing about the turkey getting overcooked,' added Callum. 'She was about to send out a search party.'

'Liam was finishing Mum's present,' Henri told them. 'It far surpasses anything you two idiots could have got her.'

They exchanged a look with each other.

'Of course, you have no idea what you got her because Hannah and Janai handled that for you.' Henri shook her head. 'Hopeless, absolutely hopeless. Anyway, will you guys look after Liam while I go and get changed. Promised Mum I'd wear a dress today.'

'Sure,' Callum said, raising his can of Coke. 'Can I get you a drink, mate?'

'Mum won't let us crack the beer open until we sit down to lunch,' Andrew apologised.

'A Coke would be great,' Liam replied as Henri kissed him on the cheek before disappearing into the house.

He endured a few awkward minutes while Andrew and Callum got all big brotherly and grilled Liam on his intentions towards Henri before she emerged again, this time with the other adults in tow. Not that he really saw any of them.

'Jesus,' he hissed as he drank in the sight of Henri.

He loved her in her usual shorts and T-shirt, he loved her in her swimsuit, he loved her when she wasn't wearing anything at all. But the sight of Henri in a hot pink, sleeveless dress that hugged her curves and finished just above her knees did insane things to his insides.

If they weren't surrounded by her family, he'd have marched right across to her and taken it off.

'We don't take the Lord's name in vain around here,' said Henri's mother, before turning back to smile at her daughter. 'See what happens when you wear a dress.'

Henri grinned and did a little twirl.

'Sorry, Fiona,' Liam said, not feeling sorry in the slightest.

She stepped up and gave him a hug. 'You're forgiven, but don't made a habit of it. Merry Christmas.'

'Merry Christmas to you too. Thanks for having me.'

'So, how's this actually going to work between you two?' Tilley asked after Liam had been welcomed by everyone else.

'Well,' Henri looked to him, 'I'm going to make sure I fly home between contracts …'

'And I'm going to take time off to go see her when I can as well.'

In between other pursuits, they'd spent the morning working out logistics. They weren't silly enough to think this was going to be easy, but where there was a will there was a way and Liam had never wanted anything in his life to work more.

'Aw, isn't that sweet?' Tilley said, pressing her hand against her chest. 'They're already finishing each other's sentences.'

'It's very sweet,' Fiona agreed, her eyes gleaming as she grinned at them, 'but if we don't eat soon, the lunch will be ruined.'

Liam noticed that while he'd been gaping at Henri in the dress, the long table had filled with food, almost like a miracle.

The kids were summoned, and everyone took their places—Fiona Forward at one end, the other empty in respect to the absent but much-loved Fred. The rest of the adults sat along each side and the children at their own table nearby, all except Joe, who sat in a highchair between Hannah and Callum, banging a spoon on the tray.

'Can you say grace please, Andrew?' Fiona asked, and everyone reached for each other's hands and closed their eyes as Henri's brother began.

Liam felt Henri's eyes on him and opened his to find her looking at him. She leaned in close and whispered, 'You sure you're okay?'

He nodded. His anxiety had completely evaporated the moment she walked out in that dress. It was impossible to have any dark thoughts with her sitting beside him wearing it.

Finally it was time to eat. In addition to the turkey and roasted vegetables, there was a leg of ham, prawns, potato bake and at least four different types of salads. Henri hadn't been kidding when she said her mom went all out. The only things missing were a green bean casserole and a yam and marshmallow one, but this was an Aussie Christmas not a Silver Ridge one.

He only allowed himself a moment's reflection before picking up his cutlery and getting stuck in.

Life might not have turned out the way Liam imagined—he'd never get over the brutal loss of his family—but maybe it was finally going to be another kind of good. Although it was Christmas not Thanksgiving, he sent up a silent prayer, thanking the powers that be for gifting him Henri.

He couldn't imagine another present that could ever top that.

Epilogue

One year later

'What's a girl got to do to get a drink around here?'

'Henri!' Liam would know that voice anywhere. He straightened from where he'd been restacking glasses under the bar and nearly whacked his head on it in the process. He didn't care. 'What are you doing here?' he asked, almost unable to believe his eyes. 'I didn't think you were coming home until tomorrow?'

Sheila didn't waste time with conversation; she'd already darted out from behind the bar and was pawing Henri like a long-lost war hero.

'I decided to surprise you,' Henri said, giggling as she stooped to ruffle the dog's fur. 'At least *someone* seems happy to see me.'

'Happy?' He shook his head and rushed around to join them, yanking her into his arms, putting his mouth on hers and showing her that happy didn't even come close.

After a good thirty seconds, he pulled back, took hold of her hands and looked his fill. 'I missed you.'

'Ditto. The last few weeks felt like an eternity.'

He nodded as he reached for her luggage. 'You tired? Want me to take these upstairs or do you want a drink first?'

'Unless you can sneak away with me …' She glanced around at the heaving pub. It was three weeks before Christmas—almost a year to the day that she'd fallen asleep in the pub. Harvest had just finished and everyone was in a mood to let their hair down.

'Not for a while, I'm afraid.'

'That's what I thought. I'll have a prosecco then.'

'*Prosecco?* Since when does Henrietta Forward drink prosecco? Who are you and what have you done with my girlfriend?'

She gave him a smug smile. 'I'm celebrating something.'

His heart thudded. 'You're not pregnant, are you?'

A child wouldn't be the end of the world, but he knew it wasn't something Henri wanted and that suited him just fine. Thanks to her he had more than he'd ever expected to have again.

She gave him a look. 'As if! Get my drink and I'll tell you.'

'Yes, ma'am.' Curious, he returned behind the bar and while he grabbed a bottle of their finest bubbles, Henri did a quick round of the pub, saying hi, before finally climbing up on the stool beside Rex.

She kissed him on the cheek. 'Hey there. How's things at the tip? Found anything interesting lately?'

'Only yesterday I stumbled across a fresh bouquet of roses.'

'Wow. That *is* interesting.' She nudged him in the side with her elbow. 'Maybe you have an admirer.'

Liam chuckled as Rex's whole face turned bright red.

'I heard about your latest donation,' Henri continued. Grant was putting on a Christmas pantomime to entertain and also raise money for rural men's mental health, and the not-so-mysterious-anymore benefactor had made a large donation for costumes and sets. 'You never cease to surprise me. I wouldn't have picked you as a theatre buff.'

The crimson fading, Rex winked and swigged his beer. 'How are you anyway, Henri girl? How long you back for this time?'

'Long enough,' she replied and then glanced around as if only seeing the pub for the first time. Her gaze lingered on the tinsel that trimmed the bar before moving on to the reindeer head that said 'Merry Christmas' when anyone walked past it, and landed finally on the large Christmas tree right next to the bar.

'Nice decorations, Liam.' She smiled at him and then lifted her hand to her ear. 'And are they *Christmas* carols you have playing?'

'Just tell me your news,' he said, leaning across the bar so their faces were mere inches from each other. He could kiss her again if he wanted to, and he did, but he didn't trust himself not to stop. 'What are you celebrating?'

'*We're* celebrating,' she said, before lifting her glass, taking a sip and immediately making a face. 'Ugh. Why do people like this stuff so much?'

'Put me out of my misery and I'll pour you a Guinness.'

'Okay.' She put down the glass. 'I'm coming home. For good.'

'What?'

'The wonderful Wendy Mann at Geraldton Air Charter has offered me a job.'

'Holy shit. Flying?'

'Yep. As you know, they do charter and aerial work and amazing tours. I'm looking forward to taking tourists out to the Abrolhos Islands, but also to Monkey Mia, Shark Bay and Kalbarri.' She met his eye with a twinkle. 'I don't want us to be apart anymore, and this way, I get to have my cake and eat it too. I get to keep flying, but I won't have to go away. Well, very rarely, and not for more than a night or two max.'

'Are you serious?'

She nodded.

This was the best news Liam had heard since … since ever.

But what if she regretted it? It had been tough spending weeks apart, but they'd managed. She always flew home between contracts, and he'd gone and visited her in various places as well. Turned out Macca and the rest of his fabulous staff managed the pub just fine without him.

'Are you going to say anything or are you just going to stand there showing off your tonsils?' Henri asked.

He choked out a laugh of disbelief. 'I … Are you *sure* this is what you want? Won't you miss the thrill of ag flying and travelling far and wide?'

She shook her head. 'Not as much as I miss you. We've made long-distance work this year, but I don't want to do that any longer. I want to be with you. Twenty-four seven. Three hundred and sixty-five days a year.'

'In that case, congratulations.' He picked up her glass and took a sip of prosecco—it truly wasn't as bad as she made out.

Acknowledgements

Every book I write is a different experience—some are easier to write and some take more time to get right—but the one thing that remains constant in my writing is the support I have from the people in my life and I'd like to take a few moments to thank the following:

Sue Brockhoff, Annabel Blay, Sarana Behan and everyone else at HQ Books Australia who work tirelessly to bring my books to you. Also to my fabulous editor Dianne Blacklock, who pushes me hard to make sure the final product is the best it could possibly be. Thanks to my agent, Helen Breitwieser, who offers me practical feedback, advice and wisdom whenever I need it.

Massive thanks to my family who encourage me to keep writing—to my mum, who is always my first reader and my biggest cheerleader, and to the boys and Craig, who have faith even when I don't. They also put up with my mood swings and anxiety when the writing isn't flowing as well as I like; I really do appreciate your love and support.

Thanks as always to Beck Nicholas—my author friend—who reads everything I write as I'm writing and helps me work through plot problems or just my own stupid doubt. I wouldn't be without you. And to all my other writing buddies, of whom I'm blessed to have many—you all rock and are without a doubt a blessing I did not expect when I started this journey.

With each book there are a few special people that help me with my research—for this one it was two wonderful pilots! Thanks to Cecil, who gave me so much insight into what it means to be an agricultural pilot and also read the final draft of this book to make sure I was on the right track. And thanks to Marty for helping me with a few other technical questions.

I'm so grateful to the bookshop owners, librarians, bloggers and book reviewers who promote my books to their customers and followers. You guys help keep the book world ticking. Readers, please remember to support your local bookshops!

Lastly, but definitely not least, thanks to my readers who kept saying they wanted more books in the Bunyip Bay series—I hope you like this one just as much as the others. Lots of love to the members of the Rachael Johns Online Book Club and to Anthea Hodgson, my co-host, and Brooke Testa, who helps us run it. I really value our book community and you all constantly inspire me to keep writing. (If anyone is not a member and would like to join, you can find us on Facebook.)

Turn over for a sneak peek at bestselling Australian author Rachael Johns's new book.

THE WORK WIVES

by

Rachael Johns

Available November 2022

Prologue

When Shaun Reid, CEO of The Energy Co, summoned all employees to the boardroom just before close of business on Friday afternoon, neither Debra Fast nor Quinn Paladino had any idea that their worst nightmare and their greatest wish (respectively) were about to come true.

Like everyone else in the building they'd been counting down the hours until the weekend officially began and the last thing anyone wanted was to listen to Shaun wax lyrical about the qualities of the new guy.

Deb had a hot date to look forward to and Quinn had her parents visiting from South Australia. How the tables had turned—Quinn spending Friday night with her family and Deb out on the town!

She was grinning to herself when Quinn popped her head over the top of her cubicle at 4.45 pm.

'It's time,' her friend announced, tapping her smart watch.

Deb groaned as she closed the spreadsheet she'd been working on. 'Why couldn't this have waited until Monday?'

Quinn shrugged. 'That's one of the many mysteries of the world. Along with why Shaun has employed yet another man to fill the Director of Sales position. So much for gender quotas.'

'So, you think the rumour's true?' Deb asked—both she and Quinn clearly disheartened by the thought.

'Of that I have no doubt.' Quinn threw a hand in the air as if she were throwing in the towel. 'But you know Shaun's a man's man. Powerful women terrify him. Come on, the sooner we get to the boardroom, the sooner it will be over.'

'Just got to finish one thing and I'll be there.'

'I'll go save you a seat,' Quinn promised.

People were already crammed into the room by the time Deb arrived a few minutes later. The massive oak table that usually took pride of place in the middle had been pushed to the front, extra chairs had been brought in and were now lined up in rows like a classroom, but there weren't enough seats for everyone. She wouldn't mind standing at the back near the door to make escaping hastily once the meeting finished easier, but as promised Quinn was guarding a vacant chair beside her.

'Over here!' she yelled, waving her hands like they were at some kind of football match.

Deb apologised as she squeezed past Mikael from Legal and Samira from Customer Service and made her way to Quinn.

'Where's Shaun?' called someone from the back. It sounded like No Mates Nate. 'Does he think we have all night?'

Murmurs of agreed disgruntlement echoed around the room as Quinn's phone pinged with an incoming text. She glanced at the screen then to Deb. 'Mam and Dad have landed. Hope this doesn't take long cos I wanted to be home to meet them.'

Before Deb could reply, the door at the front—the one that came direct from Shaun's office—opened and a hush fell over the room as everyone's heads swivelled towards it.

'Oh my God,' whispered Quinn, her jaw dropping as she gazed at the tall, broad-shouldered man who entered with Shaun.

Her whole face lit up and Deb immediately understood why. The new Director of Sales was without a doubt one of the best-looking men she'd ever laid eyes on; the problem was this wasn't the first time she'd seen him.

As the few other single employees—women and a couple of men—perked up around her, a chill snaked through Deb's body. Her heart thumping, she lowered her head and slid as low as possible in her chair.

'Good afternoon,' began Shaun, his smile so cheesy his artificially white teeth were in danger of blinding them all. 'I'd like to thank you all for coming to welcome our newest member of The Energy Co family, Oscar Darke.'

People started to applaud but every single cell in Deb's body froze. Despite the addition of beard and glasses, there was no longer any room for doubt.

'Oscar comes to us with an impressive resume of experience and lots of innovative ideas. I've asked him to say a few words, tell us a bit about himself and his vision for the future of the sales department.'

'Thank you, thank you.' Oscar clapped Shaun on the shoulder as he took his place, needing to stoop a little to talk into the mic that had been set up to add to the fanfare. 'I have to say I'm a little overwhelmed by such a warm welcome. I know you're probably all itching to hit the pub for happy hour so I'll try to make this snappy.'

With each smarmy sentence Oscar uttered, bile rose in her throat. She silently willed him to stop talking so she and Quinn could escape without making a scene. Maybe Quinn would have some idea what Deb should do.

'I'm really looking forward to getting to know you all over the coming weeks,' he concluded. 'Have a great weekend.'

'Holy smokes,' Quinn hissed, leaning towards Deb and echoing her thoughts as everyone else stood. 'It's him!'

'What?' The hairs on the back of her neck prickled. How could Quinn possibly know? And then she realised ... her friend's expression was one of glee, not horror.

'He's The One! I'm going to go introduce myself. Coming?'

Hell no!

Somehow, she swallowed those words.

'Are you okay?' Quinn asked, frowning slightly.

'Actually ...' Deb put a hand on her stomach. 'I'm feeling a little queasy. I've got to get out of here.'

'Are you going to be sick? Do you want me to come with you?'

Deb shook her head. 'I'll be fine. I just need some fresh air.'

Without another word, she hightailed it to the elevators, almost tripping in her rush to get away. *Thank God it's the weekend.* She would need every second of the next forty-eight hours to work out how she was going to handle this, because one thing was certain.

She could not work in the same office as that man.

Debra

Three months earlier

Deb didn't know who was more nervous as she turned into the carpark at Smythes Ladies College—her daughter or herself. Even though changing schools had been Ramona's choice this time, it was always nerve-racking starting at a new place, trying to make new friends, getting to know new teachers.

'What are you doing?' shrieked Ramona.

Clearly, Deb *wasn't* the only one on edge. 'What does it look like I'm doing?'

'No. No. No!' Ramona pointed ahead to where a row of SUVs that looked like they were fresh from the car dealership were cruising through the Kiss and Drive. 'Drop me off there.'

'But I thought I'd come in with you. Help you find the right classroom.'

'*Mum.*' Ramona groaned and rolled her eyes as if Deb had just suggested she wear a clown costume to school. 'I'm not in kindergarten. I don't need you to hold my hand anymore.'

'I know but ...' Trying not to show her hurt, Deb looked anxiously towards the school's vast entrance. Surrounded by immaculate gardens, the main building with its sandstone walls, steep-sloping roofs and arched windows, looked like something out of Harry Potter—a stark difference from the local Catholic high Ramona used to go to. What if she got lost?

'Mum, *please*,' Ramona implored. 'I'll be fine.'

'Okay. If you're sure.'

As Deb relented and slowed her ancient Toyota Corolla in the Kiss and Drive, Ramona pulled down the visor and checked herself one last time in the mirror. Officially, make-up was forbidden at school, but when Deb had called her out for wearing foundation, blush, mascara and tinted lipstick, Ramona had told her to take a chill pill—that everyone did it and it was hardly visible anyway. Deb hoped she was right because the last thing either of them wanted was Ramona getting in trouble on her first day. Until this summer, she'd never even bothered with make-up.

'Let me stop the car before you get out,' Deb said as Ramona reached for the door. 'Having to call an ambulance on your first day would not for a good start make.'

She was trying to be funny, but Ramona didn't laugh. 'Thanks for the ride,' she said, grabbing her bag from the floor and opening the door in one fell swoop.

'Forgotten something?' Deb called.

'What?!'

Deb leaned towards the passenger side and tapped her cheek.

Ramona shook her head. 'Sorry. No time. Wouldn't want to be late.'

Deb jolted as the door slammed and the sound reverberated around the cabin. She watched as Ramona hitched her brand spanking new SLC school bag up her shoulder and joined the hordes of girls—all dressed identically in the uniform of blue-plaid summer pinafore, white short-sleeved shirts underneath and black shoes with white socks—swarming up the steps.

What had happened to her little girl this summer? Make-up, slamming car doors, no kisses—it was like someone had snatched her sweet daughter and replaced her with a stranger.

She jolted as a horn sounded behind her and glanced in her rear-view mirror to see a long line of fancy cars waiting to pull in behind her. Blinking back stupid tears, Deb pulled out of the school grounds and rejoined the morning rush hour traffic. It went against every bone in her body to leave her precious daughter alone on her first day, which was why she'd offered to take her. She didn't normally drive to work but thought Ramona would appreciate not having to navigate public transport.

Apparently not.

Her car came almost to a standstill in the traffic on New South Head Road and she switched on the radio to try and drown out her thoughts. The office wasn't far as the crow flies from SLC but at this time of the day she'd be lucky if she made it in less than half an hour. *And* she'd have to pay an exorbitant amount for parking.

By the time she arrived at the parking tower down the road from her building, she was in danger of being late. She made a mad dash down the street and was almost at the elevator when she remembered it was her turn to buy morning coffee.

'Dammit,' she muttered as she rushed to the café next door and joined the long queue.

'Double-shot skim latte and an almond cappuccino, please,' she asked when she finally made it to the front.

'Name?' barked the guy behind the till.

As if I don't tell you every second day. 'Debra.'

While she waited, she shot off a quick text to Ramona: *Hope everything going well, and the girls are nice. Can't wait to hear about your day tonight. Love you.* She knew how bitchy girls could sometimes be—especially to a kid from the western suburbs who could only afford to be at the elite school because she'd scored a scholarship. If it wasn't for the fashion program Ramona had been desperate to join, no way Deb would have endorsed this move.

Collecting the coffees, she headed up to the thirteenth floor in the painfully slow elevator, smiling at Lexi, the receptionist, as she entered. 'How's that bump of yours going?'

Lexi rested her hands on her burgeoning stomach. 'Giving me grief. And he kicks so much at night, I'm barely getting any sleep.'

Deb offered her sympathies and then continued, not wanting to linger long enough to get into proper conversation. As much as she liked Lexi, it got boring answering phones and directing traffic, so sometimes Lexi resorted to gossip to pass the time.

'Hi, morning, hello,' she called to various people as she walked towards the finance department, detouring via digital marketing on her way.

'Quinn not in yet?' she asked Toby and Linc.

The two men in their early twenties, who both wore skinny jeans, black Converse and almost exactly the same shirts, shook their heads, not even looking up from their phones.

'She had a date last night. Maybe she finally hooked up with someone,' said Linc, exchanging a smirk with Toby. This was the only department where the employees didn't even bother trying to be surreptitious when on their mobiles in office hours.

Ignoring this remark, Deb put the almond cappuccino down on Quinn's desk. It was a miracle she could find a place among the clutter, which included make-up, bright-coloured hair accessories, a framed photo of her large family, tiny plush toys and other trinkets. The state of her desk was worse than Ramona's bedroom and that was saying something, but somehow Quinn managed to do her job, and do it well.

'See you later, boys,' she said as she left.

Neither of them replied.

There was a heated discussion happening in the kitchen between Sally, the NSW sales manager, and Steve from IT—probably The Mug Thief had struck again—but Deb kept her head down and continued to the payroll department. Her colleagues, Brendan, Garry and Ian—all middle-aged, semi-balding, married men—chorused a cheerful 'good morning' despite already being ensconced in spreadsheets.

Setting her latte on her desk, Deb slumped into her swivel chair. She couldn't stop wondering about Ramona—how her day was going, whether she'd found her first class okay, what the teachers were like, if the other students were being welcoming. Why didn't high schools have those apps where you could log in and watch your child through a camera? Lexi was constantly on her phone watching what her eighteen-month-old twins were getting up to in the day-care centre downstairs.

Then again, if SLC had such a thing, Deb would probably never get any work done. Speaking of ... She switched on the computer and began going through her emails. About half an hour later, one popped up from Quinn.

Never have I felt more in dire need of caffeine. I owe you my life!!!
PS. How was Ramona this morning? Nervous?

Deb chuckled at Quinn's dramatic exclamation as she dipped into her handbag to grab her mobile. She sent the photo Ramona had reluctantly allowed her to take to Quinn.

Why the even-more-than-usual need for coffee? Big night? Did you get lucky?
PS. No idea re Ramona, she barely said two words to me. Sent photo to your phone.

Lucky? Lucky?! Simon was lucky I didn't stab him in the eye with my chopstick before main course.
PS. OMG Ramona looks—ARGH—are you sure that's really your daughter? She may as well be wearing a straitjacket. I thought this school was supposed to be fashionable?!!?!

Smiling, Deb took a sip of her latte. When not in school uniform, Ramona favoured vintage clothing, and would spend hours scouring second-hand shops. In the last couple of years, she'd even started making clothes herself, learning everything from YouTube videos. She had a style of her own and a flair for making old stuff look cool that impressed Deb whose wardrobe was almost entirely shades of black, something which both Ramona and Quinn berated her for on a regular basis.

What happened with Simon? I thought he sounded promising.
PS. It's the program she's in not the school that's fashionable. In terms of uniform, SLC is stuck in the dark ages—or so Ramona told me when we spent an exorbitant amount buying it.

That daughter of yours is a smart chicken.
Regarding, Simon. Rendezvous? Five minutes, usual spot!

It's a date.

Deb glanced at the time on her computer screen and decided to take an early break. The way she was feeling right now, it wasn't like she was going to achieve much anyway. Listening to Quinn share antics of her latest Tinder date—or was it Bumble or Hinge?—would hopefully take her mind off Ramona.

talk about it

Let's talk about books.

Join the conversation:

facebook.com/harlequinaustralia

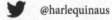

@harlequinaus

@harlequinaus

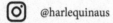

harpercollins.com.au/hq

If you love reading and want to know about our authors and titles, then let's talk about it.